Jak Lore

RULES OF
ENGAGEMENT

Jak Lore

Published by Mythic Legends Publishing Inc.
2018

First Printing: 2018

ISBN 978-1-7323539-1-6

Mythic Legends Publishing Inc.
Elmwood Park, IL 60707

www.mythiclegends.com

This book is a work of fiction. The characters, incidents, and dialogues are products of the author's imagination and are not to be construed as real. Any resemblance to places or real people, living or dead, is coincidental or used in a fictitious way.

Cover Art by Manthos Lappas and Shir Dahan

Edited by Beth Dorward

Acknowledgments

I would like to dedicate this page to those who have helped me and supported me throughout the writing of this book. I want to thank my parents who supported my desire to write this story. I thank my sisters who always asked how the book was progressing. I thank my friend Eufemio as he let me bounce ideas off him for the basics of the story.

I would like to thank the cover artist Shir Dahan for another amazing cover. It came out better than I imagined.

Finally, I would like to thank my editor, Beth Dorward who helped me get the book into this final product. Your help was invaluable in making this story the best it can be.

To all of you, I thank you.

One

The snow crunches beneath my feet. I stare at the ranch-style home in front of me. It has the same faded brick walls that the Sword of Might showed me in my vision. The same sloped roof topped with a foot of snow. A recent snowfall has covered the shoveled ground with a thin white sheet. This is the house I left Chicago two days ago to find. The white door with the green handprint is the proof. The cold winter wind blows as I approach the door, whipping my long blonde hair in its frigid embrace. Angel's trench coat, which is a bit too big for me, flutters unbundled in the wind. Even with the sleeves rolled up, my skin refuses to acknowledge the morning cold.

Standing stoic in front of the door, my fingers linger on the small handprint. They're actually two overlapping small prints. They belong to children, not an adult. I swallow, but my throat is pained from my inability to cry. My broken heart is also full of rage. Santano, my teacher, a man I trusted, destroyed everything I ever knew. I will never let that happen again. My eyes narrow and my fists clench as anger boils inside me. Behind this door is another person like Santano; an avatar. The Sword of Might tells me his name is Aran. I don't care. He'll be dead soon. I won't let him hurt anyone. I'll never let them hurt anyone. Ever.

I hear hurried footsteps inside the house, even over the wind. It surprises me. I didn't know my hearing was that keen now. I wonder what other senses are heightened, but the jiggle of the handle halts that thought. I grip the blue cloth-wrapped handle of the Sword of Might. My breathing slows and my blue eyes narrow as the door opens. A man, at least a head taller than me, comes to an abrupt stop in his rush out of the house. It's Aran, just as the Sword of Might showed me. His short brown hair bobs at his abrupt stop. In his hand is a slender blood-red blade, about the length of a butcher knife, adorned with ten small white ovals. The guard is fashioned with dragon heads, each decorated with opal eyes. There is no doubt in my mind. That is the Blood Dagger, the weapon he'll use to make his sacrifices, just as Santano had done. "You won't," I nearly growl.

Aran's flushed face contorts in confusion as he steps back, muttering something I don't care to hear. I draw the Sword of Might from its slender scabbard. No longer Angel's hefty scimitar, it's now fashioned as a straight sword. The blue cloth tail spins as I twist my wrist and thrust the point into the avatar's heart in one fluid motion. "Go to Hell," I say through gritted teeth. Aran drops the Blood Dagger as his trembling hands reach for the blade piercing his heart. I pull the sword free and slam the heel of my palm into his body to knock him over, but instead he flies back into the house and slams against a wall. The pictures shake and fall as he collapses in a heap on the hardwood floor. I stare at my hand wide-eyed. I still have that much strength? Is that my normal power now?

The steel of my sword refuses to hold onto the avatar's blood as it drips off like water. A quick flick of my wrist splashes the rest onto the floor. I hear a slight groan and see Aran convulse slightly. He's not dead yet? I walk over to him with heavy steps. My grip on the Sword of Might becomes tighter as I glare down at him. He manages to turn his face to the side and stare up at me. I can see the fear in his tearstained eye. "Cold," he whispers.

"It's warm in Hell," I answer. I spin the Sword of Might into a downward thrust and drive the blade into him again and again. His body convulses with each savage stab. The blood in his throat gurgles as he tries to scream. I shout, "Go to Hell!" over and over with each strike. I continue long after he stops moving. My heart races as I catch my breath. I pull the sword free one last time and flick the blood across the walls. I return to the entryway to deal with the Blood Dagger lying harmless on the floor, silently waiting for sacrifices that will never come. This is the last thing I need to do before I can move on. I touch my sword's tip to the crimson weapon and say, "Purify." The sword glows for a moment and does nothing else. Somehow I know why, almost as if I'm being told. Without souls it isn't tainted. I reposition the sword over the dagger. "Shatter." The blade shines and the glow accumulates at the sword's point. I drive it into the dagger and the crimson weapon shatters on contact. It's done.

I let out a sigh as I sheath the Sword of Might. Now I just have to wait for the next avatar. If it's anything like before, I have at least a few hours before I know where I'll have to go. I stand at the threshold of the door and stare out. Has it really been two days since I left? I wonder what's happening back home? I take a deep breath and can smell breakfast cooking nearby. I instinctively clutch my stomach. I haven't had anything to eat or drink in those two days, but I don't feel fatigued at all. After two days without water shouldn't I be on the verge of death? A bitter smile crosses my lips. I say, "You're the demon hunter now, Rebecca," as if that explains everything. I close the door. Since I have time before the next avatar shows up, I think I'll raid the fridge.

I pass by Aran and offer him only a sneer as I venture deeper into the house to find the kitchen. I open the fridge and find very little in the way of food. A half-empty gallon of milk, orange juice, leftover pizza, beer, and browning vegetables. I warm up the pizza and pour myself a glass of orange juice. The milk is sour. I sit at the table and anxiously eat.

Time ticks by slowly and I pass it doing something I haven't done since I was a child; practice my martial arts. Angel taught me everything I know in—I guess Heaven-sent—dreams. They were very vivid, often lasting hours, but I always woke well rested and refreshed, no matter how intense the dream may have been. My body may have ached a little, but I was always ready for the day. It still amazes me how well my dream life passed into my waking life.

Hours pass and the Sword of Might is silent. There is not a sound except for the tick-tock of an unseen clock. The only thing in the kitchen is a digital timer on the stove. The sound is coming from another room. Just how good is my hearing now? I follow the sound past the dead avatar and into the living room where I find a grandfather clock. The pendulum doesn't move, only the hands on the face. It's not even a working replica, just aesthetic, but the sound is coming from there. I look around the room and see pictures of a once happy family staring back at me from the walls. In most of the pictures Aran is holding onto a lovely young woman. They look like they're in their twenties. She's very pretty with eyes full of life. She looks happy in the pictures. I guess this was his girlfriend and maybe she left him. Figures a jilted lover would become an avatar. I trail from one picture to the next and find two kids: a bright and happy young girl that looks so much like the young woman, her mother I guess; and a younger little boy that more resembled Aran. I stare at the picture. He was a father? So, he was divorced.

There is a picture of the two siblings at a water park. The boy looks about five in the picture; the girl maybe eight. I pick it up from the counter it rests on and run my fingers over the glass. I was an only child. I never wanted a little brother or sister but did wonder what it would be like. My parents did want more children but had trouble after me. After Dad's accident, that became impossible. They decided after I finished high school they would host foreign exchange students, especially since I was planning on going away to college. I toss the picture back onto the counter with a scowl. None of that is going to happen now. Hell made sure my entire family died. At least I managed to protect these people from Aran. I could never imagine killing my own children, or Michael, for any reason.

My eyes continue to drift through the pictures and I find one of the mother; her arms wrapped lovingly around her children with huge smiles across all their faces. My heart starts to hurt. "Mom," I whisper. The tears start to form and I slam my fist into the picture, shattering the glass. "You bastard!" I curse. "You took them from me!" I take a deep breath as I wipe the tears away. My anger has been pushing my pain away. I don't want it to break. Where's the next avatar? I can't stand this. I find myself wandering the room not wanting to look at the pictures and being reminded of what I lost, but not being able to stop myself. Almost like some force is driving me to look. The pictures are mostly of their children. I watch as they grow up within the frames. I look at a picture of the girl smiling up at the camera as she stands by the baby's cradle. She looks about four, her beaming smile showing all her tiny teeth. She's so happy to have a baby brother. I see a Christmas picture. The boy is five or six. He and his sister stare dumbfounded at their gifts. They had opened each other's presents by mistake. I laugh a partial sob. Sorrow is starting to overtake my anger. Christmas wasn't that long ago and it breaks my heart knowing it was the last one I'd ever share with my family. I try to control my sobs, but I can't stop the tears. They run freely down my face, even as I curse Santano. I refuse to breakdown. I follow the pictures until I find three photos positioned in a triangle on the wall. One frame containing each child with their mother at the head. They are all smiling and a ribbon crosses the frames. A funeral card clings to the corner of each picture. They're dead. He was alone, just like me. It slaps me hard. He was a widower. He wasn't angry because they left him. He was angry because he lost them.

I can't stop it now. "Mom. Dad," I sob. I back away from the pictures and cry. I'm all alone. Everyone's gone. I back myself into the couch and turn to lean on it. "I don't want to be alone," I cry. I can feel warmth around me and the hurt starts to lessen. I move around the couch and curl up on it, still crying hard. "Please don't leave me alone." The stress is lessening, almost as if someone is holding me. I want so badly to throw my arms around that person, around Michael. "I won't, Rebecca," a voice whispers gently into my ear. I grip my knees tightly against myself. "Michael," I sob. "I need you." That small comfort, that invisible embrace, suddenly rips away and pain pierces my heart. All the hurt and anguish comes washing back in a massive wave. I cry. My mom and dad are gone. I have no one left. I want Michael, but all I can do is cry. Finally, I can cry.

Two

My clock radio makes a strange sound. It starts as a ringing and then turns into a deep hum. I must have accidentally set it to alarm instead of radio last night. I reach over to my nightstand to silence it, but my body is stiff and protests. After finding empty space I realize this isn't my bed. I start to move and remember I'm not at home. My eyes shoot open in realization of what's going on. It's the Sword of Might!

I tumble onto the floor as I fail to get up into a defensive pose. I twist onto my feet and draw the Sword of Might into ready over my shoulder. I look around for the threat but find none. There's nothing here. I sigh in relief and relax my guard. I must have cried myself to sleep. I look down at the Sword of Might and smile. It's warning me of the next avatar. I don't have to linger in my thoughts anymore. I don't have to feel the ache of my broken heart. I can focus on killing the next avatar. I close my eyes and say, "Show me."

The darkness of my closed sight is overtaken. It's strange, seeing almost ghostly images. I see a crimson red straight sword with a dragon-headed guard and ten white ovals along either side of the slender blade. I'm sure it is the Blood Sword even though it isn't the large bladed scimitar that Santano had wielded. This sword is more like mine. Disbelief sets in when I see who holds it:

Aran. My eyes fly open, breaking the vision, and I rush to the hallway to check on the body. He has to be there! I killed him and destroyed the dagger. It's over!

I stand over what should be a bloodstained floor. Divots litter the area where the Sword of Might bit into the wood. Aran is gone and not a single drop of blood is spotting the wood. He's still alive? What did I do wrong? "Where's he going?" I exclaim as my eyes slam shut. I see a young girl, about seventeen or eighteen; around my own age. Her name is Anna. She's wearing a heavy coat and hat, but I can see her face clearly. Strands of her dark hair peek out from under her hat. She has just finished cleaning the snow off her car and is throwing the brush into the trunk when the scene shifts. Her blue car is flying down the road, Route 6 towards a forested area. Aran is waiting there. She's his target!

The vision ends and I rush to the door. In my hurried panic I pull the door off its hinges before falling into Quickstep. The door grinds to a halt in midair. I'm not sure which surprises me more, the fact that I pulled it out of the frame, or for the first time seeing the world come to a standstill. I had seen cars moving slow as I ran past them on my way here, but seeing the world actually crawl to a stop is eerie. The Sword of Might forces me to focus on the task at hand, showing me the way to the road. I sprint down the street and head north on Route 6. The world around me is almost at a complete standstill as I race as fast as I can on the snow-covered fields. There is no crunch of snow as I move. No sheet left behind me. My pounding steps do not sink into the snow to leave marks. I'm actually running on top of the snow. If I wasn't so panicked this would be cool.

My grip on the sword's handle is tight, making my knuckles white, but I can't move my arm. My body aches as my lungs burn and heart pounds. My vision blurs every few seconds, only to clear and make my legs ache. I can feel pressure against my body during those moments which leave me winded and slightly confused. This isn't how Quickstep was when I fought Santano. Am I pushing my limits already? I try to reach for the Dagger of Power, the sister weapon to the Sword of Might, but my arm won't obey. What's wrong? This isn't how it's supposed to be. I hear a word echoing in my ear, "Normal." This is normal? Trees burst into view around me. "Don't be scared," I repeat the whispering words. "Don't push. Slow." I shouldn't slow down, but I do. Why isn't this scaring me? My anxiety is drifting away.

Ahead I see Anna's car. There are pieces of tire and skid marks on the road, leading to the car crashed into a tree. The car door was pulled off and is hanging in the air. The avatar is pulling Anna out of the car. I'm tired from the effort I'm putting into Quickstep, but I push harder. The avatar is pulling his sword back for a fatal strike. God, I have to time this just right or I'll miss. This was easier before. Why isn't this easy now? God, please don't let me mess up.

I fall out of Quickstep right beside them. Finally, I'm able to draw the Heavenly Weapons together and thrust them forward in a cross, catching the crimson sword and letting it bite deeply into the car. Anna screams and falls back against the wreckage as I kick out into Aran's stomach. He loses his hold of the Blood Sword and falls back into the snow, slamming against a tree. Panting, I face him with weapons raised at the ready. "Are you alright?" I ask between breaths.

Uttering incoherently, Anna scrambles to get back on her feet.

"Anna!" I almost shout.

She gasps back into the here and now. "What's going on?" she asks. "Who are you?"

"You again," Aran growls as he gets back to his feet. "Rebecca Virtue. He said you're the demon hunter."

"I killed you," I say. "How are you here?"

"You released my inner demon," he says with a grin.

I look at him quizzically. What's an inner demon?

His grin grows wider, showing his teeth. "Ready to see it?" he asks.

Santano's angry scream echoes in my ears as the terrifying visage of the Shadow of Death invades my mind. I remember the miasma of terror washing over me, unaffecting me then but terrifying me now. What did I do wrong? I feel arms around me and a body pressed close. At first I think it Anna, but the embrace is not fear. "Calm," a voice whispers into my ear. "He's not like Santano." My racing heart slows as I find I trust this unseen voice. "He'll never be."

Even as a dark aura begins to rise from Aran's feet, I remain calm, trusting what I hear. The aura clings to his body and wafts away in strands. As it climbs up his form he begins to tense. It covers him, bathing him in its malignance. A red mist escapes his lips as he lets out a breath. The aura brightens to that red color. Anna's breathing deepens as she watches the spectacle before us. I swear I can hear her heart racing. I watch more out of curiosity than fear. He hasn't made any sacrifices, so what's happening? The aura begins to invade Aran's body, turning his skin a red hue. His clothes rip as his body grows taller and wider. His face becomes elongated and twisted horns grow from the sides of his head and around his chin.

Anna screams, startling me. I realize she may try to run. I can't protect her if we're both chasing her. I spin around and take her by the shoulders. "Calm down," I

11

say. "It's okay." She struggles against me, staring at Aran's transformation into a monster. I cup her chin with one hand and force her to look at me. "Hey!" I shout. "Stop it! I'll protect you!" Panicked eyes stare at me. "Listen to me. I'm going to protect you. I just need you to stay behind me. I won't let him near you. Understand?"

"Do you really think you can keep me from that little bitch?" Aran asks in a deeper, harsher voice. He almost sounds like a totally different person. I turn around and brandish my weapons beside me. Aran stares back at me with a cocky grin on an elongated goat head, revealing stained yellow teeth. He's nothing like Santano at all. Santano's body had remained unchanged, but the flesh of his face had been stripped away until all that was left was a skull with a pair of eyes and a tongue. Aran isn't turning into Death. He's just a demon.

Looking at him, he's only grown a few inches taller, maybe topping six foot now, but his muscles doubled in size. His clothes tore from the sudden growth revealing the crimson skin beneath. His shoes barely hold together. Large toes with long sharp nails have burst from the front. His feet have grown a few sizes and his body is laced with burn scars. He has four yellow twisting horns growing out of his head and small yellow spikes jutting from his chin. His hair is slicked back now between goat ears. His eyes appear as deep yellow orbs. I turn away to look at the crimson sword embedded in the car. It's nothing like Santano's either. This Blood Sword is like the Sword of Might, a straight sword.

"Like the Sword of Might," I repeat aloud.

"Do you understand?" the kind voice whispers.

I nod. The Blood Weapons mirror the demon hunter's Heavenly Weapons. That's why Santano's sword was a scimitar. His dagger would have matched the Dagger of Power too, like Aran's did, even though I never saw it. Angel had already destroyed it, but he didn't kill Santano. That's why Santano was becoming Death and not a demon. "Santano survived," I say.

Aran stretches his body, flexing his muscles and getting used to his new girth. As he does the blood sword pulls itself from the car and flies into his hand. He looks as surprised as I do. He can call his weapons too. Aran grins sinisterly at the realization the sword will answer his call. "My power is awoken!" He laughs.

"No, it's not," I say. "You're stunted."

"You have no idea," he says. "You've unleashed the power that will destroy you both."

I shake my head in contempt. "I didn't release anything, you idiot. This is the limit of your power. You won't get any stronger. You're nothing like Santano and you never will be."

"You think you scare me you little bitch?"

"I don't care because I understand. I have to kill you twice." I move my foot and the Dagger of Power forward to create my foundation. I raise the Sword of Might overhead and lean back into my stance. I may have only held these weapons in my dreams, but it will translate to the waking world. I know how to use them and I bet he doesn't.

"I'll gut you first before I split her open!"

"She will not be your sacrifice."

Aran charges with his sword drawn overhead. I step into my upward thrust and deflect his wild swing. I shift my body and thrust with my dagger, forcing Aran to retreat. I keep pressing forward, alternating between sword and dagger strikes. Aran fumbles as he tries to keep his balance, making it difficult for him to deflect my blows. I'm not trying hard to hit him. I just want to push him back. I should use Whirlwind. That will really push him back.

With my next thrust, hurricane winds twist to life without warning. Snow rips off the ground and the trees sway into the powerful winds as Aran spirals backwards and out of my strike range. I'm too surprised to rush forward and close the gap. I didn't mean to use Whirlwind yet. I struggle a little to hold my arm steady. I don't remember this kind of power when I used it against Santano. It's stronger now? After a moment of focus I'm able to will the attack away and look back at Anna. She's cowering beside the car, pulling her hat over her head and crying, trying not to see the monster before her. She should be trying to hide. Heather, my friend and only survivor of that night, didn't have that option as I unleashed all my power against Santano. I was so strong I could have easily hurt her. If not for Úna, I would have. I could have leveled the school at that point. There was just so much power and it was so hard to control. I thought it had all gone, that my power had stabilized to something more manageable. I guess I was wrong. I look around at the snow-covered trees. Black skids mar the pavement, leading to Anna's car wrecked head-on into a tree, with Anna quivering beside it. "Great," I mumble. "Úna," I call out, "could I get some help?"

"You're asking the wrong person," she answers back, her voice thick in her Irish accent.

"I can't control it yet," I whisper as I watch the avatar rise from beneath the snow.

"Then I suggest you learn."

"Úna..."

Aran let out a deep bellow, something between a roar and a scream. "Why are you protecting her?" he demands.

"She's innocent," I answer.

"No! My son was innocent, but she still ran him down like a dog!"

"No!" she cries. "That was an accident! I'm so sorry! I didn't mean to!"

I glance back at Anna. She killed the little boy? "What do you mean an accident?" I ask. "What happened?"

Aran screams as tears roll down his face. I stare at him dumbfounded. He's crying? "Everything was taken from me! The doctors let my wife die! The jury was a bunch of idiots! They murdered my wife! My daughter couldn't take losing her family. She couldn't take the bullying and took her own life! I did everything I could, but it wasn't enough! The teachers stood by and did nothing!" He points to Anna. "That plastered bitch runs down my baby boy and barely gets a slap on the wrist? She still isn't even old enough to drink!"

"I know!" the girl cries. "I was wrong! I'm sorry! I'm so sorry! I'll never drink again!"

"I'll make sure of that!" His eyes widen in surprise. He grasps his head as it flails about, screaming in pain and anger. "Are you fucking kidding me?" he growls. "They were all in on it?" He spits foam as he screams. "I'll kill you all," he roars and with it a fan of flames spews from his mouth.

My stomach tightens. I spin around and grab Anna, hoping I can fall into Quickstep with her. The world slows around us. I can feel the heat of the flames at my back as I pull her up and away. I'm still in Quickstep when the flames hit the car. The explosion rocks the ground and forces me out as we tumble to the ground. We had barely gotten away. I almost wasn't fast enough. Anna is shaking and taking short shallow breaths. She is as wet from sweat and tears as she is from the snow.

Her terrified stare goes from her burning car to Aran. He clutches his throat in surprise. His fire breath wasn't something he knew about. His lips curl into a smile and he bursts into laughter. My eyes dart around us. The snow around us has melted and revealed burned greenery. The pavement is scorched and blackened metal and burnt plastic litter the ground. A smoke plume rises into the air from the burning car. "Anna," I say, "Hide in the trees. I'll deal with him."

Aran is smiling as I fall into Quickstep and barely acknowledges my disappearance as I close the distance. I come out in front of him, much to his surprise, and take hold of his face. I don't regulate my strength as I thrust my arm out, throwing him across the empty road. He bounces off the ground several times. I break into a sprint as the blade of the Sword of Might glows, activating Holy Strike. I'll end this with one blow. Aran stumbles to his feet and sees me rushing towards him. He breathes in deeply and exhales a gout of flames. I fall into Quickstep and instinctively leap up, completely clearing the flames.

I come out a dozen feet in the air. Was it because of Quickstep or are my legs that much stronger? "Use it," a voice whispers. It isn't Úna, but it's oddly familiar. I swing my sword in front of me and the path of the blade ignites. From the flames about a half dozen rock core fireballs plummet to the ground. I remember this, but the name escapes me. Aran braces himself as the meteors rain down. Explosions rock around him, throwing snow, rock, and dust into the air. I'm not sure if I hit him. I land in the smoke and strike with the edge of my sword, cutting into his torso. He roars as he ambles backwards. I thrust with the dagger, but he grabs my wrist before I can connect. With a powerful upward jerk, he pulls me up into the air and slams me

16

back onto the ground like a whip. My head jars as it hits the pavement. The ground beneath me buckles as the air is knocked out of my lungs.

Aran pulls back to strike, and unable to roll away with my wrist still in his grasp, I kick my leg up, slamming my foot into his middle. I knock the air out of him and he falters but doesn't loosen his hold. I try to pull my arm free as I get to my feet. Aran's grip tightens and he pulls my arm, inadvertently helping me up. I twist and spin into him, hugging close to his body and slam my elbow hard into his side. It gives me enough slack to pull my hand free and I jump into a spinning roundhouse that connects with his face, sending him crashing into the ground and melted snow. I move forward to attack with my sword, but he twists his body toward me and rips his hand into the pavement and throws rock, dirt, and mud into my face, blinding me. I start to claw the debris from my face when the voice that has been a whisper shouts, "Left!" I shift my body and feel something pass by my head. I open my eyes enough to see the slender red blade of the Blood Sword and my stomach twists. He almost got me.

I drop into Quickstep and back away while getting the dirt and mud out of my eyes. As I come out of Quickstep I see Aran's body blur before disappearing. I rub the rest of the mud from my eyes when the voice shouts, "Defend!" I raise my sword just as Aran's blurred body appears in front of me and strikes. I barely block his blow. That was Quickstep. I've never seen it like that before, even when Santano did it. I saw every move he made, despite how fast he was moving. I completely lost track of Aran when he used it. He towers over me, using his height as leverage. I cross my weapons and push back. At this point I can think of only one thing. Please don't breathe fire.

17

"All I care about is revenge," Aran growls, "and you're in my way."

"What about your family?" I ask. "Do you really think this is what they want? This won't bring them back!"

Aran smiles. "When I am Death, I can do anything."

Is that why he made the deal? To bring them back to life? Aran pushes hard against me and I push back with equal force. Suddenly he pulls his blade down. He's slow with his first thrust, making it easy to doge and pulls back for another overhead strike. I deflect quickly with my sword and Whirlwind bursts from the thrust of my dagger. The hurricane torrent slams into Aran and throws him back into the trees, but it's even stronger now. My hand twists and the winds almost go errant. I feel someone help to steady me, but my wrist hurts and my grip is weak. The dagger flies from my hand. The wind whips in all directions, kicking up the surrounding snow into the air in massive sheets. The trees sway and branches break. The powerful winds take the dagger high into the air before the hurricane dies, allowing the sheet to settle into falling snow.

I hold my aching wrist against me. It was too much to control. Why? It was hard, but I could control them before. Why can't I at all now? Without control I'm just as dangerous to Anna as Aran. Without someone to protect her, I can't use my powers. I have to beat him with skill alone. I shake the pain from my wrist before opening my hand. After a brief moment the handle of the Dagger of Power finds itself in my grip from wherever it had landed, causing residual pain to shoot up my arm.

With effort, Aran pushes off a fallen tree that partially has him pinned. With a growl he gets back to his feet and stares at me. I can't use any more powers. Everything has to be melee. I simply can't control my abilities yet and I hope he hasn't realized that. The longer this drags out, the sooner he'll figure it out though. I have to end this. I think it's still safe to use Holy Strike. It's probably the only power I can safely use.

Aran blurs before disappearing. He's dropped into Quickstep. It's strange seeing it like this, but I follow. His form blurs back into being as he runs past me. I overtake him easily and block his path. His face contorts into surprise as he comes to a sudden stop and we come out of Quickstep together. He gawks as he looks between me and where I was. "How did you?" he starts to say but clenches his teeth into a growl before dropping back into Quickstep. This time, though, I notice an instant before and follow him before he's blurred away. His distorted form is moving now, running around me to get to Anna. His body doesn't solidify until I start moving, and again I block his path. This time he reels back when I stop and stumbles as we come out. I can't let him keep moving forward. I have to push him back.

"Here's my fire," I say before slamming the blade into the ground. The flames of Eternal Fire burst to life and spread out towards Aran. I see a tell in his left leg an instant before he falls into Quickstep. I follow and watch the growing blaze slow as Aran runs from the flames. He seems to slow as I start to move and overtake him again.

"How?" Aran snarls as he takes a few steps back.

"I'm not going to let you," I say as I take the same steps forward.

I see Aran's tell and drop into Quickstep alongside him and let him move first, making sure I read his tell correctly. Aran broke left, just like his tell read, and I give pursuit. He looks back to see me giving chase and contorts his face in aggravation. Even as I pass him, he just looks ahead. He picks up speed, trying to outrun me, but I'm already too far ahead of him. I stand my ground as I fall out of Quickstep and the sword glows with Holy Strike, the one ability that is still safe to use. Aran comes out of Quickstep right in front of me and belches his flames. Shock covers my face as I reel back and will Psionic Shield into being. I can feel the push of the fires as they slam against the opaque white field and the heat on my hand and arm. I try to twist away and fall. Aran drops into Quickstep.

I can't follow on the ground like this. I push myself up so fast and hard I lift my entire body off the ground and stumble when my feet touch down. My heart is racing. I didn't push myself up; I leaped. I can't control my strength, but that doesn't matter. I stumble into Quickstep as Aran drops out, pinning Anna against a tree and pulling his sword back. Everything grinds to a standstill except for Aran. His arm inches slowly into a thrust. I push as hard as I can, my legs straining as I try to push myself to the limit. My vision starts to tunnel and my peripheral vision shifts red as pressure builds against my body. I cover the distance in a blink and Anna is in my arms. Pain erupts in my side as I fall out of Quickstep and we tumble away. Aran's blade catches my coattail as it bites deeply into the tree trunk, forcing me to stumble to a stop. I let Anna go and she falls into the snow. Barely maintaining my balance, I spin around, tearing my coattail free, and shout "Holy Strike!" I thrust the Sword of Might deeply into Aran's body.

The glowing energy of Holy Strike drains into his body and he stiffens. Cracks break along his form as the energy forces its way out. In a guttural roar, Aran is blown to oblivion. The Blood Sword clatters to the ground and begins to melt very strangely. I smell copper. Oh my God. That's not metal. It's blood! They're made of an avatar's blood! Is that why Santano's powers were all blood-based?

Soft sobs pull my reeling mind back as the tainted blood begins to evaporate. I look at Anna curled up on the ground in the fetal position sobbing, "I'm sorry. I didn't mean it." My grip on the Heavenly Weapons loosens. Aran is dead and his sword destroyed, but this isn't over. I sheath my weapons, noticing the bloody rip on my coat sleeve. I ignore it, and the pain, for now.

"It's okay," I say as I kneel beside Anna. "He's gone. He won't hurt you anymore."

"It should have been me," she cries.

I pull her into my arms and rock her gently. She cries, holding me tight, aggravating the wound on my side when I slammed into the tree to rescue her. It, however, is being overpowered by the pain seeping into my heart. She hurts so much. Something weighs heavy on her soul. "Tell me," I whisper.

"It was an accident," Anna sobs. "I didn't mean to."

"I know," I assure her.

"I was at a party. There was beer. My friends said, 'What would one hurt?' Then it was one more. Then one more." Anna sobs deeply as I stroke her hair. I close my eyes and listen. "I don't know how much I drank. Daddy didn't know. I didn't want him to know. I thought I'd be okay if I drove slowly. It was dark. I didn't see them." I can almost see it, like a distant memory. She wasn't going fast, but she was driving by the streetlights. "I tried to stop, but it was too late." The screeching tires were followed by a thud. There were flashing lights that made her head hurt. I think the airbag deployed. What am I seeing?

"I don't remember actually hitting him," she continues, "but I did. I killed him. I killed a little boy."

The memories are fuzzy. I can't see the details, but it involves her father. He's the Chief of Police. There's something about the mayor and the judge, but I don't understand. "They told me to go on with my life," she says through sobs. "They would take care of it. I tried for three years, but I still see his face; all bloody and cut. I see it every day. I wish it was me instead. I wish it was me." I understand. They protected her. They know each other. That's what Aran meant. He saw this too. They didn't let the law play out for her.

Somehow, I saw her sin. She killed a little boy and because of her father's connections, was never punished for it. That pain weighs heavy on her. She wants only to be forgiven. It's a dark spot on her soul, weighing her down. I can see it, just behind her heart. A dark and pulsating orb the size of a baseball. I want to heal her, to soothe her pain. With my hand on her back, behind her heart, I reach out for it subconsciously. I can feel it press against my hand. It stings, like little pinpricks against my palm and fingers. It's heavy in my hand as I pull it away. Only now do I realize I am looking at a sin through closed eyes. I open my eyes and look at the darkness. It's become a misty shadow that twirls around my hand. This is a sin? I'm looking at the physical manifestation of a sin, her sin. The heavy center presses against my palm and the dark mist slides down my arm and vanishes. I feel a deep pain in my heart and then it's gone. Did I just take her sin? I can do that?

Anna's crying has become soft sobs. She's fallen asleep. Now I can feel fear. I close my eyes again and caress her head. I focus, trying to see what she feels. I see Aran's demon form, but it's exaggerated; much bigger and more grotesque. "Go away," I whisper. I grasp at the memory as it delves deeper into her mind. I removed a sin; maybe I can remove a memory too. It sinks deeper as I reach for it. I catch it and I pull, but it won't budge. "Leave her be," I almost growl at it. The memory dislodges and is gone. Neither the tragedy nor the avatar would haunt her. She can now accomplish what she had been trying so hard to do. She can move on.

I lay Anna against a tree facing the road and begin searching around her car, hoping I can find a cell phone. Her belongings are strewn all around her car and in the middle of the road is her purse. I pick up the singed handbag with a little flame still burning on it. I blow it out and gather what I can find of her things. Most of it is ruined, but her cell phone still seems to work. I'm not sure exactly where I am, but I know how I got here. I dial 911 and tell the operator there was a car accident on Route 6, just north of Fredericktown. I describe the wreckage and where to find Anna. Without hanging up I lay the cell phone beside Anna. "I wish I could do more for you," I say. I brush her tangled hair from her face and let the peaceful presence around me take my hand. It guides me to draw the sign of the cross over her. I know no prayers but feel something must be said. "God keep you, Anna," I whisper.

She'll be safe now. Her sin is gone, the avatar is dead, and help's on the way. Now it's over. I drop into Quickstep and begin to move. It's all I can do. It's all I want to do.

JAK LORE

Three

-Hell's Interlude-

Satan sat atop his throne of bones as he watched the events before him. He showed no emotion as Aran fell, but the gears turned in his head as he continued to watch Rebecca. He watched as she removed the girl's sin and made a mental note. He understood what her ensuing concentration and demanded whisper was. He cast his eyes down at his gathered court. He saw disinterest and confusion among their faces. "Enough," Satan said.

Lucifer lowered his staff as the glow of the crystal orb atop it dimmed. The display which showed about him faded as his shimmering black robe no longer had light to reflect. "I don't understand," Lucifer said as he turned to Satan. "He was a poor choice. Why waste an avatar? It's only January and you've used two of your yearly six."

"It wasn't wasted," Satan said as he stood from his throne. "He was the perfect choice."

"How exactly was he perfect?" a hoarse voice called out. Eyes turned to a tall man, Balam. A cloak of bearskin rested on his shoulders, exposing a chiseled bare body. Wild, rustic brown hair covered his head and disappeared into the cloak's bear-head hood. The same rustic brown hair enveloped his perfectly shaped body. "Please explain."

"You are a god," War's voice boomed, "yet you cannot feel what is before you?" All eyes turned to the tall, hulking being of slick black metal. His body, a living suit of armor, was jagged and twisted with spikes. The toothy maw of his helmet, forever closed.

Balam turned to War. "I do not feel," he said, "I see. What I saw was a weak man led to the slaughter."

Satan inhaled and said, "I felt it."

"There is more buried within," War said, his deep crimson eyes glowing as he spoke.

"Far more, but she's afraid." Satan rose and continued, "She lacks control and fears her potential."

"I will bring it out."

Hands clasped behind his back, Satan descended the bone mound that created steps to his throne. "She entices you?"

"I want to taste her power."

"A demon hunter is not easy to find, nor unprotected."

"Chases are part of the joy. Once I have found her and tasted of her flesh and blood, she will never be able to hide from me." War raised an iron clawed finger towards Satan. "You will not stand in my way."

Satan flashed a devilish smile. "When could I give an order to a Horseman?"

"Never. I will taste her power. I will feel it thrash against me. I want to feel the pain, her pain. It will be mine. Then I will return it to her and watch it crush her."

"Such an entertaining sight that will be."

A loud churning of a stomach turned their attention. Famine scratched his massive belly, dragging his dirty nails across his pale emerald skin. "This is boring," he said. "The avatars are dead. She is the demon hunter. The cycle goes on. I don't care. She is nothing. I have defeated powerful archangels. She is only human, an insect. Not even an appetizer. Demon hunters do nothing for my appetite."

The ground shook as Famine pushed into motion. "I have land to rot, crops to spoil, water to pollute; she is of no interest to me." Famine began to fade away, each step causing the ground to shake less as his form vanished. "I return to Earth. Leave me be."

Pestilence chuckled as he approached War. "She doesn't have what it takes," he said. "You'll crush her, then the line will be gone; Death will rise. She is of no interest to me. Angel is dead and the Virtues gone—truly this time. She is the last. I am satisfied." Pestilence turned away from the eldest of his brethren. "I would like to see my old friend. We have so much catching up to do." Pestilence chuckled as he departed the court. War's chains ripped from his body, spinning around him in a sphere, hiding him within. The sphere shrank in size quickly and the first Horseman was gone.

Satan said nothing as the Horsemen dispersed. He simply began to walk away.

"Where are you going?" Lucifer asked.

"To think," Satan replied. "The hunter is the hunted. I would concern myself elsewhere, lest you draw the wrath of War."

Understanding the warning Lucifer nodded absently and turned to the waiting court. "We are adjourned. Leave the demon hunter be." He struck the butt of his staff on the ground and vanished in a bright flash. The court began to disperse. Baraqyal, however, stood her ground. Staring blankly at the floor she struggled to control the storm within. Her hair shifted in an unseen breeze. "My demonic," she lamented. So lost in her

26

thoughts, she was unaware of the snow forming above her head until it fell in a heap. She screeched in surprise over the laughter of another angel. "Baradiel!" she shouted as she wiped away the melting snow. "You know I hate when you do that!"

"I couldn't resist sister," the fair-skinned Baradiel said. Unlike most of his kin, he still preferred the simple white gown of Heaven and walked barefoot. His wings looked of ice just beginning to melt. He preferred to display his wings as they helped to keep the lord of hail cool. "It was too easy. Only your body was here." Baraqyal discharged a bolt of lightning around Baradiel, but he didn't flinch. His white hair waved in the discharge of power as violently as his gown. "You're touchy today."

"I'm in a bad mood," Baraqyal replied. "You wouldn't understand."

"Should I care to?"

"It's been two centuries since Demonic Angel was exorcised by that stranger."

"He was certainly unique. He was the only demonic that could never be truly exorcised. I always wondered why he never returned on his own, like he had always done before."

"I searched for those answers, but always came to a dead end. Finally, Satan calls him back from Purgatory and I'm summoned to Earth only to watch that little bitch end him again. I haven't felt so helpless since the Fall."

Baradiel raised an eyebrow. She felt helpless over a demonic? "Demonics die all the time sister. Rarely is it that a demon hunter has only one demonic, they die so often."

"He was different."

"Well, he was stubborn. Come, walk with me."

Baraqyal fell in step with the taller Baradiel. "I want to go to Earth," she said

"What's stopping you?"

"What I want to do. Satan will not allow me."

"And that would be?"

"I want to fry the little bitch."

"It's not exactly forbidden, just ill-advised," Baradiel mused. "Just give it some time. War will bore."

"It's not like you'd care either way. Her demonic is your—" Baraqyal stopped short and looked around. "Where is her demonic?"

"Still waiting for me," Baradiel said with a smile. "Satan summoned his court, so I decided she could wait."

"That must be fun for her. You must let me hear her scream. It would be a small consolation."

Baradiel smiled. "I can do better. Be her guardian."

Baraqyal nearly stopped in surprise. "What? Why?"

"I cannot leave."

"Why not?"

"I'm working on something very important. If I were to leave it would be ruined. Centuries would be wasted. I'm at a very crucial moment and this is the only place I can access the amount of energy I need."

"Rebecca hardly had any sin. Even with the murder her demonic isn't strong. You wouldn't be on Earth long. She's too weak to defend herself."

"Yet she insists I go to Earth, alone. She is much too weak to defend herself, but that doesn't seem to matter. I want no part of whatever plan she is brewing, but as her guardian I must."

Arms crossed, Baraqyal looked over the ice angel. "What exactly are you working on?"

"Being her guardian would allow you to circumvent any decree Satan has laid upon you," Baradiel said as he stepped in front of Baraqyal, halting their walk and ignoring her question. "It would give you an opportunity to hear the real thing scream."

"Yes, it would." Baraqyal pondered the offer for a moment. "Demonics are impatient. You'll take her to Earth and watch her die. You just don't want to babysit."

"Babysitting would be easy and not interrupt my progress. She truly is planning something."

Baraqyal let out a deep breath as she stared up into the darkness above. "You've wet my curiosity." Her lips curled into a smirk. "Either way I'll get what I want. War shouldn't be too much of a worry, as long as I don't get in his way."

-End Interlude-

JAK LORE

Four

I run without regard to a destination. I push myself to stay in Quickstep for as long as I can, keeping myself down to a comfortable speed. I learned the hard way running at top speed, which I have no idea what that is, isn't a good idea. Once my body reaches its limit, I'm forced out of Quickstep. The first time that happened on my way to Aran, my body collapsed and I vomited. I'm still not sure how long I laid there before I was able to move again, but I'm glad I ran on the shoulder. I was racing past cars like they were standing still. They whizzed by me once I was on the ground. I drank the holy water in Angel's trench coat to soothe my rasping throat. It's all I had. My body had to recover from that stress before I could fall into Quickstep again. I realized quickly how much strain this ability puts on my body.

I run in and out of Quickstep for as long as I can, but eventually my body can't take anymore and I just stop, resting on the shoulder of a highway. It doesn't matter. I have nowhere to go without an avatar to fight. I'm just running. Cars whisk past me now as they return to their normal speed. My hair and trench coat whip in the wind they create. I try to button it to keep it from whipping around but find there are no buttons or zipper. There are button holes, but the buttons are missing. I tie the sash looped through the jacket

30

instead. I guess Angel found it easier to get inside in a pinch if he couldn't bundle up.

Out of Quickstep my body ached. It's not a painful ache and feels good, like when I ran with Michael. My heart twists. Michael. He's gone. I'll never see him again. Once more I feel loving arms around me. It takes the pain and apprehension away, like his embrace used to. "God, Michael. I miss you so much." A painful jolt hits behind my heart and through to my shoulder blade. The embrace is suddenly gone and all the emotions that were held back come flooding in, hitting me like an angry wave. My face contorts as tears fall. I can't help it. I bury my face into my hands as I fall to my knees. "Michael," I cry. The pain sharpens again and I hurt more. "Becca," I hear a whisper too faint to recognize.

A blazing horn pulls my attention behind me. I find myself staring at the large engine of a truck idling on the shoulder. I can't stop crying and manage only to wipe my tears away as someone gets out of the massive vehicle. He's a tall, thin man with a scruffy beard. His brown hair is long and wild, longer than Michael's had ever been. He needs at least a good brushing. His shirt is dark and loose on his body and his jeans dirty. He puts a pair of shades on to hide his tired eyes. For an instant they look like they're glowing.

"You okay?" he asks. His voice carries concern. "What happened?"

I stutter, unsure of what to say.

"Do you need a ride somewhere?"

What do I say? I have nowhere to go until the sword tells me.

He kneels down and offers his hand. I look up at him. My lips still quiver but my sobs are finally subsiding. I wipe my tears away. "Yeah," I say. "Where are you going?"

"I'm heading up to Lansing, Michigan, but I got to stop for the day soon. A few miles up the road is a truck stop where I'll be camping out. It'll only take a few hours to get to Lansing tomorrow."

Right now, I don't have a purpose. I'm just wandering. I take his hand and get back to my feet. "That's fine," I say as I wipe away the last of my tears. "I'll go with you."

He leads me to the side of the great engine and helps me in. He closes the door and walks around to get back to the driver's seat. We lock ourselves in and carefully, but aggressively, he pulls off the shoulder and back into traffic. Horns blare and he waves them off.

"Sorry," he says with a smile. "Sometimes while driving a truck you just have to pray."

I try to smile back. "It's alright."

"I'm Dennis. You are?"

"Rebecca."

"Hope you don't mind my saying, but you look like you've been through Hell."

"You could say that. I'm sorry, but I don't want to talk about it."

"I understand, but it might do you some good. You know, share the hurt. It's easier if you don't have to carry it alone."

He's right, but I have no one to talk to. All my family is dead. Michael, who had worked so hard to win my heart, is gone. My circle of friends is destroyed. I really have no one to turn to, no shoulder to cry on. I'm alone. "I lost some people close to me," I say finally.

"I'm sorry, Rebecca," Dennis says. "I know how hard it is to lose loved ones, even if it is their time."

"It wasn't their time. They were taken."

"That makes it harder. You know the saying though. If it's God's will—"

"It wasn't God's will!" I shoot back. "What happened to them was not His will." I stare at Dennis, realizing I shouted at him. I sink back into the seat. "I'm sorry. It's just..." I don't know how to finish.

"Don't worry. That saying usually comforts people, even if they can't grasp how His will works. Personally, I never liked it."

"I never gave it much thought until now. I don't like it either."

"God's will isn't the only will though, you know? Sometimes there are other, more malevolent wills at work. Sometimes they undermine His and win. Or at least come close. Evil never really wins, does it?"

I look out the window, watching the world rush by. "It shouldn't."

"Even if they were robbed, they're in a good place, right? I mean—well, you know."

I offer a weak smile. "Yeah, I know they are."

"They're at peace now. We're still here, fighting the good fight. Theirs is over. Remember them, love them, mourn them, but never yearn for them."

I look at him puzzled. "What do you mean yearn for them?"

"Cling to the past. They can hear it, you know; when you cry out for them, when you yearn to touch them again. It makes the spirits restless."

I give him a funny look for a minute. I sigh and smile. "I get it. Dwelling just makes the hurt last longer. I just wish it was that easy to move on."

"It takes time to heal when your heart is broken."

I nod in agreement.

"Let's get our minds on something a little more positive. You like Country music?"

"It's alright," I reply as Dennis reaches for the radio.

33

"If you think it's only alright, you haven't listened long enough."

I laugh a little as a song plays. I'm not sure who's singing or the song, but it's upbeat. Dennis asks me if I know the words and starts to sing along before I can answer that I don't. He goads me along and I pick up on the chorus. The song is over much too soon, but I know the next one better. We sing Country songs the rest of the trip.

We pull into the truck stop just as Dennis reaches his daily driving limit. He's grateful to really be able to stretch his legs after so many hours on the road. I was only with him for less than an hour. We have a bathroom break and decide to meet each other inside the restaurant. I wash up and splash water onto my face. Staring into the mirror, I see only exhaustion. My cheeks are still a little red from crying and my hair is disheveled. I comb my fingers through the strands to tame it a little and let out a sigh. My left arm is stiff. I must have hit that tree pretty hard. I search my pockets, looking for money. I want to eat but have no money at all. Anything I did have was left at home. Home. I just want to go home.

I walk into the restaurant looking for Dennis. He's sitting in a booth with two glasses of water and looking at a menu. I let out a sigh. I was so looking forward to a good meal. I go over but don't sit down.

"It's alright," he says with a smile before I can say anything. "My treat."

"Thank you, but I—"

He raises a hand in objection. "Rebecca, it's alright. I never expected you to pay. God knows what you've been through. Let me be nice."

My face warms with a smile. He makes me feel good. Little by little, my burden isn't so hard to bear. "Thank you," I say as I sit down, feeling the Sword of Might shift against the seat. Discreetly I position it to be more comfortable and keep it hidden. I open the menu and begin looking through it. It's nice of Dennis to buy me food, so I don't want to get anything too expensive. The waitress comes for our drink order and Dennis orders a pitcher of water. I think that's strange but say nothing of it and order orange juice. The waitress smiles almost the entire time. This restaurant, with only a few patrons, is quiet and welcoming. The waitress returns shortly with our drinks. I take a sip of my orange juice while Dennis pours himself a glass of water. In one long swallow he empties the entire glass.

He sighs in satisfaction and returns my amused look with a sheepish grin. "Sorry," he says. "I'm just really thirsty."

"Looks like it's been ages since you had a drink," I say.

Dennis bobs his head in mock contemplation. "You could say that."

Dennis manages to make me laugh while we wait for our orders to be taken. It feels good and seems like forever since I last laughed. When the waitress comes back Dennis lets me order first. I try ordering one of the $4.99 meals, but he interrupts saying I can get something more expensive.

"It's fine," I tell him. "I appreciate you buying me dinner and the ride. I don't want to abuse your kindness."

"Then just don't order the lobster," Dennis laughs. "That is a little out of my budget right now. Maybe tomorrow."

I can't help but smile. He's being so kind to a total stranger. I decide to order the chicken skillet instead. Dennis orders steak tips and we spend the rest of the afternoon talking. Amazingly, he doesn't talk about anything that would be a soft spot for me. He doesn't ask about school, friends, family, or even a boyfriend. Almost like he knows I've lost all of those. Mostly he tells me about his travels across the country and I share my trips abroad with my parents as I grew up. We talk about current events, laughing at the recent Y2K bug scare; share our tastes in music and movies. We don't seem to have too much in common, but it distracts me from the here and now and for that, I'm grateful. I feel like the weight I've been bearing is slowly being lifted, making my body ache a little under the reduced pressure. It's still early, but I'm a little sleepy.

The sun has set and given way to night by the time we head back to the truck. The days are so short. Dennis opens the door for me and says, "Listen, why don't you take the bed. I can sleep up front."

I shake my head. "No, you need your rest more. You're driving." I look up at the starry sky. "I'm not quite ready to go to sleep yet anyway. I mean, it's not even six yet, is it? I'll sleep in the chair."

"At least let me get you a blanket if you're going to stay out here for a while."

"It's okay, I'll be fine."

"It's already pretty cold and the temperature drops at night. I doubt you know the extremes you can take. I'll get you a blanket, just in case."

I smile and nod. Why argue with him? He digs around the truck for a minute and hands me a thick black blanket. It smells fresh. I wrap it around me to show him I'll be alright and warm, though I'm not cold at all. Satisfied, Dennis goes inside to rest and I close the door behind him. The street is clean of snow, but the grounds aren't. That's fine. I don't want to take a walk anyway. Looking at the top of the trailer, I wonder how high I can jump. I'm not really sure of the limits of my powers. I wrap up the blanket so it won't get in my way and get ready to jump, deciding to start small and aim for the hood of the engine. I make it without struggle, then onto the cab, and finally over to the trailer. Except for a few patches of snow, the trailer is clean but for the expected dirt. I put the blanket down and lay on it.

I stare up at the starry sky for a long while just thinking. I'm calm for once, my mind not a jumble of emotion. The Sword of Might is quiet. There are no threats to face. What am I supposed to do in the meantime? Can I... go home? I sit up and rest my arms on my knees. I look at my hands and trace the light scars on them, scars that are remnants from before I became demon hunter. I grip my shoulder. I haven't checked yet, but there will be a scar there too. I was stabbed by Demonic Angel's dagger when I finally met Angel face-to-face. Demonic Angel came to kidnap me as Santano's last sacrifice. Even with Angel's help, I was only able to rescue Heather. I feel bad for leaving her at the steps of the school that morning, after I beat Santano. She's the only one that knows the truth. She saw it all. I hope she'll be okay. I pull the cloth away and look at my shoulder. The scar is more pronounced than the ones on my hands. It's a little rough. I guess I have my battle scars.

I sit on the side of the trailer and look out over the snow-covered landscape. I watch as the wind washes a sheet of snow over the field. It's cold, I can tell, but I'm not. It's at least twenty degrees and I'm not the least bit cold as the wind hits against me, taking my hair in its caress. Not even a shiver. I exhale, watching my breath turn to vapor. I wonder if I'll get sick. I look back over the field. Except for the roar of the line of engines, everything is peaceful.

"Hell plots against you, Sweetness," Úna's Irish voice almost whispers.

I'm used to her invading my thoughts. It's just normal now. "I know," I answer without looking for her.

"You need to be vigilant, Sweetness. Not everything is as it seems."

"I can handle it."

"Can you? As I recall, you beseeched me."

"I didn't want to hurt her."

Úna sits beside me, her thin legs dangling beside my own. "I am not your guardian."

I look at her freckled face as she stares back at me with her intense green eyes, brought out starkly by her short frizzled red hair. "You protected Heather when I fought Santano. If not for you, she would have died with everyone else. If you're not my guardian, what are you?"

"Someone with something to gain. I can guide you, but I cannot protect you. That is the angel's job."

"What angel?"

"The angel who watches over you. That is who you should have called if you needed help."

"I haven't met any angels."

Úna cocks her head. "Do you not hear the whispers?"

"Yes," I say after a moment. "A little bit. I guessed it was just a part of my powers. It's an angel?"

"You must listen better, Sweetness. There can be no more hand-holding. War is on the hunt and you are his prey."

I swallow and my stomach twists. War. That monster of slick black metal and glowing red eyes. I look back over the snow-covered field. "Let him come," I say. "It's my destiny to stop them, right? Let him come."

Úna shakes her head. "It is not that simple, Sweetness. These abominations, these Horsemen, are unlike anything you will ever face. You are not ready."

"Yes I am. I have to be."

Úna slides off the trailer's side and finds her feet on invisible ground about a foot from where my feet dangle. She hooks her thumbs into the belt loops of her cut-off jean shorts and looks at me. "If you face any Horseman now, you will die. As you said, you have no control of your power yet. You must learn that control first. Though your angel can protect you, guide you, he cannot help you understand what you truly need to know."

"And what is it that I truly need to know?"

"To discover that, you must find the one that will teach you."

"Who is that?"

"He is the master of warfare; the lord of combat and sovereign of protection. You must find the First."

"A True Form, like you?"

"Yes."

"His powers were stripped like yours, weren't they?"

"Only the Fourth remains, Sweetness."

"Where can I find him?"

"You will find him waiting for you where First Blood was first shed."

"What does that even mean? Úna, I can't waste my time chasing riddles."

"It is not a waste. There is much for you to understand. This is simply the beginning. You must find the First before War finds you."

"I'm ready to fight War. I've beaten Santano. War will be no different."

"War and Santano are two very different beings. You are not yet strong enough to face him."

"Yes I am."

"You are not."

I stare at her for a long moment. She's always had so much faith in me, always pushed me forward, even when I thought I wasn't ready. Now she wants to pull me back? "I'll try to find the First," I say with a sigh, "but I can't run from War either."

"You must. He knows not where you are now, but should he draw blood you will never again be able to hide. He will chase you to the ends of the Earth."

"I won't give him the chance. I'll destroy him like I destroyed Santano."

Úna shakes her head. "War is no avatar." Strong winds whip snow from the ground in a whirl and Úna vanishes.

Five

I contemplate what Úna said for a long time. War isn't an avatar. How much stronger could he be? He made two more sacrifices than Santano did. He'll have more experience but shouldn't have much more power. I held back and Santano still couldn't keep up. As long as I let loose, War shouldn't stand much of a chance. I guess it doesn't matter right now, though. I have no idea how to find him or the First.

Eventually I go inside the truck. Curled up in the seat, I wrap the blanket around me and stare out the window. With nowhere to go, I should try to relax and get some sleep. I'm tired. The night is long and I eventually drift off, though I'm not sure I actually slept. Hearing Dennis get up the next morning, groaning about his head, rouses me from my half sleep. Something seems off though.

"Good morning," I say as I stretch in the seat.

Dennis jumps back. "Who are you?"

I stare at him in disbelief. He doesn't remember me?

"Oh, wait. I remember; Rebecca, right?"

"Yeah."

"Sorry. Last night is a little vague." Dennis opens a cupboard and fills a glass with water. "I feel like I have a hangover." He drinks the entire glass in one gulp and pours another.

"All you had at the restaurant was water, no alcohol at all." I assure him.

Dennis puts the empty glass down and catches his breath. "Feels like one."

"Maybe it's food poisoning?"

"Must be. I don't drink." He rubs his temples as he disappears into the bathroom. After rummaging around for a bit, he comes out with a pair of pills and swallows them with another glass of water. "I'm sorry, refresh my memory. How far are you going again?"

"Lansing."

"That's my last stop before I head back. I'm going to grab some food before we head off." He holds his stomach with a groan. "Hopefully I can keep it down."

Dennis stumbles out of the truck and heads to the restaurant. I sit dumbfounded. Why didn't he remember me and why does he have a hangover? Something's different about him today too, but I can't put my finger on it. Eventually Dennis returns and hands me a hot breakfast sandwich and cup of coffee. Not wanting to be rude, I don't tell him I don't drink coffee and put it in the cup holder. He does the same and drops a bag with bottled water on the floor. He bites into his sandwich as he sits down. "Sorry," he says, "I want to get an early start. This is my last round for a few days."

"No problem."

He reaches into his pocket and pulls out a card and coin. "You know, I never play these things, but I had a horrible urge to buy this ticket." He begins to scratch the game area. "I don't know why. You never really... win... anything."

"What's wrong?"

He looks at the card in disbelief. "I just won a thousand dollars."

"Congratulations!" I cheer. "I guess it's a good thing you listened."

"I guess so." He slips the ticket into his overhead visor. "I'll cash this later. I want to get going."

With sandwich in mouth, Dennis lurches the truck into motion. He munches away as he drives. I eat my sandwich slower. I'm not hungry, but I'm not so overly full that I can't eat. I try the coffee, to be polite, but the bitter taste makes my face scrunch up.

"There's sugar and cream in the bag," Dennis says.

"Um, could I just have one of the water bottles instead?" I ask sheepishly.

Dennis laughs. "Sure. Not a coffee drinker, huh?"

"I never really cared for it. You can have it."

"Thanks."

I smile. "Well, you did buy it. So thank you."

Dennis shrugs as I open a bottle and take a long drink. "Hey," Dennis starts, "this is going to sound weird, but can you fill me in on yesterday?"

"What do you mean?"

"I can recall bits and pieces, but it's mostly a fog."

"That's weird. What do you remember?"

"The last clear memory I have is seeing someone huddled on the side of the road. It gets hazy from there. Was that you?"

"Yes. You stopped and offered me a ride."

"You were crying, right?"

"I was."

"I remember; death in the family. You don't have to talk about it."

"Thank you."

"Was I... singing yesterday?"

I smile. "Yes. You have a great singing voice."

He flushes a deep red. "Oh God. I can't believe I did that."

43

Now I'm officially confused. He seems like a completely different person today. He seems so much younger now too. I've only now noticed he seems in his twenties. Still older than me, but younger than I first thought.

"I never sing in front of anyone," he says. "I get too nervous."

"You hid it well. You have a lovely voice. You were hitting all the high and low notes. You're definitely not an amateur."

"Mom always said I should have gone to Nashville."

"What stopped you?"

"I don't know. Afraid I wouldn't be any good?"

The Sword of Might vibrates slightly, sending a tingle from my stomach to my heart. That was different, not the way it felt when it warned me of an avatar. It doesn't feel like a threat. I decide to ignore it, at least for now. "That's not a reason not to try," I say. "Can you play anything?"

"Guitar. I was kind of nerdy and didn't have many friends in high school, so it helped me through my Friday nights."

"You've never sang for anyone? Not even a girl you liked?"

Dennis is silent for a moment. "Her name was Carol." He tries to hide the pain in his voice.

"Did she like it?" I ask, already guessing the answer. "Girls like romantic gestures like that you know. I'd question her taste if you didn't sweep her off her feet."

Dennis smiles with tears filling his eyes. "She loved it."

"So what happened?"

"She died. My song was the last thing she heard."

"I'm so sorry. What happened?"

44

Dennis is silent for a long moment, shifting uncomfortably in his seat as he stares down the road. His eyes glisten as tears threaten to form. "It was five, maybe six years ago now," Dennis says finally. "It was prom night. I wanted to ask Carol, but had trouble getting the courage. Someone else didn't, so I decided to stay home. Just a typical night for me, messing around with my guitar and writing songs. My mom called me to the phone. Someone wanted to talk to me; said it was important." The first tear finally brakes free and runs down his cheek. "It was one of Carol's friends. She was on her way to the hospital. Carol had left early with her date and some friends, but there was an accident. I found out more details over the next few days. She had gotten into an argument with her date and had demanded to be taken home. It's why they left early. She didn't like the fact that he had gotten drunk. I'm not sure who was driving, but there was a head-on collision that only she survived. Everyone else either died at the scene or on their way to the hospital. Carol had fallen into a coma. I didn't know what to do." He takes a pained swallow as he wipes the tears from his cheeks. "This must seem pretty weird, huh? Crying over something that happened five years ago?"

"If you don't want to, you don't have to go on," I offer.

"It's okay," he says. "I always say share the hurt. Maybe I should take my own advice for once."

I nod and let him continue.

"We weren't total strangers, you know? Yeah, we didn't hang out, but we did talk in school and the more we talked the more I fell for her, but I always felt out of place. Like I said, I was nerdy. She wasn't. The only thing we seemed to have a similar interest in was music. After the accident I could barely sleep and did the only thing I could think of. I wrote music. Carol inspired a lot of what I wrote, but this one was actually for her. I was begging God to not let her die. A few days later a mutual friend of ours came to my house. He told me to get my guitar. Carol wanted to see me. We went to the hospital and one of her friends pulled me aside. She told me Carol's parents were on their way and wouldn't let anyone else in. She told me not to screw up because Carol wanted to see me last. I didn't understand until later.

"Her friends left us alone. She smiled at me when I came in and motioned me over. She was weak, but she was awake. She wanted to know for certain if I liked her. Of course, I said yes and was so sorry I hadn't told her sooner. She wanted to know why I never asked her out. I told her because I didn't think I was good enough for her. She had me come close and told me we were both idiots before she kissed me. That was my first kiss. She told me she knew and regretted listening to her friends for so long. She wanted to make the first move."

Dennis struggled with his tears, trying to keep his emotions in check and control the truck at the same time. Has he never told anyone this story? It must have been so painful to hold onto those feelings for so long. He smiled and laughed a little as he continued the story. "I never knew she walked by my house almost every night. She would go out of her way and listen to me sing and practice before going home from wherever she was. She said she would imagine I was singing for her. I was performing a private concert just for her every night and never knew. She wanted it to be true just once, that I was singing just for her. I told her about the song I wrote when she had the accident. She was all smiles and wanted to hear her song. So, for the first and last time, I sang just for her. She loved it and was in tears. She was kissing me when she died."

46

I wipe away my own tears. Dennis takes a pained breath before adding more to the story. "I wanted to sing it at her funeral, but her parents were furious with me. They felt because I was there instead of them, Carol died alone. Her friends defended me, but it didn't matter. I wasn't allowed at the funeral."

"You were the one person she wanted to see."

"I think that's what ticked them off. I was more important to her than they were."

"She couldn't die without telling you."

"I never sang after that. I couldn't stand being at school, so I dropped out, sold my guitar, and got my CDL. I've been driving ever since."

"Could you still sing it?"

"I'll never forget it. Why? Do you want to hear it?'

"I'd be honored if I could."

Dennis thinks it over before he nods. "Maybe she'll be able to hear it too." He clears his throat and takes a deep breath. "I heard Heaven may be welcoming a new angel, tonight. So beautiful she'll be, in flowing gown with wings of white. God, do you have to take my angel tonight? Heaven's halls will fill with her laughter. A heart so pure and touch so gentle, gone forever, is something I can't handle. Angel, are you really leaving tonight?" I see something, very faint. A soft echo follows the next verse. "Oh, why must you leave? Why couldn't I see what was in front of me? Your smile and your laughter, is this the way it has to be? Oh how I'll cry if Heaven gets a new angel tonight." I see the outline of a face framed by light brown hair. An arm stretches out over his. Is that Carol? Oh God, she stayed to be with him? "So young, her future so bright," they sing together, "gone on such a joyous night. I never got to say, I love you. I wonder, do you love me too? God, are you really taking my angel tonight?" Her hair is pulled back into an elegant braid. She wears a silver bracelet and a gorgeous blue dress. She's pale, though, like a ghost. "Now I sit alone with my tears. Why God, couldn't I overcome my fears? Today my heart is breaking, because her soul you'll be taking. Please God, don't take my angel tonight." Tears run down his cheeks as well as mine. Carol leans her head against his shoulder. There is nothing below her waist. "I heard Heaven may be welcoming a new angel tonight," they continue. "Heaven is welcoming my angel tonight."

Carol leans in and kisses his cheek. "Thank you," she says. "I always wanted to hear it again." She holds him in her arms as she begins to fade. "I only want him to be happy," her voice trails off, almost lost on a nonexistent wind.

"Wow," I say. "That was beautiful. I see why she liked it."

"Thank you," Dennis says as he wipes his tears away. "You're the first person I ever told this to, you know. I didn't even tell my parents. It's funny. I actually feel a little better."

My thoughts drift to Michael. "I guess you were right. It helps to talk about it; to cry sometimes."

Dennis watches me wipe my tears away. "You can relate, can't you?"

"Yes."

"Is that why you're on the road too?"

I nod, trying to keep the memory at bay.

"Do you want to talk about it?" He rubs his arm where Carol had placed her hand. I wonder if he could feel her and not realize it. "I understand if you don't want to. It took me a long time to tell somebody."

I struggle not to cry at the memory of Michael's sick form kneeled in front of me. His eyes were so distant, but he still managed to smile at me. I love you was the last thing he said.

"Fire," I choke. "My boyfriend died in a fire."

"I'm sorry. You never got to say goodbye, did you?"

"I got to say goodbye before he had to go to Heaven." That has to be the hardest thing I ever experienced. To be able to hold him, only for a moment, just to have him slip through my arms and watch his spirit travel up the light to Heaven. It's a painful memory and takes everything I have to keep from sobbing, though a few manage to slip free. "Michael," I whisper. "I miss you."

There is a pinch in my stomach and behind my heart. It physically hurts. I feel a little weak. "I'm sorry," I say. "It was very recent."

"I understand."

"It must have been hard to carry that all these years."

"It was. You stop noticing the pain after a while, if you don't think about it."

I look out the window, half expecting to see Úna in its reflection, but I only see my own pained face staring back at me. There is no one I can tell my story to, not the real story. I'll carry that secret forever. How will I manage this growing pain without any hope of release?

"I've been running from her," Dennis says suddenly.

"What do you mean?"

He looks at me in surprise. "Sorry, I didn't mean to say that out loud."

"What do you mean you're running from her?"

"I've never been to her grave. She made me feel accepted, but all I could do was sing for her. I feel dead now."

"You gave her the one thing she wanted and let her die in peace, in the arms of the one she loved."

"How do I tell her I'm sorry?"

49

"Go and say hello."

"I owe her at least that much." He shakes his head. "All I've done since she died is run. Run from one city to the next; from state to state."

"Haven't you run from her memory long enough?"

"I don't know how to stop."

"Just park."

Dennis thinks about that for a minute. He signals and then pulls onto the shoulder, parks, and cries. I let him cry for many long minutes. Had he been holding onto that much sorrow? That much pain? Did he never grieve at all? He cries like I did in Aran's house. When Dennis finally stops his head is resting against the wheel. I can't see Carol caressing his head, but I can see the subtle movement of his hair as her hand runs through it. I wonder if Michael is with me too. Could he be the angel Úna hinted at?

"I'm sorry," Dennis says as he straightens himself and clears his throat.

"Are you okay now?" I ask.

"Yeah, I'm a lot better."

"Good. You must have really needed that."

"I did. When I wasn't allowed to go to her funeral I was so angry I never cried. I just kept moving. I'm going to her grave when I get back home. I hope she'll forgive me for waiting so long."

"I know she'll forgive you."

Dennis begins to make his way back into traffic. "I'm going to buy another guitar and practice a little first. Then when I go, I'll sing her song to her."

"I know she'll like that."

"Me too. I want to do something more with my life than just drive this truck. Maybe I'll write some songs and try to sell them. See where I can go from there. Thank you, Rebecca."

"For what?"

"For helping me through her death. I never really faced it until today. Thank you."

I smile. "You're welcome."

-Hell's Interlude-

Baraqyal arrived at the first circle of Hell, the place where demonics are born and almost always picking a fight they couldn't win. She soared relatively low to the ground. There were plenty of air currents this low in the atmosphere and gliding in Hell was much easier than actually flying. The first circle was hardest, however. Even now, Baraqyal could feel the tiring of her wings and the unnatural weight of her body. Soon she would become short of breath and be forced to land. In a weakened state, this circle could be as dangerous to a powerful being such as herself as it is to the damned souls plummeting from the maw of the River Styx above. No matter where one stood on this plane, the Gates were always within sight.

Winded, Baraqyal decided to land despite the bestials below. They were rabid, shallow creatures, broken from the torment of their sins and reached blindly for anything that came within their reach, including each other. Baraqyal's hand crackled with lightning and she hurled a lightning bolt to scatter the rabid creatures. They fled into hiding, dragging souls or beaten brethren with them. They were cowards with short memories. They would always return, often in greater numbers.

A twisting storm churned overhead; the Vortex of the Damned, the end of the River Styx, forever casting forsaken souls into damnation. The deafening roar of the storm, though so far away, always echoed in one's ear here. Baraqyal clenched her fist. Lightning slipped from her hand in a clash of thunder that drowned out the ominous storm above, at least for a time. The crack of lightning also acted as a deterrent to the savage demons that inhabited this un-claimable level.

Baraqyal wondered what this demonic's personality would be like. Would she be like the others, before Demonic Angel? He was not like the rest. Born unafraid, like those before him, he was also born incredibly strong. He had actually come to Baraqyal instead of the other way around. Demonics always called for their guardians to fetch them after their will had been broken. Not Demonic Angel though. His power was great for a newly born demonic, with power to dress and delve into the depths of Hell to fetch his guardian himself. He was very domineering and unafraid; certainly a handful. Baraqyal wondered when exactly she started becoming enamored with him.

"Baradiel," a weak voice rasped. Baraqyal searched for the origin of the voice. It was Rebecca's voice. It rasped again. "Baradiel." Baraqyal followed the cry to a dried ravine. She couldn't help but wonder if this place ever had water. "Baradiel." The sound was muffled, coming from beneath something. Baraqyal spied several bestials surrounding and pawing at stone. She approached and hurled a lightning bolt over their heads. They scattered following the boom. There was an alcove in the bedrock. A slender olive toned hand poked out. A partial face peered from the shadows, its eyes a pretty green, its long hair jet black.

"Who are you?" Rebecca's voice asked.

"I am Baraqyal," the angel answered.

"Where's Baradiel?"

"I am here in his stead. We wish to make an exchange."

52

"I don't care who guards me," the demonic said, "but I need Baradiel."

Baraqyal placed her hands on the alcove and forced the stones apart, revealing a bruised and naked demonic. Physically she looked like Rebecca. As being the physical representation of their sins, all demonics look like their demon hunter but differed in varying ways. This one's skin tone was darker, and her hair and eyes a starkly different color. Baraqyal noted this demonic hadn't been fighting but hid almost straight away. "Shall I fetch him? Inform him you refuse?"

Demonic Rebecca looked up at the callus angel before her, ignoring the gathering bestials waiting for the angel to leave. "I said I didn't care who my guardian is," the demonic said. She struggled to stand, using the stone walls for leverage. "Guard me if you must, but I need—" The demonic stopped midsentence and looked Baraqyal up and down with a curious look in her eyes. "Maybe," she said finally. "I might be able to use you after all."

Baraqyal's eye trained on the demonic standing up to her. "What are you going on about?" she asked.

"Take me to safety first, guardian."

Baraqyal huffed a laugh and pulled Demonic Rebecca into her arms. She turned and beat her wings to create powerful gusts and crashing sounds, frightening the waiting bestials and sending them skittering once again into the dark. "Talk," she said as she began to walk. "Baradiel mentioned some plan."

"In short," Demonic Rebecca said as she wrapped her arms around Baraqyal, "I need you to masquerade as Rebecca's guardian."

Baraqyal stopped abruptly and laughed. "What?"

"I want you to pretend to be Rebecca's guardian. That's why I wanted Baradiel. They're both guys."

"I can assume a male form." Baraqyal looked around, spying a rock face where she thought they would be safe. "Hold on. I'm going to have to give you my full attention for this."

Through struggled pain, Baraqyal took to the heavy atmosphere and headed to the rock face. She was breathing heavily when she landed and put the demonic down. Baraqyal supported herself against the rock face. Demonic Rebecca slid to her knees and rested against the hot stone.

"Why would you want me to masquerade as Rebecca's guardian?" Baraqyal asked. "More importantly, how would I even manage that?"

"It's simple really," the demonic said. "She doesn't understand."

"Understand what?"

"Anything. She doesn't know the Rules of Engagement. She doesn't know about me or that her sins make me stronger. She's sinned already. I can feel it. Murder, I think?"

"Yes. She killed the avatar in cold blood, before he had fully committed."

"And she'll do it again. She'll jump to the conclusion that it's okay, that she is doing a good thing, saving people. She doesn't realize that their soul is still white, or that they're still human."

"She'll figure it out eventually. Raphael will guide her. How could I replace him when he is already with her and guiding her?"

"She's pushing him away."

Baraqyal's eyes perked.

"She can't readily see or hear him. She yearns for another angel and that pushes Raphael away. It'll allow you to slip in, you who she doesn't know. You'll be able to keep Raphael's voice silent and hide her from him.

Guide her astray, to sin and strengthen me. You can sever her tie with Heaven."

Baraqyal jumped and stumbled. "Break her tie? Is that possible?"

"She would be siding with Hell. Her powers would be greatly diminished and her miracle lost."

Baraqyal laughed. "She would lose her Sainthood? Wouldn't War just love that?"

"What about War?"

"He's decided to hunt Rebecca and force her to her miracle so he can fight it."

The demonic's eyes widened and her breath quickened. "You can't let him do that."

"That's not really my place."

"Then you have to protect her from him. They can't be allowed to fight. He can't bring out her miracle!"

"Why are you so scared?"

"She has too much power as it is, even if she can't call it all. It's crushing me and takes all my will just to push back."

"I'm not following."

"If she accessed that form it would destroy me and all future incarnations of me! Her sins wouldn't matter anymore. Every demonic would be crushed by her power when they're born. Even her children's demonics, long after she's dead. It would be an end to us!"

"Demonics are part of the agreement. She can't—"

"They won't survive! They'll be born and die almost instantly! Don't you understand? If future demonics are to survive, I must survive. I must be able to withstand the pressure!"

Baraqyal stared on bewildered. Slowly, realization etched itself on her face. "I thought the Cornerstone was Demonic Angel."

"I'm what's important now," Demonic Rebecca insisted.

Baraqyal breathed in deeply. "You realize you'll be left unguarded. I can't take you to safety in my kingdom. I have to go now, while there is distance between Rebecca and Raphael."

"I know. You have to protect her from War and separate her from Raphael."

"This has never been done before," Baraqyal smiled, "but I've grown accustomed to doing things not done before."

-End Interlude-

Six

We reach Lansing by late morning. Dennis stopped at an oasis and cashed his lottery ticket on our way in. He drops me off near a hotel and insists I take a few hundred dollars of his winnings. I do need the money so don't offer much resistance and thank him for his generosity. As Dennis drives away I see Carol's ghostly figure in the passenger seat. She smiles and waves to me. I smile and wave back. Hopefully they'll both be happy now.

"Michael," I whisper. "Are you with me now?" The cold wind blows and sends pain through my joints. It feels odd. With nothing else to do I rent a room for the night. Once inside I place my hand on the Sword of Might's pommel as I close the door. "Show me the avatar," I whisper. The sword shows me nothing. Frustrated, I take my trench coat off and throw it onto the bed. Then I have a thought. I close my eyes, steel myself, and say, "Show me War." Red paints the outlying darkness. A bemused growl echoes in my ears, "So the mouse hunts the cat." It's the same as from my dream, when the Four Horsemen chased me. It's War's voice. "Let the game begin."

Barbed chains rush towards me in sharp contrast in my vision and paint my sight red. I feel the sharp chains scrape across my flesh and tighten around my body. I gasp as my eyes fly open. The guard clicks loudly against the scabbard and I pat my body, looking for the chains and cuts. There's nothing. The chains weren't real, but it didn't stop my heart from racing. It was like his presence was in the room. It was heavy and frightening. I can still hear him chuckling in the back of my head. I shake the laughter away. I'm scared. Through gritted teeth I say, "I will beat you."

Why am I shaking so much? I can do this. I know War will be stronger than Santano, but I walked all over him. Heaven helped, but they just guided my powers. I can figure that out on my own. I rummage through the trench coat's inside pockets for a vial of holy water. I find it almost instantly and splash it on the door and windows saying, "God, protect me from evil tonight." I know it's not a real prayer; I don't know any, but hopefully it'll keep War at bay while I prepare. I doubt the few attacks I know will be enough to beat him. I have to read Angel's journals. He said he wrote down everything he knew.

I sit on one of the beds and pull out Angel's bundled journals. They're bound three at a time. I unbind them so they'll be easier to read and study. I notice a long card next to the phone on the nightstand. It's for room service. I'm a little hungry and I'm not sure when I'll get to eat again, so I skim through the double-sided card and order a pizza. I begin to leaf through the pages of the journals while I wait. Angel had written so much; it's difficult finding entries that hold clues to his powers. Mostly I find notes of Angel's powers diminishing. On one page he noted the number of fireballs his Meteor Strike created was falling. That's what the power I couldn't remember was called. I used it against Santano, but for the life of me I couldn't remember it when I was fighting Aran. Angel noted he could force the number of

58

meteors back up, but it was taxing. I look around a bit more near that entry, but there's no mention of the number of fireballs he could actually generate. When I used Meteor Strike against Aran I generated about half a dozen fireballs. I remember generating more against Santano but can't remember how many. I just remember it was different.

I find one journal Angel had only started to write in. It held only one entry. The last one he wrote. It's dated December 1999, last month.

I've been given warning of the New Year's avatar. This one will be in the United States. The travel to Laredo will be straightforward, but it's been about a decade since I crossed the northern Mexican border. Hopefully the route I usually take has been left relatively untouched. It'll make crossing the border easier. After some meditation I was able to discover that Satan plans to raise an avatar in or around Chicago. I can take the Greyhound in New Mexico or Arizona to Chicago. Satan has not finalized his choice yet, but he has determined the location. The last avatar almost managed to make his fifth sacrifice and start the Collection. I have to make sure that doesn't happen again. The aberration has insisted I won't see the next millennium and that has me worried. She may be right. I feel my powers are nearly depleted. What happens when I finally fall?

There's no more. I run my fingers over the written words. An aberration? I wonder if it was a True Form. I turn to a fresh page and rummage the nightstand for a pen. Luckily, there is one and it works. I think it's time to start making my own notes.

Psionic Shield - A shield that does not let harm pass through. I can reach through it.

Shield - I am not sure about this shield or if it even has a name. It can expand around me, but blocks my view, and can almost completely encircle me.

Quickstep - Allows me to move really fast. I'm not sure exactly how it works, but avatars have it too.

Whirlwind - Creates powerful hurricane-force winds. I am not sure of its limits.

Psionic Camouflage - Makes me invisible by bending light.

Meteor Strike - Throw Meteors. Unknown base or max number. 6 so far.

Holy Strike - Killed Demonic Angel with this.

Cosmic Crush - This creates some kind of void that implodes on itself, destroying whatever it touches.

I stare at the page with only a handful of powers. I have more than this. I used them against Santano but for the life of me I can't remember them. Why can't I remember any of the powers I used then?

There's a knock on the door followed by, "Room Service." I get off the bed and answer. A bellhop is there to greet me with a square box on a pushcart. He looks max twenty, only a little older than me. His bellhop hat sits atop a crew cut of dark brown hair. His brown eyes are bright and his smile big. I can't help but think this is his first job. I try to smile as we exchange pleasantries. I'll never know what that feels like, to have my first job. After I lock the door I head back to the bed and open the plain pizza box. I put a few square pieces onto a paper plate and pour a cup of generic cola that came with the order. I always thought they had a bitter taste, but it'll have to do. Sitting down I pick up another journal and begin to leaf through it, jumping entries and trying to find new attacks. When I do, I write them into the journal I claimed for myself. I have no idea what most of the attacks are.

Meteor Punch ~ Sounds like a condensed Meteor Strike.

Force Shock ~ Unknown

Flame Strike ~ Something with fire.

Impact ~ I remember Gerald using this. It caused an explosion when the dagger struck. I should probably throw it first.

Consecration ~ Consecrate neutral and blasphemed ground. Angel could do this inside blasphemed ground.

I lean back against the headboard and take a sip of the cola to wash down the pizza grease. "Blaspheme ground," I ponder. It sends a shiver through me. Demon hunters were supposed to lose their powers on it, but Angel didn't. The entry said that the demons were surprised Angel had his powers on the blasphemed ground at all, though he could feel it slowly suppressed. Why was Angel able to keep his powers? What would happen to me? Would I lose my powers? Angel doesn't seem to talk more about it. I had read something about Pestilence trying to give him something earlier. I wondered if Angel knew how to summon the Horsemen. He wrote so much and that is so specific, where would I even start looking?

"Concentrate...Align," a voice whispers.

I reach my hand out over the books, but I don't know what to do and curl my hand into a defeated fist. "I don't know how," I whisper back, unsure of who I'm even whispering to.

"Close... eyes. I... show you." He's hard to hear—I think it's a he—but I know what he wants me to do. I close my eyes and take a breath. I'm tense. "Quiet... mind," the voice whispers. I take a deep breath and hold it, trying to force the shaking of my body to stop. I breathe out slowly, letting the tension go with it. I can see a faint light in the darkness. It's where I think my hand should be. I hear the voice whisper again but can't understand it. Outlines of a hand appear in my darkened vision and I feel it rest atop my hand as I watch it fall into the light. It gets brighter and I can see the outlines of the books on the bed. I can feel an arm embrace me and a body press against my back. It makes me think of Michael. I lean back into the embrace; becoming more relaxed. My hand moves at the bidding of the invisible hand. A white sheen begins to waif off the books, all equally bright.

"Focus," the voice whispers into my ear. I can feel his breath on my neck. It's so warm. I find it easy to relax and focus in the warm, welcoming embrace. The glowing sheen of light around the books grows dim. Slowly the books vanish into the darkness, except for one. The sheen grows, making the yellow book appear and glow in the darkness. I pick it up off the bed. The light that is my hand, and the glowing book, move in the darkness as I manipulate what I can't see. Not with my physical eyes. This is a whole new way to see and it's kind of scary.

I press the book against my body as all the lights fade. Another arm embraces me. "Don't fight... War," the voice says. "Kill."

I put my hand around the invisible arms holding me. "I know," I answer.

The embrace reminds me so much of Michael, how he used to hold me. But this is all in my head. As much as I want it to be Michael holding me, he's gone. He died in the school's basement. There's no one in the room with me. I am alone and when I open my eyes I know this will all go away. So I keep my eyes closed and rest in my mind's illusion. I don't know who is whispering to me, but I know it isn't Michael. It isn't his voice. I feel I can trust it, but I don't know what it is. Angel or True Form? I wonder; does it matter?

I want to stay in my delusion longer, but it's time to come out and face reality. I'm alone in a hotel eating pizza. At least the food is decent. I open my eyes and the feeling of being held lingers. I am being held. I can see the arms in white robed sleeves holding me, though they aren't physical. I can see through them, but I can also feel them. My heart skips a beat. I think of Dennis and Carol. She was holding him and he could barely feel her. I can see and feel these arms.

"Michael?" I ask as I turn. A painful surge of electricity rushes through my body and forces me to jerk away. I can feel the pain run through Michael too. It is Michael, right? I look around the room. It's empty and looks like I'm alone, but there is someone else here with me. "Michael," I ask. "Is that you?" I reach for where he was sitting behind me. "Michael? Say something." My hand is shocked and I pull back. I try to shake the pain away. It burns. No, it isn't Michael. He would never hurt me. My eyes narrow. "Whatever you are, get out!" I demand. Another shock, this time to my chest, knocks the air out of me. Something slams into the wall, making the pictures shake. I reach for the Sword of Might and pull it free of its sheath. "Get out!" I shout.

Another shock; this time to the base of my skull. The lamp on the nightstand is knocked over and the stand itself shakes. The drawers slide out and the sheets on the second bed are pulled. I take a swing with the sword as whatever that thing is retreats. The curtains are nearly pulled down and the window flies open. I thrust the blade through the open window. "Stay out!" I shout. A shock runs through my hand and makes me drop the sword. I shut the window and lock it. I catch my breath as my breathing creates fog on the window.

"Great," I say. "Just great. What in the world was that?" I go to the bed and search for more holy water. I try to bless the window again, hoping whatever I chased away will stay out. I guess my first attempt didn't work so I do the door again too. I don't think it was a demon. I would probably be dead right now if it was. It may have been a ghost. It made me completely lower my guard. I was helpless in its embrace. I shiver. "Ew," I groan. "A ghost was coming on to me? Ew! Ew! Ew!"

I run to the bathroom, strip, and throw everything into a pile on the floor. Hastily jumping into the shower and turning it on, I shriek as the cold water hits my body. I'm in too much of a hurry to get any ghost jizz off me that I don't give the water time to heat up. I scrub furiously. My skin crawls thinking about how some strange ghost was probably grinding against me. It's disgusting. Oh God. How many times had something like that happened and I just couldn't feel it? Gross!

When I finally decide I'm clean I turn the shower off and dry myself. It's been almost a week since I last bathed and it feels good to be clean. I step out of the shower and stare at my clothes on the floor. I've been wearing the same thing for just as long. I pick up my shirt and smell it. The stench assaults my senses, causing my nose to wrinkle. "This is how I smelled?" I ask myself. "Gross." I look at the sink. I have to wash them. They're all I have to wear. "This sucks!" I pout. "I don't want to spend the night naked. What if something happens? I can't fight like this!" I'm flustered but go about washing my clothes anyway. "That ghost better not have damaged the curtains. The last thing I need is a peeping Tom!"

I wash everything as thoroughly as I can. I wring out as much water as I'm able to and hang everything over the curtain bar to dry. I wrap a dry towel around myself. It almost isn't big enough to cover me, which says something about its size since I'm a small girl. I comb my hair with the hotel supplied comb so it doesn't tangle as it dries. Holding the towel in place I look at myself in the mirror. The scar on my shoulder is very apparent. It really mars my body. My first of many battle scars. How did Angel hide all of his?

I sigh and leave the bathroom. It doesn't matter. I have more important things to worry about. Making sure the towel doesn't slip to expose me, I go to the curtains and make sure they aren't broken. I can't afford to replace them. Aside from a few pulled rings and bent pole, they're fine. I pull them closed and go back to the bed. I pick up the journal that I found during my— whatever that was. I sit down with my legs curled under me and flip through the pages. This journal seems more like organized notes. There are prayers and... spells? Was that wall Angel created at school a spell? That's interesting. I flip further into the book. A list of demons he has encountered and how to deal with them. That'll be useful. There's also a list of plants, their properties, and where to find them. I definitely have to read this one. I thumb through the pages until something catches my eye. *Summoning the Horsemen?* is the page's title. My stomach tightens. Angel had at least thought about facing them. Maybe he did?

From time to time I have encountered the Horsemen. Sometimes it was their specter where their influence was great. Other times it would be their dispatched minions to carry out some order. I have even encountered cultists trying to contact them.

Where rain was ever scarcer, I would see the specter of Famine trudge along, scraping his fingers on the ground where crops tried to grow. The crops would wither and the soil rendered infertile. I would see him trudge through the rivers that towns pulled their drinking water from, drying the banks. I had even seen him reach into people's stomachs and devour whatever he found, leaving only hunger pains behind.

Where anger and hate hold sway and violence is as common as the rising and setting of the sun, I have seen the ghost that is War. His very presence drowns out rational thought and feeds prejudice. His chains indiscriminately end the lives of the defeated, hanging onto life. Many would have survived their wounds. Others he will simply watch linger and grow their agony into death.

The dark miasma of Pestilence permeated villages and towns stricken with epidemics. His powers blocked the magic of the healers and would mutate or strengthen disease against medicines. I see him over the beds of the sick, vomiting more poison into their bodies. I would see him caress the nursing staff and breathe into them disease. All but Pestilence would ignore me. I think he still views us as friends.

I gasp in shock. They were friends? What was Angel doing that he became friends with an avatar? Then again, Santano was my teacher. There were no signs of evil in him. He tricked us all. How long was he practicing before he became an avatar? Years? How many potential avatars are leading normal lives? Thinking about Aran, who had a family, I'd guess all of them.

Where their presence is felt strongest, I see them. War-torn battlefields, regions of drought and famine, lands facing epidemics; they are there making matters worse; their influence growing stronger and spreading. I have found cultist groups that try to bring the Horsemen into areas where their influence is weak. Pestilence will answer me if I call him, but not the others. At best, their specters will laugh at me. But I have found a way to make them pay heed to me. I know how to summon them. I've learned doing so is a mistake.

I thought I found a means of destroying Famine and I summoned him. I was wrong. I could not hurt him in any way. He was too powerful. I can only assume it's because of the power I've lost over the decades. I had beaten Pestilence once. I thought I could beat his brethren too.

"Aha!" I shout. "They can be beaten! Angel beat one! I'm stronger than Angel! I should be able to beat them too!" I can't help the grin on my face. They aren't invincible. I can beat them. I just can't hold back.

I found summoning them to be easy. I wonder if other demon hunters had known and tried their hand. How many died in their attempt? How many knew better? I can't give up. I have to keep searching for a way. I have to try again.

To summon any of the Horsemen, seek a place where their influence is strong. Violence and hatred. Hunger and wastefulness. Hopelessness and illness. As these things reach a height, their specters will appear. Call out to them. Call out that the demon hunter challenges them and they will answer.

I close the book. I'll find War where there is anger and hatred. Where there is only violence. I need to go somewhere violent. I spy the remote on the floor and pick it up. I press the power button and the television hums to life. I start flipping through the channels, looking for the news. There's always something violent going on somewhere and the news is always eager to show it.

I cycle through the stations once before I find a news show. I sit and watch it while eating the pizza and cleaning my hands on the towel around me. There is a lot to take in. I don't know the area. During commercials I look for other broadcasts. I watch the news well into the night. It looks like there's a gang war in Detroit. That should be violent enough.

-Heaven's Interlude-

Across from the hotel a baby-faced, innocent-looking angel sat. His curly, dark brown hair covered his face as he cradled his burned hand. He obeyed when she ordered him out, but she had mistaken him. She had hurt him. This demon hunter made it difficult to get close. She was hard to guard, constantly pushing him away. Rebecca's guardian, Raphael, watched as she drew the curtains closed. He wondered what had gone through her mind after she pushed him out. He placed his hand on his shoulder and cast a simple healing spell, trying to stop the bleeding staining his white robe and blue tunic. He had felt the sting of the Sword of Might before. They all had, but not like this. Not intentionally from the demon hunter. It would take a few days to heal even with magic. He was unsure about the burns he had sustained when she tried to touch him. That was a new sensation.

RULES OF ENGAGEMENT

"This is going to be problematic," he said.

-End Interlude-

Seven

The air is utterly still and a pitch darkness surrounds me. My footsteps don't make a sound as a single ray of light shines down on me like a spotlight. In the distance I can hear a growl, like the breath of a great beast, and the rattling of chains.

"I look forward to our game," War says, his voice loud in the silence. I draw the Heavenly Weapons and look around into the blackness. The grotesque sound of ripping flesh pierces the emptiness. "Let us enjoy the chase," he says. I step on something slick. I look down and see blood. I back away from it as it pools in front of me. "Where shall we meet? Some place familiar?"

Rattling metal echoes in the distance and lights above me come on one by one, illuminating lockers. I stare down the hall and recognize it. This is the high school. I walk to my locker and it rattles as I approach. "No," War says as the marks of powerful claws rip into the locker door. "Not here." The marks race down the lockers on both sides of the hall. "Some place exotic perhaps?"

I step back and a twig snaps under my foot. I look down to find the ground covered in leaves and vegetation. The lights shatter and the lockers tear away. Trees burst from the ground and reach high into the sky. The moon appears and shines down on me. "Tell

70

me," War's voice echoes around me, "where would you like to die?" Barbed chains shoot out of the darkness and twist around the trees, trapping me between them. There are vicious heads attached to each chain; hooks, spikes, clamping beaks, and they come at me from all angles. Instinctively I surround myself with my white shield and the heads beat hard against it.

The ground shakes and giant metal fingers emerge, tearing away the trees. The chains pull back and the dark steel fingers arch towards me in the center of a palm and press against the shield. War chuckles as his large, imposing, and horrific face comes out of the darkness. He is a giant and I am literally in the palm of his spiked hand. The pointed fingers of his gauntlet press against the shield, forcing it to shrink as my arms are pushed inwards. I strain against the pressure as I fall to my knees. The shield is cracking. "Such fun we shall have," he gloats.

I push back, trying to expand the shield, but I can't. The pressure is crushing me. Under War's calm, sadistic chuckles, the shield breaks and his sharp fingers no longer have resistance.

I jump in my seat, nearly screaming. My heart is racing and goosebumps crawl along my body. War's calm and taunting laughter echoes in my ears. The rocking of the bus must have put me to sleep. I look out the dirty window as the world races by. A passing sign says thirty miles to Detroit. I rub my eyes and look out the window again. Glowing red eyes on a wicked black helmet stare back. I jump and the face vanishes. War's taunting laughter echoes again. "Show me your strength," he says.

Angry that my mind is playing tricks on me I want to strike the window but fight the urge. Instead I move to a different seat. Breaking the window would just get me thrown off. I peer down the crowded bus from my seat in the back. Honestly, I was surprised by how many people were waiting when I got to the station. The first bus didn't leave until nine and the trip was going to be a couple hours or so. The bus is pretty full, but I see a couple empty seats. I make my way to the front and end up sitting next to a guy who looks around my age with a purple Mohawk and several piercings on his face. Normally, he isn't someone I would sit beside but what could he do to me now? He looks at me as I sit down and I give a nervous smile. He laughs to himself as he adjusts his headphones.

I sigh; glad he didn't try to strike up a conversation. I want to read Angel's journals. I've found he wrote more organized notes into three separate journals. I guessed these were the notes he fell back on and kept them updated. At least six centuries of knowledge were in these writings. It would give me a leg up against Hell and its avatars.

Angel went into detail about each power; what they did, their limits, and how to command their strength. Each is divided into one of three categories; Sword of Might, Dagger of Power, and Demon Hunter. He had a plethora of powers and abilities when he began, but they dwindled over the years. Next to many of the entries is a note, *Faded* or *Lost*. It makes me worry. I have a time limit. Eventually my powers will fade too. Angel did tell me this power is passed to the eldest in our bloodline when the current demon hunter dies. I'll have no successor, so it's a safe bet I have a good lifetime at full strength, so about seventy or eighty years, give or take. The thought of not growing old is nice, but not the cost. I would gladly grow old to have my family and friends back.

"What ya reading?" the guy with the Mohawk asks.

I slam the book closed. "Were you reading over my shoulder?" I ask.

"Yeah. And? You sat next to me babe."

"Don't call me babe. I didn't sit next to you because I thought you were cute. I wanted to move to the front of the bus. This seat was empty."

"Sure thing." He snatches the book from my hands. "So what is this anyway? Occult or something? You a witch?"

"It's none of your business!" I say as I reach for the book.

He keeps it out of my reach and opens it. I'm fast enough to simply snatch it from him. Why didn't I? "Never heard of these plants," he says as he flips through the pages. "These for love potions or something?"

I reach out with lightning speed and snatch the book away from him. It takes him a second to realize that I moved and have the book now. He looks at me in amazement as I tuck the book back into an inside pocket. He leans into my space and says, "Wow, you're fast. You're definitely not a normal chick. That much I can tell. What else you got under there?"

I lean away from him, regretting my choice to sit next to him. "Nothing you would be interested in, trust me."

"Oh, I don't know. I'm pretty freaky myself. So, what are you not wearing under there? Mind if I peek?

I'm shocked and react instinctively, angrily. I slap him. Blood splatters on the seat in front of us. I see a flash of War's face and hear a low growl. The Mohawk haired guy holds his face and curses. Blood flows between his fingers. "Crazy bitch!" he shouts. I sit in shock. I didn't mean to hit him that hard. "I think you knocked some teeth loose!" Teeth? I knocked his teeth loose? How hard did I hit him? "You are a freak. I'm out of here."

So shocked, I'm unable to move as he pushes past me. "I'm sorry," I manage to say, but I don't know if he hears me or cares. I sit staring at my hand. I hit him hard enough to cause damage with a simple slap. I lost my temper and couldn't control my strength. I hurt him. I look out the window. There is blood splatter on it too. I lack control completely. It was just a light tap and I knocked his teeth loose. What damage could I do if I was really mad? No. I can't let that happen. I have to control my emotions. I always have to maintain total control. If I don't I may end up hurting someone I'm trying to protect; or worse.

Angel had written about using meditation to keep his mind clear and emotions in check. It's not something I'm very familiar with but spend the rest of the trip trying to do. I don't need to lose control and hurt someone. All I know about mediation comes from cartoons and movies, so there's that issue. I sit cross-legged in the seat with my back straight and rest my hands on my knees. I close my eyes and take deep slow breaths. I try to let my mind rest and not think about anything and focus only on my breathing. Slowly it becomes quieter. I feel befuddled, hot, dirty, and achy. I'm not sure if I am doing it right or if these feelings are normal. It's becoming a little hard to breathe, like there's a weight on my lungs. My heart starts to race when I find I can't move or open my eyes. I'm trapped in the meditation. I can feel my muscles twitch as I try to force my body to move. It's becoming painful. The noise of the bus begins to filter back in, but it's loud, so loud. It hurts my ears. I want to cry out. My lips part and I try to call for help, but it barely comes out as a mew. I'm not even sure I heard it.

Strong hands fall on my shoulders and squeeze me tightly. The bus comes into stark relief against my closed eyes. It's smoky and I can look around, but my head isn't moving. I can see the hands on my shoulders, like a misty gray negative. The hands go to my head and force me forward.

"Don't move," the voice says. It's like an echo. "You're starting to astral project."

"I'm what?" I ask. I'm panicked and don't realize at first that I'm able to talk again.

"Hold still. You don't want to be forced back into your body."

"Who are you?"

"The bus will stop soon. Take a deep breath and exhale."

I do as he—I think it's a he—tells me.

"Relax your body. Don't fight the sensation."

I try to relax. I feel weightless, like the only thing keeping me down are his hands.

"Keep breathing. You need to slow your heart rate."

I keep breathing. Deep inhales. Steady exhales. My heart is still beating fast. I don't know how to slow it.

"We're out of time. I'm going to try to keep you aligned, but your thoughts will be befuddled. Repeat 'Stay still. Rest.' Or you may not like where you find yourself."

"Wait, I don't understand!"

"Just repeat it and don't stop."

Not sure what's going on, I begin to repeat the phrase. There's pain in my shoulders as he presses down. I only manage to get through a couple repetitions before my head hits the chair in front of me. I'm able to move again, but I hurt all over and am nauseous. My eyes ache and my vision can't keep up with the motion of my head. I'm mumbling something but can't

75

understand it so stop. There are snickers. I've fallen out of the chair.

I sit down and rub my temples, attempting to at least rub the pain in my head away. What did I do wrong? I was reciting something. I need to be reciting it. What was it? Everyone is filing out of the bus, but I just sit there, probably looking as confused as I feel. I know I'm on a bus, but I don't know where I am. I can't remember why I came here in the first place. What am I looking for? A guy with a purple Mohawk walks past me. He has dried blood on his face and shirt. I think he's missing a few piercings. He won't look at me. I hurt him. I hit him and hurt him. I can't remember why I hit him, or if he deserved it, only that I regret it. Why am I so confused? What was I doing? What was I saying?

Finally I'm willing to get to my feet, but my knees are wobbly. Each step feels like the floor is farther away than it actually is. I make my way towards the exit using the seats for support. It seems like they're farther away than they are and my hands keep slamming into them. I hear creaks and cracks as I hit them and one seat actually moves. I'm hitting them too hard. I'm too strong and have to be careful. I have super strength, but that's silly, isn't it?

When I finally make it off the bus the snow hurts my eyes and makes me squint. I scan the terminal and I see a sign that reads Detroit. I'm not in Chicago? That's right. I had to leave Chicago, but I don't remember why. Was I following someone? I came to Detroit for something but can't remember what. I see the guy with the Mohawk talking to two men. One of them has a tattoo on his neck. It looks like the head of a bird with lightning behind it. It's a Thunderbird tattoo. I heard about them on the news yesterday. They're in a turf war. War. That's right. I'm looking for War. I'm the demon hunter. That's why I came to Detroit. I can't remember how yet, but the Thunderbirds can lead me to War. I take a deep breath. My steps are slow at first, but steady. My legs still ache, but don't feel so weak. "Sorry about your face," I say to the guy with the Mohawk. He sneers at me.

"You did that?" the man from the Thunderbirds asks.

"Yeah."

He looks to the guy with the Mohawk. "You didn't say your fight was with a chick."

I realize the guy I hit is probably trying to join the Thunderbirds. Gangs value strength, right? So, I have to look tough. "I knocked a few of his teeth loose too."

The two men laugh. "Seriously?" the Thunderbird asks. "Either she packs one hell of a punch or you have a glass jaw."

"I'm strong," I say before the guy with the Mohawk can answer, but his face is contorting in anger. "I pack a good punch." The feeling in my body is beginning to return. I don't feel so numb, but I'm still a little confused.

The Thunderbird looks me up and down. "I don't know. I think maybe he just has a weak jaw. Look—"

"You little bitch!" the guy with the Mohawk shouts as he throws a punch.

It takes us all by surprise, but I'm fast. I reach up and grab him by the wrist and tilt my head away, both instinctually, though he doesn't come close to hitting me. He tries to pull away, but I hold him tight. I'm scared though. Why am I scared? "Let go!" he shouts. I oblige and he falls back onto the wet ground.

The second guy laughs out loud. The Thunderbird looks at me with a curious look on his face. "Okay," he says. "So the trench coat isn't for looks. You're fast, definitely, but have you ever been in a real fight?"

"My fair share."

"Who wins?"

"They die."

He looks me over again before turning to his friend. "¿Qué piensas? Podría haber tenido suerte?"

"Esa es una gran suerte Storm."

"We'll take you with us," the Thunderbird says. "Let's get moving you two. Play nice with each other."

We all fall in line and follow the Thunderbird. I think his name is Storm; it's the only thing that was said in English. He leads us to a deep red car with slightly tinted windows and a hood ornament of a bird. From my vantage point I think it looks like a hawk. The underside of the car is marred with sludge and salted snow. Mohawk and I sit in the back while Storm and his friend ride up front. I'm nervous as Storm shifts the car into gear. What exactly am I doing? What do they think I'm doing? What was the point of approaching them and trying to impress them in the first place? Caressing my cross, I pray I'm not making a mistake. Things are slowly becoming clearer and my recent memory is returning. The numbness of my body has been replaced with a dull ache. I remember this started on the bus when I tried to meditate, but I'm not sure exactly what happened.

"So what's your name?" Storm asks.

"Rebecca," I answer, glad we're about to exchange names. "You're Storm, right?"

"Si. Where're you from?"

"Chicago."

"Long way from home, aren't you? Why come all the way out here?"

I'm not sure exactly what he means, but try to play it off. "I have my reasons."

Storm shrugs. "You'll have to share those reasons if you want in."

I try not to look surprised. He thinks I'm trying to join? Is that what I'm trying to do? It isn't what I wanted. "I'll tell who it concerns." I say, trying to hide my worry. God, I'm making a mistake. How do I get out of this? "So I know your name," I say, trying to change the subject so I don't panic. "What about your friends?"

"Call them whatever you like babe."

I furrow my brow. Only Michael was ever allowed to call me that. He isn't Michael. I shift in my seat and lean towards the front to stare at Storm through the rearview mirror. "Firstly, it's Rebecca. Not babe. Not doll. Not toots. Rebecca. Got it?"

Storm smiles. "I like you. You may actually fit in."

I'm not sure that's a good thing, but at least I think I have enough of an attitude to make them give me some respect. Granted, the attitude probably comes from the fact that I know they can't lay a finger on me. A couple weeks ago and I would have kept my mouth shut and kept walking if a gangbanger said anything slightly offensive to me. Today I willingly got into a car with three of them. I'm having second thoughts about this poorly laid out plan, but it's too late to back out now.

"Where are we going anyway?" I ask.

"Initiation," Storm answers. "That's why you came here, isn't it?"

"Yeah," I stutter.

"You're tough, so I'll vouch for a fight. Just don't screw it up. Make me look bad and I'll be damn sure to have a turn with you."

What does he mean by that? "I can handle myself."

"For your sake, I hope so."

I don't want to break the pursuing silence. I'm strong and fast, but this isn't me. I'm agitated. I need to keep this attitude up, but I don't want to overdo it either. I'm glad when Storm turns the radio on, though I don't care for his choice of music, particularly the excessive, rattling bass. I can't even hear any music as the car thumps. I have to endure it for a good twenty minutes before he pulls into a lot and parks. We get out and I look at the building. It looks like an abandoned store. The signs are missing and the windows are boarded. We follow Storm inside. I'm nervous. I don't know what to expect.

We enter through the door and behind the boarded windows are dozens of men and a handful of women. I swallow nervously. These are all gang members, aren't they? The girls look me up and down as I walk by them. I can hear them whisper about how I was going to get it and laughing about how hard I was going to get it. I was pretty. What are they talking about? What am I going to get? I'm just going to fight, right? I can handle that.

There is a lot of shouting and jeering ahead of us. I'm not sure what's going on. "Time!" someone shouts over the crowd. "Can you get up?" A few minutes pass. "Get this waste of space out of here!" I recognize the voice, but I can't place it. I see a couple guys carrying a third who is bloody and beaten away.

"What happened?" I ask.

"He didn't get in," Storm answers.

They beat him up? I would have to let them beat me up to join? I shake my head. No. I'm not trying to join. I'm trying to find War and need their help to do it. That's why I came looking for them in the first place. This joining is a mistake. All these violent people in one place. Violence is normal for them, but is it good enough? If I call to War and he answers, what would become of these people? My stomach turns. I really didn't think this through. Not at all. I know nothing about gangs. I'm in way over my head.

We break through the crowd and find ourselves at the center of a fighting ring. There's fresh and dried blood splattered on the floor. "Who's the blonde?" someone asks. He has the same tattoo on his arm that Storm has on his neck. He has different tattoos on his other arm, mostly tribal, but I can make out one barbed wire cross that looks familiar. His features are purely Hispanic, more so than even Michael's were. Wait a minute, I think I know him. His hair is longer now, about shoulder length and all pulled back, but there's no mistaking those unearthly gray eyes of his. That's Jorge. I begin to look around the ring, hoping she isn't here too. Hoping that I can recognize her if she is.

"Her name's Rebecca and she's something else," Storm says as he pats me on the back. "You should check her out. Let her fight."

Laughter breaks out in the crowd, but Jorge just stares at me and I stare back. He recognizes me.

"Golden Girl?" Jorge asks. "Is that you?"

"Where's Andrea?" I demand.

"What in the world are you doing here?"

"Wait, you know her?" Storm asks.

"She shouldn't be here."

"Move!" I hear someone shout. A girl bursts through the crowd. She looks nothing like Jorge, but I know it's her. She's older now, but I recognize her nonetheless. She has lighter skin than her brother and doesn't look as exotic, but there's no mistaking her ethnicity. She's cut her hair. It's a lot shorter than it used to be. Even though I haven't seen her in years, it looks strange on her.

"Andrea!" I shout as I meet her at the ring's edge.

"What are you doing here?" she asks.

81

I'm at a loss for words. What do I say? "It's a long story," I decide on.

"I'm happy to see you, but why did you come here?"

Jorge grabs my arm and tries to pull me around. "You need to go Golden Girl," he says. "You can't handle this."

I pull my arm out of his grip. "You have no idea what I can handle."

"I know you can't handle this life."

"I've changed."

"I doubt you've changed that much."

"You'd be surprised how much I've had to change. I guess I shouldn't be surprised at how hard that is for you to believe Jorge. You haven't changed at all."

"You don't know a damn thing about what's going on!" Jorge shouts as he points sternly at me.

Andrea gets between us. "Stop it, both of you!" she shouts. "Rebecca, please come with me."

Andrea pulls me into the crowd as Jorge shouts, "Send her away, hermana! She'll just get hurt here!" My fists clench. I'll get hurt? He has no idea what I'm capable of. I stare after him as he calls out to a man named Frankie. The guy with the Mohawk comes into the ring. I force Andrea to stop where we are. I'm angry and don't want to keep moving.

"What's going on?" I ask.

"This is an initiation," Andrea answers. "Rebecca, why did you come here?"

I turn back to look towards Frankie. He's squaring off against someone, but his stance is all wrong. I can tell just by looking, he doesn't know how to fight. His opponent does and it's painfully apparent when his first punch easily connects with Frankie's face.

"Rebecca," Andrea says. "Let's go. You don't need to watch this."

"I came here for a reason," I say, almost sternly.

She stares at me for a short moment. "Please don't. Whatever you think— You can't handle this. You'll get hurt."

I turn back to her with wide eyes. My mouth is agape and can't form words. Andrea thinks I can't handle myself? Does she really think I'm the same little girl I was when we were ten?

"Weak," I hear a deep voice groan.

"I'm not weak," I say. Andrea stares at me with her face contorted in worry.

"I never said you were," Andrea says. "But I know you, and this time I have to stop you."

Frankie falls back into the crowd who just push him back into the ring. Someone follows behind him and punches Frankie in the kidney. He falls to his knees from the pain and gets kicked in the back. The two men circle him a couple times as Frankie struggles to get back to his feet.

"He's not a fighter," I say.

"Neither are you," Andrea says. "If he can't stand up, they'll just toss him out. You won't be that lucky."

I watch as Frankie manages to get back to his feet only to have the third and final attacker tackle him to the ground. Frankie rolls onto his side as he cradles his head. The three men start to take turns punching and kicking Frankie as he gets into the fetal position.

"Andrea, you have to stop this!" I exclaim.

"I can't," she says. "There isn't anything I can do. He knew what he was stepping into."

"That doesn't mean they can beat him to death!"

Something hits my foot and draws my attention to the floor. A bloody piercing, still with flesh on it, rests at my feet. I watch the three men beat Frankie who isn't even trying to fight back anymore. The air is thick with

83

the scent of sweat and blood. The crowd's cheers egg the fight on. They don't care. To them, this is fun. This is normal. If he dies, who cares? It's just another life they'll take. I look back to Andrea. She's shaking her head, silently pleading with me.

"Fine," I say as I untie the Heavenly Weapons and push them into Andrea's hands. "I'll do it myself."

"What are these?" She asks.

I remove my trench coat and give it to her as well. "Family heirlooms. Don't let them out of your sight." I hold my cross as I walk towards the ring, Andrea staring after me in bewilderment. "Please," I pray, "don't let me hurt them too badly."

"Rebecca, wait!" Andrea calls after me. "Think for once!"

I push my way through the crowd, ignoring her. They don't stop me as they cheer. "This time won't turn out for you!" Andrea shouts. She's having a harder time breaking through the crowd.

"It will," a deep voice groan in delight.

I size up the situation as I come to the front of the crowd. Frankie is on the ground trying to protect his head. One of his attackers is facing his back to me and kicking with his right foot. The other two are attacking Frankie from behind and so facing me. They're alternating between punches and kicks. Once, this was a fight I would not have gotten involved in. Now I'm the demon hunter, so this will be easy. I just have to pull my punches a little.

I run at the one facing his back to me. He's supporting all his weight on his left leg as he kicks Frankie. I kick his left leg out from under him and he crashes into the floor with a painful grunt. I keep moving before anyone can register what's happening. I step over the first man and move left towards the second. He barely has time to acknowledge what's going on when I grab his hand. I pull his arm forward then back and twist his wrist. The quick motion and forward footwork twists his body with his arm, flipping him and slamming him onto the ground with a loud thud. The third man moves to attack me. I raise my arm and block his punch before striking with my other hand, slamming the heel of my palm into his stomach and forcing him to buckle over. I strike the base of his neck with the edge of my fist and he slams face first into the ground.

"Hold on! Time out!" Jorge shouts as he breaks into the ring. Everyone quiets down and the three men pick themselves up and move away from me. "Where the Hell did you learn that?"

"You wouldn't believe me if I told you," I answer as I relax my stance.

"I didn't ask for your help," Frankie coughs.

"Oh shut up!" I almost shout. "You were in way over your head!"

"He's right," Jorge says. "This wasn't your fight Golden Girl. It was his."

"That wasn't a fight, it was a beating; and quit calling me that!"

"Well it's true! You're the pampered little white girl you always were; looking at everything through your rose-colored glasses; living in your own little privileged world! This is reality chica! You don't belong!"

I'm fuming to the point I'm almost seeing red. I can't stop myself as my body suddenly moves on its own. I slap Jorge and he hits the floor. There's dead silence as everyone stares at me with hate-filled eyes. Andrea calls out to me worriedly. Storm tries to help Jorge up, but he just pushes Storm away. Jorge looks up at me and we exchange angry stares. I see the blood coming out of his nose and side of his mouth and my anger leaves. I did it again. I lost my temper and hurt someone.

"Jorge," I stutter, "I'm sorry."

He wipes the wetness from his face and looks at his bloodied hand. "You know what?" he asks with an angry smile. "It's okay. It's fine."

Andrea finally breaks through the crowd and stands beside me. "Hermano, cálmate," she says as Jorge gets back up. "Ya sabes cómo actúa primero y piensa más tarde."

Jorge ignores her and addresses Storm. "You brought her here for the initiation, right?"

Storm nods.

"Apparently she can fight and packs a punch; no idea where she learned that."

"No, por fa," Andrea pleads.

What, I wonder? Have me fight?

"But that's not how girls get in, is it?" Jorge addresses the gang. There are murmurs of agreement among them. "I think we can make a little exception for Golden Girl here though."

"What exception?" I ask; worried about where this is going.

"You start with three and there's no limit. If you can't fight them off for five minutes, you'll still get in...after you're sexed in like every other bitch."

Jorge grabs Andrea and begins to pull her out of the ring. She resists as she pleads with him. Storm steps in and together they quickly remove Andrea as she calls back to me, "I'm sorry!"

I don't understand what's going on and no one will answer me. Suddenly, someone grabs me from behind, pinning my arms to my sides. He holds me tight and lifts me off the ground. Two men rush me as the ground falls away. I kick my legs up, catching one of the men under his chin. He stumbles back as the second grabs my ankles before they can come back down. I let my knees bend as he pushes my legs against me, then I push out sharply. The strength of my legs takes him completely by surprise and he falls back into the crowd. I slam the heel of my foot into the shin of the man holding me. He lets out a scream and I pull his arms apart. My feet find the ground and I pivot just enough to grab him and throw him over my shoulder. He hits the ground with a loud thud as the air is knocked from his lungs. The man I pushed into the crowd runs at me again with two people following him. I back pedal a bit to give myself room to move. One of the men takes a wild swing that I duck low under. I sweep his legs out from under him, sending him face first into the floor. I come up and pivot into a straight kick into the second man's stomach. He falls onto his back and slides across the floor. I hope I didn't kick him too hard, but I don't have time to worry. The third man moves in to punch me, but I block both his strikes before returning with an open-handed thrust. Hitting just below his sternum, he falls forward as he's thrown backwards.

There's almost a roar over the angry shouts of the crowd. Four men rush me from the crowd this time, two by two on either side. I focus on the two closest to me, moving in quickly with a block and knee strike to his stomach. Now with control of his body, I pull him towards me and push him into the two men coming up behind me. The last man throws a punch, but I step outside it and deflect his strike while twisting and locking his arm. I kick him in the stomach and throw him into the trio, knocking them the rest of the way to the ground and tangling them up.

It's getting harder to control my strength as they start to come at me in groups of three or four at a time.

I'm trying to stay on the defensive and keep moving. I can't stay in one place or let them surround me, but that's getting harder to do. I'm trying not to use my full strength against them, but I have to move faster and faster in order to deal with the sheer numbers they're throwing at me. Moving so fast I can't help but hit harder. My strikes are starting to draw blood. My heart is racing as I listen to the angry slurs they throw at me. I even understand some of the Spanish ones. My pulse is pounding as the rush of adrenaline washes over me. I'm smiling. I'm enjoying this? Yes. Why shouldn't I? Jorge wanted to stack the odds against me and they can barely lay a finger on me. They're angry and I'm almost laughing.

I'm becoming more aggressive. I just don't care as much anymore. I'm having fun. I see a punch coming in from the corner of my eye and instinctively raise my hand to block it, but instead catch it. I hold a firm grip on his fist as he tries to pull free while dealing with other attackers at my side. I pull him along as I deflect blows, flip opponents, and kick them back into smaller groups. I pull him towards me as I move and twist his arm behind his back, using him as a shield to take a punch that I could have easily dodged. He takes it hard to the chest; he's taller than me after all. With a smile on my face I push him forward into another guy hard enough to knock them both to the ground. There's something echoing in my ears over the chaos, but I don't listen. I feel a heavy presence hanging over me and the fight as a whole. I feel as if I'm being watched. Almost as if I'm showing off to whatever it is that's watching me. I want to show it how good I am. How strong I am. That's when I realize it's War. He's watching me. "Hurt them," I can hear him whisper. They deserve it, don't they? I'm happy War is watching. I want him to watch. I want him to see what I'll do to him. I'll hurt him like I'm hurting them.

My blows land fast and hard and elicit empty sounds from my attackers. I hear the snapping of bone followed by a scream. I see the misshapen arm in my hands and freeze. I broke it. I broke it with my bare hands with so little effort I didn't even realize I did it. I wish it was an accident, but it wasn't. What have I done? I let go and move back in panic. Arms lock tight around me and lift me off the ground. Two quick blows follow, one to my face and one to my stomach. They hurt, but I don't think they drew blood. My body is slammed onto the ground and I'm punched and kicked. They're shouting angrily at me, but I can't make out what they're saying. I'm still reeling from what I did and can only refuse to lay prone on the floor. Hands claw and pull at my body, trying to position me so I can't fight back. Some are trying to cop a feel while trying to twist my arms behind my back and push my head down, but I resist. No, something's wrong. They're not hitting me anymore. They're pulling at my body and clothes. My shirt rips and someone pulls on the back of my pants. I hear War laughing. Oh God, I know what Jorge meant now. I know what they're doing!

I push myself up and pull my arm free. Throwing my arm up, I toss the men beside me away. I strike out with my other arm, my forearm burying itself into someone's middle and sending him and the men around him down like bowling pins. I gather all my strength and force my body up, throwing the group off me. My elbow flies back into someone and I hear a sickly crunch. I rocket my fist out into someone reaching for me. I strike without regard to my strength and he flies through the crowd, knocking them down as he barrels through them. His body slams into the wall, cracking it as he hits, blood flying from his mouth. He lies still face down except for some twitching. I'm not sure if he's dead or alive. Everyone has backed away and stares at me. I adjust my clothes while holding my ripped shirt and bra together. Someone cries out in pain behind me. A man writhes on the floor holding his face as blood seeps around his hands. "Turn him over!" someone shouts repeatedly as a few people try to get him off his back. He's the one I elbowed. The crunch was breaking bone. I lost control and people got hurt; badly this time. I feel sick and lose strength in my legs. I feel like I'm hyperventilating as I fall to my knees. My heart pounds in my chest. I watch as more than a few men limp away. My adrenaline is falling and I can feel the ache of my body now. I have to pull myself together. I'm not safe like this. I get back to my feet and everyone surrounding me backs away. I watch as the one with a crushed face is led out with a bloody shirt held against his face. I look around and find Andrea and Jorge staring at me. I try not to look distraught as Jorge takes a few steps towards me. He looks around at the damage I did before addressing me. "Where the hell did you learn to fight like that? How the hell did you do that?"

I'm the demon hunter. It's the simplest answer. I'm trying not to shake in fear at what I've done. They can't see me afraid, so I decide to be mad. "Tell your boys," I hiss, "to never touch me again."

Jorge bobs his head absently. "Right." He seems at a loss for words.

Andrea walks up beside Jorge and smacks him with my sheathed sword. "Is she in now?" she asks as she draws the Sword of Might in show. "I'm betting she can use this too, since it belongs to her."

Jorge watches as Andrea hands my weapons back to me, but I notice her shaking. "Those are yours?" he asks.

"Yes," I answer.

Someone comes up to Jorge and whispers in his ear, but I can hear everything.

"She really messed a lot of people up," he says. "Marco and Daniel may not make it." I take in a sharp breath. I may have killed them? "If she can do that again, she might be the answer to our problem. I think you should consider making her an Elemental."

My brow furrows in confusion. What's an Elemental?

"We'll discuss it, like normal," Jorge says, "but I agree." He stares me up and down before reaching for his wallet and hands Andrea a credit card. We both look at him in confusion. "Rebecca needs new clothes," he says. "Make sure you get at least a few outfits in our colors."

"Your colors?" I ask.

Jorge ignores me and addresses his sister. "Bring her back home when you're done."

She nods and leads me out.

Eight

As we head outside, Andrea is shaking, but it doesn't seem to be out of fear. Her breath is quickened and she's smiling ear to ear as she searches for words. "That was amazing!" she says as she leads me to her car. "I've never seen anything like that before."

"Hopefully you don't have to again," I say as we get in. "How are you not freaked out? I punched somebody across the room."

"Oh, I'm terrified," Andrea laughs as she starts the engine. "But I know you won't hurt me."

"I'm glad," I say as I buckle in. "I don't want you to be afraid of me. I know I should say I'm sorry; I want to say it, but I'm not."

Andrea puts the car into motion as she responds, "You shouldn't be. You know what they were going to do to you if you lost, right?"

"They were going to rape me."

"That's how girls get in. I didn't think you knew, stepping in."

"I didn't. I didn't understand what Jorge meant."

"I know it's been six or seven years since I moved away; I don't think we were even twelve yet. The Rebecca I knew would never have stepped into that ring, but you always had a knack for barreling ahead blindly when you set your mind on something. I thought for sure this was going to be the one time it wasn't going to work out for you. Boy was I wrong."

"I do that?"

"All the time."

I think back over the last few days. I didn't think when I mentioned Angel to all my friends, when I saw him for the first time, the man I spent my entire life dreaming about, teaching me and training me in my dreams. Is that what go them pulled into that mess? Is that what got them killed? I sure wasn't putting too much thought into breaking Angel out of jail. I just knew I needed to save my friends and he was the only one that could help. What consequences am I going to face from that? I haven't really thought that far. "I guess I do," I say. "How did you two end up here, like this?" I ask, trying to change the subject so I don't have to think about those consequences, at least right now. "I mean, I'm not really surprised about Jorge, but this isn't like the Andrea I knew."

"Of the three of us, I'm the one who's changed the least."

"What do you mean by that?"

"Jorge's my brother, and yes, the leader of the Thunderbirds, but not because he wants to be. He tried being good. He tried doing things the right way. That's not what fate wanted. I'm around them a lot, but I'm not one of them, and I don't want to be. I wish things could be so much different. And now you are one. You can handle what I thought neither of us could. I guess it's just me. Why come all the way out to Michigan though?"

"I'm looking for someone."

"After what happened, I'm sure Jorge will be willing to help."

"I guess that was the plan."

"Who is he?"

"He's..." I trail off, unsure of what to tell her. I'm not sure how long I stare out the window trying to think of an answer that makes sense.

"What's the matter, Rebecca?" Andrea asks as she pulls into a parking lot.

I look at her, unsure of how long I've been silent. "It's hard to explain. I've been surrounded by a lot of death recently."

"I guess that explains the sudden silence. I'm sorry."

"I don't mean to come off as cold, I'm just still dealing with the losses. I'm glad I ran into you again. I just wish it was under better circumstances."

"You're here now," she says as she parks, "so let's make the best of it. Jorge's been teaching me to just roll with the punches."

Andrea moves fast to get out of the biting cold wind. It doesn't bother me, but I keep up.

"Wow, the wind really picked up!" Andrea says after entering the store.

"Just like home," I say.

"How are your parents?" Andrea asks as she heads for the women's section.

"They passed away recently."

"I'm sorry. My mom died of cancer a few years ago."

"That must have been hard. What about your dad?"

"What about him? I haven't seen him since Mom died."

"Why not? What happened?"

"That's right, you wouldn't know. My parents divorced after we moved here. The last time I saw Dad was Mom's funeral. Jorge got into a big fight with him and that was the last time I heard from him. He still pays my child support, but I'll be eighteen this year, so that'll probably stop."

"I never realized your parents were having so much trouble," I say as we begin going through the clothes racks. "I never imagined your dad to be the type of person to abandon his kids though."

"I think Mom got full custody, so I guess he didn't have much of a choice. I remember when he tried to see us, it usually ended up in some kind of fight between him and Mom, and eventually Jorge. Eventually he didn't try to see us much. I guess he just got tired of it."

I feel bad for her. She's lost both parents, but only one is dead. She'd be alone if not for her brother; even if he is the biggest jerk I ever met. Andrea picks out some yellow tops for me to try on and says, "Make sure you pick out a few things that are yellow and white. Those are the Thunderbird's colors."

"At least it's a decent combination," I say as I pick out some white blouses I like. I try to keep in mind that whatever we buy I'll have to fight in, so it not only has to fit well, it can't be too restrictive or loose. I have to make sure it can't be grabbed or caught on anything. If I can't move or fight freely in it, I can't have it, no matter how cute it is. The trench coat is already a big enough hazard for me to deal with. It's too big, but it's the only thing that can carry everything Angel left me. I still have no idea how it all fits in those inside pockets. Everything else is empty.

With a few different outfits in hand, Andrea points me towards the dressing room. Once inside I place the trench coat and Heavenly Weapons against the wall. I'm finally able to get a good look at my clothes. The rip in my shirt is pretty bad, but my bra is still intact enough to keep my dignity. I decide to try on the pants we picked out first and shimmy out of mine. I don't have much trouble getting the first pair on and they aren't too long in the legs, which is something I sometimes have issues with. I'm not a leggy girl so sometimes pants are either too long or too short. These seem to fit well.

"You're scared," an Irish accented voice says.

I jump and spin around. Úna replaces my reflection in the mirror, but she's wearing what I'm wearing and admiring herself. "Jeez, don't you ever knock?" I ask.

She looks at me and then knocks on the glass. "You're scared and distracted."

"What do you think?" I ask, modeling the white pants and ignoring her accusation.

Úna appraises them. "They will stain easily."

"They're white. Of course, they'll get dirty easy."

"I mean with blood. That's hard to get out of white."

I sigh in agreement and take them off.

"Your attention is being vied for," Úna continues.

"I guess I'm just a popular girl," I tease, trying to lighten the mood.

"Don't become lost in your fears. Don't lose your focus in the shouts."

"You think this is a mistake."

"You're vulnerable. Hysteria hangs about you. It's hampering you in all ways and every part of your being suffers from it. He will feed on that chaos."

The next pair I try on fit fine and aren't a solid white. "I'm just off my game today," I say as I take my torn shirt off to try on one of the yellow tops that looks like it'll match well. Úna mimics me as she tries on the same outfit. "That's all. I'll be fine. You seem to be enjoying trying on my clothes." Úna doesn't answer and I adjust the yellow top before facing her. She looks good in my outfit, but I have no idea how I look since she's robbing me of my reflection. Everything seems to be resized just for her. "What can you tell me about War? What can I expect?"

"I don't know. He isn't mine. He belongs to The First."

"If he's a True Form, why doesn't he just come to me like you do?" I ask as I take the top off and try on another. "You don't seem to have any problem doing it."

"We agreed to help you to your ascension. We did. I was chosen to help you until you find your feet. You haven't."

"Will he help me?"

"Yes."

"But I have to find him first?"

"He can't help you if you don't want it. To prove your desire, you have to go to him. He can help you reach your full potential."

I take off the top and try on a different one; white with long sleeves. "I already know how to do that. Why do you think so many people are getting hurt?"

"Power and potential are two different things, Sweetness."

"And to reach my potential I just need to control my power."

"I'm glad you think it so simple. I suppose then we do not have to worry about your sins."

"My sins? What do you mean?" I turn to face her, but only my reflection waits for me. "Úna?" I call. "I hate when you do that you know!" Not feeling like trying on any more clothes, I get back into my things. Seeing the rips in my shirt only makes me madder. I throw it down and tear off the tags on one of the shirts that I liked. I'll make sure it gets paid for at the register, but I'm not wearing that anymore. I throw the clothes I don't want into a bin and head out to find Andrea. I hear her voice and she sounds hostile. She's arguing with someone. I find her being confronted by three men. They're all on the taller side and imposing in their leather jackets. Two of them have visible tattoos on their neck. One of the three, the Hispanic one, is wearing a black and yellow bandana. He seems to be the leader of the trio. I have no idea what's going on, but I doubt they would do anything in a store. I take a breath and calmly approach them. After Úna, I almost want to pick a fight.

"This is my home," Andrea says. "I won't be bullied out by some spastic little man!"

"We've been nice up until now, chica," their leader says, "but that's starting to run out."

I throw the clothes into the shopping cart and look at the three men. "Is there a problem, gentlemen?"

They start laughing. "Looks like they picked up a nice little rubia."

"Damn, she's fine," one of the other two says. His neck tattoos are visible even against his dark skin. "I think I should make an offer. I'd love to tap dat ass."

My anger rises. I want to punch him across the store, like I did in the fight. Not wanting to kill someone else though I reply with, "You couldn't afford what I'd do to you."

"Hey, don't worry. I'm up for anything you got, muñeca," their leader says. "¿Como se llama?"

It takes me a second to translate what he said. Just who are these people? I don't like how they're crowding us. "My name is trouble if you don't back off."

"Then maybe you can give us a three for one deal?"

I pull my coat open enough to reveal the Sword of Might. "Maybe I need to make my point clearer." They stop smiling and take a step back. "Trust me, it's not for decoration."

"We're about done being nice," the Hispanic man says. "Let T-Bird know, he got a message coming."

"I don't take well to threats," I say. "You need to leave."

98

"Don't worry puta, we're going. You'll get yours. We don't take kindly to threats either."

I watch them as they walk away, making sure they don't try to do something after I lower my guard. Eventually I lose sight of them and can only assume they've left the store.

Andrea lets out a sigh. "Wow, thanks for that backup. I guess that sword comes in handy."

"Who were they?" I ask.

"Members of Black Lightning."

I nod, looking back towards the front of the store. There's the other part of the puzzle. The other group I need. "I heard about them," I say. "Your rivals, right?"

"Yeah. We should go."

"That's a good idea."

We head to the register to pay for the clothes. I hand the cashier the tag for the shirt I'm wearing, explaining that I couldn't wear mine anymore. He just nods as he scans the tag. I can tell he's nervous.

"Storm said he was taking me to see T-Bird," I ask as we unload the clothes. "Is that Jorge?"

"Yeah," Andrea answers.

I can hear the rapid thumps of what almost sounds like a heartbeat. Looking at the cashier I notice that he's rigid as he scans the clothes and won't make eye contact. Did he see what happened? I pick up one of the white and yellow shirts before letting out a sigh. "What was I thinking?"

"That's one thing that hasn't changed about you," Andrea says. "You never thought things through. If you can do it, you start without thinking about the consequences."

"That's gotten me into more trouble than ever lately."

"I don't know how it always works out for you, though. Even now. No matter how bad a situation you put yourself in, you never seem to stumble into more than you can handle. Even when it looks like its way beyond what you can handle."

That was true once. Handling what I'm in now is something I'm finding hard to do. Andrea pays for the clothes and we head out. The wind isn't blowing so fiercely now. Andrea comments something, but the Sword of Might pulls my attention away as it vibrates and hums. This is different, sending a chill of dread down my spine. I want to do something, almost need to do something, but my brain is trying to process so many unknown signals that I'm unsure what to do. Suddenly everything becomes clear as a roaring engine fills the air. I react instinctively and draw the Sword of Might as a car screeches to a halt in front of us. I see a gun pointed out the window and move my sword lengthwise in front of me. I don't have time to brace the sword as shots ring out. The blade jerks in my hand as a bullet pings off it. Andrea screams and I pull her to the ground as hot pain burns my arm. My shield encircles us in a protective dome before we even hit the floor as more shots fire. I can feel the bullets pinging off the shield.

"I got her!" I hear someone shout. The tires squeal as the car takes off. That voice belonged to one of the men from Black Lightning, the one I threatened. He tried to kill me for that? My breaths deepen as my eyes narrow on the shadow of the swerving car as it tries to speed away. The shield collapses as I get to my feet. I pull the Dagger of Power from its sheath and throw it at the car while shouting, "Impact!" The dagger strikes the rear of the car and the resulting blast throws the entire back end up and rips out both tires before slamming back down onto the street. The metal of the car sparks as it's dragged across the pavement before jerking to a stop. I hold my hand open and the Dagger of Power rips from under the car and returns to me.

"How did you do that?" Andrea asks.

I turn towards her, unsure of how to answer. I didn't think. I just reacted. Andrea is supporting herself on the ground with a bloody hand pressed against her side. "Oh my God," I exclaim. "Are you alright?"

"Behind you!"

The Sword of Might gives me the same sensation as before just as Andrea shouts her warning. I spin around and hear the sound of a gunshot. It feels like the sword is pulling me to one side, so I fall in step with it as something flies by, barely missing me. I keep moving as another fast object just misses me, followed after by a loud bang. Only now do I realize that the world has slowed, but the bullets are still moving fast. I reacted so instinctively I didn't realize I fell into Quickstep. I push forward before another shot can be fired, sprinting towards the Hispanic man. He's the one leading this. His friends are still in the process of getting their guns out.

He fires a third shot before I can close the distance completely, but he hasn't seemed to acknowledge that I'm no longer where he's aiming. I come out of Quickstep as I grab his face and throw him across the lot. He slams into a parked car, denting the door with his body and shattering the windows. I hear chains scrape across the pavement, prompting me to fall back into Quickstep. I move to dodge whatever caused that sound, but there's nothing to dodge. The other two men are still in mid-spin from my sudden appearance and attack. They're practically standing still. I take a few strides towards the man with the neck tattoos and jump into a kick before coming out of Quickstep. I connect under his chin and try to control the force of the blow, but still hit him much harder than I intended. His head jerks back with an awful crunch. Teeth and blood escape from his face as he flies back a few yards and drops his gun. He hits the pavement with an empty thud and bounces a couple times. He isn't going to be getting back up and I can only hope that I didn't kill him. God, please don't let him be dead.

"You damn bitch!" the last one shouts. I fall into Quickstep as I turn to face him. The world slows, but his shots don't. The world jerks back to normal as one of the shots grazes me and makes me stumble. I try to fall back in but can't. I'm forced to move around him, using the Dagger of Power as a pivot against his gun to keep him from taking better aim and landing a direct hit. Even with my increased speed and agility, I can only do so much at such close range. The trench coat weight may not be affecting me, but its sheer size is. It's too big for me to move like I need to and it finally catches up to me. I step on its tail and struggle to stay on my feet, even as burning pain shoots through my thigh and my leg becomes wet and warm. I fall to the ground, scraping my hands. I roll as shots hit the ground. After several shots ring out I hear the clicks of the empty chamber. He tosses the empty gun aside and pulls another from inside his jacket. He starts to shoot as the white shield forms around me. A bullet manages to sneak by and hit my shoulder before I'm fully protected. I roll over, hugging my hand to the new wound. The shield holds strong, protecting me from the barrage. I can feel each bullet as it pings harmlessly off the shield.

"The hell is this?" he demands as he empties his second gun. I get up to one knee, bearing the pain in my leg and shoulder. It hurts to move and I don't think I can go into Quickstep. Unsure if he has any more guns I take the Dagger of Power in both hands hoping I can keep whirlwind steady, but the man turns and runs.

With a sigh of relief I let the shield down. He's not even looking back. He's done with this fight. Sirens blare in the distance. Help is on the way.

Pain shoots through my leg as I get to my feet. "It's over Andrea," I call back to her as I sheath the Heavenly Weapons. "Help's coming." Pressing my hand into my bleeding shoulder, I stumble towards her. She's lying motionless on the ground as blood pools all around her. She isn't moving. My heart drops. "Andrea!" I push through the pain and run to her. I roll her onto her back to find she's been hit near her neck and is bleeding heavily. Her eyes are closed and I can't tell if she's breathing. "Andrea!" I cry as I check for a pulse. It's weak, but she has one. She's still alive! If I don't stop the bleeding she won't last, but I don't know how. I start to panic. I don't know what to do. "Help!" I shout. "Someone help!"

I feel a presence around me. A nonexistent voice urges me to calm down. I can use Angel's ointments! He used them on me when I was stabbed. I'm not sure how they work, but they helped. I reach into the coats inside pockets. What color did he use? I'm having trouble getting my fingers around any of the jars, like they're just beyond reach. Time is ticking and I'm getting frustrated. If I don't do something soon Andrea will die. I hear a faint whisper, but I can't understand what it said. "I didn't hear you! Tell me again!" It's faint, but I can just barely make it out. The light pink one! My hand immediately wraps around a jar and I pull out the exact one I was after. I twist the top off and dig my fingers into the semi-solid material and massage it into Andrea's wound, staining my fingers red with her blood. I scoop out more with my other hand and massage it into Andrea's stomach wound before applying pressure to both. The flow of blood is already slowing, but I can't be sure if that's because of the ointment already sealing the wound, or because she doesn't have much left to bleed.

"Hold on Andrea," I say. "Please hold on. Help is coming."

Squealing wheels turn my head. Three police cars pull up and officers are getting out.

"She needs an ambulance!" I shout to them. "She's been shot!"

The police rush to us and push me out of the way. I feel helpless as they radio for help. I can do nothing now but wait. I hold onto my cross with bloody hands and pray, "Please help her pull through."

Nine

Two officers hover over Andrea and begin treating her wounds. A third comes to tend to me. She helps me to her squad car and lets me rest on the hood. I limp a little but am grateful to finally be off my feet. She goes into her car and comes back with some kind of first aid kit. It's not like one I'm used to seeing. Blood making my body wet and sticky, she helps me out of the coat so she can get to my wounds, but I won't let her take it away. I huddle it around my waist to hide my weapons. The movement is painful. She starts to dress my wounds and applies pressure to stop the bleeding. It shoots pain through my entire left side and I stifle a cry. "The paramedics are on their way," the officer says.

I can already hear the sirens of the ambulance. The officer's talking to me, but I'm barely paying any attention to her. My eyes are locked on Andrea. The officers around her are frantic and call the paramedics over as soon as they arrive. They rush a stretcher over to her and block her from my view. My hand grips my cross as the minutes crawl by. When the paramedics finally hoist Andrea up her shirt is cut open and hanging off her sides. Her torso is covered in blood and an oxygen bag covers her mouth. They're squeezing the ball to push air into her lungs. I gasp as my heart drops and my stomach twists into knots. She's dying. The ointments weren't enough.

As they carry Andrea they pass one of the shooters. He's in a neck brace and being strapped into a stretcher. My teeth clench. This is their fault. They shot at us because I defended us. I scan the parking lot for the other man, the leader of the group. I find him with a couple paramedics hovering over him. I grip my hand on the curve of the hood, not regulating my strength. I want to go over there and throw the paramedics off him. The sounds around me are drowning out as my eyes narrow on that bastard. My teeth clench so tightly that my lips curl to reveal my teeth. I can hear a voice in the back of my head but ignore it. I shrug my shoulders, unwelcoming the gentle hands on them. I want to pick that murderous scum from the ground and demand why. Demand vengeance if my friend dies. I want to crush that little—

"Call it," a voice breaks through my haze. "He's gone." It's one of the paramedics. I hear the echo of my name screamed at me and I snap back to reality. "The autopsy will determine if it was the broken neck or crushed jaw that killed him." I crushed his jaw and broke his neck? I killed him? I shake my head. I didn't mean to. I was just trying to protect us. I just wanted to stop them. I didn't want to hurt them. I wasn't trying to. A voice whispers comforting words that I barely pick up. I feel hands on my shoulders again, but there are none there. I glimpse my hand clutching the car and find the metal crushed in my grip like plastic. It takes a little effort to free my hand. No one's noticed yet, so I move over to cover it. The voice is trying to tell me not to worry, but I can't help it. My thumb is caressing my now bloody cross. "I'll be okay," I whisper. "Andrea needs you more. Please help her."

I feel acceptance and the warm hands are gone. My angel will protect Andrea. My angel will save her.

-Hell's Interlude-

The paramedic came back with a white tarp. He handed it off to his partner who was distracted for a moment. She smiled and said, "He isn't going anywhere. I can handle this myself. Why don't you go check that guy out? They look like they could use a hand." The paramedic agreed and left his partner to the body. She unfolded the tarp as her eyes followed the light only she could see. She was careful not to let her angelic eyes too close to her host's human eyes. She just needed to be able to see the angel. The shapeless light was enough. She threw the tarp over the body as she watched the light descend into the ambulance with Andrea as it sped off. She kneeled by the man's head as she adjusted the tarp. "I really must thank you. Killing you myself may have drew attention, but War's hold had to be broken. I must remember to have you rewarded later." She pulled the tarp over his head and patted it. "Now that the sun is away, the storm gets to play." She stood up and brushed the snow and dirt from herself. "Let us make sure the demon hunter is calm for her trip. Can't have her lashing out in fear."

The possessed paramedic made her way to Rebecca as she gave those trying to help her a hard time. Baraqyal took a breath behind the human façade. It was time to start the charade.

"Hey, what's going on?" Baraqyal asked.

"She won't let me examine her," the paramedic said.

Baraqyal noticed Rebecca pulling the trench coat around her waist. "I'm fine," Rebecca said. "I'm not in shock. I just..."

Baraqyal nodded in the paramedic's body. Rebecca worried about the Heavenly Weapons. She hadn't yet realized her ability to hide them. "Honey, you've been shot," Baraqyal said as she placed a soothing hand upon Rebecca's shoulder. She had to release the anxiety. "You're not fine. We need to get those taken out of you, but before we can move you, we have to stem the bleeding. We can see where you've been shot. Let us do our job and get you into an ambulance."

"Can't we just skip that part?" Rebecca asked.

"If you keep bleeding, you'll pass out." Baraqyal began to tend to the easiest accessible wound; Rebecca's leg. "You seem fine, but we don't know how much internal damage there is. This is all we're going to do here." She showed Rebecca the bloody bandages. "Let us tend to your arm so we can get you to the hospital."

Reluctantly, Rebecca relaxed her arm, her face scrunched with pain the whole time. The first paramedic, frustrated with Rebecca, wasn't as tender as she could have been. Rebecca still tried to keep the Heavenly Weapons hidden. Once the paramedics were satisfied, Rebecca was loaded into an ambulance and taken to a nearby hospital. The possessed paramedic smiled as she pulled her gloves off. Rebecca's wounds weren't life-threatening so she wouldn't be taken to the same hospital as Andrea. Baraqyal looked around for a new body. It was time to change hosts. She spotted a police officer taking some statements from a small group of people. Still in his prime; late twenties to early thirties maybe. He was in good shape, but not too physically imposing. Though the stress of his work was beginning to show in his beard, he was physically fit. A much better vessel than she was currently in. Baraqyal smiled. He would do perfectly.

RULES OF ENGAGEMENT
-End Interlude-

Several hours have passed since I arrived at the hospital. In that time, I've had x-rays and the bullet in my thigh was removed. They left the bullet in my arm alone and the one that hit my shoulder went clean through the little space between the bones. All my scrapes and cuts were cleaned and bandaged, and I received a number of stitches. My bloody clothes are sitting in a clear bag and the Heavenly Weapons are bundled inside my trench coat. I'm wearing a pair of disposable scrubs so I wouldn't have to sit, and potentially leave, in just a hospital gown. I told them I just bought several outfits when we were attacked and waited for them to return those clothes to me. I've asked about Andrea, but she's been taken to another hospital and no one has any information for me. I stare at the x-rays, wondering about the bullet in my arm. It's lodged near the bone and the doctors said it would be safer to leave it than to remove it, so it remains. I wonder what I'm going to do now. I don't have anyone I can call and I don't have anywhere to go. I have no idea how to get in touch with Jorge and tell him what happened.

As I'm lost in thought, there's a knock on the partition separating my room from the next and a voice calls out, "Rebecca?"

"Come in," I say as I sit up in the bed. Storm comes in followed by someone I don't recognize. He hunches over slightly with his hands in his pockets. He has a slender face and short black hair that is slicked back. He has a spotty beard, mostly around his chin and a long pointed nose. He has one ear pierced with a diamond earring.

"This is Rain," Storm says.

"Hi," I say as Rain goes to my bag of bloody clothes.

"You are one lucky girl," he says as he lifts them up.

"Is Andrea alright?"

"Well, she's not dead yet," Storm answers. "She's out of surgery, but they're not sure if she's going to make it. Right now she's in a coma and T-Bird is beyond pissed."

"What happened?" Rain asks. "Why did they attack you?"

I look down at my hands as I try to find something to do with them. "They were harassing Andrea at the store. I got between them and we ended up threatening each other."

"They were intimidated by you?"

"I did threaten them with my sword."

"Sword?" Rain laughs. "I guess whatever works."

"They should have known better than to shoot at you in the first place," Storm says. "Hitting Andrea was too big of a risk."

"What do you mean?"

"That's T-Bird's story to tell," Rain says.

"When are they letting you out?" Storm asks.

"I don't know. I'm still waiting for them to bring the clothes we bought. They're all I have right now."

"You look around my cousin's size," Rain says. "I'll get you some clothes."

"Where're your weapons now?" Storm asks.

I point to them wrapped in my coat.

"We'll take them," Rain says as he picks them up. "Let's not give them a reason to hold you."

"I'll leave you my jacket," Storm says as he takes his jacket off and throws it over a chair. "We're lucky nobody's found them yet."

"Yeah," I say as I glance at the x-rays. The Heavenly Weapons are visible on the film, but nobody noticed them, just like in the pictures of Angel. Only I could see them. I still don't understand that.

There is another knock on the partition and a police officer walks in carrying a few bags. Storm and Rain eye him as they step out of his way. It's hard to gauge him as he's wearing shades. I never realized how intimidating that looked until now. It was especially intimidating in my current situation. I'm in no condition to really defend myself if I need to, not in such a cramped place. He's a little shorter than Rain, who is easily the tallest of the group. The officer has short soft brown hair growing out of an old crew cut. Gray dots his thin beard. He's either growing it out or overdue for a shave. He's in at least his late twenties.

"Gentlemen," the officer says to them before addressing me with a warm smile. "I believe these are yours, Miss Virtue."

I take the bags and find the clothes we bought. "Thank you," I say, my guard slightly lowered. "I really needed these."

The officer looks over the hospital bag with my bloody clothes inside. "I certainly understand." He turns to Rain and Storm with that same warm smile. "Do you gentlemen mind if I ask your friend a few questions?"

"Naw," Storm says. "We were on our way out."

Rain pulls a notepad from his pocket and writes something on it. "Give me a call when they release you." He hands me the sheet, which has a number on it, before he and Storm leave, taking the Heavenly Weapons with them.

"Are you doing alright?" the officer asks.

"I'm doing better," I answer.

"I'm glad to hear it. How's your friend doing?"

"I'm worried about her. I heard they're not sure if she's going to make it."

"Miracles happen if you pray hard enough. She has good people looking after her. They'll do their best."

"I hope it's good enough."

He takes out a notepad. "I'm afraid I have to ask you a few questions."

I nod.

"Do you know the people who attacked you?"

"No."

"What about your friend?"

"I don't know. Maybe? They were harassing us in the store. I stood up to them."

He scribbles into his notepad as he says, "I take it they didn't like that. They retaliated."

"Yes."

"The three men that attacked you, they were noted members of Black Lightning. Are you affiliated with the Thunderbirds?"

"What? No! I never said that!"

He smiles, not threateningly, but kindly. "No, but the company you keep tells a different story."

"What does that mean?"

He puts his notepad away and pulls up a seat beside the bed. "As you find allies in unlikely places, the file against you also grows."

My heart starts to sink. What is he talking about?

"You must be careful in stepping before War," he says. "You may find it's a bit more than even you can handle."

My heart is pounding. He knows more than he's telling me.

"You need to be careful. Think about what it is you're trying to do or you may end up regretting your actions."

What is he talking about? Nervous, my hands instinctively clench into fists, gripping my hospital gown. Is he going to arrest me? I'm the victim here! I can't fight my way out if he does. This is a hospital.

There are lots of patients and doctors that'll get hurt if I fight, not to mention all these fresh stitches I have.

"I understand your fear," he says as he places a hand on mine. "You've been through so much and have the scars to prove it." I'm not sure why, but his touch is somewhat comforting, even though I want to pull away from it. "You're strong, Rebecca, but you're not alone. You've never been alone."

"I don't understand what you mean," I say, my anxiety beginning to rise again. He takes my other hand and the stress almost melts away. It's very eerie.

"Of course you do, my little hunter," he says with a gentle smile.

Little hunter? That catches my attention. "Wait, are you...?"

"I know things are loud right now. There is so much commotion. So many voices, it can be hard to hear, can't it?"

I nod, almost absently.

"It can be hard to focus, but I can help if you let me."

I nod again. "I need help."

He takes his hands and caresses my ears while saying something in a language I don't understand. "Gloria in omnibus. Tantum audi me." The words echo in my ears.

I don't feel different. I'm not sure exactly what he did, but I don't question it. I just trust.

"You must learn to be more careful," he says as he turns to leave. "They know who you are and will find out what you've done. What do you think happens next?"

He disappears past the curtain and I sit and stare. The events of days ago play back in my head. Slipping into the jail that night, looking for Angel. Finding him and committing to freeing him. I remember my movements as I took out each guard in turn, until all five were unconscious on the floor. I trusted all that training in my dreams was good enough. It was. "I broke Angel out of jail," I say. "And attacked five cops to do it." Then it hits me. "I'm such an idiot!" I exclaim. I gave them everything they need to find me. My name, birthday, social security number, everything. Why didn't I think! I have to leave while I still have a chance to slip away.

I get to my feet and dump my new clothes onto the bed. My body strains with the lingering pain of my wounds as I get out of the hospital gown and into real clothes. Once dressed I peek out of the curtain to see what I have to deal with in order to get out. There are a few police dotted throughout the floor, but they don't seem to be doing more than talking to one another. I don't see any doctors and the nurses are mostly busy on their computers. There looks to be two exits that I can see; a main entrance and a trauma entrance. I'm closest to the trauma. I hear the mention of my name and look towards the source.

In the center of the room is what looks like a huddle area for the nurses. The space is large and mainly empty, surrounded by a wall on one side and computer desks on the other. The administration secretary, who I had talked to earlier and given all that damning information to, is talking to a nurse as she examines a piece of paper. I can't see it from my vantage point, but I notice one of those domed mirrors on the ceiling. I can see the nurse through it. I strain my eyes and focus on the paper's reflection in the mirror. As I focus more details come out as everything else in my field of vision slowly blends out. Almost like it's enlarging, I can see what's in her hands; my wanted poster. They know. I'm running out of time.

I blink and find that my eyes hurt and my vision is a little blurry. I rub the pain away and my vision focuses back to normal. What just happened? What did I do? I shake my head. It doesn't matter. I have to get out of here. I look for a phone in the room, finding one on the right countertop, and call Rain. I hope they haven't left yet. After a few rings Rain answers. "Where are you?" I ask, trying to hide my panic.

"We just got to the car," Rain says. "What's up?"

"I need you to pull up to the trauma entrance."

"What's going on?"

"I have to leave. Just have the door open."

"We're on our way."

He hangs up and I finish getting ready. I can't believe I'm putting my wellbeing into the hands of these people, but what choice do I have? I just hope I'm too hurt to use Quickstep. I put on Storm's coat, wincing in pain as I pull my arms through the sleeves. The partition between my room and the next can move, which gives me an idea. I just hope the room's empty.

I take my bloody clothes and extra linen in the room and make a human shape under the covers on the bed. I also pocket a few first aid pieces; gauze, tape, and the like, shoving them into my side pockets. Making sure my curtain is closed as tight as it can, I move the partition back enough to squeeze around it. The room isn't empty, but the patient is sound asleep, so I move as quietly as I can and pull the partition back into place.

I peek out around the curtain and see the same nurse talking to a policeman. My window of opportunity is shrinking. I look around the room for anything that may help me sneak by. There's a hat in the clear hospital bag resting on the floor. Silently I apologize to the sleeping patient and take it out, finding a scarf as well. I hear people announce themselves as they enter my room. I put the scarf and hat on, hiding my blonde hair completely. With hands in my coat pockets I exit the room and head to the trauma entrance as the police make demands to my decoy. I'm out the door by the time they realize I'm gone.

Rain is standing beside a double-parked red car holding back passenger door open. I don't want to look back towards the hospital and a beeline towards him. I risk Quickstep and push into a jog as the world slows. I'm in the car and pull the door closed as I come out of the ability. Rain curses, taken by surprise. He gets into the car and I start to calm as we pull away from the hospital.

"How did you do that?" Rain asks.

"Where are we going?" I ask, ignoring his question.

"T-Bird's place," Storm says. "He wants to talk to you."

"Good. We need to talk."

I sit back into the seat as Rain and Storm talk in Spanish. I don't bother listening. I don't know enough Spanish to even try piecing together what they're saying. Storm is wearing my coat, so I just stay in his. The Heavenly Weapons are in the backseat beside me. I pull the Sword of Might into my lap and sigh. The more the reality of what my life has become sinks in, the more depressing it is. I guess it's no surprise I have a warrant. Jailbreak and attacking an officer are felonies, right? How many years am I even looking at? I want to cry. The police on a constant look out for me will make it harder to fight the avatars when I find them. Angel had the experience to deal with this, but I have no idea what I'm doing. How do I stay low and out of sight like he was able to do?

I look out the window and absently begin caressing my cross, mostly cleaned of blood now. It's always been a habit, but it's probably going to come close to compulsive now. I just don't know what to do. I just barrel head on, like Andrea said. That almost got her killed. It caused me to end up joining a gang. It caused my friends to focus attention on Angel. I wonder, is that why Santano targeted them? Is it my fault their dead? How do I fix this?

The Sword of Might begins to hum in warning. There's danger. Blue lights flash through the car and Storm curses. "Just let me handle this," he says as he begins to pull over.

"You were seen," a voice says. "They were notified. They come for you."

"No, don't stop!" I shout.

"Why not?" Storm asks as he starts to slow.

"They need a reason to search us," Rain says. "You're fine."

"I have a warrant!"

Storm steadies his speed. "For what?"

I repeat what the voice tells me. "Assault of an officer. Prison break!"

"Are you serious?"

"Two more just showed up," Rain says. "¡Pisalo!"

"¡Maldición!"

Storm presses the pedal hard to the floor and the car tears off as the engine roars. It fishtails a little before finding traction. The police cars tear off in pursuit. I watch as several more squad cars tear onto the road behind us from side streets. Horns blare and tires screech as Storm runs through a red light.

"How many?" Storm asks as he weaves around traffic.

Rain starts to count out the cars behind us. "Six," he says.

"Six? Already? Damn chica, what else you do?"

"Just let me out!" I exclaim. "They only want me!"

"What, you want us to take the whole thirty seconds it's going to take to stop and let you out?" Rain asks. "They'll be all over us, unless you plan to jump and kill yourself!"

"I'll survive!" Storm tears around a corner, throwing me against the door. Rain tumbles but is caught by his seat belt. "We'll kill someone like this!"

"Take a left up here! I have an idea!" Rain shouts as he points out a direction.

Storm makes a sharp left and throws me across the back seat.

"You won't evade them," the voice whispers. It's more distinct now. It's so much easier to hear than before. "You'll have to fight."

"Fight?" I ask. "No, I can't!"

"Down the alley!" Rain shouts to Storm.

"¡Eres loco!" Storm shouts back. "That's a dead end!"

"Just do it!"

"¡Mierda!" Storm curses as he makes a hard turn into the alley.

I watch out the back window as the squad cars slam on their breaks to try and make the turn. I hear the crunch of metal as several cars screech out of sight. A few do manage to make the turn and continue the chase.

"The construction site!" Rain shouts. "Tear through the fence!"

Storm fights the wheel as he makes another sharp turn and rips through a fence surrounding the construction site. The metal skeleton of a building is erected and a concrete-filled foundation. Dirt and gravel kick up behind us and the near foot of snow slows us down as we barrel towards the structure. The car suddenly fishtails as the tires switch from the snowy dirt to the smooth, but snow-covered concrete. Storm curses as he fights for control, causing the car to spin and slam into one of the metal supports. The driver side airbag deploys, stunning Storm and making him lose complete control of the car as it twirls around the beam before coming to a halt. Rain is jerked to the side and I hear the crunch of glass. I fly across the backseat and slam into the door.

"Are you guys okay?" I ask as I try to find my bearings.

"Define okay," Storm groans, but Rain doesn't answer.

"Rain, are you alright?" I ask as I pick myself back up. He responds with a groan. I reach over the seat to shake him and find the window cracked and blood smeared around his head. I call out for him to wake up when something large slams into the ground kicking up a cloud of snow.

"The hell was that?" Storm exclaims.

The lights of the police cars pierce the cloud of snow and I hear them slam into each other as they skid to a stop.

"The building," the voice says. "It's going to collapse."

"What?" I shout. Two more objects slam into the ground, one crushing the hood of the car and rocking us.

"I'm stuck!" Storm exclaims as he wrestles with his seatbelt buckle.

"You can't save them," the voice tells me. It's more a whisper in my ear now than a faint voice.

"Yes I can," I say back as the building starts to roar. I find purchase with my feet and burst through the roof of the car.

"¡Dios!"

I grip the Dagger of Power tightly at my side and raise my hand. I can feel the white field surround us. The building screams as it comes down, slamming against the shield. Pressure shoots through my arm and my knees buckle against the force, almost knocking me down. I steady myself and strain to focus as the shield visually fluctuates against the mass of the beams. Each fluctuation jars my body and makes my head pound. Sweat covers my brow as I focus to keep the shield up. I'm afraid to release the Dagger of Power, worried that doing so will release the shield, but I can't push the shield out. My body is straining against the piling weight of the beams. My vision is going in and out of focus and I'm starting to see double. I raise the dagger and mentally push against the barrier with both hands, using the Dagger of Power as a focus.

My arms strain to extend and push the shield out. The beams move, some sliding off the shield. My head is pounding and my body feels weak. The shield is starting to crack. With a guttural call and final push, I force the shield out as it shatters. For an instant I black out as pain shoots through my head. Foggy sight returns as something large falls towards me. It's one of the beams! Instinctually I reach out to catch it and barely succeed. My feet press into the metal of the car, creating divots, and the tires blow out. I struggle to control the massive weight. Twisting at the waist, I throw the beam away and feel a sharp pain in my side. The beam disappears into the snow cloud, blowing more snow and dirt into the air. I sink back into the car holding my side.

Storm stares at me as I take a moment to push the pain away. My hand is covered in blood. I'm hurt, but I don't have time to deal with it. Rain is hurt too and the police are still out there beyond the whiteout. We might be able to use this to get away if we move fast. I shoo

Storm's hands away from the buckle and break it with a twist.

"We have to go," I say.

Storm stares at me with a look of fear and disbelief.

I kick the side door open, sending the entire thing flying into the cloud. I hear it slam against something and the police yell to one another. Storm shakes his head and exits the car. I get out and pull the entire driver's seat from the car so I can pull Rain free. I hand Storm the Heavenly Weapons and take Rain into my arms.

"I think I see someone!" I hear someone shout. The snow is starting to settle.

"Storm, my dagger," I say. He hesitates and I repeat myself in more earnest. He hands the dagger to me and I grip it and his hand. "Just trust me, okay?" I can see him most clearly and he slowly nods. "I'll get us out of here," I say as a green mist seeps from the dagger's handle and begins to surround us. Storm watches as the mist encircles us but makes no attempt to break away. Once enshrouded in its magic, Storm vanishes momentarily before reappearing in my green hazed sight, just as I know I had done for him.

"What did you do?" Storm asks.

"I made us invisible," I answer. "It won't last long, but we can use this to get away."

"Just who are you?"

I'm silent, looking for an easy way to explain it. The answer is simple, but to Storm it will be insane. "I'm the demon hunter," I say.

Ten

The dagger's power fades after a few blocks. Storm hails a taxi and we get in; Rain in the back with me and Storm up front. The driver glances at us in his mirror and says, "Is your friend alright? I can take you to the hospital." Storm slams the door behind him and places some money in the man's hand. "You drive and don't ask questions."

"Yes sir," is the driver's response as he heads down the road.

I cradle Rain's head in my lap as I tear into the gauze I took from the hospital. I have to stem the bleeding and am careful not to apply too much pressure to his wound.

"Storm," I call. "I need you to go through the inside pockets. There are jars of colored ointments."

Storm pats the pockets. "They're empty," he says.

"No they're not. Just put your hand in and pull them out."

He rummages through the pockets in surprise. "Where is this stuff coming from?" He hands me a red colored ointment. "These pockets are empty."

"Those pockets are not empty," I insist as I take the jar, unsure of what this one does.

He digs into the pocket again and pulls out a green jar. "I have no idea what kind of trick this is."

RULES OF ENGAGEMENT

I rub the ointment onto Rain's head, hoping that it will help. I need my coat and a proper place to treat him. Storm directs the driver as he makes a phone call. He's talking Spanish, but I hear the English word T-Bird. I can only assume he's either talking to or about Jorge. I don't pay attention to the conversation and focus my efforts on Rain instead. I worry he may need stitches. I can only guess how bad the wound is by how much he's bleeding. I'm trying my best to not let it onto the seats, letting it stain my clothes instead. So much for this outfit. I keep my hand on Rain's pulse to make sure it's not weakening. The fact that it's still fairly strong relaxes me. I use all the gauze I had taken, adding clean over the blood-soaked.

After about twenty minutes we pull over. I look up to see Jorge waiting for us with a towel in hand. He must not have been waiting long. He's wearing a plain black sweater instead of a jacket and doesn't look cold yet. He opens the door and tells me to wrap Rain's head with the towel, then helps me lift him out of the car and into the house. Storm lags behind a few minutes talking to the driver.

Jorge has a place prepared on the floor. There's a blanket to lay Rain on and folded towels to rest his head. None of it is white. The blanket is a dark red color, which will hide the blood well, and the towels a deep brown. There's a first aid kit on the side with a bucket of water and several rags, as well as a few bottles of water and a bottle of hydrogen peroxide. This isn't the first time Jorge has done this.

"How's he doing?" Jorge asks as we lay Rain on the blanket.

"He still has a strong pulse," I say, "and I think the bleeding is slowing down."

"What happened?"

"He hit his head against the window when we crashed."

"Storm filled me in a little. I have help on the way. We just have to make sure Rain stays stable until she gets here. How about you? Are you okay?"

"Rain's more important right now. Storm has my coat. I need it. There's medicine in there that can help."

Storm comes in and closes the door behind him. "Dale la chaqueta," Jorge says.

I understood that. Storm does as instructed and gives me my coat. I think for a minute, trying to remember the colors Angel had used on himself. I believe they were yellow and pink. I reach into the pocket and fish around for the two jars and my hand finds several. There are three yellow ones and two pink ones. They aren't the same. The color consistency is different. There's a very bright pink one and a soft pink one. The yellow has a very bright one, a light one, and a more earthy tone one. I'm almost certain Angel used the light pink one, but I'm not sure about the yellow one. My hand drifts over the three yellow ones when I feel pressure on my hand as I go over the bright yellow jar. I take that as a sign. I use a rag and water bottle to begin cleaning Rain's head. Jorge helps prop Rain's body on his side so I can get to the wound. He watches intently as I wash away the blood to reveal a split in Rain's head about two inches long. I have Storm keep a flow of water on the wound to wash away the blood as I use tweezers to probe for glass shards.

"You're definitely not the same girl you were back then," Jorge says into the silence.

I offer him a quick glance and ask, "What do you mean?"

"You used to squirm at the sight of a worm. You couldn't stand the sight of blood. Now here you are covered in it and digging through an open wound like this is second nature to you."

"I told you I've changed," I say as I begin combining the ointments to apply.

"What's that?" Storm asks.

"Special salves. They'll help with the healing and infection." I wash the blood from one hand and dig into a pocket for a suture kit. I'm glad Rain's unconscious. This part is going to hurt. They watch the precision I learned over the years in my dreams with Angel as my teacher. They were incredibly vivid; enough to actually teach me. I'm not sure how he managed to prepare me like that, but he did. Everything he taught me in those long dreams is accurate.

As I begin to wrap Rain's head in a bandage Jorge says, "You've earned it."

"Earned what?" I ask.

"The respect. You deserve to be an Elemental."

"What's an Elemental?"

"A position of power in the gang. Elemental is the name we gave it and it stuck. You get a street name noting it so others know you have authority. We chose Lightning for you."

"So Storm and Rain are part of these Elementals too?"

"Yeah. That's why they were checking in on you."

I don't like the name. I don't like nicknames at all, short of Becca, but don't want to argue it right now. "How many are you?"

"Six including me. You make seven."

I clean my hands of what's left of the blood and dry them. As I do I notice a dark haze around Rain's body. It's similar to the mist that was around Anna's heart. Storm starts talking, but I don't pay attention and focus on Rain. It's in Spanish anyway. The haze takes on a darker, heavier form as the world around me begins to drown out. It's covering Rain's body, enveloping him. The mist is so thick around his head and hands that I almost can't see them. It's his sin and he has a lot of it. What has he done to cause so much?

When I had taken away Anna's sin, it had been accidental. I didn't know it was something I could do and am still not sure how I did it, but it seemed to help her. I wonder if it will help Rain too. I just have to figure out how to do it again.

I run my hands along Rain's face and around his head. It's gotten heavier with the weight of his sins. My hands almost completely vanish into the mist. I lace my fingers through the darkness and pull it away. It's warm in my hands. The strands cascade away from my fingers and I try again. Strands of darkness fall from between my fingers as what is in my grip runs down my arms. It feels wet, almost like water running down my arms. I take bigger handfuls and repeat the process. My eyes are starting to sting, but I continue to focus. I can taste copper on my tongue as it and my teeth begin to ache. I blink hard, realizing I've been so focused I wasn't blinking. The mist around Rain starts to fade and my arms are warm and wet. My mouth and jaw hurt and I can taste the copper of blood. The surrounding world comes crashing back and I hear my name being called.

"What was that about?" Jorge asks.

"I just thought it would help," I answer. Accepting that there is nothing more I can do for Rain, I finally take a much-needed breath only to have pain shoot through my side.

"You're hurt too," Jorge says as he kneels beside me. "Let me see."

He prods my side, making me grimace with pain. He lifts my shirt to see the gash. "This looks worse than Rain's."

"I can take care of it," I say, but I'm unsure if I can.

Jorge presses a wet rag to the wound and says, "Don't worry. We'll patch you up. We have a friend who helps us at times like this. She does good work, like you."

"You're being unusually nice to me."

"You saved my sister. She'd be dead if not for you."

"She never would have been shot if not for me."

"Bull shit," Storm says. "As far as they knew you were nobody and they still shot at you. They were just looking for an excuse."

"Well it's time to stop playing nice," Jorge says. "They want a war they just got one."

War. The whole reason I'm in this mess in the first place. I wanted to use Jorge and his gang to call War. Now I guess I'll get the chance and I hate the price I've had to pay for it. But if I can beat War, then maybe I can stop all this pointless violence. If he's not there to push everyone along then what point will there be to continue?

The doorbell rings. "We'll continue this conversation later," Jorge says as Storm goes to answer it. "Right now, our priority is making sure you're in fighting condition."

"Wait, what?" I ask.

-Heaven's Interlude-

Andrea rested under the watchful gaze of Raphael. His hand laid over her heart, ensuring that it continued to beat strong. He kept her from flat-lining during the long surgery and ensured the bullets were removed with minimal trauma. Andrea's body was healing well. The intubation tube could be removed tomorrow. The various wires monitored her vital signs, ready to send an alert should her life tilt closer towards death than it already was. It wouldn't. Raphael had done much of Andrea's healing already. The guardian he was waiting on would just have to continue the healing process, though Raphael was uncertain of when she would wake.

Raphael was growing anxious and increasingly impatient. He wanted to get back to Rebecca. He normally didn't mind leaving his demon hunter to their own devices, but Rebecca was different. She was very green and had already made serious mistakes. He didn't like leaving her alone. On top of that, their bond wasn't strong. His words struggled to get through to her. Her emotions were very strong but unfocused, making it difficult to discern them. Something had happened while he was gone. He could feel Rebecca's panic, but was unsure the reason. She was in pain, but he could also sense an uneasy safety. He wanted to get back and find out what was going on.

A ray of sunlight pierced through the gray winter sky and shined through the window. Raphael breathed a sigh of relief. The guardian angel he requested had finally arrived. The light gathered in the room and formed into a humanoid shape. The wings of the figure spread out partially before folding around the being. The light dimmed to reveal a young man in a brown jacket and black slacks. His white wings folded neatly behind him.

"About time," Raphael said.

"Apologies Prince Raphael," the angel said as he respectfully bowed. "The Choir is still in a bit of disarray following the Horsemen incident. They sorely need your guidance."

Raphael reached out and placed the angel's hand over Andrea's heart. "This whole situation took us by surprise, but they'll have to fair without me for the foreseeable future. I know it's been awhile, but there is a protocol in place."

The angel examined Andrea as he aligned his energy with hers. "I apologize on behalf of the Choir."

Raphael laid his hands upon the shoulders of the young angel. "You don't need to apologize for the shortcomings of your superiors. Is this your first charge?"

"Yes sir, but I passed my training with some of the highest marks."

"That's good. This may be a difficult charge. You are healer trained, correct?"

"Yes sir."

"Good. Once she's healed you'll work alongside a category two guardian and begin that training as well. Follow their lead. Once she's settled in a secured life your trial will be over and you may leave her and return to Heaven for further orders. Until you are notified otherwise, she is a level three."

"A level three?" the angel bows. "Thank you for your faith. I will not let you down."

"Don't hesitate to use everything at your disposal if you feel the need. The demon hunter will be upset should this woman pass on."

"I won't hesitate."

"Very good. Godspeed." Raphael took a turning step and moved into the astral plane.

-End Interlude-

Eleven

I walk through the darkness, Sword of Might firmly grasped in my right hand. I can see shapes moving in the blackness but am unsure of what they are. I hear a growl in the distance and the sound of chains dragging across the floor. My legs are heavy; not like they're made out of lead, but like they're sloshing through thick mud. There's pain around my wrists, then around my neck. Barbed chains ensnare me, cutting into my flesh and pulling me down to my knees. Whatever I'm trudging through is warm to the touch, but it isn't mud. Eyes, crimson and piercing, appear high above me as large as the moon. They glow as the voice of War echoes, "Show me your wings."

Powerful claws rip down my back and I scream.

I tumble onto the floor, finding myself wrapped in something. I rise to my feet and rip what encases me in half. Panting, I look around, searching for threats in the small room. I catch a glimpse of myself in the vanity mirror. Standing in Andrea's flowery pink pajamas, I hold two halves of a blanket. I sigh and let them fall to the ground. It was another nightmare.

Jorge let me stay the night in Andrea's room after I was stitched me up by their friend. He let me use whatever clothes of Andrea I liked as well, since I lost everything I had running from the police. I repay him by ripping one of Andrea's blankets in two. This is going to be fun to explain.

I look at the clock on Andrea's nightstand. It's barely six in the morning. Jorge and Storm are probably still asleep. I wonder if Rain has even woken up yet. My back aches a bit so I stretch to loosen the muscles, but it only makes the pain worse. I'm surprised the rest of my stitched-up body doesn't hurt as badly. My muscles loosen from the tightness of sleep, but the stretching does little to lessen my body's pain. I'm not supposed to bathe for a few days, but I don't think a quick shower will hurt the stitching that much.

The house is eerily quiet as I make my way to the bathroom. I lock the door and let the water warm up. I take off the pajamas and check them for blood before folding and laying them on the toilet seat. My body is sore, but my back is by far the worst, followed by my side. A piece of metal was removed. The stitching site was barely swollen and looked too healed to have only been done the night before. The stitching on my leg had skin growing over it already. I'm able to pull the stitching out of my arm, leaving only scar tissue. The scrapes on my hands are completely healed. What's going on? How am I healing so fast?

The shoulder stitching is about on par with my side. The pain from these wounds is more of a dull ache, but the pain on my back has been growing this whole time, slowly becoming a burning sensation. Why, of all things, does that hurt so much? I only hit the floor. I turn around and look over my shoulder into the mirror. What I see horrifies me. Deep red claw marks run from my shoulder blades to the small of my back. I look away and start to take deep breaths. I'm shaking and brace myself against the door. War is not haunting me in my dreams; he's attacking me in my dreams. He can hurt me.

"...controlling your dreams," the voice of my angel whispers. It's not as clear as it was yesterday, but still easier than it had been. "...let him. Fight..."

I take a deep breath and hold it for a moment, trying to calm my racing heart. I let out a long exhale. "I know," I whisper.

"Do you?" The Irish voice of Úna asks.

I look over my shoulder to find her reflection in the fogging mirror instead of my own. I pull down a towel and wrap myself in it. "Úna!" I complain. "Could you not do that when I'm naked?"

Úna shakes her head in light laughter. "So it seems your sight is no better than your hearing. I urge you to reconsider this course of action Sweetness."

"Úna, we've already had this discussion," I say as I check the temperature of the water. "I know I don't have full control of my powers yet, but even my angel just agreed I should fight him."

"Did he now? Can you even see your angel? Do you know the name by which to call him?"

I lower my head and sigh. "No."

Úna wipes the encroaching fog from the mirror as I move to face her. "Yet you still insist on summoning the most violent and destructive force on the face of the Earth?"

My stomach drops. I never thought of War that way. I look at Úna but don't answer. I'm not sure what to say. Úna shakes her head. "Stupid girl. As it stands War will crush you beneath his boot. You may still have a chance, but you better try harder to make contact." Úna turns in the mirror and fades as she walks away, my reflection returning as she does so.

RULES OF ENGAGEMENT

The steam in the room quickly overtakes the mirror, blotting out my reflection. I turn around and reach my hand out. I feel my hand pass through something cool, but only briefly. "I should be able to see you, right?" I ask. "Why can't I? Why haven't you told me your name?" I wait for my angel to answer me, but I'm given only silence. I lean forward and rest my head against the door. I feel so alone. "Michael, I wish so much that you were here right now," I say. "I need you." Pain runs through my body and I feel pressure pushing against me. The pain, or the pressure, I'm not sure which, makes my knees buckle. Again? What is causing this pain? "Please, talk to me," I beg. I wait in the silence, hoping, praying for something to show I'm not alone; that I'm not ignored. The shower kicks on, beating against the porcelain tub. I sigh and offer a weak smile. I don't know why we can't talk, but at least I'm heard.

Since my wounds are so well healed, I take a longer shower than I originally planned. The stitching in my leg practically falls out, leaving a swollen scar. I run my hand over it, looking at the new mar on my body. I guess this is going to be my normal from now on. Just a scarred-up warrior. I let the water beat down on my body for a long time, until the hot water is used up and starts turning cold. The pain in my back has left. By the time I step out I can smell breakfast cooking. I go back to Andrea's room to get dressed. I rummage through her clothes for something that fits well. Andrea is taller, bustier, and curvier than I am, so it takes a little time. Eventually I do find a pair of straight leg denim in the back of her closet that isn't so loose that a belt can't fix. She has a few of those to choose from. A yellow blouse completes the outfit.

I walk into the kitchen to find Jorge at the stove. Rain and Storm are sitting at the table with a coffee cup in front of them.

"¡Finalmente! ¡El baño!" Storm says as he heads out of the kitchen and past me.

"Just in time for breakfast," Jorge says. "Did you sleep well?"

"No," I answer. "How are you doing, Rain?"

"Headache and dry mouth," he answers. "They said you patched me up."

"Yeah, I did," I say as I get a glass of water from the sink. "You should be okay, but you probably want a doctor to check the stitching in a few days. Make sure you're healing well."

"Always good to have friends with medical knowledge. Thank you." I sit down as he continues. "What happened to you and Storm? I heard we avoided a close one."

"We did. The building collapsed."

"I saw on the news this morning. They reported no casualties, so you can bet they'll be searching the hospitals."

Jorge sets down plates of food. Breakfast looks like chorizo and eggs. Reminding me of Michael, I smile.

"You had this before, huh?" Rain asks.

"Yeah. How'd you know?" I say.

"You smiled. You knew what it was." He tears a tortilla apart and picks up a chunk of food with it. "I guess it's something you like."

"I had it at my boyfriend's before," I smile remembering. "I had him teach me and my mom how to make it."

"Where is this boyfriend?" Jorge asks as he hands me a fork and sits down.

My smile fades as quickly as it came. "He died— geez, it's already been a week."

"Sorry to hear that. What happened?"

"I'd rather not talk about it right now."

"That's fine. I want to talk you about a few things."

I give him my attention as I eat, trying to focus on Jorge and not the memories the food brings back.

"I wanted you to come with me to see Andrea, but since they're looking for you primarily in hospitals right now, you three need to lay low for a while." I don't like it, but I understand. "Eventually they'll move on when they can't find you," he continues. "In a couple days we'll be meeting with the other Elementals to go over your status and make it official. You're going to be Lightning. Most won't know you as anything else, so get used to it. We're going to do the same. And I want you to get into the habit of calling me T-Bird, not Jorge."

"What if I don't like the name you gave me?" I ask.

"Tough. You need a street name. You can come up with any alias you want. I recommend it. Rain can help set that up for you once he's a little better."

"Until then all we can do is lay low," Rain says. "I'll get some safe houses in order. We'll need them."

"Good," Jorge says. "When I get back from the hospital I want to talk to you privately, Lightning."

I look at him for a minute. I hate nicknames. I hate that name. "Yeah, sure. Whatever." I get up and place my still half full plate by the sink. "I'm sorry, but I'm not hungry right now." I head back to Andrea's room. Nobody tries to stop me. I guess since I'm trapped in this house for a while, I should do more research. "Oh, by the way, T-Bird," I say on my way out. "Sorry, but I ripped your blanket in half."

The look on his face makes me feel better.

JAK LORE

-Hell's Interlude-

Demonic Rebecca struggled to stand, her knees weak and wobbly. "So close," she groaned. "I need just one more good sin. I'll be able to move then." She could hear the bestials below. Content to fight amongst themselves, they had long forgotten about her. Without Baraqyal, she was loathed to try and move around too much and risk drawing their attention back. She was still unable to defend herself and had no one to protect her. She didn't want to call Baraqyal back if she was in trouble. That could ruin everything. Demonic Rebecca was unsure how much longer she would go unnoticed on the mountainside before the bestials below picked up her scent. It was inevitable and she had to be strong enough to defend herself by then.

Resting against the rocks, Demonic Rebecca listened to the growls and roars of the bestials below. She stared out at the Vortex of the Damned as souls descended from the River Styx. Watching the tortured souls plummet she couldn't help but envy them. Wingless spirits broken in their descent, an eternity awaited them. "I am better than they," Demonic Rebecca said. "I will prove it. I will earn my existence." She reached out towards the falling souls. "I will have what they have. I will find a way."

Demonic Rebecca was startled as a massive shadow and the guttural sounds of bestials ascended above her. Two bestials were locked in battle. One was an avian. Panic set into her core. She struggled to her feet. She had to find a place to hide. It already struggled in flight. She wasn't safe if either landed on the mountain. Using the rock face for support she tried to move away. She didn't travel far before the two bestials slammed into the mountainside, throwing her onto her back. The two

136

continued to fight unaware that easier prey was before them. Demonic Rebecca could see the bestials more clearly now; a large tan bat, half the size of an adult human, and a large dark wolf. She crawled away as fast as she could as the savage demons clawed and bit at each other. The bat tried several times to become airborne, but struggled for lift.

As Demonic Rebecca tried to scurry away, another shadow cast over her. A red-eyed raven landed hard on the ground before her, panting and stumbling. This bestial, nearly as large as she, now blocked her path. Its eyes locked on her. It cawed loudly as it turned to advance towards her. The bat bestial flew over her head and slammed into the raven. Demonic Rebecca threw herself against the ground as the wolf leaped over her and into the pair with gnashing teeth. Demonic Rebecca cowered away, looking around frantically for something, anything, to defend herself with as the wolf tore into the flesh of the avians, taking great effort to maim their wings.

The raven tumbled to the mountain's edge with a missing wing and one side of its dark feathers coated in blood. The wolf bestial took a vice grip on the bat's throat and shook it from its feet, slamming it into the ground and mountain said before hurling it into the dazed raven. The bat collided into the advancing raven, pushing them to the edge of the mountain. Their broken wings flapped furiously to keep them from tumbling over the side. The wolf bestial darted forward and threw its body into the struggling mass and sent them over the edge. The wolf watched their descent before turning its attention to Demonic Rebecca.

The wolf bestial rushed forward with teeth bared. "Back off!" Demonic Rebecca shouted. The bestial screeched to a halt, surprising her. It obeyed? The bestial eyed Demonic Rebecca with a low growl. She could see its nose taking in her scent. Its jaws moved, as if trying to remember how to speak. Slowly, it uttered a word. "Rebecca."

Demonic Rebecca was taken aback. She eyed the bestial. "You know my virtues?" she asked. She pushed herself up into a kneeling position and stared at it. Reaching out tentatively she asked, "Who are you?"

The bestial let Demonic Rebecca caress its face for a moment before it began to growl. She pulled her hand away just as it snapped at her. It bared its teeth again and hackled its shoulders. "Enough!" Demonic Rebecca shouted, causing the bestial to back down. Using the mountainside for support she forced herself to stand, unstable as she was. "Think!" she demanded. "Who are you? How did you die?"

The feral dark brown eyes of the bestial showed a hint of intelligence, running up and down the demonic's naked body, studying it. Thinking.

"Remember," Demonic Rebecca said. "You were human. You died."

"I...died," it repeated.

"Yes. Now think. Remember. What is your name?"

The bestial just breathed. Silence between them for minutes. Then it rasped, "Nicholas."

Demonic Rebecca's eyes widened as a cautious grin curled her lips. "Nicholas Rannulf."

Upon hearing the name, the bestial's head began to shake, almost as if in pain. It snorted and growled, struggling to repeat the name it had heard. The screech of other bestials took Demonic Rebecca's eyes from the wolf to the sky. Several winged bestials approached. Demonic Rebecca pressed herself against the mountainside and gritted her teeth. The avian bestials, numbering about half a dozen, landed. Catching their breath, they were not quick to attack. The wolf bestial placed itself between them and her. The avians growled and cawed. The wolf bestial rose onto its hind legs. Demonic Rebecca watched as the muscles and limbs of its body changed. Its front paws lengthened into strong, nimble fingers. It staggered on its hind legs only for a moment before their shape changed to accommodate a bipedal posture. The wolf did not howl. Instead it let out a powerful roar and threw itself at its winged opponents.

Using tooth and claw it tore into its winged adversaries. The winged bestials descended upon the outnumbered wolf and took to the air with their prey. Taking advantage of the struggle of flight, the wolf twisted and turned, breaking their hold and allowing him to latch onto them. He twisted their limbs and shredded their wings, leaping from each avian as they fell from the sky, no longer able to fly. The wolf fought with a controlled savagery that it did not fight with before, but victory would be short-lived. The wolf made short work of the avians, and upon eviscerating its final opponent, it plummeted to the ground with it, unable to make the leap back to the mountain. The wolf had beaten them all.

-End Interlude-

Twelve

I make the bed, fold the two pieces of the blanket and lay them at the foot. I grab my coat and remember what Storm had said. I squeeze the inside pockets and find no resistance, even though I know they're not empty. I stick my hand in just to feel what's inside, but my hand just moves around without finding anything, even the bottom of the pocket. That's strange. I peer inside the pocket and see nothing but a deep darkness. It doesn't even look like the inside of a pocket. I stick my hand inside and it disappears into the darkness. When I think about Angel's journals, which I know are inside, my hand finally wraps around something and I pull a journal out. Okay, that's freaky. Do the pockets have some kind of inter-dimensional space?

The inside of the coat has pockets and the outside has one on either side. The outer ones used to have buttons to keep closed, but they're missing. To my surprise, all the pockets have the deep darkness. It's so strange. I've rested my hands in the outside pockets before but never found anything, but then I was never looking for anything. It was just a place to put my hands. I slip them inside the outer pocket wondering what I'll find. At first I find nothing, not even the bottom of the pocket. It's eerie and unsettling, but then my hand grasps something. It's hard to the touch. Plastic, I think. I pull out a pair of binoculars. How did I not find this before? I put my hand in several more times, pulling out a flashlight, a few water bottles, and a small mirror. How did all that fit and I not notice?

I begin to dig around in the other pocket. I don't find anything at first but then my hand touches something large and soft. I take a good grip and begin to pull it free. It slips easily from the large pocket, but I'm shocked by what I pull out; a tightly rolled and tied sleeping bag. This is absolutely impossible. It's longer than the pocket is deep, yet here it is. I begin to empty out all the pockets entirely.

Half an hour later, at least, what I've pulled out is insane. The bed is completely covered and so is the surrounding floor. Among the many things I find are duct tape, matches, flint and tinder, flares, a tarp, even a fishing pole. I also find small bags of various substances. Some are easy to tell what they are, like gold and silver flakes, while others are just strange: a foul-smelling substance, small carvings, and even bone fragments. Why in the world would Angel be carrying such strange things and how does it all fit?

I shake out the trench coat, trying to make sure it's empty. I look over the coat but find nothing special about it. Is this just another extension of the demon hunter's power? Will it extend to my clothes too? I look over the items for some things I can experiment with. I choose a sewing kit, a water bottle, and a bundle of maps. None of them are too big, but they vary enough.

I put the sewing kit into my front pocket. It fits, as it's small, but physically takes up its space. Its presence is visible. I can't get the water bottle in my front pocket at all and the map bundle will only go into my back pocket so far. This isn't working. Is it because these clothes are Andrea's and not actually mine or does the type of clothing matter?

I pull some of Andrea's spare jackets and pullovers out of her closet and begin filling the pockets. They fill up quickly and the items poke out. This didn't happen with Angel's coat. Maybe I have to wear them first? I put on a coat and try again, but the result is the same. Now I wonder if Angel did something. He said the Dagger of Power has utility abilities. Maybe Angel used that, though I don't remember reading anything like it. I unsheathe the Dagger of Power and press it against the pocket. Then I start to take shots in the dark.

"Magic Pocket." Nothing happens. The pocket still bulges out. "Deep Pocket." Again nothing. "Hidden Pocket. Magical Pocket. Dimensional Pocket. Secret Pocket?" Nothing works. Everything stays the same. I repeat the commands on an empty pocket and try to place items inside, but I get the same result. If Angel used the Dagger of Power, I have no clue what the command word could be.

I pick up a journal and flip through the pages. I can only hope that whatever power Angel used he wrote it down. I just have to find it, which will be easier said than done. I've actually found more journals and even scrolls. I hope I've found everything. I gather all the relevant papers and books together and begin to lay them out neatly on the floor. At least now I know how to find the information I need. The question is can I do it on my own this time?

I sit on the floor in front of the journals and scrolls. I take a deep breath and close my eyes as I try to remember exactly how to do this. I walk myself through the steps first. My mind has to be clear and it won't be if I'm thinking about what to do next. After I go through the steps a few times in my head, I force all thoughts out. I focus only on my breathing for a few minutes, letting the silence of the room overtake me. I reach my hand out over the books. There is already a faint glow in the darkness, so it's working. As the glow of my hand brightens, the glowing outline of the books slowly begins to appear.

This is taking longer now that I don't have help, but I continue to focus. The white sheen begins to waif off my hand and I begin to move it about the books. I focus on the light, keeping in the back of my mind what I'm looking for, though that's a little vaguer than before. One by one the glowing books begin to dim while others brighten. This is different. This isn't how it happened last time. There are too many still glowing. Does more than one hold what I need? The glow of everything begins to dim as I become distracted with the change. I try to regain my focus, but the lights are dimming too fast. I reach out and grab a couple of the ones I saw were getting brighter before I became distracted. The light's gone and I only have a few pieces to sift through. A scroll, a journal, and some folded sheets of paper. I guess I'll just start with the easiest.

I spend a few hours trying to find the secret of the trench coat. After using that trance thing—I have no idea what to call it—I find more things to research from. It does pay off, but I'm not any better than I was before. I think the pockets were created with spells, but they're all written in Latin. I can't read it. If it weren't for notes Angel had written in English, I probably wouldn't have figured that much out. I learned that some of these odd things I found are actually material components for the spells. Some of them aren't made out of pleasant things either and I really don't want to touch them. I guess I won't have to, since I don't know how to use them.

A lot of the spells have drawings and diagrams and are actually pretty math heavy. From studying the diagrams and formulas I think I figured out which spell Angel used to create the pockets, but I have no idea how it works. It looks like Angel had to decide the dimensions when he created the pockets. At least now I know they hold a finite number of items. That would explain why all the pockets had something in them. I just need to figure out what that limit is.

I don't know how much time passes as I pour over all the information I can find and understand. Angel was able to use magic so it stands to reason I can as well. A knock on the door pulls my attention. I look at everything I pulled out of the coat laid out on the bed and floor and groan. "How am I going to explain all this?" I wonder aloud. "Just a sec!"

Jorge doesn't wait and comes into the room. He sees everything laid out and exclaims, "What the hell is all this?"

"What I said wait for," I answer.

"No, seriously. Where did all this come from? I thought you were in here all day. Where'd you get this stuff?"

"Um, my coat."

He sighs and mumbles something in Spanish.

"No, really. Watch." I take the sleeping bag and push it into the pocket I pulled it from. Now that I know the space is limited I want to make sure I return things to where I found them. I fold the coat over and toss it to Jorge. His face is already stunned but goes starker as he feels the pocket.

"Okay," he says. "What kind of trick is this? Where is it?"

"I'm not sure exactly," I say as I show him the spell charts I think are responsible for it. "But I think Angel used this to make it."

"Okay, back up. What is this and who's Angel?"

"Angel was the demon hunter before me. All of this belonged to him. This I think is a spell he used on the coat, but I can't read it."

"Right." He closes the door finally. "Kind of what I wanted to talk to you about. Storm told me what happened, I think. So what's a demon hunter?"

I let out a sigh. "I'm not really sure how to explain it," I say. "I'm kind of still learning."

"Then where's this Angel guy?" Jorge asks. "You said he was the one before you."

"He died protecting me."

Jorge scoffs. "Protecting you? After what I've seen you do and what Storm told me, why the hell would you need any protection?"

"I've only had these powers for about a week now."

"A week?" Jorge laughs. "Aren't you just full of surprises?" He tosses my coat back to me. "We have a lot to talk about. I'm skeptical to believe what I've been told, but I've seen you do some incredible stuff already. So why don't you put your toys away and have a seat? Start with what exactly happened last night."

I look at him and sigh. "I hope you're ready for the truth then." I put what I'm studying aside and begin to put everything back in the pockets I pulled them from to the best of my memory. As I do I tell my story, starting with the police chase and working my way back. I tell Jorge why I came here in the first place.

Jorge shakes his head as I finish my story. "I'm going to need a drink after this," he says. "Everyone's dead?"

"Everyone," I answer. "I'm the only one left."

145

Jorge takes a deep breath. "None of this sounds possible, at all. Even what I've already seen you do is pushing the limits of what I'm willing to believe, but I'm going to."

"I know it's all hard to believe, even for me and I lived through it. Sometimes I wake up expecting to be home, that this was all just a dream, but it isn't."

"If only half of what you say is true, I think we can help each other."

"What do you mean?"

"I think we can give you what you want if you give us what we want."

"Yeah, I guess that is why I came here. I'm not really sure what I was thinking."

"Do you ever?"

"No, I guess not. That has to change."

"Look, we'll continue this later. I need time to take this all in. Here, I forgot to give these to you earlier." He pulls a medicine bottle from his pocket and tosses it to me. "You must be in a lot of pain."

I hand him back the bottle. "Thank you, but I don't need these."

"Are you kidding? You're full of stitches. They're vicodin. They'll take any edge off. Just take one or two. You'll be fine."

I decide not to argue and keep the bottle.

"I don't know about you, but we haven't eaten since breakfast and it's almost five. We're starving. You have a taste for anything?"

I'm taken aback. It's almost five? I look out the window and see how dark it is. I've lost complete track of time—again. What's going on with me? I touch my stomach realizing I'm not hungry, even with as little as I had for breakfast. "I'll eat whatever you make," I say.

"Ordering a pizza," Jorge says. "You have a problem with sausage?"

I shake my head. "Sausage is fine."

Jorge leaves and I lock the door behind him. I lick my lips. They aren't dry. "What's going on with me?" I wonder aloud. "I've hardly had anything the last few days and I'm not even thirsty."

"My gift to you," Úna says. I turn around to find her sitting on Andrea's dresser with a vine of grapes in her hand. "We have gifted to you our Nirvana."

"What's Nirvana?"

Úna smiles. "Finally, a meaningful question, yet difficult to answer. Put simply we have given you gifts beyond the scope of the demon hunter. I have given you freedom from natural hunger. Your body will not devour itself. The Third has gifted you freedom of illness. Your body will not succumb to disease of natural or unnatural origin. The Fourth has gifted you with an ageless life. Eternal youth and vigor. You will not grow old. You will not wither."

"You mean I'll live forever?" I gasp. I'm not sure if that's a good thing.

"That will be up to you, Sweetness. Every living creature is designed to self-destruct; to destroy themselves. A select few are able to override this design, but that is the exception to the rule."

"What about the First? Did he gift me anything?"

Úna pulls a few grapes from the vine and eats them one at a time. "His is not a gift to give, but a power to earn."

"How did other demon hunters earn it?"

"We do not help the demon hunter."

"But didn't you just say—?"

"We help you. We helped Angel. We help no other."

"Why?"

"You are not ready to understand the answer. You still have much to learn before you can even begin to understand."

"Then why don't you teach me instead of telling me how much I don't know? I'm trying to learn on my own, but I don't know where to even begin."

"With your angel. You are focusing so much on War that you are missing opportunities to commune with your guardian."

"I can't ignore War. He's attacking me in my sleep. I'm actually safer awake."

"Who do you think will protect you, guide you, and teach you? Who will prepare you and fight by your side if not your angel?"

"You could. You could teach me. You could help me commune with my angel."

Úna shakes her head as she puts the nearly empty grapevine down. "I am already bending the rules. Sweetness, you are one of the few that even know of us. One of fewer that can even commune with us. Even the mighty beings of Heaven and Hell do not know of the True Forms. Those that do... well... let's just say there is no love lost."

"I'm not sure I follow."

"Don't worry. I don't expect you to yet. What you really need to focus on is contacting your angel and learning the Rules of Engagement. It is vital to your success as the demon hunter. If you are not careful, sin will overtake you. You must always beware your sins."

-Interlude-

Detective Jeffery Cragoff sat alone in his study. He dragged his hands down his face before finally breaking down and taking more painkillers. His body still ached from the wounds he received at the hands of the demon that abducted his son. He was given paid leave while he recovered, but it didn't stop him from pursuing the case on his own, even if he was no longer officially on it. Paperwork of the Angel–Santano case littered his desk. Though they were still waiting for forensics, Jeff knew the unidentified body was that of his son, Jason, even with Angel, Santano, and Rebecca unaccounted for. If Jason was still alive, Jeff was sure he would have heard from his son. After a week he hadn't. That left three people potentially alive and unaccounted for.

Jeff sorted through the pictures of the crime scenes and stared at photos of the torn remains of the unidentified victim. They were barely recognizable as human. His wife, Hellen, clung to the hope that they belonged to someone else; anyone else. She wanted to believe her son was alive, not torn to shreds so he couldn't even have a proper funeral.

Jeff laid a folder atop the pile and spread out the pictures of Angel he had gotten from Rebecca. The murders then were only beginning and Angel was the prime suspect. At first he couldn't see the large bladed sword upon Angel's back. Rebecca is the one that called his attention to that detail. He still couldn't see it clearly, but it became clearer every day. It appeared as a ghost-like object now—there but not there all at once. Jeff took a marker and drew a circle around the sword. It stood out more, but was still far from a solid object, coming in and out of focus. "I don't understand," Jeff said. "I know you're there. Why won't you stand out more? Why can't anyone else see you? Why could only Rebecca?" The door of his study opened and Hellen, red-faced from tears, came in. Jeff stood up and embraced her. She was quivering and pouting. He realized this crying was recent and stronger than before. He knew her hope was gone and tears began to well up in his eyes despite the fact he had known from day one. He guessed he harbored just a little more hope than he thought. The forensic office had called.

"It was Jason," Hellen cried. "All of it was Jason. How could someone do that to him?"

A painful lump lodged in Jeff's throat as he tried to stay strong despite the tears rolling down his face. "We'll get him," he said, his voice forced and in pain. He couldn't stop his tears and fought to keep from wailing in despair.

Hellen cried in her husband's arms. Jeff's upturned lips trembled as tears rolled down his face. Everything they lived for, everything they had built their entire life around was destroyed by a single act. Their miracle baby was gone. Jeff vowed to bring his son justice. His killer, whether it be Angel or Santano, wouldn't get away with it.

"I'll get the bastard that did this," Jeff promised.

Hellen spied the pictures of Angel on Jeff's desk. She picked up one of the photos and stared at him. "It's because of him all this happened." Her fingers tightened on the picture. "Him and Santano. My baby is gone because of them." Tears fell anew down her angered face. "I hate them!" she shouted as she tore the picture to pieces. She slammed her hands on the desk and threw everything off. She moved to sweep the remaining on the floor when Jeff threw his arms around her and restrained her. She struggled in his embrace for a moment before twisting in his arms and held him. She cried angry tears for several minutes. "Get them for this," Hellen said. "Promise me you'll get them for this."

"I promise I'll get them," Jeff vowed.

Jeff's private line rang, drawing his attention to the vintage rotary phone, which was a gift from Jason. Not many people had that number, so Jeff had a good idea who was calling and why. He thought about letting it go to the answering machine, not really wanting to talk to his Chief right now. Opting to answer, he picked up the receiver and greeted who he knew was on the other end.

The chief laughed sadly. "Could have been the pizza boy."

"Treading lightly there, boss," Jeff laughed with equal sorrow. He knew what was coming.

"I think a certain level of decorum is called for right now. I was hoping to get you before forensics did."

"They already called."

There was a momentary silence between them. "I'm sorry, Jeff. He was a good kid. You raised him right. He didn't deserve that."

"No, he didn't."

"We'll get 'em. They won't get away with this, I promise you."

"I know we will."

"We're both on our private lines, so I want to be honest with you."

"About?"

"You're my best detective, Jeff. You know that. You've solved some of our most difficult cold cases, but this is becoming an FBI matter. Once they take over, you're going to be restrained, especially since one of the victims is your son. They're going to see a conflict of interest."

"You're not pulling me from the case, are you?" Jeff asked. "Chief, you know that's bull!"

"You don't gotta tell me. That's why I'm going to give you a few months paid leave. I need you out of this bureaucracy that's about to slam down on us. I'll feed you info as I can, but you're going to have to go rogue for this."

"You want me unofficial?"

"I want you to get dirty. Some very powerful and dangerous people are also interested in this case for similar reasons as yours. This may go against your ethics, but if you want to get these bastards, put it aside. I know you won't like it, but they have a pretty deep network that can help you."

"What are you talking about?"

"How bad do you want these guys Jeff?"

"More than you know."

"You'll get a call on this line from the contact. If you're willing to do anything, say yes to him. You can't back out if you do. I won't be able to protect you after that. Be sure you're willing to go there."

Jeff took a deep breath. "How off the books are we talking about?"

"We're screwed if we get caught kind. I can keep the FBI off your backs, but you guys have to do this on your own. Work with him, but watch your back, understand?"

"Yes, I'll be careful."

The chief hung up and Jeff turned to his wife. "What were you talking about?" she asked.

Jeff looked at the pictures and reports strewn across the floor. He found the picture of Angel he had circled. "I'm being given a special partner," he said as he picked it up. "I'm still working the case, but don't tell anyone anything about what you just heard, especially the FBI." He showed the picture to Hellen. "Do you see anything in the circle?"

Hellen stared at it for a moment. "Yeah. A target for a bullet."

Jeff looked at the picture. She couldn't see the sword.

-End Interlude-

About an hour passes and I hear the faint sound of a doorbell. I look out the window and see a car idling in the street and can already smell the pizza. That's a pretty strong scent. I go to the front room just as Jorge has finished paying. He sets the pizza on the coffee table.

"You were watching out for it huh?" Jorge says. "Guess you were hungrier than I thought."

"I heard the doorbell," I answer.

"Funny. The things hard to hear in the living room. Sit down. We all need to talk."

I sit and take a slice. The doorbell wasn't loud, but I did hear it. Something similar happened in the hospital with my vision. How heightened are my senses now?

"T-Bird filled us in on what you told him," Rain says. "You are one hot mess, if that's all true. I'll make some phone calls, see what I come up with."

"It's only a matter of time before they get a search warrant," Jorge says, "so you can't stay here. You have to hide out for now."

"My cousin can hide us," Rain says. "At least until we get our alibi's set."

"Alibis? For what?"

"How about the police chase last night? I'm sure my blood is all over the place. The car belongs to Storm. It's a little sticky right now."

"They have more than enough to hold," Jorge says. "I wish you had just waited in the hospital. Our lawyer could have gotten you out on bond, but this news you may have actually fought back."

"Sorry that I thought getting arrested was a bad thing," I scowl.

153

"It's not the end of the world," Rain says as he fumbles with a strand of cheese. "What we need to focus on now is getting our stories straight."

"They got DNA," Storm says, "so can't say the car was stolen; we weren't in it."

"You took off out of your room," Jorge adds, then shrugs, "People do that all the time. Just not before they're getting read their rights. How'd you know to leave anyway?"

"Would you believe an angel told me?" I ask sheepishly.

The trio look at each other for a moment. They each nod as Jorge says, "Yeah, we can roll with that."

"Nobody else will," Rain says. "You got jittery with the cop, so decided it was time to leave."

"What about the chase?" I ask.

"That's where we're at a loss. That is what it is. We ran."

I look at the half-eaten slice in my hand and sigh. Police chases, hospital escapes, alibi planning. What's my life coming to? This is not what I expected when I became demon hunter.

Thirteen

Metal creaks beneath me with each step. The floor is hard and a damp musty scent assaults my nose. I press forward despite the darkness. Then I hear that familiar guttural growl. "I see you," War says. "I smell your fear. What is it that frightens you so?" I can feel his breath on the back of my neck, sending chills down my spine. I pivot into a spin as I draw the Sword of Might and strike. I hit nothing and War chuckles. "So many things you fear," he says. I feel movement behind me and react. The blade bursts into flames as I thrust. The fire pushes to the tip of the blade and erupts into a single fireball. It's bigger than the fireballs I've released before. I've only seen Angel use this power. It's Meteor Punch. The fireball strikes something and explodes, forcing me to brace myself to stay on my feet. It's so powerful I can't help but smile, but it doesn't last.

Shadows dance against the light of the flames. Some are human shaped. Others I can't tell. "What is it you fear most?" War asks. "Is it the unknown?" I send another fireball in the direction of his voice. It travels farther this time before striking something in the darkness and exploding. "Perhaps your own inadequacy?" I swing the Sword of Might in an arc, loosing several fireballs at once. The meteors fly into the darkness and hit the unknown, creating a raging fire

155

that illuminates my surroundings. Bloody body parts hang from hooks in the butchery I find myself in. Severed bodies lie atop chopping blocks with fresh blood seeping from the carcasses. The floor is slick with diluted blood and guts, and bone chips litter the base of the chopping blocks. I wretch as I realize the bodies aren't of animals, but of people; men, women, and even children. My heart aches as I throw up a little, tears escaping my eyes. "Is it pain and anguish that makes you quiver?" War asks. I turn at the sound behind me, almost forgetting to raise my sword. "Perhaps you fear something more terrifying?" The ground begins to tremble beneath my feet. My heart beats through my chest as the ground around me buckles as if something is burrowing beneath the metal floor. "Perhaps you fear the same as the rest of humanity." Suddenly everything is silent. There is no creaking of metal. The ground doesn't shake and the air is deathly still. I can hear only my own heavy breathing, feel only the pounding of my heart, and smell only the scent of blood. War breaks the silence. "The monsters in the dark."

Something bursts out of the ground, knocking me down. Its screech is high pitched and pained. It's a massive serpentine-like creature. Its dry, cracked body is a dirty rust color and banded like a worm. All along its massive length, ten times longer than I am tall, protrudes spikes that wave about perpendicular to its body. Its featureless bullet-shaped head stares down at me. My breath is heavy and my heart is beating so hard and fast it feels like it'll burst from my chest. Goosebumps lace my arms and my body trembles. Its head splits open six ways as it screeches again, revealing rows of pointed teeth down into its throat.

The monster shoots towards me with its screeching maw open. I push myself against the floor and throw myself away from it. It slams into the ground, shattering the metal and burrows into the earth. I feel the ground quiver beneath me but can't tell where the creature is. The flickering light of the fires cast shadows all around, making me unsure of what's around me. Fear gripping me, I pivot around looking for signs of the creature. The ground near me explodes as the monster emerges, knocking me face first into the wet floor. I struggle to my feet as the creature circles me and rears its head up like a snake. I pull the Sword of Might back to unleash its power, but the creature's maw splits open again and from its throat, thorn coated tendrils erupt. They wrap tightly around my legs and waist, holding me still. They grip my wrist so hard it twists my arm and forces me to drop my sword. The thorns cut into my neck as I use my free hand to pry at the tendril around my throat. I pull my weight back as it tries to drag me towards it. I let the tendril go and it tightens around my neck, making it hard to breathe. I hold my arm out and the Sword of Might finds itself in my grip. The blade shimmers and I slice through the thorny tendrils. Now free, I collapse to the ground and cough as I try to amble away, but the creature seems unfazed. It comes at me again and I don't have time to react.

Light shines down and forces the creature to stop. It appears to cause the creature pain as it writhes around and screeches. A glowing figure descends from within the light and motions towards the monster. The figure speaks, but I can't discern its voice. The serpent writhes around violently as light starts to escape it. The light becomes so bright I have to cover my eyes. The screaming of the creature is slowly replaced with the sound of birds. The air around me becomes warmer and the ground soft. A gentle breeze caresses my body, soothing my pain. I open my eyes to find the butchery has been replaced with a clearing of tall grass and flowers. The sun shines down brightly, warming my body. My eyes widen as they fall upon who came to my rescue.

"I thought something a little more serene," he says with a smile and outstretched hand.

"Angel?" I ask as I take his hand.

"No," he answers with a frown and helps me to my feet. "This is the image you have projected upon me."

"I don't understand. Who are you?"

"I am your guardian."

"You're the voice I keep hearing?"

"Yes, though I don't think you can hear me clearly."

"Why do you look like Angel?"

"You are not ready to accept me fully. Until you do, I am unable to reveal myself to you."

"But I do accept you. Why wouldn't I?"

"There is a difference between being religious and being faithful. You still hold doubt in your mind and pride in your heart. You must cast them aside."

"I don't understand."

"You must not pursue this course of action."

"I have to. War is hunting me."

"And you him, but you are not ready. No demon hunter has ever had the strength to stand against a fully realized Horseman."

"But I'm stronger than any other demon hunter, aren't I?"

Angel sighs. "It's true that you have immense power, but so do the Horsemen and we don't know the limit of that power."

"Then what am I supposed to do?" I cry. "Am I just supposed to run from War for the rest of my life? Am I just supposed to kill avatars forever? The Horsemen have to be destroyed!"

Angel is silent for a moment. "I'm not sure they can be."

I'm taken aback.

"The Horsemen are different from angels and devils. They don't originate through Man. They don't originate through God. I don't know their origin. I don't know what binds them to existence. I don't know if there is a way to destroy them."

"Úna thinks they can be killed."

"Úna," he repeats. "This is another being I am unfamiliar with. I'm not sure I trust her."

"She helped me accept myself as demon hunter. She still tries to help me. She's just... cryptic."

"She is not an angel. She is not of Heaven."

I stand in shock. "She's a demon?"

Angel shakes his head. "She is something different, similar to the Horsemen."

"They're connected. Úna is something called a True Form. It's where the Horsemen stole their power from."

"Interesting. Regardless, she has valid points that I do agree with."

"Like?"

"The foolishness of hunting War and the need to bridge the gap between us."

"I've come too far to stop now and War is getting closer, but I'm not sure what to do and I'm scared."

"I'm here to help you; to guide you. You simply need to call out to me."

"Then tell me your name so I can."

He speaks words that don't sound like words at all. It's more akin to music. He sighs. "You're not ready to understand my name. Rebecca, you must open your heart to me. Pray. Commune with me."

My hand goes to my cross. "I'm not sure I know how to pray."

Angel cradles my chin with his finger and lifts my head. "Yes you do. From the heart, not the mind. There are prayers designed specifically to commune with different angels. You can start there. Listen to my voice, Rebecca. Open yourself to me so that I may help you."

I wake up in the early morning just as the sun begins to peek over the horizon. I rub the sleep from my eyes, momentarily forgetting where I am. I sit up in the bed and stretch. I'm a lot calmer than I have been, despite the terrifying dream. Even the red marks around my arms and soreness around my neck don't alarm me as much as they probably should. I guess finally being able to talk to my angel settled my nerves. I touch the cross around my neck and think about my dream. I couldn't see my guardian, so he looked like Angel instead. I couldn't even hear his name. He's my protector and teacher, but we have no connection and I don't know why. I have to find a way to make one. I have to bridge that gap. He said there were prayers attuned to angels, so I guess I need to start there.

I go to Andrea's dresser and look over the journals and scrolls that lay atop it. I wonder aloud what my guardian said, "Prayers from the heart. How exactly do you pray to an angel, especially if you don't know the angel you're praying to?"

I gather some clothes together and decide to think about it while I shower. I wonder if Angel had written any prayers down. I'll look later. Hopefully I can find something with that technique. I really need to name it. I'm showered and dressed in about a half hour and begin gathering all the books together. I need to mark them so I can keep track of what I'm looking for in which. I don't get far when there's a knock on the door.

"Lightning, you ready?" Jorge calls through the door. I groan to myself at the use of the name and move to open the door.

"Ready for what?" I ask.

"It's time to get moving, remember. Rain has the safe house ready and I pulled the rest of the crew together."

"On such short notice?"

"We've learned to be fast and precise. You'll meet the rest of the crew, do your thing. Cast out any doubts. Afterwards you, Rain, and Storm will head to Maria's place. That's Storm's cousin. She'll take care of you. This is an official meeting, so wear our colors. I know Andrea has something you can wear. Rain had Maria set some clothes aside for you at her place. They're yours."

I agree, though I'm not looking forward to this. This is starting to become overwhelming.

The four of us drive together to an auto garage. There are a few cars in the lot already and the place looks closed. Jorge leads us to a side entrance which is propped open. Storm is the last one in and closes the door behind us. There are already three men in the building waiting for us.

"This the supergirl we heard about?" one of the men asks. He has a large muscled body and shaved head. His black beard is thick and his colored tattoos are bright against his dark skin.

"Yeah," Jorge says. "Guys, this is Lightning."

The man walks up to me and stares down at me. He's at least six feet, if not more, and the tallest of the group.

"Don't look like much," he says and shrugs. "Whatever. Least she's pretty to look at."

"Hey!" I protest. "I'm more than my looks!"

"Don't mind Hail," one of the other men says. "He was the odd ball out 'til you. I'm Hurricane."

I greet him and turn to the last member. He puffs on a cigarette and doesn't look at me. Exhaling a cloud of smoke he says, "What the hell she let you do that the other bitches wouldn't to make her an Elemental?"

"Took out two of the guys that tried to kill my sister," Jorge says. "How's that for a start? Lightning, this is Ráfaga." I repeat the name. I've never heard it before. "It means Gust."

"Sounds kind of cool in Spanish," I smile.

Ráfaga looks at me for a moment and takes another drag of his cigarette. "The way I heard it, you blew their car up."

"That's not too far from the truth," I admit sheepishly.

After a moment's thought, he smiles. "Nice."

"Still don't explain this," Hail says. "She walks in, throws a little weight around, and you bend over backwards for her. I get she saved your sister, but isn't that why we're all here?"

"That's exactly the reason," Jorge says, "but you have no idea what she can do. None of you were there at her initiation. She didn't get sexed in. She fought, like all of you. I stacked everything against her and she still kicked everyone's ass. She's the reason Daniel and Marco are dead."

"I heard the stories," Ráfaga says as he stomps out his cigarette. "Sounds like something out of cartoons really."

"I know it's hard to believe," I say. "It doesn't sound possible and a few weeks ago I would have agreed, but it's true. I did kill your friends and I'm sorry. I didn't mean to, but I freaked out and lost control. People tend to get hurt if I lose it."

"I know this is unusual—" Jorge starts.

Hail interrupts. "No shit! We haven't even had an official vote and you not only already gave her a name, you're having her use it! Besides being lucky what has she done to earn it?"

"You act like I want this!" I shout.

Hail gets in my face and shouts back, "Then why are you here?"

Jorge gets between us and pushes Hail back. "Don't be her demonstration," Jorge says.

Storm nudges me towards the garage. "She'll show you what she's bringing," he says as he instructs everyone to follow us. Inside the garage is an old beat up station wagon with rust all along the bottom of the body and resting on completely flat tires.

"This the junker?" Jorge asks.

"Yeah," Ráfaga answers as he walks over to it. "Complete trash. Engine is locked and everything is rusted. Not much to salvage and a pain to get here so quick."

"Lightning," Jorge calls to me, "time to prove what you can do. Trash it."

The three men laugh at Jorge's request. It makes me more annoyed than angry. I look at the car and consider using the Heavenly Weapons to completely obliterate it but decide my hands would be a better display. I set my coat and weapons aside. Hail laughs and jokingly asks if there should be a time limit. I smile at him and say, "Five minutes should be enough." I remember how easily I crushed the body of the police car. I didn't even notice. Now I'll see what I can actually do. I guess this will be good practice in letting go when I fight War.

I force my fingers under the hood and pull it open and completely off the car. I walk around and flip it onto its side. The shouts of disbelief are in both English and

163

Spanish. With a little bit of effort, I pull the engine out of the car, pieces of metal flying free and bolts rolling on the floor. Dirt and grime drips from the engine as I toss it aside. I pull the rest of the parts out of the car, including the radiator and battery, base and all. I pull the wheels out from the inside, bending and snapping the parts that keep them in place. The entire front end of the car is almost completely dismantled before Jorge stops me.

"So are we ready to vote or do we need to make a stronger case?" Jorge asks.

"That's not possible!" Hail says in disbelief. "That engine weighs three hundred pounds! It takes two guys to lift!"

"Screw the engine," Ráfaga says. "She tore that car apart with her bare hands!"

Hurricane shoots his hand up. "I officially believe every story I heard. I vote yes."

Storm throws his arms around the other two. "Well guys, you going to make it unanimous?"

They stutter and mumble a yes. I notice Rain standing behind everyone, more fear on his face than anything. He pushes it aside when he notices me staring at him. I can feel the tension coming off him as we stare at each other. I look at the car parts surrounding me. The engine is resting on the floor. The ground beneath it has cracked. I look at the destroyed front end and then my dirty, oil-soaked hands. My stomach twists into a knot. I just tore apart a machine. What Jorge saw and was trying to show was my worth to them. That's not what Rain saw. He saw me do something in only a few minutes what would take them hours to do with tools. Jorge sees an asset in me, but am I really?

"Now that that's out of the way, time for business," Jorge says.

"Yeah, this is going to be weird," Hail says. "The fact that she's a beast doesn't change the fact she got no homies."

"Not going to matter for what we have planned."

"Which is?"

"Take out Black Lightning."

"¿Verdad?" Ráfaga asks.

"Yeah. Lightning here is our trump card. You've seen what she can do. They won't stand a chance. Then maybe we can get this to end."

"What are you talking about?" I ask as I try to get the dirt and oil out of my hands in the garage sink. "End what?"

"Sergio. Help us with our man, we'll help you with yours."

I stare at everyone for a moment. What else did I think was going to happen? I guess Sergio is the leader of Black Lightning. They need to take him out to win. "Yeah," I agree. "I'll help. I'll fight your war so I can kill mine."

"Anybody want to explain that?" Hail asks. "Don't make much sense."

"Lightning here is a demon hunter," Jorge says.

"Lo siento, ¿qué?" Hurricane asks.

"Just roll with it. She has special powers. She took out three would-be assassins and did it without a gun. She saved Storm and Rain's life. She can end this. She can end Black Lightning."

"Sounds unbelievable so far," Hail comments.

"I'll contact Conrad for one last brawl. This should attract a little visitor that Lightning wants some one-on-one action with. Not only will Andrea be safe, we'll actually control Detroit."

They break into smiles, but I'm lost. "Wait," I say, "I'm a little confused. What is one fight going to do? What does Andrea have to do with any of this, and who is Conrad? I thought you said Sergio was the leader?"

"Wait, she don't know?" Hail asks. "How the fuck do you bring her here, induct her into this, and she doesn't know?"

"Know what?"

Jorge looks at me. "We'll talk about it later. There's still a lot we need to work out, but Hail's right, you need to know. You should know to be here."

"Then why don't I?"

"I'll fill you in later, when we have time to sit and talk."

I take a deep breath. "Fine. Figure it out, then come tell me."

Angry, I gather my things and step outside. I sit on the hood of Jorge's car. Everything is finally starting to come together. Úna and my guardian don't want me to face War at all, but I have to. I'd much rather fight him on my terms instead of his. I guess my worry is I'm not sure what's going to happen when I call him or if this will even be enough. What if it isn't? What will I do then? Will I have to go to an actual war zone? Are there any wars even being fought right now? Would I even be able to survive an actual warzone? I'm not invulnerable, I just heal fast. I can be hurt. Plus I had medical attention. How long would it take if I didn't? The scars I had yesterday are gone now and the last of the stitches fell out, leaving a scar which will probably be gone tomorrow. My worst injuries are taking about three days to heal. I dig around in my pocket for my journal and pen. They find my hand after a few seconds and only them. This was the first time I knew exactly what I wanted and found only that. I can't help but smile. I

166

think I'm starting to understand how the magic works, but I'll need to experiment more to be sure and find the limitations.

I take this time to write down my thoughts and ideas, as well as my worries. How does Andrea fit into all of this? She said she wasn't a member of the Thunderbirds, but those men in the store targeted her. I thought it had to do with me or Jorge, but maybe I was wrong. I fill a few pages when a blue car pulls into the lot and parks. A customer I guess. I put my journal and pen back into their pocket and slide off the hood. The car idles for a few minutes before the engine cuts off. A woman in a thick winter coat gets out. It reminds me of the cold weather and I tie my coat closed. Her hair is completely hidden under her hat, but her features are starkly Spanish. She sees me and comes over with a wave and smile.

"They done already?" she asks.

I look back to the garage before answering her. "I'm not sure. I can find out for you."

"That's okay. They shouldn't be long." She offers her hand. I accept and exchange a quick shake. "So you're the new addition?"

"Yeah. I guess I am."

"You sure stick out from the rest of them. Guess Hail isn't the black sheep anymore, though we could just call you the white sheep." She laughs and I'm just uncomfortable. Was that a racist joke? "Oh lighten up. They would have all thought that was funny. Hail would probably had made a joke himself."

"I'm sorry. I'm still getting to know them, um..." I stumble at her name, never having gotten it.

"Maria, Rain's cousin. You're Lightning, right?"

"Yeah. I guess I am." I hear the distant sound of a door close and turn my attention back to the garage. "I think they're done," I say.

"Are you sure?" Maria asks as she stares at the garage.

A moment later the group comes around the side of the building. Greetings are exchanged with Maria before Jorge addresses me. "Just lay low for a while. I'll swing by later and bring you up-to-date."

"Looking forward to that," I say. "When can I go see Andrea? Nobody's told me how she's doing."

"She's still improving. She seems to be out of the danger zone, but still in a coma."

"Can you at least tell me where she is?"

Jorge laughs. "No. The last thing we need is for you to be sneaking around. Just stay with Maria. I'll come by when it's safer."

I sigh in defeat. "Fine. I'll do it your way."

"Yes, you will. Now get going."

Everyone disperses and I get into the car with Maria, Rain, and Storm. Rain sits in the front with his cousin, talking to each other in Spanish, while Storm sits in the back with me. I turn to Storm and ask, "So who are Sergio and Conrad?"

"Conrad is the leader of Black Lightning," Storm says. "Sergio, well, that's T-Bird's place."

"What does Andrea have to do with all of this? It's more than she was just shot."

"There's a lot more. You have to wait for T-Bird."

I sigh and stare out the window for a while. Storm has entered the conversation between Maria and Rain, but they're all talking Spanish. I wonder if there's a spell to help bridge language barriers. I decide to take out my journal and continue writing, adding that to my research list. Being able to understand what everyone around me is saying will keep me out of the dark and on even ground with them.

Fourteen

We pull up to a small white house outside Detroit. The sidewalk has been shoveled, but everything else is buried under several inches of snow. I take up the rear as Maria leads us to the front door. As soon as she puts the key in a dog starts barking. "Sí, sí. Tranquilo, soy solo yo," Maria calls out as she opens the door.

"Lo tienes encerrado, ¿verdad?" Rain says.

"¿Te parezco estúpido?"

"You know I don't know what you're saying, right?" I ask.

"They're talking about her dog," Storm answers. "It's mean."

"He's not mean," Maria says. "He's protective. He doesn't like strangers."

The inside of Maria's house is small and quaint. Everything looks secondhand and restored. There's a large gate separating the living room from the hallway and locked behind that is an equally large white pit bull with large brown spots. It's pacing and eyeing me intently.

"¡Tranquilo!" Maria calls out to him.

I feel a presence about me again. "Soothe his fears," the voice says.

I hesitate before approaching the snarling animal.

"Don't get too close," Maria warns. "He doesn't know you and will bite."

"I'll be careful," I answer as Maria disappears into another room.

I stop several feet from the gate. The dog is jumping onto his hind legs, but not slamming his body into the gate. Its ears are pressed back against its head and is baring its teeth as it snarls.

"Calm... project... calmness..." the voice says.

I take a deep breath and repeat, "Calm." That's easier said than done. The dog is frightening. I also have no idea how to project my own calmness, provided I can actually find it. I feel hands lay on my shoulders, but there's nothing I can see. "Breathe," the voice whispers. I take a deep breath and exhale slowly. As I do, my fear and worry of the animal lessens. By the end of the second breath my fear is gone. I close my eyes and focus. From the center of the darkness a cool shade of blue fans out. When I open my eyes, a faint light outlines my entire body momentarily before disappearing. I take another breath and envision that glow around me. Using my hand I act as if I'm pushing it from me to the dog. I see the faint blue light surround the dog and it stops jumping. It's barking starts to lower into a whine and then it calms and sits down, poking its nose through the gate. Its right ear still lays flat against its head, unlike the other. Tentatively I reach my hand out and it licks me. It paws and whines at the gate. I undo the latch and jump when Rain and Storm shout, "No!" I had forgotten they were there. The dog jumps into my arms and begins licking my face.

Maria rushes back towards us shouting, "¿Qué es? ¿Que pasó? " She stares bewildered as her dog presses its body affectionately against me as I pet him. "What's going on?"

171

"I'm not sure," I admit. "I just… did what felt right." I smile as I ruffle the dog's face. "He's very friendly."

"Not to strangers. He wouldn't let Rain touch him for six months. He still doesn't like Storm."

"You're not going to do anything to Storm, are ya boy?"

He looks at Storm, growling a little as I pet him. After a moment he stops and just relaxes into the attention.

"Can we put him away?" Storm asks. "I'd like to not get bit."

"I don't think you will," Maria says. "What did you do to my dog?"

"I… calmed him down," I say. "What's his name?"

"Taurus," Maria answers.

My smile fades and Taurus seems to sense my shifting mood. He stares up at me and whines. "I had a friend who named her dog that; for his birthday."

"His adoption. He's a rescue dog. Don't know what his name was before." Maria scratches behind Taurus' left ear. "He likes this though. He can't feel or hear out of his other ear. That's why it droops. His last owner would beat him and drag him around by the ears." She sighs. "Storm actually helped me rescue him."

"See?" I say to the Taurus, "You have Storm to thank for Maria."

Taurus looks at Storm with a hyper wagging tail and barks once. Storm, however, hides behind Rain.

"I'm going to put him up for now," Maria says. "Then I'll make us some breakfast."

Rain leads us into the kitchen as Maria takes Taurus away. Storm and Rain talk to each other in Spanish, which frustrates me and reinforces the idea of a language spell. I don't like not knowing what they're saying. Michael and his parents had always told me there were only two reasons someone would talk

172

another language around someone who couldn't understand. To show disrespect, whether meaning to or not, or to hide something. It makes me think of him and miss him so much my heart hurts. I wish he was here to stand up for me.

Suddenly I become light headed and am forced to sit down. Maria walks in and sees me dazed. "Hey, are you okay?" she asks.

"Yeah," I answer. "I'm fine."

"A little food will help." She goes to the fridge and takes out eggs while Rain and Storm are already cutting up potatoes and onions. The dizziness subsides rather quickly, but I'm not really hungry. I'd rather study. I try to say something but Úna interjects first. "Don't be rude." I look about for her and see her reflection in the kitchen window. She's sitting at the table with me in the reflection, but she's not physically here. "You may not hunger," she continues, "but you still need sustenance. You still expend energy. Like a crocodile, your metabolism has slowed, but you still use energy. Build your reserves when you can or you will become sluggish."

I sigh. Terrific. I'm not hungry but I still have to eat. Isn't that how people get fat? I stand up and ask Maria to point me to the bathroom. I want to talk to Úna without having to explain her.

Úna is already in the mirror when I arrive in the bathroom. She's silent and expressionless as I lock the door behind me.

"How do you expect me to fight if I get fat?" I ask as I lean on the sink.

Úna cocks her head to the side. "How would you get fat?"

"Eat when I'm not hungry? That's how people get fat you know."

"There are many ways for one to become fat, Sweetness. Not all involve food. Yes, I am saying for you to eat even without the pains of hunger, but I am not suggesting you commit the sin of gluttony." She points at me accusingly. "Nor should you practice the sin of vanity."

"I am not being vain!"

Úna laughs. "Liar. Your concern is that of your figure. Is it not already marred?"

Úna's image twists and bends until she's unrecognizable; just a blur of color. The swirl melts into a moment in time that changed my life forever. The twisted crimson dagger of Demonic Angel rips through the air and cuts deeply into my shoulder. The scar that was left behind begins to burn, causing me to press my hand against it. A howling wind blows the scene away, replacing it with another moment from my past. It's night and the wind blows the loose snow around like a white wave. A dark blanket lays spread over the dirty trailer top. I sit over the edge and trace the light scars on the back of my hands. I glance at them and instinctively try to cover them, but one is always revealed. The sound of water against glass pulls me back to the mirror as the scene is washed away to reveal another. This time I'm standing with a towel around myself and staring into a mirror in another bathroom. This was the hotel I stayed in. My thoughts, which were silent then, are loud now. "How did Angel hide his scars?"

"Enough," I say as I turn away from the mirror. My voice nearly brakes and I can already feel the tears welling up in my eyes. "I get it alright." I turn back to the mirror. The scenes are gone and Úna has returned with that emotionless face she always has. "But you don't understand. That isn't why I said that. I saw what

Angel had to endure. What I'll have to and have endured."

Úna comes out of the mirror then, face-to-face with me. "No, you do not understand! Angel's trials are not your trials! You are from a different time and place. Your life, your ascension, your powers are different than his. You are not the same."

I back into the door at Úna's sudden burst of anger. It surprises and scares me. She takes a breath before continuing, calmer now. "There is so much you do not know or understand. You have erred so much already."

"I'm doing the best I can with what I have."

"It is not enough. You can do better. You are moving much too fast. You—" The wall shakes as the sound of someone hitting it rings out, silencing Úna. She looks behind me. I turn but no one's there. "As you wish," Úna says with a chide smile. "After all, she is your charge. But you would both do well to heed my words."

"Who are you talking to?" I ask.

Úna returns her gaze squarely to me. "Let me ask you this, Rebecca Virtue. What happens when you sin?"

I swallow worriedly. Úna's never called me by name before. "I don't know what you mean," I answer with obvious worry in my voice.

Úna gives a disapproving glare and harrumph. "Then maybe you should learn. Your sins are vital to the Rules of Engagement."

"What are the Rules of Engagement?"

"Unfortunately something you did not have the opportunity to learn." She points between me and an unseen figure. "You two need to talk."

"You mean my angel. I'm trying. Help me, tell me how."

"I can't. Only you can make that journey. And Rebecca, since you are so concerned with your figure..."

Úna snaps her fingers and my stomach twists and churns and I feel queasy. I'm hungry. "Perhaps this will be more towards your liking."

"Úna, wait!"

No sooner than I say those words does Úna disappear and is replaced by my own worried reflection. My stomach churns and I find myself growing hungrier and hungrier until I'm starving. I feel weak and nauseous as I return to the kitchen. The smell of food cooking only makes the nausea worse. I've gone days without eating this past week and never felt like this. Úna's been keeping the hunger away all this time. That was her gift. Now that I've made her mad she's taken it away. I'm so thankful when Maria finishes cooking and serves me a plate. I try not to wolf down the food and I even take seconds, but it doesn't do much to ease the hunger. I find an opportunity to insert myself into the table conversation, which has been almost exclusively in Spanish. They say something I kind of understand. It pulls the conversation into English, mostly. Maria eventually asks about my personal life. Where I'm from and how I came to be here. How I know Jorge and Andrea. I omit a lot, mainly the demon hunter stuff, but Maria does seem interested in Michael. Talking about him makes me miss him more. It makes me wish he was still here with me. Those thoughts cause me physical pain and I leave the topic of Michael, stating that he's dead and it's still too painful to talk about.

After we eat Maria shows me the room I'll be staying in and the clothes she picked out for me. It's not much, but it's more than what I have. I thank her and decide to lock myself away for now, apologizing for my reclusiveness and hoping I don't offend her. She assures me it's alright so I take her word. What else can I do? Over an hour passes before my hunger pains finally start to subside and I feel full. My stomach hurts a little. I guess I ate more than it could handle. I really made Úna mad. She's turned her gift into a punishment. I wonder if she'd come if I call her? I don't understand half of what she's been saying, but she expects me to. The fact that I'm not is frustrating her. I should apologize to her but I need to make her understand too. I am trying but I have no idea what I'm doing. Something is between me and my angel and I'm not sure what. I need help to get past that and Úna is the closest thing to a teacher I have. She's the only one I can turn to.

I decide to leave it be for now and give us both time to process. Maybe she'll come to me as she usually does and we can talk. In the meantime, I'll study and utilize my coat's magic pockets. I found spare clothes Angel kept army-rolled inside. I know how to army roll and decide to switch out Angel's spares with my own. Then I break out the books and scrolls. I've learned if I reach into the pockets with intent I can pull out exactly what the magic is holding, but I'm still not sure if the pockets are linked or not. I bundle and categorize the various works and label them in my journal. Hopefully this will give me stronger intent to retrieve them in the future.

Before I know it, night has fallen. I've lost track of time again. At least it's not being wasted. I smell food cooking and the hunger starts up again. I missed lunch and didn't notice. If this is what'll happen every time I smell food this is going to be a big problem. I won't wait too long before I try to talk to Úna.

I eat, have awkward conversation, and lock myself back into my temporary room. Some hours later the house goes quiet. Looking at the clock I see it's almost midnight. They've gone to bed. I suppose I should too, but I'm not tired and not looking forward to the dreams that await me. I guess I'll just study until I'm too tired to focus. Maybe then I won't dream.

I spend most of the night looking for information on prayers for angels. I learn about some angels and what they did, as well as dozens of prayers. I don't realize night has passed until the rising sunlight assaults my eyes. I've been up all night and don't feel tired at all. I decide to take a break and enjoy the sunrise. Everything is covered in blinding snow and the outside world seems peaceful and eerily quiet. Being the middle of winter, no birds are singing. I enjoy the calmness and bask in the warm sunlight magnified through the window.

I pull myself away and sit on the bed. What I really want to do is see Andrea. I know I can make it to her without being caught if I just knew where she was. Besides, this may be my last chance to see her. I haven't found anything in my notes that might be able to help her but want to at least say goodbye. I wish there was a way to find her on my own. I could sneak in an out with my powers. Wait a minute. Why didn't I think of it before? The Sword of Might! It has Clairvoyance! It can show me Andrea.

The sword shows me Andrea sleeping in a hospital bed. She's on oxygen and hooked to an IV. Her vitals are stable and she looks peaceful. The vision moves to outside the room, showing me the number. It then moves through the floor and to an elevator, showing me the floor. The next movement is much quicker as the vision moves outside the hospital and centers on its name. Next is a bombardment of information as the vision flies through the city and lifts to an aerial view. I see the paths I can take and have an idea of where the hospital is. The vision fades and I shake my head. "Wow, that was freaky," I say, "but at least I can find her now."

I slip out the window so I don't wake anyone. Once I hit the ground I fall into Quickstep to get away from the house and not leave any tracks, traveling as long as I can before dropping out. Using Psionic Camouflage, I continue to retrace the steps I had seen and continue on foot.

I make it to the hospital without incident and calmly walk inside, still enshrouded by the dagger's magic. I make my way to Andrea's room and close the door behind me, letting the concealing magic fade. She's sleeping just as the Sword of Might showed me. I pull a chair next to Andrea and take her hand. I look at her for a long moment, trying to find the words to say but have trouble finding any at all. "I don't know what to say except I'm sorry," I finally say with a sigh. "I didn't mean for any of this to happen. I was just— you were right. I just keep going without looking back or slowing down. I don't think. My powers made me cocky, which made it worse. You paid the price." I shift in the chair. The room is a bit warm. "I told your brother everything. Well, almost everything. He hasn't told me everything either, though. I'm not sure if this is a good idea or not, but I don't know what else to do. He wants to help me, which means I have to help him. People are going to get hurt." I take a deep breath. This room is very warm and starting to bother me. "I'm scared, Andrea. I don't know what I'm doing and the only person that can help me I can't talk to. I feel like everything is going out of control." I squeeze her hand. "I'm not rushing this time. I'm trying to plan so I don't make matters worse. I have to make this right with you. I'm just not sure how." I feel so hot, almost burning, but I'm not sweating. This heat feels like it's coming from inside me and trying to get out. I notice the tempo of the machines change. Andrea's pulse and blood pressure are rising to a normal state and her oxygen level is going up. She takes a deep breath and opens her eyes.

"Andrea! You're awake!" I cry as I throw my arms around her.

"Ow! Ow! Ow!" Andrea cries as she pushes me off.

I pull away. "I'm so sorry!"

"What happened?"

"You're in the hospital. You almost died."

Andrea looks at the ceiling for a moment as she thinks. "They shot us."

"Yeah, but you're okay."

She looks at me. "What about you?"

"I'm okay. Your brother's been looking after me."

"How long have I been out?"

"A few days."

Andrea stares at the ceiling for a short time. She takes a deep breath before taking off the oxygen mask. "What has Jorge done?"

"Nothing yet."

"Yet," Andrea says with a weak scoff. "He's going to kill Sergio. Maybe he should."

"Andrea, what's going on? Jorge mentioned Sergio; talked about dealing with him. And he talked about you. How do you play in all this?"

"I'm the reason the Thunderbirds exist. And that's because of Sergio."

"I don't understand. What do the two of you have to do with Jorge's gang? I thought Sergio was connected to Black Lightning."

"He is. I met Sergio a couple years ago, my sophomore year I think. He had a thing for me and pestered me every day. He was cute, yeah, but he had a bad attitude. I didn't like him, but I decided to give him a chance. I went on one date with him and we didn't hit it off. Not even close. Things went from bad to worse

180

after that. He didn't want to take no for an answer. Eventually Jorge took it upon himself to make it crystal clear that Sergio needed to leave me alone. After that Sergio and a few of his friends jumped and raped me."

"Oh my God."

"Jorge and his friends almost killed him. They chased him out of town. They trashed his car and burned his house down. I'm not really sure how Conrad is related to Sergio. I mean, Conrad is black and Sergio is Mexican, like me. But somehow they're connected. Conrad came down from California and is a high-ranking member of a very big, very dangerous gang. A year after Sergio left, he came back with Conrad and started Black Lightning. They threatened us at first, vandalized our home and stole from us."

"Why do all this?"

"Because he still wants me, I guess. It got worse every day. Jorge had good friends though. They did their best to protect us, but it was never enough. I wasn't safe on my own street. That's why Jorge grew the Thunderbirds. That's why he's still trying to make them bigger." Andrea begins to cry. "They were always just fucking with us. Trying to claim me like some fucking animal!"

My teeth are clenched and my anger is rising. My breaths are deep and shallow as Andrea tells me her story. Why didn't Jorge tell me this? "He'll learn you're not an animal," I say angrily.

Andrea tries to laugh as she wipes away her tears. "You've changed since we were kids, you know that? You've become so strong. Stronger than I ever thought."

"I've seen some horrible things. I'll see more horrible things."

"I guess I wasn't the only one who had it hard. I wonder what Jorge plans to do."

"Fight, though I'm not sure what one fight is going to do."

"What do you know about a fight?"

"It's still being planned."

Andrea sits up a little. "How would you know that? He would have only told his inner circle, like Storm. He wouldn't have told you."

I take a deep breath to acknowledge what the fact is. "They're calling me Lightning."

"What?" Andrea exclaims as she sits straight up in shock. She grimaces and holds her neck and stomach. "Are you telling me he made you an Elemental?"

"Yeah, he did." I don't try to hide my displeasure.

"What in God's name did you do?"

"Save you, among other things I'd like to not talk about."

Andrea lies back down and stares blankly in disbelief. "Wow. You've changed so much. I really don't know who you are anymore."

I slump back into the seat. "You're not the only one."

"It's not a bad thing, Rebecca. I guess I should start calling you Lightning though, huh?"

"I'd rather you didn't. I hate nicknames. I hate that name. I just want to be Rebecca."

"You're so much more than that now."

"You have no idea. I should get going. There are things I have to do."

"Where's Jorge? Shouldn't he be with you?"

"He doesn't know I'm here. I do need to talk to him though." I stand up. You need to get some rest. Just let God watch over you."

Andrea smiles weakly. "He hasn't let me die yet."

I leave Andrea to sleep. Leaving the hospital is as easy as coming in. I can't help the scowl on my face. Learning what Andrea, my friend, has been through and knowing Jorge didn't even mention any of it has me livid. I'm tired of being in the dark. It's going to stop. I fall into Quickstep as soon as I get outside and push my limits. I'm going to see Jorge.

I ring Jorge's doorbell and impatiently bang on the door. Jorge opens the door and is surprised to see me.

I push him out of the way as I force my way inside. "Why didn't you tell me what he did to Andrea?" I demand.

"Who?" Jorge asks as he closes the door.

"Sergio!" I shout.

"I was!" he shouts back.

"When?" I demand.

"Before I took you to see him! Why are you so pissed?"

"Because you didn't tell me what happened to my friend!"

"Wasn't very high on my to-do list! That's why I told you to wait! Who told you? They know better!"

"Andrea told me!"

"She's in a coma and you don't know where she is! Why did they even let you out of the house?"

"I don't need your permission to go anywhere or see anyone!"

"What's gotten into you? Yes, you do!"

I grab him and shout, "No I don't!" I throw him away from me and through the house. I take a step forward as aggression fills me. How dare he try to order me around? I feel something move past me and suddenly I'm slammed against the door. For a moment I see a dim light in the vague shape of a person holding me back. I'm surprised and angry. "Let me go!" I shout. A warm feeling washes over me and I hear the word War whispered. I shake my head and can feel myself start to calm down. The light fades and I can clearly see Jorge staring at me in shock from across the house.

"What am I doing?" I ask myself.

"...attacking... mind..." my angel whispers. I'm only hearing every other word, but I think it's enough to piece together.

"War's attacking my mind?" I ask.

"Yes."

"Oh God," I say as I fall to my knees. "That's what's wrong with me." I start to cry. He can't get me in my dreams anymore, can he? My angel can protect me there. Now he's messing with my emotions? "How do I fight that?" I scream.

"Okay," Jorge says, pulling my attention to him. "While you have your meltdown, I'm going to have a stiff drink. A really stiff drink." He gets up and disappears into the kitchen. I curl up on the floor and try not to cry. I feel so helpless. "Please, talk to me," I beg. "Say something. Anything. I don't know what to do. How do I defend against this?" I'm crying. I can't help it. I feel so scared and so angry. I feel hands on my back and the intense feelings begin to lessen, but they don't go away. I'm breathing fast and deep. I look up and examine my surroundings. I'm alone in the room except for the easing presence around me. I begin to control my breathing and calm my emotions. I hear two distinct words whispered in my ear. "Call. Her."

He's right. I need someone that I can talk to. Someone that can help me. Right now there is only one person that can. I call out to Úna. Jorge jumps at my shout. "Where the hell the bottle go?" he asks. I look around the room and find Úna sitting on the arm of the couch. She's examining a bottle of alcohol.

"He's got good taste," she says as she drinks directly from the bottle.

"Úna, I'm so happy you came," I say.

She looks at me. "You kneel. Warriors only kneel in defeat. Are you defeated?"

"I'm not winning."

"But are you defeated?"

"No."

"Then don't act like you are."

I nod and rise to my feet. I take a deep breath and relax my body. "I'm sorry, Úna. You're right, I'm not ready to fight War, but he doesn't care. We are going to fight. The question is on whose terms?"

Úna swishes the liquid in the bottle around. "I suppose that is one way to look at it. What are your terms?"

"I don't want to be caught off guard. I want to have a plan ready and choose the place to fight. I want to know as much as I can before facing him."

"You do not give yourself much time."

"I know. That's why I need your help."

"I am not your teacher."

"But you can see and hear him. Maybe he can teach me through you."

Úna stares at me with a stern look. "No."

"Just for a little while."

"I cannot."

"Why?"

"One Horseman is arguably too much for you now."

"I don't understand."

"We are tied to the abominations, but mine is different. It is why I was chosen for you."

"You're not making any sense."

"If I do too much, Famine will sense me. He will find you without hesitation."

"There must be some way you can help me."

"Your mind is clouded and your heart longing. You must bring them into line to commune with your guardian. Clear the storm and release the past."

"Who are you talking to?" Jorge asks, making me jump. "And why is my tequila in here?" I look back to where Úna sat to find her gone and the bottle left on the end table.

"She says you have good taste," I say.

Jorge groans into his hands. "Had to be a psycho girl."

"I've told you a lot, but not everything. I will, but you have to too."

"Fine, but we got to get you back to Maria's. You can't stay here."

Jorge and I get into his car and drive off. His teeth are chattering in the cold and I just sit and buckle in.

"Damn girl, aren't you cold?" he asks.

"No," I say. "I guess I don't get cold anymore. I can tell how cold it is, but it doesn't bother me."

"Whatever. What was that meltdown back there?"

"War."

"What about it?"

"I mean the Horseman."

"Okay. We're going to call him and you're going to kick his ass, right?"

"That's the plan, but he wants to fight. He's looking for me."

"I'm not seeing the problem there."

"He doesn't know where I am, but he can get into my head. He's been giving me nightmares and playing with my emotions. If I don't keep a clear mind he makes me go off."

"So you took it out on me? Fair enough. I did mess with you a lot when we were kids. Guess I deserved it."

186

"No, this time was different. Before the emotions just went wild. They weren't directed at anything. They were this time. War made me direct them and it was at you. I couldn't stop myself. I was going to attack you."

"I'm glad you didn't, but what stopped you?"

"My guardian. We have a lot of trouble communicating and I can't see him at all, but somehow he managed to become solid enough to touch me physically. He pushed me against the door and stopped me."

"I don't think I want to know the details. You're scary enough as it is."

"I scare myself too sometimes, but you need to know."

"They were supposed to wait for me. Who told you what happened to Andrea?"

"She did. I went to visit her. She's awake."

Jorge breathes a deep sigh of relief. "That means she's going to be okay. I guess you strong-armed the information out of Rain and Storm?"

"No. One of my powers is Clairvoyance. I can find people. I've used it a few times. I'm not totally sure how it works though."

"Why didn't you use that to find this War guy?"

"It doesn't work on him. I guess it has limitations. Andrea told me what happened with Sergio. What he did. Why didn't you go to the police?"

"She did. The fucker's dad's a cop. Evidence was 'lost'. Everything got dropped."

I bite my lip. A crooked cop and a crooked son. I remember Jason talking about crooked cops on the force. How hard it was on his father when one of them turned out to be his partner and best friend. He testified anyway and promised Jason, all of us, that he'd do the same with any of us if he ever had to. He wouldn't cut us any slack.

"You didn't see any other way," I say, "except to take the law into your own hands."

"Sometimes the wrong way is the only way."

I don't want to believe that, but I'm not going to argue it. I guess I don't have much room to talk. "So he started Black Lightning to get back at Andrea?"

"I think more to get back at me."

"Andrea said you almost killed him."

"She stopped me. She was at a house party and I got wind Sergio was showing up with some of his friends. I went with Storm, Rain, and a few other of my boys. We caught Sergio and his friends trying to rape her. Again. I lost it. We fucked them up, but Andrea pulled me off him before I could finish him. When he got out of the hospital, he had no home. We torched it and put him in a cab at gunpoint. Told him if he ever showed his face again he was dead. Hard to kill someone with an army though. We had to grow to match."

"You've done all this to try and protect Andrea."

"It's not enough. She'll never be safe with Sergio and I'm running out of options. You know it's funny. I've been praying, trying to find a way out of this mess and then you show up. You have all these powers and abilities. It could put an end to all of this. It's like God dropped you in my lap or something."

I stare down at my clasped hands. "I'm not sure I would look at it that way."

"I was coming over tonight to tell you the story. Let you know what we're fighting for. We're meeting with Conrad and Sergio tomorrow."

"How many of us are going?"

"Just you and me."

"Why just me?"

"Because you're my trump card. I need you to protect me and control the situation."

"How am I supposed to do that?"

"Make them afraid. Use your powers. Break some bones, punch through a wall, toss a car, I don't care; just let me do the talking."

"Jorge, you need to know I don't have full control of my powers yet."

"You can control them enough to get a point across, can't you?"

I hear War's distant groan and anxiety enters me. "Yeah, I can."

"Wear our colors and remember to use our street names. Show respect."

My fists clench. I hate that name; Lightning. It isn't my name. I take a deep breath to calm my already rising anger. Damn you, War. "I will."

Fifteen

After dropping me off, Jorge left to see Andrea. He came back to Maria's later that afternoon. The Elementals filed in shortly after. I was made to join the meeting. They planned terms of the fight and I really didn't like what was being suggested. Jorge had a better understanding of what I was going through and helped me maintain control of my tail-spinning emotions. Barely. I lost it at one point and slammed Maria's couch into the floor. She made to always be on the other side of the group after that. Jorge promised to replace her couch and repair her floor. I spent most of the night apologizing to her, but I doubt that fear will ever go away. I guess the silver lining was everyone agreed with enthusiasm to Jorge's plan. They also agreed to Jorge's new rule: keep me happy.

I'm still angry when we go to meet with Conrad and Sergio the next morning. I'm so ashamed of my outburst last night that curbing my anger is easier right now. I don't think War can pick which emotion to influence. He gets them all. Rain parks a few blocks away from the restaurant we're going to be meeting at. Jorge and I walk the rest of the way alone. The entire length of the walk the Sword of Might emits a constant drone of danger.

"Try not to act so tense," Jorge says.

"I'm sorry," I say. "It's just I think we're in danger."

"Of course we are. Have you been keeping an eye out for what I told you?"

"Yeah. I've seen at least one group on every block."

"Just stay on guard and we should be fine. Feel free to flex if they start trying to bluff, just don't go overboard and don't draw on them. I don't feel like getting shot at."

Jorge points someone out to me as we approach the restaurant. A man in a long coat is standing outside and smoking a cigarette. He has a short buzz cut and there are visible tattoos on his face and hands.

"Conrad?" I ask.

"Yeah, that's him," Jorge answers. I can hear the disgust in his voice.

Conrad sees us. He takes one long puff of his cigarette before tossing it onto the cold ground and going inside. I take one last look around before we follow. Mariachi music plays in the background. I take a quick look around the otherwise quiet restaurant. There's an elderly couple enjoying breakfast, barely noticing we even came in. By the door are two fairly large men eyeing us. One of them snickers. At another table are two young men having an early drink while trying to watch us discreetly. I notice tattoos on one of them, but they're partially obscured so I can't make them out. In the center of it all with a smirk on his face sits Conrad and someone else. He looks about my age. "Sergio," I state. Jorge only nods. So that's Sergio. Andrea was right. He is kind of cute. I can only imagine how bad of a personality he has. I follow Jorge's lead and sit at the table opposite Sergio. He eyes me up and down with a wolfish grin and gestures a kiss at me. I sneer in disgust.

"What have we here?" Conrad laughs. "Is this some kind of peace offering? Not what I was expecting from you."

"Excuse me?" I say. "Do you want to repeat that?" I can already feel my anger rising and take a deep breath to try bringing it under control.

"This is Lightning," Jorge answers. "She's the one that took out your wannabe assassins."

"So this is the little magician I heard so much about." He looks me over. "You're pretty, I'll give you that."

"You tried to kill us," I say without breaking eye contact.

"Wasn't the intention. Send a message, yeah, but they weren't supposed to kill her. You actually did me a favor. One less to do myself."

"You killed them?"

"Only the one that took off like a pussy. You put the other in a lifelong wheelchair."

My emotions take a sudden shift to the opposite extreme. At least someone survived me. A waitress comes and places a basket of chips and salsa on the table. She asks if we would like anything to drink. Conrad orders a round of beer for the table. She starts to say something, gesturing to me, but backs out. She's scared. She knows who Conrad is. My mood is dropping fast and I can already feel tears building. War has my emotions swinging to the extremes. If I don't stay mad, I'll start crying. "Not for me," I say before the waitress can leave. "Water is fine."

Conrad laughs. "What kind of straight arrow did you find? Is this a joke?"

"She's always been a bit of a Golden Girl," Jorge says. "Doesn't change what she can do to you though."

"Cut the crap. You're overplaying your hand. This—" he points directly at me, "doesn't scare us."

My emotions swing again. There's the anger. "Give me a minute," I threaten.

"What exactly are you trying to game here, Birdie?"

"What do you think?" Jorge asks. "What has this ever been about?"

"Then butt out," Sergio says. "This is between me and the bitch."

"She is not a bitch," I say sternly, my rising anger almost making me growl it. "She doesn't like you and never will. You're the one that needs to back off."

"She just needs to learn her place, like you."

"Excuse me?" I shout as I shoot up. "Who do you think you are?"

Everyone around me moves except for Conrad. He just sits with a mocking grin on his face. The two men drinking alcohol have gotten up and reach for what I can only assume are guns. I look directly at them and say, "Try it. See what happens."

Conrad waves off his men. Reluctantly, they sit back down. He looks at me. "You can sit down too."

"It's okay, Lightning," Jorge says.

I take a breath and sit down. I don't want the anger to take full control.

"So you're serious about this?" Conrad asks. "You know you can't win, right?"

"Neither can you," Jorge says, nodding towards Sergio. "Seriously. What do you think will happen? After everything you've done? She's not going to suddenly like you."

"That's cute," Sergio says. "You think I like her. Does she too?"

"Then what is this about?" I ask.

"I want her. And I'm going to get her."

"She's not an animal to own."

"You're all animals. You just don't know it."

"What did you say?"

"You just have to be tamed and broken."

He's worse than Nicholas. At least he never spoke down to girls. "You're a pig!" I shout as I push the table into them. They almost fall over and can't push the table back.

"T-Bird," Conrad grunts, "control your whore."

Jorge crosses his arms and grins. "Don't you know anything about lightning? It can't be controlled. And it packs a punch."

"Point taken. Apologize to the lady, Sergio." Sergio starts to protest, but Conrad interrupts. "Now."

"Sorry, Lightning," Sergio hisses. I let up on the table and they breathe a sigh of relief. "How did—"

"Shut up, Sergy," Conrad interrupts, obviously not happy. "Fine, you're serious. You have my attention."

"We both know how this is being fought. Let's ante up."

"You don't have much to ante."

"That's where you're wrong. I got Andrea." I clench my fist and grind my teeth. So we're really going through with this? "If you win she's yours," Jorge says. Yup, we're doing this.

"Looks like someone finally came to their senses," Sergio says.

"If we win you hike your asses back to California and stay there. Both of you. Disband."

"Ballsy," Conrad says. "But that's two-to-one." He looks at me. "Throw her in."

"I'm not a bargaining chip!" I exclaim.

Jorge puts his hand on my shoulder. "Reel it in, Lightning. Right now you are. You know you are."

"Not like that." My anger is starting to skyrocket again.

"Just roll with it." Jorge says as he offers me a knowing smile. He turns to Conrad. "Deal. The two of you for the two of them."

"Fine. We got just the place too. You aware of that new factory Ford started building? They're not anymore and it's abandoned."

"No guns."

"Won't need any. I hope this is worth it for you, 'cause you're going to lose." Conrad and Sergio get up to leave and the two other tables get up with them. "See you in a week; Thursday. For the last time."

Once they're gone, Jorge calls Rain to get us. "I didn't like this plan before," I say. "I really don't like it now."

"Nothing's changed. You go off on them like we planned and we won't have a problem."

"You're treating me and Andrea—"

"Pull yourself together!" Jorge shouts. "You're letting him get to you again."

"After how they talked—"

"War! You're letting War get to you."

Outside, I take a deep breath. "I know, but I'm still mad."

"You think I'm happy? All of this is riding on you. I know with you we can win, but I still don't like it. I don't trust them."

"I know you don't care if I hurt them, but I do."

"Even after listening to that?"

"So a little less. God, I hate these mood swings!"

"You're not the only one, but you need to keep it together. Remember, we're outnumbered. You need to take them out. They've been toying with us and pulling their punches, but he isn't going to do that after today.

He's mad and will probably truck people in. You embarrassed him."

"I know," I say with a smile. That did make me feel good, but the smile doesn't stay. "You don't have the numbers. You're going all out to try and protect Andrea."

"Yeah, but I'm at the end of my rope. We need the kick-ass person you've become. Andrea needs that person."

I stand in silence for a moment, my storm of emotions finally calming. Everything rests on my shoulders. Without me they have no hope. "I'll be ready."

Once we get back to Maria's I set to work. I still have a lot to learn and not a lot of time to learn it. Jorge tells Maria to help me in any way she can, but otherwise to just let me be. I ask her for labels and a radio. She digs out a portable radio and gives me leftover Christmas labels. They remind me of last Christmas, the last I'm sure I'll ever have. I let out a sorrowful sigh and take them. I thank her and tell her not to offer me any food or water. It'll just distract me. She finds that odd but agrees. I don't need Úna's power starving me.

I disappear into the spare room and the first thing I do is plug in the radio and find a classical station. I study better to that than anything with lyrics, especially if I really need to study and not just go over homework, like now. Lives depend on my knowledge. After finding a station I begin to empty my pockets onto the bed. I don't need to empty everything, just what I know I'll need. I set everything neatly into separate piles; journals, ointments, first aid, and all religious items. I then begin to place labels on all the vials, jars, and journals. I go through the labels quickly and am forced to pull out the duct tape from my coat and finish labeling with that.

Going over my notes, I label everything the best I can. This should make things easier to retrieve from the magic pockets. It also helps me stay organized. I use the trance ability I've been perfecting several times to better label the journals. Once everything is labeled I focus on all the combat notes, especially those of the Heavenly Weapons. I just wish I had a safe place to practice.

I study well into the night and don't notice the sun rise the next morning. I'm too intrigued by what I'm learning, now that I have a better study system. According to Angel's notes the Heavenly Weapons are indestructible, though he noticed them beginning to wear as he did. Luckily, damage to the blades was always minor and for the most part repairable. Even under extreme pressure and abuse they never broke, even when a normal sword would shatter. He could use the Sword of Might as a lever to lift things weighing in the tons. Angel could also use several abilities at once, but the number dwindled as time wore on and became more difficult. He had entire sections devoted to different martial arts he had learned and abilities he used or modified. Sometimes he spontaneously learned new powers as he needed them and could then learn to master them.

A knock on the door startles me. Instinctively I reach for the Sword of Might and rush to my feet. Andrea walks in. I smile in relief and lower my sword.

"Wow," Andrea says. "I thought I was tense."

I lay the sword down and hug her. "Yeah, I'm really nerved up," I say as I'm careful not to embrace her too strongly. I don't want to hurt her again. "But I'm happy to see you. They let you go?"

"Yeah. They finally cleared me." Andrea walks past me into the room and looks at everything laid out on the bed. She turns back to me and asks, "What's all this?"

"Only part of it. I'm still trying to figure out what everything is. All this was given to me and there wasn't much time to explain everything to me. I'm trying to do it on my own."

Andrea looks over everything on the bed and picks up a small cross. "Jorge said you were here preparing. I guess praying doesn't hurt. God knows I've been."

"Did you really agree to Jorge's plan?"

"Didn't you?"

"Barely. I still don't like it."

"Me either. I think he's being stupid."

"Then why?"

"Because I trust my brother? I know you're really strong, but you're still just one person. You can't beat them, but maybe you can still win."

"What do you mean?"

"Kill them."

Shock befalls my face.

"I know how it sounds, but just listen." I can tell she's scared when she turns her back to me. She picks up the Sword of Might and pulls the blade partially free. "You've changed, I can see that, but at the same time I think you're still the same person I knew as a kid. You're moving forward and not thinking, like you always do. That's not going to work this time. We live in a different world now. Moving here was the worst thing to happen to me. My life was already falling apart, but it took an express trip once we moved to Michigan. I know your life's changed too, even without you telling me that it has or how." Andrea pulls the sword free and faces me. "I've seen how you can handle yourself. You fight better than anyone I've ever seen and I doubt you carry this for looks. How many people have you killed with it?"

I sigh and look away. "Is it that obvious?"

198

"Yeah, kind of. I have no idea what you've gone through, but you don't know what I've been through either."

"Only what you've told me." I take my sword from her and return it to its sheath. "You have changed though. You've changed a lot."

"I will honor my agreement, but I don't want to be his plaything. I doubt you want to be Conrad's either."

"We're not going to be."

"I don't think I have what it takes to kill someone, even Sergio. You do."

"I can't just murder someone."

"It's not murder!"

I hear Andrea's cry, but another voice overlaps her own. It's the voice of my angel.

"It's not?" I repeat.

Andrea looks at me as she wipes away freshly fallen tears.

"There is... between murder... killing," the voice says.

"Do you mean a difference?" I ask to the unseen voice.

"Rebecca?" Andrea asks. "Are you okay? Who are you talking to?"

I look at her, realizing how I must seem. "It's hard to explain, but don't worry. I'm okay." I look at everything laid out on the bed. "I need some time to think about this."

"I'm sorry, I know how this sounds. Maybe it is wrong, but what other choice do we have? I'm scared Rebecca. Aren't you?"

"Of course I'm scared."

"You sure don't act like it."

I take a breath and just look at her. I know I have to really be careful so I don't hurt anyone, much less kill someone. Now Andrea is asking me to do just that and it seems like my angel thinks that's fine. It isn't murder, but it is murder, isn't it? How can it not be? I had to have misheard him since he's already so hard to hear. I need to talk to him. Úna said I need to clear my mind and there's only one way I know of to do that.

"I need to meditate," I tell Andrea.

"You meditate?" she nods with a half-smile. "I guess I could see you picking that up."

"I've noticed it helps when I'm scared or confused, but it works better if I'm alone. I need the quiet."

"Sure. Do you want something to eat first? It's almost lunchtime."

"No, I'm—" My stomach twists and growls in protest. I'm starving. This is why I didn't want food mentioned. I groan in annoyance, "Úna."

"Who?"

"Nothing. Let's eat first. I've been so busy I haven't eaten all day."

-Hell's Interlude-

Demonic Rebecca huddled against the rock face. There she was relatively safe. She was far too high for her scent to be picked up by most bestials. The biggest threats were the aerial bestials, luckily the dense atmosphere made flying strenuous. It seemed anything on that plane had difficulty flying. Even Baraqyal was winded after a short flight. It offered Demonic Rebecca at least a little safety. She caressed her olive-toned legs. They didn't feel so jelly-like and weak now. "Strength is coming," she said, "but slowly. I have enough strength to walk for a short while, but certainly not enough to defend myself. That I won't for a while, not at this rate. What is taking so long? I can feel the sins, but I'm having trouble absorbing them. I'm not sure what exactly Baraqyal is doing, but at least my virtue is sinning."

Demonic Rebecca stood up and stretched her body. She tested out her balance and coordination with a few jabs and rocking a defensive stance. Though she had little trouble maintaining her balance, she was not satisfied with her performance. "I know I should be stronger than this, so what's wrong?" The sound of shifting rocks caught Demonic Rebecca's attention. Her tension rose as she took a frightened ready stance. Her emerald eyes scanned the surroundings and she strained to listen. She could hear heavy breaths that were not her own. Something was climbing the mountain. She knew she could not outrun or fight it off. There was nowhere to hide either. She gritted her teeth. "Don't call her," Demonic Rebecca said to herself. "Deal with it yourself, you coward. The pain is better than the alternative." The black fur-covered claw of a bestial gripped the ledge of the cliff. Demonic Rebecca readied herself. She would not lie down and let this thing do what it may without a fight, even if that fight would be a poor one.

A wolf bestial pulled itself up, but to her surprise it was different from the other bestials she had seen, aside from open wounds and blood matted fur with missing patches. It looked far more powerful than any bestial she had seen and looked equally man and animal. Other bestials were more animal than man, if they were man at all. Demonic Rebecca remembered Nicholas change before her eyes and realized that this bestial had undergone an even further evolution. She found herself wondering, was this even a different bestial?

"Nicholas?" Demonic Rebecca asked. "Is that you?"

The bestial looked at her and approached on all fours while repeating her words verbatim. Demonic Rebecca stepped back but the bestial reached out quickly and with its claw firmly on her waist, held her still. She pried at its hand for a moment before realizing it simply didn't want her to move. It smelled her, taking in her scent. Traveling up her legs, it focused on her crotch and nudged her with its nose. "Down boy," Demonic Rebecca said as she pushed its muzzle away.

It grabbed her arm and pulled it aside as it stood tall on its hindquarters. Staring down at Demonic Rebecca, it bared its teeth with a low growl. "You may be stronger than me," Demonic Rebecca said, "but I'll still claw out your eyes."

The bestial slammed Demonic Rebecca against the rock face and pinned her arms over her head. Demonic Rebecca moved her head about as the demon sniffed her head, neck, underarms, and around her breasts. She felt its tongue against her flesh and kicked out, forcing a bit of air from the bestial.

"Don't even think about it," Demonic Rebecca threatened.

The bestial roared, its hot breath assaulting her face. She returned her own roar. The bestial gritted its teeth as a deep growl escaped its throat. Its grip on her arms was tight, but Demonic Rebecca bared the pain. With its muzzle so close to her, she slammed her head into its nose as hard as she could. The bestial howled and released her as it gripped its muzzle.

Demonic Rebecca struggled to remain on her feet when she hit the ground. Enraged, the bestial backhanded her and sent her sprawling towards the cliff edge. It moved forward to grab her as she struggled for balance. Overstepping, the bestial lost its footing and took them both over the side of the mountain. It held her close as they fell. Dirt and rocks flew into the air when they slammed into the ground. Demonic Rebecca bounced off the bestial and rolled away, hitting her head against a jutting stone. Her head spun as she struggled to get up. She wiped blood away and could see blurry figures approaching. She knew they were bestials.

"Terrific," she groaned. "Out of the frying pan and into the fire." Demonic Rebecca watched the bestials as they approached, her vision becoming clearer. There were three. Her heart raced and she could feel Baraqyal's presence. "Stay put!" Demonic Rebecca shouted. "Don't you dare come to my rescue." Demonic Rebecca trembled as she gritted her teeth and tears graced her face. "I'll bare it. It's not like I can die here after all, right?" She was sobbing. "It's better than dying." She wiped her tears away and shouted, "Come on then!" The bestials charged and she refused to look away. She would stare her fate in the eyes. "My turn will come," she whispered.

The wolf bestial charged between them with fur bristled. "She's mine!" it roared. It rose onto its hind legs, towering over its opponents, visibly intimidating each. It looked back to Demonic Rebecca and said, "Run."

With that distraction the momentarily cowering bestials attacked, but the wolf tore into them. Demonic Rebecca didn't hesitate to run as well as she could. This bestial, whoever it was, had decided to claim her as its own. She could only imagine what that meant to it. Then she smiled. It claimed her. It was gaining intelligence. It could be bargained with.

The storm descended without warning, casting a whiteout as it did, bringing traffic to a sudden stop. Baraqyal stood atop a building with her fists clenched. Her hair and clothes fluttered lightly in the cold ethereal wind that emanated from her body. That wind pushed its way into the physical world as the storm. She could feel the distress of her demonic charge but was ordered to stand her ground. Reluctantly, Baraqyal did as ordered. It was strange feeling her charge in distress. Demonic Angel had always been very powerful. He seemed to fear nothing.

"This is just great," Baraqyal complained. "I've forgotten how helpless demonics are. Raphael is working hard to close that gap too. Even with my spell, it's only a matter of time before they make meaningful contact. He hasn't left her side either. What am I going to do?"

The clicking of metal echoed over the ethereal wind and Baraqyal immediately took notice. She turned to see smoke shifting in the air. Within the mist a man of emerald green with long dark hair took shape. A three-piece suit shifts into shape on his body. He wore a doublet with silver and jade embroideries. His long-tailed coat was decorated with gold and onyx and lined with black-brown fur. His crane-headed cane tapped loudly as he approached, walking proudly with one hand resting at his hip. Baraqyal smiled. "I was expecting you sooner, Nebiros."

The young man smiled, revealing sharp teeth. "I thought to give you a chance to return on your own," he said in a hoarse voice as he adjusted the loose linen tied around his neck. "You were ordered to remain in Hades."

"I'm here in service to the demonic."

"Isn't Demonic Angel dead?"

"I serve the new demonic now."

"Ah, a trade was it?" he smiled as he moved to stand beside Baraqyal. "You are aware you have disobeyed a direct order?"

Baraqyal looked out over the city with arms crossed and a grin on her lips. "I'm under the protection of the

Rules of Engagement. As long as I am, there's nothing he can do."

"No, there isn't; and it's a waste of time to even try to bring you back."

"You already know that, so why are you really here?"

Nebiros turned to Baraqyal with a friendly smile. "It's my job. I have to at least investigate and report what I have found. I'm sure he will find my report very interesting."

"I'm sure he will."

Nebiros turned as Baraqyal stayed overlooking the white buried city. She placed her hands on her hips as she wracked her mind to solve her predicament when a thought occurred to her. She turned to the Field Marshal as smoke began to appear around him. "Nebiros," she called out to him. He stopped and turned to her, casting curious red eyes upon her. "Satan will only send you back, you know."

"Indeed," he answered. "No doubt he will want more information, so I will see you again."

"Since its information he'll want, I may be persuaded to give that to you now."

"What is it that you need in exchange?"

"Asmodeus."

-End Interlude-

Maria reluctantly joins us for lunch in the kitchen. She tries to keep herself busy by making the food and getting us drinks. The topic of the couch is glossed over, Maria saying that she's waiting for a new one to be delivered. She makes us ham tortas full of lettuce and tomato. I'm so hungry I have two. I don't want to be rude and run back to the room as soon as I'm done eating. I also want to spend time with my friend. I worry it'll be the last time.

Andrea shows off her stitches, lamenting about the scars they'll leave. She asks about mine, but all I have to show are the scars on my shoulder and hands. Everything else has healed completely, not even leaving a faint mark on my body. I'm glad I won't have scars like Andrea.

My hunger finally passes an hour after lunch and I excuse myself back to my room. Andrea presses me about what exactly I'm doing. All I can think to say is I'm trying to come up with a battle plan. Like she said, I need to stop running forward blind. Once back in the room I close and lean against the door, wishing it had a lock. I let out a stressed sigh. There is so much resting on my shoulders. More than I'm even acknowledging. I'm the demon hunter. The fate of the world rests on my shoulders, but this fight is what's stressing me out? Go figure. I need help. I need my angel, but I don't even know his name. I look at all the books laid out on the bed. How did Angel contact his guardian? How did he learn their name? I stand over the books and use the trance, which I've decided to call Insight Trance. I want to find anything Angel has on contacting or interacting with his guardian. Everything goes normally at first. Everything has a glow that one-by-one dims, but nothing is brightening. Suddenly everything goes out, leaving only the glow of my hands. I open my eyes with a heavy heart. There's nothing. No clues at all. That doesn't make any sense. I find myself caressing my cross. My angel said I can commune with him through prayer. How do you pray to an angel, especially if you don't know its name? Honestly, I've never heard of or thought about praying to an angel. I just didn't think that was done, but I guess it is. I pick up Angel's pocket bible and wonder if I can find any clues in here. I'm sure I can, but I just don't have that kind of time. What I might have is time to learn to make my own prayer.

I go through Angel's bookmarked pages in Psalms. I've never actually read any of these before, only recited in church. There are a lot of references to music. Are these supposed to be sung? They don't really sound like songs. Maybe I'm wrong and these aren't actually prayers? Looking at the clock I see I've wasted enough time. I have to try something.

I clear the bed and sit cross-legged. I close my eyes and take a deep relaxing breath. I focus only on my breathing as I let everything around me slip away. I'm not sure how to start. I'm not even sure if he's in the room right now. "Please, give me a sign if you're here," I plead. I wait, hoping for a sound or sensation. A chill enters the room and then leaves. I guess that's my sign. I take a deep breath. "Dear God, I am lost. Please help your angel to find me. Help me to hear his voice. Help me bridge the gap between us." Something comes over me. It's scary, but I feel love. Thoughts fill my mind that aren't my own and my lips ache to open and my tongue to move. I open my mouth and speak the words that long to be spoken. "Glorious Archangel of God, great prince of the heavenly court, my guardian dear. You are my guide, my consoler, and my refuge. I beg you, light my way and guide me in my suffering. I humbly pray you heal my soul and guide me with your grace of purity in my time of ill. Amen." I let out a deep breath and feel like a weight has lifted. My mind seems a little clearer now.

"Pretty intense, isn't it?" a voice asks. I recognize it, but it's not the voice I'm expecting.

I open my eyes and find Heather sitting cross-legged across from me. She has her hair down and is wearing

207

her favorite outfit. She smiles warmly at me, but something seems off, aside from the glow about her.

"Heather, is that you?" I ask.

"No, I'm afraid not," she says as her glow fades. "This is just the form I'm taking." She looks over herself. "Shapeshifting isn't my best ability, so I hope I have the body right for as quickly as I formed it. At least for a short time we can talk."

"I don't understand."

Heather climbs off the bed and looks over the scrolls. I move to sit on the side. "I had no idea how thorough Angel was," Heather says. "He left much for us to work with."

"I can't read it."

"It's in Latin. I'll teach you."

"Who are you? How are you taking Heather's form?"

"Physical projection is a talent taught to all in the guardian class, but we aren't shapeshifters. It helps us bridge gaps with our charges and more directly guide them if necessary. Your prayer helped bridge our gap and gave me the power to take on the form of a living person you know and trust. Luckily, there's still a few."

"You can only take the form of living people? Then Angel is still alive?"

Heather shakes her head. "That was a dream. You projected that form onto me when you couldn't see me. I'm sorry, but Angel is dead."

"I thought since you said..."

"It's more complicated than that."

I look hard at Heather. "So you're my guardian, right? You've come to me as Angel and now as Heather. Are you a man or woman?"

"Neither. Angels are spiritual beings. Though we may prefer to embody one gender over another, we do not possess a sex. We're able to choose our sex at will.

That's not what I'm here to talk to you about. My time is limited so let us begin."

"You're going to teach me to read those scrolls? They're spells, right?"

"They are, but that's not what I'm going to teach you. You need to know the Rules of Engagement. Your heart is torn with your task at hand. You know very well what you may have to do, but you struggle with the Law of War and the sixth commandant of the Lord."

"What's the sixth commandant? I don't know them by order."

"You probably couldn't recite them all in any order honestly, but that's another lesson. Thou Shall Not Murder."

"That seems pretty clear-cut."

"What is murder?"

"To kill someone."

"I see. So animals are exempt then? Nor could you defend your own life with deadly force. God has said death is a suitable punishment for certain crimes, but from your definition God is condoning the breaking of one of His own commandants."

I'm speechless. I stutter as I try to find something to say in my defense.

"You must understand, to kill and to murder are two different things. To kill is to simply take a life. It doesn't bestow a right or wrong, but merely states an act. To murder is to take a life illegally or immorally; any life. When law and morality conflict, morality wins, for law should be built upon morality."

"What makes an act moral or immoral?"

"Taking a life in order to survive, such as to eat, is a morally acceptable act. To take a life for selfish gain, such as an avatar does, is not. That is murder."

209

"I understand that killing an avatar isn't murder, but—"

"No, you don't. You think that simply because a human chooses to become an avatar that the taking of their life is justified. The last avatar was committing grievous sins, yes, but you did as well. You took his life with anger in your heart and contempt for his life. You judged him without knowing him. You murdered him and in doing so damned his soul."

I sit in shock. Killing the avatar was wrong? I murdered him? "What about Santano?" I ask angrily. "Did I murder him too? Was killing him wrong too?"

"No."

"I don't understand! Why was killing Santano okay but not the other avatar?"

"Santano left no alternative. He had committed to his course of action, denying God entirely and turning his soul black. Aran had not yet done so. His anger, his judgments, were justifiable. Yours were not. While you were angry at Santano, your anger was at what he had done to you and your friends; your anger was justified and well placed, but you should not hold onto your anger. Let it go; forgive the avatars. All that you meet, including Santano. Otherwise that anger will grow and consume you. You will be prey to the sin of Wrath."

"This is confusing."

"I know. Your understanding of what is right and wrong is being challenged. You've lived your entire life by Man's Law, not knowing or understanding God's Law. As demon hunter you must live by both. When they conflict, and they will conflict quite often, it is God's Law you must follow. Your powers are tied to Heaven, and thus Heavenly Law. For now, understand this. There is a time to take life and a time to protect it. Do not carry anger in your heart and take life only as a last resort, when every other option has been exhausted."

"What about Sergio? I still don't know what I should do about him. I can't just kill him, can I?"

"I saw the sin within him. If you cannot wrench him free of Wrath, you must take his life so others can live. If he will not repent, then he must be punished, and that punishment is death."

I sigh. "That's not what I thought you would say."

"Rebecca," Heather begins but trails off. Her body is beginning to glow. "It seems I have less time than I thought. Rebecca, I won't tell you not to sin. Sometimes that cannot be avoided. I wish I had the time to better explain this to you, but know the magnitude of the sin can be controlled. As demon hunter, you must control it. Don't hate or judge. Weigh the balance and do what you must. Always, forgiveness is key. Not just for them, but for yourself." As the glow of her body becomes brighter, Heather begins to fade. "I leave you with this. Keep your heart and mind open. Understand the teachings. Do not just accept their face."

The light is warm and overtakes Heather's body as a pillar. The light fades, taking Heather with it. I flop down onto the bed and groan. This just keeps getting harder and harder.

Sixteen

-Heaven's Interlude-

Raphael watched carefully over his charge in the days that followed. She went sleepless nights and ate only when she was reminded to. The sever hunger pains that the reminders brought on were sudden and unable to be held at bay by Raphael's power. He was unsure if that was because of the being Úna or their own rift. Either way it was frustrating. His power of influence fluctuated dramatically over Rebecca. The less sure of herself the greater the fluctuations.

Rebecca worked hard to prepare, to the point of mental and physical exhaustion. After a few days Raphael was able to make her rest. He put in place a mental barrier to protect her dreams from War. Raphael touched the cross about Rebecca's neck and wondered how such a small thing could hide an entire bloodline from the sight of the divines. Yet there she laid; the one that shouldn't exist. The last demon hunter. That fact may not matter soon. Demon hunters have challenged the Horsemen in the past, but never have the Horsemen sought after a demon hunter. Once summoned, Raphael knew Rebecca would not stand a chance against War, but perhaps that's a blessing in disguise. Rebecca wasn't ready to see or hear him, but if she found herself in grave danger, he could manifest himself in response to the Guardian's Plea. She would be forced to accept him then. All that would be left then would be to survive War.

Raphael took a breath. A presence he recognized had entered the room. "Asmodeus," he said.

Manifesting through the wall opposite the bed, a tall man of Persian descent carefully stepped. He was handsome, with long, wavy, dark brown hair, pulled into a pony-tail with a green ribbon twisting through it. His beard was well trimmed and maintained. His gait had a limp, which he supported with a slender oak cane with a bronze tip. "The tales are true, she is pretty," Asmodeus said as he stood opposite Raphael and admired the sleeping demon hunter before him.

"What are you doing here?" Raphael demanded.

"I have brought a gift." With a swirl of his hand, a small box appeared wrapped in a red bow. Asmodeus set it upon the nightstand. "She is beautiful. You could never guess the strength she possesses. She is so small and meek."

"She's the demon hunter, Asmodeus. I advise you to tread lightly."

Asmodeus smiled. "Of course, brother. I know she is yours. I would never try to challenge that." Asmodeus cocked his head from side to side as he examined Rebecca. He frowned. "She is heartbroken. Can you not feel how her flesh hungers?" Asmodeus reached his hand towards her and Raphael reached out and took hold of Asmodeus's wrist before he could touch Rebecca. Asmodeus stared at Raphael with an amused grin.

"I am not going to harm her," Asmodeus said.

"I know your Carnal Touch when I see it, Prince of Lust," Raphael said as he let Asmodeus take a step back.

"I had no ill intent. I was actually trying to help."

"At what price? Nothing from you comes free."

"It can," Asmodeus said. "Tell me, how much faith do you have in her?"

"The same I have for all demon hunters."

"She's not like other demon hunters though, is she? I understand you are facing some—unique—problems."

"What would you know of these problems?"

Asmodeus smiled. "What do you think incited this war she finds herself in? This war she means to use. It is my domain. I can help you."

Raphael eyed Asmodeus cautiously. Something wasn't right. "Why?" Raphael asked.

"Think of it as—" he tapped his shorter left foot, "starting our journey on the right foot."

"What journey? What are you planning?"

"I'm planning nothing, but I do see our paths crossing in the near future. She will meet an old acquaintance and also someone close to me who I have not seen in a very long time."

Raphael's eyes narrowed. Asmodeus' premonition power wasn't spontaneous. Something, or someone, had to bring her to his attention first. Raphael crossed his arms. "I'm listening."

"I fear it's too late to actually stop this battle, but I can quell it. What my mark starts, it can end. I can't stop the fight, but I can dampen the negative energy, perhaps enough that War won't even take notice."

"And in return?"

"Don't teach her the method by which to bind me."

"And leave her open to you? Not a chance."

"You have my word, I will not hurt her. Will you not teach her?"

"Can you guarantee War will not appear?"

"Of course I can't."

"Then why would I leave her defenseless against you?"

"You are her guardian. Why would she be defenseless? Oh, that's right. That's another problem you face. What if I told you I can help with that too?"

"If you could, why would you?"

"Because neither one of us can help her alone. I need your help and you need mine. Will you hear my proposal?"

"Go on."

"The only chance of averting this disaster is to lay a new mark." Asmodeus points at Rebecca. "On her. It will take some time to charge, so will require a delayed trigger."

"What exactly will this mark do?"

"That is where your assistance is required. A gamble is required."

"What kind of gamble?"

"An exceptionally powerful mark is needed. Upon activation, Rebecca will absorb the marks tied to this quarrel between the factions and override them. Lust is lust, after all, whether it is for flesh or power. Without the lust, the tension will subside. However, that lust must be replaced. That is where the gamble comes in. I propose a game. Should you win, you will become the object of her lust. Of course, it would only apply to a mortal visage; the form of her ideal man. Wouldn't that help her communication with you?"

"Should you win? What would you get?"

"Lust, of course, but she will help decide lust for what."

"Can you guarantee War will not appear if I agree to this?"

"Of course not, but upon agreement, the effects of the mark will start. It will make it harder for him to find them. I will help you deal with him, should he appear, however. Do we have a deal?"

"On one condition. The effects of this mark, regardless of outcome, are bound by the Law of Time."

"As you wish. The mark will expire after a year and a day from the conclusion of our game. Now to determine what her fascination shall be."

Asmodeus passed his hand over Rebecca's body and motioned pulling from her head. A slew of cards of varying colors pulled from her mind and rested neatly facedown above her, divided into same color decks. The colors represented core beliefs and moral understanding within the varying fetishes, philosophies, and sexualities. Asmodeus ran his hand over the decks before choosing the deck of her green certainties. Raphael's brow furrowed as Asmodeus fanned the cards before him and scanned over them. What certainty did he mean to tempt?

"I choose this one," Asmodeus said as he plucked a card free. The remaining folded back into a deck and burst into white fire. "Now I will apply my mark and we shall play," Asmodeus said.

"Our deal is enacted," Raphael said.

"You will not teach her to bind me. I will aid in War."

Raphael nodded and hoped he wasn't making a mistake.

-End Interlude-

I sit apprehensively in the backseat of the car with Storm. Jorge rides in front and Rain drives. The silence is thick and heavy. I'm restless as I sit with my arms and legs crossed. Today is the day it all comes together. Andrea's life will be safe once we beat back Conrad and Black Lightning. I'll summon War and kill him, which will hopefully quell the violence in the world. Since I made contact with my angel he— she— it has been a little more helpful. What pronoun do I even use? Does it have a preference? After appearing to me as Heather the voice has sounded more feminine. I guess it doesn't matter. It's been helping me prepare for the fight all week. I've managed to learn new techniques through Angel's journals. He developed some kind of pressure-point style martial arts that's designed to incapacitate opponents without hurting them. That'll be useful. I could feel the angel guiding me as I practiced and it was able to answer simple questions, but we're still a long way from having conversations.

We pull into a crowded parking lot. There are people waiting out in the cold. They're dressed for the weather but I can make out yellow and white on them. There are dozens and there's a good range of ages among them.

"This is a lot of people, but aren't some of them kind of young?" I ask.

"We need everyone we can get," Jorge says. "Conrad will bring at least double. Why do you think you're so important? They agreed to this because they can crush us in numbers alone."

We get out of the car and I look over everyone. While they don't look as nervous as I am, I can feel the tension in the air.

"They don't seem too nervous," I say.

"They are, but they have faith in you," Jorge says. "Remember, a lot of these guys saw your initiation. Others have heard about the things you've done. You've made a reputation. This is where you earn it. You are up for this, right Lightning?"

"I wish I had more time to prepare, but I can even the odds."

"Don't be afraid to hurt them. They won't be afraid to hurt you."

"I've gotten better control, but I'm a little worried. I'm not sure how long I can hold that control once the fight starts."

"Then don't. You want to get this guy's attention, don't you?"

I don't answer as Jorge climbs on top of a car. He's right, but I wish he wasn't. He starts to address his people, I guess to give them a morale boost. As he begins his speech my angel whispers into my ears, "Don't be afraid. I am with you."

I look around at everyone, taking in the weapons they've brought. Bats, chains, pipes, primarily blunt objects. "I fear for them," I whisper back. "They're counting on me, but how do I protect them all?"

"Sometimes sacrifices must be made. Only war will beget War."

"What about once he's here?"

"I will come if you truly need me."

"I mean them. How will I protect them? Can I protect them? I won't be able to hold back and it doesn't take much for me to hurt someone."

"There will be casualties."

"Does there have to be?"

Storm taps my shoulder, interrupting my private conversation, and motions me to go with Jorge. He's gotten off the car and is waiting for me. The two of us are to lead the charge. "Are you ready to do this?" Jorge asks as I fall in step with him.

"Yeah, I guess."

"Don't guess. I need you ready. You're our Ace."

"That's not what I mean. I just wonder if what I'm doing is right."

RULES OF ENGAGEMENT

"Sometimes it's not about right and wrong." We stop at the entrance to find the door secured with a hefty chain. "Do the honors?"

I take hold of the locked chain and pull it off the door, ripping the handles out along with it. A lot of the murmurs are in Spanish, but I'd imagine they are the same as the ones in English; shocked surprise and hope. The doors pull open, but there are no handles to do that anymore. I slam my hands into the doors and force them inwards. The hatred inside hits me like a wave. I can feel the sudden shift in tension and even my own emotions begin to swing. War's presence is already strong in the building, pushing everyone's adrenaline up.

We enter the building and my emotions swing between worry, excitement, and anger. The more I think about what's about to happen the more worried I become. When I look behind me at the dozens of people who have Jorge's back and will risk their lives for him, excitement begins to take over. Then I look at Jorge. His face is stern as his eyes lock straight ahead. This is all for his sister, the only family he has left. It should never have needed to come down to this and that thought makes anger overwhelm me. I take a deep breath trying to calm the storm of emotions. I can't let War get the better of me. I can't let him get the better of us. I fear today mine are not the only emotions he's manipulating.

We step into a large room with partially built machinery and exposed walls. I spot Black Lightning across the room with Conrad and Sergio leading the way. Conrad raises his fist as the vast number of men behind him wait. Jorge comes to a stop and we wait. I can't see all of Conrad's men, but already we are outnumbered. I take a deep breath.

"Are you ready for this?" Jorge asks.

"Yeah," I answer. "I'm ready."

Jorge raises his fist, signaling to Conrad that he's ready. They throw their fists down in unison. With a battle cry, both sides surge forward. My stomach tightens as everyone washes around me and into the empty space. I can feel the hate in the air as I fall into Quickstep with a sprint. Everything slows to a crawl as I dash across the open floor and into the ranks of Black Lightning. I have to break their numbers. I fall out of Quickstep in front of the first person that completely blocks my path and throw both fists into his torso. I hold back to not kill him, but still send him flying and knocking down half a dozen men. I can hear War's distant roar. Looks like I have his attention.

I pivot and strike another man, throwing him into the rushing crowd. I step into another pivot and slam my fist into someone's hip, sending him crashing to the ground. People fall over him and spill across the floor while others step over them. One jumps off the pile towards me with a wild swing of a bat. I duck low under the swing and he lands flat on my back. I grab his arm and leg and throw him into the crowd as I get back up. A chain races at me and I raise my arm in defense. It wraps around me and I grab it tightly. I pull my arm back, forcing my attacker forward off his feet and send him down with a throat drop. I kick out and hit someone in the stomach, sending him tumbling into men behind him. I move away to evade an attack and am struck in the back. It hurts, but only unbalances me a bit. I spin around and catch the bat as he swings again and rip it from his hands. I take him by the shirt and hurl him over me.

I decide now is a good time to make a retreat and fall into Quickstep. I duck under blows that have slowed to almost choreographic levels as I make my way to open ground. I look around as I move to watch the now slow battle around me. Someone in our colors lies on the ground being beaten by three men. I move towards him and come out of Quickstep behind one of his attackers as I reach for the pipe. I force him around and slam my open palm into his sternum, sending him flying into the crowd. Using the pipe to deflect the swings of a bat and two by four, I move forward and kick both men in rapid succession. The men fall onto their backs and slide across the floor.

I want to tend to the man on the ground, but I'm being rushed by several men. Using the pipe, I deflect several wild attacks. Pulling my punches to not hurt them, I strike at specific pressure points. It's time to try out this paralyzing technique I've been practicing. I drive my knuckles into the points hard and fast, tensing my arms to not hit too hard. Legs lose their strength and collapse, unable to hold the weight of the body. Arms go limp and hang at their sides, releasing their hold on their weapons. The Sword of Might hums in my ears and the vibration pulls me to the side. I pivot and sidestep a man that tries stabbing me in the back with a knife. I kick the back of his knee and grab his shoulders, then slam his back down into the ground. I jam my knuckles into pressure points in his shoulders and twist slightly temporarily disabling his arms. I wasn't expecting them to use knives, but that means I can too. The short, slender blade of the Dagger of Power shimmers as I draw it, activating Keen Edge. A slight smile crosses my lips. With this I can even the odds.

I fall into Quickstep and make my way to help those outnumbered. I pick out someone being held by two people and beaten by a third man with a club and rush to them. I come out of Quickstep beside the third person and slice his club in half as he swings it. The sudden imbalance causes him to stumble and I jab him with an open hand, sending him flying and tumbling before he hits the floor face first. I drop into Quickstep again and run behind the other two before they can react. I come out and elbow one in the kidney and kick behind his knee. As he falls I chop the base of his neck and knock him out. The last man pushes the beaten one away and throws a punch. I shift to the side and grab his wrist. I pull him forward and slam my knee into his stomach before throwing him across the room and into another group.

The Sword of Might sends me a warning and I hesitate. A chain wraps around my neck and smacks my face, pulling me back against someone. They press their body against me and tighten the chain, lifting me off my feet. With my airway cut off I can't breathe and with my feet dangling I can't find purchase to kick or shoulder throw. I can't get a good grip on the chain either and panic starts to set in. I reach back and find a hand. I grip the wrist tight and twist. I feel bones crush and the man screams. The chain falls from my neck, allowing me to breathe again. I spin around as soon as my toes touch the ground and punch into the man's gut. As he flies back I see a flash of War's visage and hear him roar. I take a moment to catch my breath as my teeth clench and my brow furrows. I shake my head, trying to push the feeling away.

The Sword of Might's warning vibration pulls me around and I follow the motion it wants me to make. I raise the Dagger of Power and catch a large pipe. The anger I was trying to push away takes a firmer hold. The blade shimmers and slices through the pipe with ease. I grab the man and push out, throwing him through the air. I fall into Quickstep and chase after him. I come out next to him and throw him into the ground. I continue running as my eyes narrow on the next group. There are a good half-dozen people circling at least two others. One looks like Rain. I run into the circle, taking the legs out from under one man and slamming my fist into him before he actually falls, forcing him hard into the ground. I pivot back and slam my elbow into another man's side, forcing him to buckle over. A rising kick into his chest knocks him onto his back and almost forces him to roll over. I turn back to deal with the next person, but it turns out I'm not needed. Ráfaga is beating two with a staff. He's nowhere near as good as Michael was, but I guess that doesn't matter. It works. Rain has someone with a bloody face in a headlock. He hits the man a few times before I see the brass knuckles. Rain then breaks the man's neck. It snaps me out of my frenzy. I hear War's chains scrape across the ground, but he's still nowhere to be seen.

Ráfaga is going for a killing blow against someone he knocked onto the floor. I reach out and stop his strike before he can deliver it. "That's enough," I say. He stares at me for a moment before pulling his staff away. As the beaten man tries to get up Ráfaga pushes him with his foot. "¡Vete! Cabrón!"

"Have you seen T-Bird?" Rain asks.

"Not since the start of the fight." I say.

"That was awesome," Ráfaga says. "Seeing all those guys flying. That was you, right?"

"Yeah," I answer as the Sword of Might pulls me to a distinct location and giving me a vague image of sharp metal. I give myself over completely and react instinctively, plucking a knife right out of the air. There's blood smeared on the blade. After a quick scan my eyes lock onto the stunned owner. "Excuse me," I say before falling into Quickstep and covering the distance. I come out before he can react and jam my thumbs into pressure points in his hips, cutting off the connection to his nerves. His legs give way and he falls. I kick out as he collapses and send him flying across the floor.

They keep coming, wave after wave, but one by one I take them down, never staying in one place. The adrenaline flowing through me fills me with excitement. I'm a little disappointed when Ráfaga steps in and hits one of the men on the side of the head with his staff, knocking him out. A gurgled scream draws me to Rain. A trail of blood flows from a man's throat as Rain pulls away from him. I didn't notice the blade attached to his brass knuckles before.

"Chica, how did you do that?" Ráfaga asks as he smashes his staff into someone's face.

"Lightning, we have to find T-Bird," Rain says.

I look at the man drowning in his own blood and kneel next to him, wishing I could save him. This is murder, isn't it? I always thought it was; now I'm not sure. "Did you have to kill him?" I ask.

"What do you think they're going to do to T-Bird if we don't find him?" Rain shouts.

"But he wanted me to run ahead."

"We were with him," Ráfaga says, "but we were separated."

"He needs you now," a voice whispers. I look for it before realizing it's my angel.

"We need to find him," Rain says.

My thoughts turn to Andrea. She'll be lost without Jorge. He's all she has left. "I'll find him," I say.

Rain grabs my arm before I fall into Quickstep. "You know what needs to be done," he says. "Can you do it?"

I stare at him, unable to offer an answer. I pull my arm away and fall into Quickstep.

I focus on finding Jorge, ignoring the mobs around me as I move about. He needs me more. Ahead of me I spot a large ring of people facing out, like they're standing guard. I look past them and see Jorge inside. He's being held up by two men. His face is locked to the side as blood flies from his mouth. Conrad is in a punching motion with brass knuckles on both fists. Jorge's face is bloody and swollen. How long have they been beating him? Sergio advances with a knife in hand and a grin on his face. They plan to kill him!

I push myself harder as I race for the ring. My sudden appearance falling out of Quickstep surprises the men standing guard. They're too slow to react to me as I push off the ground and leap into the air, kicking the face of the one in front of me with a spin kick. I push off another man and push into the inner ring. I dash towards Conrad and grab him, pulling my weight around into a hard pivot and throwing him back into Sergio. I turn and press my thumb into the shoulder of one of the men holding Jorge. He lets go as he goes down with a grunt of pain. I thrust my hand into his chest and throw him back. I grab onto Jorge and push off the ground, spinning us around and driving my knee into the other man's face. With Jorge free I fall into Quickstep and race out of the circle through the opening I had made. Once clear I come out of Quickstep and help Jorge down to his knees.

"Where did you come from?" he asks as he looks up at me through blood-soaked eyes.

"Rain asked me to find you," I say.

The Sword of Might vibrates again, warning me of a new threat. My head shoots up in response, unsure of where or what the warning is. I spin around in response to the cock of a gun and draw my sword, deflecting several shots with the flat of the blade just in time. The sword vibrates sharply in my hand as the bullets ricochet into the crowd. Sergio stares at me in disbelief. I fall into Quickstep and see his face change to surprised fear. I come out in front of him and the Sword of Might shimmers. I thrust the blade into the barrel of the gun, slicing the metal like paper, followed by a swift kick that sends Sergio tumbling into the crowd.

Several men rush me at once from all sides. I defend myself against them, using Keen Edge to disarm them and take them down as quickly as I can. There's too many and my strength is becoming harder to control. Adrenaline races through me when someone spits up blood. I stumble and struggle to control my anxiety before War manipulates it. In my distraction I'm grabbed from behind and put into a half nelson. I flex my arms and break his hold before he can lift me from my feet and throw him over my shoulder. I need to get out of this crowd.

I leap over them and land a few yards away. Spinning around I find myself staring down the barrel of a gun. I momentarily freeze as I stare up at Conrad. I see the hammer pull back and I quickly shift to the side as the bullet grazes my face. Conrad's surprise doesn't slow him down as he follows after me and fires again. I'm able to evade this shot completely, but he follows my movements and continues to shoot. I deflect his arm with my free hand, sending the shots into the crowd. I can hear the thuds of people hitting the ground and the scent of blood becomes thick in the air. Conrad takes aim at my legs while taking wild swings between shots. I make a few strikes with my sword, trying to disarm him, but Conrad twists around each thrust.

A bullet grazes my leg, causing me to stumble and letting a second hit my shoulder. I deflect the third with the Sword of Might and unleash Meteor Strike in frustration. Several meteors burst from the flaming arc and strike the floor, the explosion knocking Conrad onto his back. His gun skitters across the floor. I emerge from the smoke and press my foot to his chest and the tip of my sword to his throat.

"Enough!" I shout. "You're not going to win this."

"Says you," he replies calmly.

Something strikes the side of my head and I hit the ground. The Sword of Might tumbles across the floor and pain erupts throughout my body as I'm beaten with a two by four. My anger rises as I'm being beaten by a growing number of people. I can hear War's growl of contentment. The scraping of his chains across the floor echoes in my ears. I feel a lust for blood; the hunger for violence growing.

I call the Sword of Might back to me and cut into the weapons hitting me, slicing through them as I rise to my feet. Fueled by anger I move to attack faster than they can react. I punch one in the sternum hard enough to send him flying through the crowd. I swear I heard a pop when I connected, but right now I don't really care. I take a long step and connect my heel to the jaw of another attacker with a roundhouse. I hear the crunch of his teeth as the force of the kick sends him spinning into the ground. Someone manages to hit my face. My teeth crunch under the metal of his knuckles. I taste blood and my anger rises faster. I catch his second punch and don't care to regulate my strength. I crush his hand and brass knuckles as I glare at him. He screams in anguish as I pull my sword back and aim for his heart. I stop just short as I come back to my senses. I was about to kill him.

I release him and back away. What happened? How could I lose it so much? "He's here," I hear someone whisper. I can't tell who the voice is over the roar of the fight. I scan the room, searching. The attacks don't stop, but I'm more focused on finding War than fighting back. With only the faintest outline, I finally see him. War lumbers slowly through the crowd, uncaring and unseen. People move through him, but no one notices. He's like a specter in the room. He's being called to this fight. It's working. War is beginning to manifest. That's why I lost it. His influence is slipping into the room itself, not just into me. I have to find Jorge. War's here. This fight's over.

I fall into Quickstep and head back to where I left him. He isn't far removed, but I don't like what I find. Both Jorge and Sergio are beaten and on the ground. Conrad is standing over Jorge while looking down on him, gun in hand. Tornado is on the ground nearby clutching his neck as blood pools around him. Sergio's trying to stand and looks like he's nursing his leg. I race towards them and come out of Quickstep near Sergio, thrusting both fists into the back of the man standing guard over him. Conrad points his gun at Jorge's head after realizing what's happened and I place the tip of my sword at the base of Sergio's skull.

"Enough!" I shout. I hear War's grunt of surprise, almost as if he heard me. "It's over Conrad!"

"Kill him, Lightning!" Jorge shouts.

"You know there's only one way this is going to go," Conrad says.

"It doesn't have to!" I shout. "You can leave! You can stop this!"

Conrad laughs at me. "Are you that naive? That's not how it works."

Tears are welling up in my eyes. "You don't want to be here in a few minutes."

"Kill him!" Jorge shouts, more frantic now. "Forget me! Protect Andrea!"

"It doesn't have to end this way!" I exclaim.

"This is the only way it can end," Conrad says.

My stomach is twisting and my heart races. I'm scared and excited at the same time. I feel War's presence more strongly now. I want to get everyone out alive, but they're determined to not let that happen.

"You wanted this Sweetness," Úna says.

"No, I didn't," I deny without looking for her. I'm too afraid to take my eyes off Conrad.

"You wanted War," she says, stepping out from behind Conrad. "You knew this was the only way. You wanted this."

"No," I plead.

"You sin. You give her power. You must make a choice now, Sweetness. How will you call him? Who will you save? Who will you lose?"

I tighten my grip on the Sword of Might. I have one chance to save their lives. I fall into Quickstep. Conrad barely has time to acknowledge my action before I come out behind him with my sword pressed against his throat and dagger against his arm. The white field appears and creates a physical barrier between the three of us and the rest of the fight.

"Enough," I say coldly.

Conrad is speechless. Jorge stares at the field around us.

"I am trying very hard not to kill anyone. You are not who I came for."

"Who the hell are you?" Conrad finally asks.

Jorge starts to laugh. "She's the goddamned demon hunter you fucking hellspawn!"

Conrad lowers his gun as Jorge laughs. "Demon hunter, huh?" Conrad says. "Fine. I guess I'll be the demon that kills you."

229

Shots hit the ground around me, causing me to pull away. Conrad spins around and backhands me with the gun. I stumble a bit but don't fall as he grabs me and pushes the gun into my face. My hand pushes against the gun as my ears ring. The bangs of the shots are loud as bullets fly past my head. I jab my fist into Conrad's chest, pushing him back. He struggles to stay on his feet and haphazardly aims his gun. I'm still reeling from the ringing in my ears and instinctively pull my arms around me before the shots continue. A smaller field encircles me as the larger one dissipates, protecting me from the bullets. I can feel the shots ping sharply off the field like little pinpricks on my body.

"Beat it down!" Conrad yells. I feel blows fall against the field, but they aren't strong. I push my arms out, making the shield expand and pushing them back. A space in front of me opens to reveal Conrad aiming at me. He fires before the shot becomes clear.

I panic as I raise the Sword of Might in defense. The first shots ping off the opening shield. With a clear path between us the next shots hit truer, deflecting off the blade of the sword. They ricochet and pass through the protective field. I'm barely able to deflect the rapid shots as Conrad advances. I force the shield around to block the shots, but it only leaves my backside open as several people rush into the barrier. I shrink the barrier to close the opening, trapping myself inside, but it'll keep more from coming in after me. I just have to deal with these three.

One makes an overhead swing with a wooden bat. I thrust my sword up and the blade bites into the wood. I smash the pummel of the Dagger of Power into his hands, making him release his grip on the bat. With a quick flick of my wrist, I force the bat off the Sword of Might and kick his feet out from under him. Unable to break his fall, he face plants on the ground. I react quickly to the swing of a large plumber's wrench with an unmoving stance, catching the oversized tool with the Heavenly Weapons. I slam my foot into his stomach and send him crashing through the field. It lets him pass through. I wish I had known about that earlier.

The last one rushes me swinging a pair of large knives erratically. I can't stop him without seriously hurting him and in that moment I don't really care. I take a step back to strike but hold my hand. That is too much force. War. His very presence is starting to influence my actions. The man takes advantage of my hesitation and throws one of his knives at me. Taking me by surprise I fall as I haphazardly deflect it with the Sword of Might. On my back the man throws himself at me with the other knife bearing down. I catch him with my legs and kick him away and through the field. An angry scream pulls my attention and I can barely brace for the hit. With a blood-covered face, the first man attacks me again, landing a blow against me with his bat. It hurts enough to make me buckle a little but isn't strong enough to take me down. He pulls back for another angry blow and I punch him with my dagger hand. I hold back enough to not do serious harm, but hard enough to send him through the barrier.

I can now take a moment to catch my breath. I can feel Black Lightning pounding on the barrier. I'm surrounded and will be overwhelmed as soon as I drop the field. My anger and excitement start to rise. Anger at how hard they're making this for me. Strangely, excitement over the thrill of this fight. I know it's War and try to shake it away, but it's hard. The longer and harder I fight, the stronger these emotions are taking hold. I want to unleash more power but am fighting against the urge.

I hear Conrad's voice over the crowd. "Keep the bitch occupied. I'm taking Jorge out." Shock befalls me. Is he serious? Even after everything he's seen me do, he's still hell-bent on killing Jorge? My grip on the Heavenly Weapons tightens and my teeth clench. Úna's right. I have to make a choice. Conrad won't stop until Jorge is dead. "Fine," I breathe as I sheath the Dagger of Power. "Have it your way." I widen the field, pushing everyone around it back and creating an opening. People are already rushing the opening but slow to a crawl as I fall into Quickstep. I use Clairvoyance to find the quickest path to Jorge and go. I weave through the crowd, feeling the ever-thickening tension and hate. I run past Conrad, forcing myself to stay on target. The urge to stop is overwhelming, but Jorge needs me. He's in no condition to fight.

As the sword showed me, Jorge's defenseless on the ground and being beaten by Sergio and another man. I come out of Quickstep just offset behind Sergio. I grab him by the back of his shirt and with the lingering momentum hurl him away from Jorge. I pivot into a roundhouse and connect with the other man in the chest, sending him hurdling away. Using Eternal Fire I surround us in flame to push back advancing enemies, leaving a swath open between Conrad and myself.

Conrad stares at me with hate filled eyes as he orders his men to stand down. I stand defiantly between him and Jorge, raising my sword to a ready position.

"Take him out, Lightning," Jorge coughs. "You know it's the only way." His voice is ragged and he has trouble taking deep breaths.

"Bitch, you need to get out of the way," Conrad threatens. "You have no idea who you're dealing with."

"Neither do you," I say. "This is your last chance. Or I can't be held responsible for what happens next."

Conrad responds by opening fire. I anticipate this and raise my hand to summon Psionic Shield the instant he made a move. The green hue ripples as it stops the bullets. "You want to see what I can do?" I whisper through clenched teeth. "Fine. Then watch." I lower all my guard and let the anger take hold. "Watch me War!"

The Sword of Might shimmers and I drop Psionic Shield. I map the path of every shot that's fired as I rush forward with enough force to cause the surrounding flames to wave. The blade of the sword cuts into the bullets and I close the distance of several yards in only a few steps. I thrust the point of the sword into the gun, slicing it to pieces. I slam my hand into Conrad's chest and rocket him away. I close the distance with Quickstep and grab his ankle. "Andrea is not a piece of property!" I shout as I slam him into the ground twice like a rag doll. I throw him across the room to the exclamation, "Jorge is doing everything to protect her!" I chase after him as he tumbles across the floor, leaving bloody splatter in his wake. I'm way overdoing this, but I don't care. I catch up to Conrad as he stops tumbling and kick him hard in the stomach, lifting him off the ground. "I'm not a prize to be won!" I begin to beat him as each blow juggles him in the air. "But you don't care!" Blood splashes around us and onto me. An angry smile crosses my lips as I unleash Eternal Fire and Meteor Strike randomly around us to keep his men at bay. "I'll return the pain you caused tenfold!" My hand finds Conrad's throat and I slam him into the ground as I scream, "You're just like an avatar!" I spin the Sword of Might to face the blade down, and with a frightening smile on my face say, "And I'm the demon hunter!"

Without hesitation I drive the blade through Conrad's heart. I stare down at him as he clutches the blade in his chest. Blood bubbles and spurts from his mouth, painting his teeth and lips crimson. He reaches up for me, his fingers scraping against my neck. I pull his hand away and stare down at him with a smile as he stares back at me with hate.

"Kill... you..." he gurgles. "Hate... you..."

My smile fades. His eyes, even as life leaves them, carry no fear or remorse. Only hatred. I understand what my angel meant now. I shake my head. "I don't want to be like you," I say. "May God forgive me. I forgive you."

Conrad's body goes limp and he no longer struggles for breath. I pull my sword from his body, the blood sliding off like water. Even in death, his eyes hold only anger. The Sword of Might sends a vibration through my arm. There are several rapid pops of a gun, but I'm not sure of the direction. I throw my hands up to raise my shield around me. I follow the sounds of Sergio's angry sheiks as the shots continue to ping off the shield. Even after emptying the clip he continues to pull the trigger relentlessly. I take the Dagger of Power as the shield drops and point it at him in warning, but he just charges. My hair and coat whip about as I unleash Whirlwind. Sergio tries to stand against the powerful winds but is whipped off his feet along with everyone near him. It's time to put an end to this.

I look for War and find him standing over someone. His translucent form is hard to see. A chain with a sharp point hovers over the body on the ground, bobbing in tandem with his weak breathing. War, though, doesn't seem to notice his intended victim, almost as if his chain has chosen its own. "War!" I shout. The sudden killing blow is averted as the chain seeks me out. "I'm the one you want! I am Rebecca Virtue, the demon hunter! I summon you!"

The chain fades as War's ghostly visage begins to look around. His head moves in several directions at once until he lays his sights on me with those piercing red eyes. I steel my resolve and shout, "What are you waiting for? Come and get me!" War begins to move from several places at once. His ghostly bodies align into one being and his body begins to solidify. His heavy steps start to echo and people begin to take notice and stop fighting. Some move from his path while others, who don't understand what they are seeing, simply try to impede his way only to have War walk through them, unnerving everyone who sees, including me. I take a few defiant steps forward, away from Conrad's body. War and I finally stand face-to-face. He's much larger than I had envisioned him.

The entire weight of his being seems to drop all at once and weighs me down. All the turmoil of emotion inside me washes away, shaking my resolve and instilling fear. Air and smoke push from around his body as the ground, or perhaps reality itself, buckles around him. His form is instantly solid, no longer the transparent ghost it was. He towers over me, terrifying in his sheer size. Everything has led up to this moment. Everything around us has stopped and all eyes lay upon us. Finally face-to-face, I find myself terrified.

War stares down at me and my knees tremble. My lips quiver despite my effort to scowl up at him. My entire body is shaking. Fear and anger begin to swell up inside me. War's chest expands as if he takes a breath. "I was enjoying our game of cat and mouse." His rough, booming voice is far more terrifying in person and elicits a frightened breath from me. My stomach twists and jumps. His crimson eyes glow with each word he speaks. "You called. I answered. Yet you tremble before me." He seems to take a breath. "How I have looked forward to this moment. To finally bear witness to the body of your miracle."

I try to hide the concern that falls on my face. What's he talking about? War holds his arms out. "Strike me. I will not retaliate. Show me your power." The sounds of confusion around us drag me back to a nightmare. All around me was death. All I could hear were screams. Michael was in this monster's grasp. Without mercy, he tore Michael apart right in front of my eyes. I know it was a dream, but with the pain of Michael's loss still fresh in my heart, it may as well have been real. Tears swell up in my eyes again and I clench my fists tight. I can't stop my body from shaking, both in fear and anger. My throat is tight from the sobs I try to hold back. My teeth are clenched tight in rage. I wipe my tears away and can hold it in no longer. The pain in my heart is too much and I cry out in rage and sorrow as I strike with all my unbridled power.

My fist creates a shockwave against War's metallic body, rocking everyone near us. My fist crumbles and pain races through my arm. My hand is shaking and my knuckles are cut and bleeding. Worse, War didn't move. "You hold back," he says in annoyance. "Do not." I take an uncertain step back. My heart is racing. What's going on? I didn't hold back, did I? I look around. That shockwave didn't just push people back. It knocked them down. If that was me holding back, what will happen if I don't?

"I am growing impatient," War says. "Strike!"

Taking deep breaths, I steel my resolve. I lash out with a kick, creating another wave of force against his body as I feel something in my foot pop. I can't help crying out in agony. I try to limp away, but my foot hurts too much to put any weight on it. After only a few steps I collapse and instinctively cradle my foot. War lets out an annoyed groan. I look back over my shoulder to see him tower menacingly over me. His body casts a shadow that seems to consume me.

I can't hurt him? Oh my God. Why can't I hurt him? Was Úna right? Am I really just not strong enough? I look out at everyone surrounding us, watching and waiting. Oh God, what have I done?

Seventeen

Despite the pain I force myself to stand and face War. I can't put weight on my foot and drawing the Sword of Might is difficult since I can't maintain a good grip, ultimately forcing me to switch to my left hand. Úna was right, this was a mistake. I overestimated myself. I'm not ready to fight him, but that's not a choice anymore. I'm going to fight War.

The sound of a gunshot makes me jump. War's dark metallic flesh ripples under the force of the bullet, but there's no wound or blood. War slowly turns his attention to the shooter. It's Sergio. "She's mine you freak!" he shouts. I can only stare at him flabbergasted. Is he serious? Did he not see what just happened? War points his hand at Sergio. I question his intention, but War says nothing. Instead, a small projectile shoots from his hand and hits Sergio in the shoulder. Sergio moves under the force of the strike and it draws some blood, but he seems unhurt. Sergio glares at War as he simply lowers his hand and returns his focus to me. I look between them. What's going on?

"You son of a bitch!" Sergio shouts as he raises his gun against War. Gnarled black spikes burst from all around Sergio's body, some reaching three feet in length and anchoring him in place. A pained groan escapes his lips. My eyes widen in shocked horror. My heart drops

238

and my stomach twists. I take a step away despite the pain and raise the Sword of Might in defense. Sergio is dead, just like that. There's a sickening crunch as the spikes retract into Sergio's bloody body and he crumples into a heap on the floor. A deafening silence follows. The Sword of Might is shaking in my grip and takes both hands to steady. My good leg shakes under the stress and weight of my body. As War stares down at me, my teeth all but chatter. I've seen his chains in action before, but never anything else. I guess I thought that was his only weapon and I could handle that. But this? This is something totally different. It was fired like a bullet but is far deadlier. Would I even be able to avoid one of those? I grit my teeth and swallow, pushing back my fear. No, I can't think like that. I can dodge—

A sudden angry war cry breaks the silence. Black Lightning is charging War. I scream at them to stop, but their anger drowns out my plea. War remains motionless and fixated on me as countless black chains burst from his body and encircle us. My stomach drops and I brace myself, unsure of what is about to happen. His horrible, nightmarish chains circle us for a moment, halting the enraged men in surprise. Various sharp and spiked heads press against the outside of the sphere War's chains make around us, ready to strike. Realizing what's about to happen, I plead to War, "Please don't do this."

The chains lash out into the crowd. Their agonized screams fill the room as the chains twist and cut into their bodies. The razor chains pull back, tearing blood and flesh from their victims. It doesn't deter them, making them angrier and focus their attacks on the chains. The vicious heads in turn lash out, striking, slashing, and stabbing at anyone that gets too close. The chains aren't trying to kill and barely fight back.

They're just trying to keep their victims occupied while others in the sphere dive into the ground and erupt in all the exits, trapping everyone inside the room. The attacking chains and sphere surrounding us retract into War and he turns away from me. What's he doing? Why is he turning his back to me? His right hand closes into a fist and a long, black serrated blade grows steadily from the top of his wrist until it scrapes across the floor. He approaches a small group of people that raise their weapons against him. "No, don't!" I shout.

In one quick and powerful motion, War cuts his sword into an upward arc. The effortless swing rips through the bodies of the charging men as if they were made of paper. Their cuts aren't clean, and not all are dead. Their screams of agony torment me as they writhe in agony. A few still have enough of a body to attempt to pull themselves to safety. War ambles away, leaving them to die slow deaths. Gunfire fills the air and War's body ripples, absorbing the bullets. He approaches the shooter as he empties the clip and panic covers his face. He throws the empty gun at War and turns to run. War pulls back to strike and I unleash Meteor Punch. The explosion throws the man to the floor and is hidden by the smoke. I begin to limp towards them when suddenly there is a scream. It grows louder as I hear bones popping, then silence. Something large flies out of the smoke with a trail of crimson following behind and lands at my feet. It's the upper half of the man. I move back in such a start that I almost fall over. The Sword of Might sends a warning through my being and I barely have enough time to raise it in defense.

A whip-like blade of serrated metal arches from the smoke and knocks me from my feet. The whip-like blade comes down and I roll away as it slams into the ground, shattering the concrete floor and making me choke on the debris-filled smoke. The bladed whip lays silent beside me as my lungs clear. Slowly, it retracts back into the smoke cloud. I can make out War's shadow. He pulls his arm and sends the bladed whip into a mixed group of fleeing men, both Thunderbirds and Black Lightning. Once they were on opposing sides, but the gang war is over. There is only one side now. Against War.

The sharp metal wraps around a man's neck and pulls him from his feet, dragging him back to War. At the Horseman's feet, War places a large heavy foot on the man's chest and stomach. The slack on War's whip tightens as he slowly pulls, cutting into his victim and ultimately pulling the man's head, and parts of his spine, from his body. Seeing the grotesque mayhem before me, I vomit a little. I've been through so much, but this is by far the worst. What have I unleashed on these people? I can barely move my foot and my hand is tingling. I can't fight until these wounds are healed. I reach into my inner pocket with certain ointments in mind. The jars come to my hand immediately. I slather the ointments onto my hand and ankle. I need to push through the pain and remember the vicodin Jorge had given me. I desire it as I return the ointments and the bottle comes to my hand. I swallow a handful of pills.

"Are you satisfied now, Demon Hunter?" Úna says. There is no love or playfulness in her voice. No Sweetness, as she had always called me, or even Rebecca. She's never called me Demon Hunter before. I find her staring at me with anger in her eyes. "You have unsheathed a weapon you cannot control. Now he will not stop until his bloodlust is sated. These sins are on your soul. You only make her stronger. This is what you wanted."

"No, it's not!" I scream.

241

A cry of agony pulls me from Úna. A small body struggles in War's grip, his head enveloped completely in the Horseman's hand. That isn't a man. He's barely a teenager. War squeezes the small skull in his grip. The boy's body spasms as he struggles. Blood oozes between War's fingers. There's a crunch and the boy's body goes limp and his crying stops. War lets the body fall into a heap and begins to move again. "It is what you have," Úna says. I stare at the body on the ground. His face is misshapen with blood dripping from every pore. One of his eyes popped out of its socket but is still connected by a strand of tissue. My fingers dig into the ground as I clench my hand into a fist. How could I let this happen? He was just a boy. "That's enough!" I scream as I fall into Quickstep. I run at War as fast as I can, everything around me coming to a halt; everything except War. He turns his head slightly to look at me as four of his chains blur into existence. I have no time to react as they slam into me, wrapping around my body and limbs. They slam me against the floor and swing me across the room into a wall before throwing me away like refuse and forcing me out of Quickstep.

The world spins as I try to stand. War attacked me in Quickstep, something I haven't been able to do since I fought Santano. War is faster than me? "You are slow," War says. I look at him and see double for a moment. Several chains point at me, each equipped with a baseball-sized metal sphere. "You taunt me." The chains lash out at me. I dodge the first few strikes, but one manages to connect with the side of my knee, causing my leg to buckle. A second strike comes, but I reach out and take hold of the chain. The barbs cut into my flesh as I stop it, only to have it wrap around my arm and throw me off balance, allowing another to strike my shoulder. Another sphere slams into the side of my face, making my teeth rattle. The chains whip me across the room and into a group of people. War completely turns his back to me and lumbers away. I see Rain help Jorge limp over to me. Someone tries to help me to my feet, causing me to instinctively pull away.

"Tranquila. It's just us," Ráfaga says.

"What the hell is that thing?" Rain asks.

"That's War," I answer as I spit out a little blood.

"That's what you want to kill?" Jorge asks.

I nod while nursing my knee. It hurts a lot, but it isn't knocked out of place.

"What's the plan?"

I support myself on Ráfaga and work the pain from my knee and foot. "I kill him." I look back to War as he pushes two heads together. Their skulls collapse under the pressure and bloody brain matter oozes between his fingers. "That was always the plan."

"Well it's a sucky plan," Ráfaga says. "He's kicking your ass."

Someone attacks War from behind, slamming a two-by-four as hard as he possibly can into War's back. The board splinters against War's body, but he remains unharmed. He turns and grabs the man by the arms. In an effortless motion, War rips the arms from their body and slams the severed limbs against the man's torso, shattering his limbs and body upon impact. The man falls in gurgling agony. I stare at the horrid spectacle before me with tears in my eyes. War kicks the destroyed body across the room towards me. The man lands at my feet with his agonized eyes staring up at me, begging for mercy as a sickening gurgle escapes his throat. He's still alive.

With tears running down my face I drive the Sword of Might into his skull, giving him the mercy he wants. I stare at War, trying not to cry; trying not to scream. He simply stares back; an emotionless killing machine. I move as I fall into Quickstep, running as fast as I can. I will Holy Strike into being, making the blade of the Sword of Might glow bright. My arm won't move to strike as I close in, so I decide to move behind. Suddenly I'm off the ground and out of Quickstep, which is jarring and causes the world to spin. There's a hand at my throat and my weapons clank on the ground as the magic of my attack dissipates. I try to pry the hand off, but War is holding me in an iron grasp. I didn't even see him move.

War brings me close and slams his head into mine, cutting my face and I think breaking my nose. Blood flows from my nostrils as War slams me onto the ground, forcing the air from my lungs. He kicks me like a soccer ball, connecting his boot to my ribs, and sends me flying through the building. Crashing through a wall, I end up in another room. I can't move. I'm in too much pain. I wonder if my ribs are broken. I cough the blood out of my mouth as I choke on it. I've bitten off more than I can chew. I can't do this on my own. I need my angel. "Please," I say weakly. "Help me."

-Heaven's Interlude-

Raphael's ears perked. He was being called. He could feel dire distress. Rebecca was in pain. She needed him. He looked at the tiered game board. They had played Babel for well over a day. He looked at Asmodeus, who was beginning to make his move.

"You win," Raphael said as he stood. "I must go."

"I see," Asmodeus said as he placed a pawn on the dissipating game board. "You are being summoned."

Raphael took a few steps before being stopped by a spiritual tether linking him and Asmodeus in place. "I've forgotten how much I miss those times," Asmodeus said as his cane changed shape. Its material shifted from wood to silver metal. He pulled his hand along it and the cane split in two, connected by a length of chain.

Raphael's eyes narrowed on Asmodeus and his golden sword blazed into being. "You wanted to separate us. Why?"

Asmodeus smiled as he rested the chain behind his back, positioning the two canes into a ninety-degree angle, with one point towards Raphael. "I asked for your help," Asmodeus said. "Now I get it." Raphael fell in step with Asmodeus, their weapons locking and shifting, but never parting as they moved. Raphael was not interested in a prolonged battle. He could hear Rebecca's cry, "Help! Please, I need you now!" Raphael tried to ignite his blade, but its magic had been nullified. He couldn't answer the Guardian's Plea. He realized in that moment what game Asmodeus had in mind from the beginning: a duel.

"Babel was a distraction," Raphael said as he moved around Asmodeus, his weapon sliding along Asmodeus' cane.

"It was, but not for why you think," Asmodeus said as his leg shifted and matched the length of his left, but the foot became that of a rooster.

A jumble of words echoed in Raphael's ears. "...can't do this..." Rebecca's voice echoed. "...need you..."

Raphael tried to disengage and shift directly to his charge, but he couldn't. "Why can't I attend to my charge?" Raphael asked. "How are you keeping me?"

"The mark is being charged. I will keep my word, but this must be finished. Your Guardian powers are sealed until there is a victor."

Raphael narrowed his eyes and spoke a word in Angelic, "Repulse."

Asmodeus was pushed away, but returned with his own Angelic response, "Bind." Raphael tried to move only to find his feet bound in place. Asmodeus smiled a friendly smile. "You were not the only one drawing a rune, but you made only one. Disarm." Raphael's sword tore from his hands. Asmodeus made a simple hand motion as Raphael began to trace a shape. Raphael's hands instantly bound together and he was pulled to his knees, but his fingers continued to trace as he chanted an incantation beneath his breath. Blue energy blazed over his body, burning away the binding magic. He rose back to his feet as his hands were enveloped in flames.

Raphael rushed forward as Asmodeus backed away, his hands and fingers moving erratically. He was building two runes at once. Raphael thrust his hand out, sending a torrent of flames towards Asmodeus, who raised one hand and blocked the flames with a thin opaque field. Asmodeus kept moving around the room as Raphael threw torrents of flame at his enemy. Unaware of what Asmodeus was doing, Raphael began etching a protective rune in his mind in preparation for whatever Asmodeus could be planning. Asmodeus rushed forward through the flames and struck the ground. Energy bursts forth and Raphael saw the now glowing circle. "Mystic Purge!" Asmodeus shouted in the Demonic tongue. Raphael felt the magic being ripped from his body and mind, effectively stripping him of his rank and power.

Asmodeus planted both hands on the ground and kicked his feet into Raphael, pushing the archangel nearly onto his back. The clawed talons of the rooster foot cut into Raphael's flesh, drawing blood. Asmodeus got back onto his feet and began to draw another rune with his hands. Raphael found his footing and did the same, but Asmodeus finished first. He circled his mouth with his fingers and blew hard. The outline of his fingers glowed and his breath was magnified many fold into the strength of a hurricane wind. Raphael tried to hold his ground and finish his rune, but the force was too much for his newly weakened body. The Mystic Purge seemed to have sapped his superior strength as well as his magic. Raphael couldn't stand and was blown away by the gales. Asmodeus stood his ground as he held his hands apart and started to trace with them and a foot, as well as tracing a fourth rune in his mind. Raphael rushed forward, the rune he was etching with his hands ruined, but the one in his mind untouched. Raphael inhaled deeply, Asmodeus only then realizing what was about to happen and altered his left rune ever so slightly, not noticing Raphael tracing several runes with his individual fingers.

Raphael forced the air from his lungs and blew a cone of flame from his lips. Asmodeus finished altering the rune and raised his hand, creating a field to block the flames. Raphael heard Rebecca call again for help and pointed his index finger at the field. A pointed energy shard shot from his fingertip and shattered the protective field, allowing the flames entry. Asmodeus was consumed by the fire but forced himself to finish tracing his runes as he was set alight. Raphael pointed his fingers at different parts of Asmodeus' body; wrists, legs, arms. Each finger shot bright energy that latched onto Asmodeus' limbs and made them heavy. Raphael circled around the fallen angel and guided the energy to bind him. Asmodeus was forced to the ground and Raphael held the bindings tight. Taking this moment to plan his next move, Asmodeus stood and turned with his hands stretched out, the same way Raphael's were. Raphael stared up in confused surprise as he realized that Asmodeus was standing above him. Panic was starting to overtake him. "I need you," echoed in his ears. This duel was taking too long. When Raphael tried to move, he saw that the magical tethers traced from Asmodeus fingertips to him. He had been bound by his own spell and Asmodeus had somehow become the owner of the binding. "I'm trying," Raphael whispered back.

Asmodeus smiled and said, "Not enough it seems. I'm sure you're familiar with a displacement spell, but what about this?" Asmodeus tugged at the tethers, tightening them a bit more. "This is a more closely guarded secret. It's a new type of reversal spell which allows me to take ownership of your spell. I've been working on perfecting it." Asmodeus inhaled deeply, Raphael narrowing his eyes as he knew what was to come next. Asmodeus exhaled, blowing a cone of fire on his helpless captive. Raphael could feel the heat of the flames and could already see the flaws in the Demonic spells used against him. His fingers were not bound, as was in his casting. "Hold on!" he shouted mentally towards his charge as he drew a rune and cut the bindings. He stood and reached through the flames, which were not nearly as hot as his own, and gripped Asmodeus by the scruff of his pearly shirt.

"It needs more work," Raphael said as he raised his right hand, already with the finished rune. He clenched his fist and it burst into flames. Suddenly, pain shot through his heart and rippled through his being. His heart burned in pain and his body became heavy and weak. Asmodeus smiled at Raphael's sudden bout of pain and finished the rune he had started. Winds surrounded his fists and he punched Raphael in the chest. The swirling winds slammed into Raphael and hurled him away from Asmodeus and into a tree, which surprised both of them. Blood splashed from Raphael's mouth, which brought a look of delighted surprise to Asmodeus' face. Raphael stumbled as he tried to brace himself against the tree only to pass through it and land on the ground.

Raphael tried not to panic. He had been pushed from the celestial plane, to the material plane, and then to the astral plane. There were ways to force a celestial onto the material plane, but he didn't see nor feel such a thing be done. Then instantly return to the astral realm? He had never heard of such a thing. The strain in Raphael's heart was so great his breaths were ragged. He could feel the weight of the tree bearing down on him, though it no longer physically impeded him. He could feel his strength slipping away in a manner that was different than what the mystic purge had done.

Asmodeus kneeled beside Raphael. "That was quite unexpected," he said.

"What did you do to me?" Raphael struggled to ask as he clutched his chest. Fear was rising in him, but he couldn't place why. It almost didn't feel like his own fear. His hands hurt and were bleeding. His entire body ached. He had never experienced anything like this before.

"I'm not so sure I did this," Asmodeus said. "I would love to take the credit though."

Then Raphael placed the fear and panic. "Rebecca!"

Asmodeus lifted Raphael's chin. "Thank you. The mark is charged." He traced a rune on Raphael's forehead and said something in Demonic. "Can't have you remembering all my tricks, you know? Don't worry, War will be dealt with."

Asmodeus faded as he strolled away, his rooster foot returning to the shape it had been earlier, causing him to lean onto his cane as he hobbled away. Raphael let lose a painful and remorseful cry, unleashing the

249

remainder of his runic and angelic powers together and tearing away the material land around him. With the physical tree holding him down now gone, Raphael struggled to his feet. He stumbled around, unable to jump directly to his charge. Something was very wrong. Unfurling unsteady wings Raphael took flight. "I'm coming," he whispered, praying his charge could hear him. Praying that she could hold on.

-End Interlude-

Eighteen

Screams of agony tear at my heart as I lie on the ground. Pain shoots through my ribs with every breath, so I try not to breathe too deeply. I have to continue this fight with broken ribs. Úna bends over me into my field of vision. With hands on her hips she stares at me with stern displeasure.

"Get up, Demon Hunter," she says. "You have a fight to finish."

I wipe blood from my face and stare at it. It has taken so much for anyone to hurt me, if they could hurt me at all. War isn't even trying and has already done so much damage. "I can't do this alone," I admit.

"Then call your angel, but be mindful of who it is you cry out to."

I take a few painful breaths. "Help! Please, I need you now!"

"Get up, Rebecca," a voice whispers.

I strain to get up as pain shoots through my ribs. I wipe fresh blood from my face and look towards the carnage. "Please," I say, "I need you. I can't do this alone."

"You are not alone. Pour the holy water upon yourself."

I reach into my pocket and pull out a couple vials of holy water. I pull the corks out with my teeth and let the water cascade down my face and body. The voice says something in a sing-song tone and my body momentarily goes numb. The pain is gone. I look at my hands and watch the cuts close. I turn out my palms and the Heavenly Weapons shoot through the hole in the wall and into my hands. The blade of the sword ignites as soon as my hand closes around the handle and I unleash Meteor Punch, blowing the wall away.

War turns towards me as the dust settles and I see a young boy in his clutches. I gasp. He couldn't be older than thirteen. War has his sharp fingers pierced into the boy's shoulder while his other hand grips the boy's head. The boy cries as he tries to pry the cold, uncaring hands off.

"Let him go War!" I shout, my body shaking in fear. "He's only a child!"

"War does not see age or guilt. It does not see right or wrong. It does not even see warriors. It sees only the weak crushed beneath the strong." War puts pressure against the boy's head, distending his neck. The boy cries for his mother, apologizing to her. My grip on the Heavenly Weapons tightens. "Strong and weak is all war can see. Which are you?"

War snaps the boy's neck at an awkward angle, causing his body to go limp. My heart breaks as my tears mix with the blood and dirt on my face. I scream as I spin the glowing Sword of Might into a downward thrust. I drive the point into the ground, releasing the explosive power of Holy Strike. Wood, stone, and dirt burst into the air as I unleash the hurricane winds of Whirlwind and send the powerful gale towards War, carrying all the debris with it. I fall into Quickstep and can still feel the pull of the gale. I dash forward, letting the force of the hurricane take me. My sword already poised to release Holy Strike.

RULES OF ENGAGEMENT

As I fly through the debris War comes to life. He throws the lifeless boy away from him and deflects my blade with his gauntlet. His second blow knocks the wind out of me and pushes me back into the gale, which catches me and throws me back at him as I'm forced from Quickstep. War uses an overhand strike to my back and slams me into the ground, causing me to lose my grip on the Heavenly Weapons. A powerful kick sends me flying across the room and tumbling over the floor. I dig my fingers into the ground, tearing up the linoleum and stone as I halt my momentum. I lock my gaze on War as I get to my feet. Loose serrated blades slither from his gauntlets as he whips them around his body, gaining momentum for a strike. I reach out my left hand and the Dagger of Power shoots into it as War rears back for an attack. The white field appears around me as War brings his whip-like blades down. The ground buckles beneath me and I can feel the immense strain on the shield. "Help!" I plead. "I can't keep this up!"

The shield shatters after two other powerful strikes, sending a shock through my mind and body. War's hand reaches for my face before I can react. "I felt it," War says as he slams his knee into me. "Where did it go?" He tosses me aside and I tumble to a stop. Battered and bruised I struggle to stand. My eyes burn, my face wet, and my mouth awash with the taste of copper. War's head jerks to the side as a makeshift flail slams into the side of his head. His chains burst from his body and latch onto the person that attacked him, pulling them to what they know will be their death. Still, the man fights back, swinging his flail at War. If they won't give up, there's no way I can. The chains melt away as an ignited Sword of Might rips through them and into

253

my hand. "You will fight me," I demand. "I'm the one that called you."

"There it is again," War says. "That burst of power."

I dash towards War, my blade still ignited. War returns my charge and closes the distance quickly. I thrust my blade into War's body, but he fades away. I hear War's heavy feet plant firmly behind me. I turn to strike only to have War's elbow slam into my face. It knocks me off my feet and he grabs my foot while I'm momentarily airborne. With an overhead swing, he slams me hard into the ground, making the stone shatter beneath me. My grip is barely strong enough to hold onto my weapons.

"It is beginning to surface," War says. "How do I pull it out?" He whips me like a rag doll and sends me tumbling again. A trail of blood paints the floor. I stand again on unsteady legs as the world shifts in my double vision. What do I do? He's just too strong. The hunger demon, the avatar, even Santano; they were nothing compared to War. "I need you," I whisper. I can feel panicked urgency, but I'm not sure it's mine. I feel a pull on my body. I can barely make out a muffled whisper, "I'm trying."

"Please," I beg as I try to steady myself. "I can't do this alone."

"Almost there," the voice whispers, clearer this time. "Call for me."

"Call your angel!" Úna screams.

"I'm trying!" I cry.

War is attacked by several people and for a moment he doesn't respond. He just stares at me. His head cocks to the side, as if in contemplation. Suddenly War reacts to his assailants. He slams one onto the ground and traps him beneath his boot. An open-handed thrust causes blood to erupt from the mouth of another man.

254

War takes hold of the third as he tries to hit him with a plumber's wrench. War pulls the man's arm back at a painful angle and begins to twist his head. The one at his feet is ripping the nails from his fingers as he tries desperately to crawl away.

"Stop it," I plead as I shamble forward. Something is building inside of me. "Leave them alone." War locks eyes on me as he puts more weight on his foot. Chains lash out of his back and slice into those behind him. "I said stop it," I declare. Something in my core has pushed to my throat and I scream, "Let them GO!"

An unearthly force escapes my lips, my scream turning into something else. Like a banshee's wail, the force of my cry knocks War back, releasing his victims to flee. War begins to advance again, but I feel the power still growing. I inhale and scream, this time to let it go, forcing the power from the back of my throat. It's stronger this time, the space before me rippling in the wave. It hits War with enough force to push him back. Exhausted, I can scream no more and the power fades. War stands and looks at me. He then looks to the surrounding gang members ready to defend themselves and I tense. How can they still be so willing to fight? War looks back to me and slowly approaches. "I understand now," he says. My already racing heart manages to beat even faster. "You have buried your power without knowledge of how to call it forth. But there is a means to make you dig."

War stands before me, unthreatened by the Sword of Might raised against him. "What are you talking about?" I ask. War reaches for my sword and wraps his fingers around the blade. I hear the burning of flesh, the smell of molten metal, and see smoke rising from his hand. Searing pain erupts in my left hand so intense that it causes me to drop the Dagger of Power. War's chains

255

wrap tightly around my right hand to prevent me from releasing the Sword of Might. I hug my hand to my body and see the burning flesh across the center of my palm and fingers. "Share in my pain," War says as he takes the blade of the sword and pierces his left side. A piercing, burning pain sears my left side in the same area he's driving the sword deeper into himself. I feel fresh blood and smell burning flesh. I realize what's happening. Just like the destruction demon, War is redirecting damage, but the destruction couldn't do this with the Heavenly Weapons. Why can War?

I try to pull away as I cry out in pain while War lets out a euphoric groan of pleasure. Is he enjoying this? My legs buckle under the pain and I collapse. War takes a handful of my hair and pulls my head back. "I will pull your miracle out of you."

I stare up teary-eyed at the shifting double image of War. He wants something I just can't give.

"Tell me you need me now," a voice whispers. Is it my angel?

"I need..." I whisper between sobs. "I need..."

"Pull her away!" someone shouts.

Hands grab me and help me to my feet. I hear the thud of something hitting metal and the vibration traveling along my sword. I hear the cry of pain as the blow is redirected, but another blow follows anyway.

"No," I plead. "Get away."

Hail is punching War and I can see the pain on his face as each is returned with War's power. "¡Deja la!" Storm shouts as he tries to pry War's chains from my hand.

"Do you want to see my Sonic Scream?" War asks.

War inhales and raises his head. He lets out a deep guttural bellow. The space ripple is easily visible as loose debris and dust lifts up and is carried by the distortion. It ripples through my body, shaking it from the inside out. The distortion carries people away. Walls crack and glass shatters as the distortion waves wash over them. War releases me as he takes another breath. He lets out another bellow as he sweeps his head from one side to the other. The shockwave is centered before him this time, crumbling walls and slamming anyone caught in its path back, including me. I barrel through battered, partially built machinery, which breaks much of my momentum and slam into a wall before face planting onto the floor.

"Say you need me!" a voice shouts. It sounds desperate.

"Focus!" Úna exclaims. "Call your angel!"

"I need my angel," I say.

"Call for me!" the voice shouts.

"Hold on!" a fainter voice says. I'm so confused. The world is spinning and fuzzy.

War's chains rip from his body and dart at me. I raise my arms to defend myself, unsure of what I can do. Someone tackles me and pulls me out of the way as the chains slam through the wall behind me. I look up to see Storm. "He's too strong!" he exclaims. "We gotta get outta here!"

Looking at his blurred shifting image, I know he's right and nod. Storm helps me to my feet. This isn't a fight I can win. I have to retreat. I turn open my palms and War glances towards me as the Heavenly Weapons find their way into my grip. He tosses something from his hand. I don't immediately see what they are as they roll between people, but explosions ensue. Chaos follows as people try to run from the explosions. War flings his hand and releases several tennis ball sized spheres. One rolls near me.

"Grenades!" Storm shouts as he throws me aside. The explosion tears into his body, ripping him apart.

"Get behind me!" I shout as more spheres explode. Everyone nearby begins to head towards me as War flings his hands again, releasing more grenades. I unleash Whirlwind and collect the spheres before they detonate and blow them safely away. War turns his attention back to me, flexing his fingers as a sphere appears between each of them. He flings them at me as everyone gathers. I move forward and hold the Dagger of Power out. The white field appears and shields us as the spheres explode against it. My arm shakes with each explosion, but the shield holds. Something heavy slams against it, causing my knees to buckle under the force and the world shifts. Each blow sends ripples through my body and makes my head hurt. The shield can't handle this. I grip the Sword of Might tight and the blade ignites. The shield shatters as I release my hold over it, reducing the mental and physical shock from its destruction. I move forward and thrust. War deflects with his arm like a shield just before the gout of flame from Eternal Fire releases. War transfers the burning of the flames back to me, making my arm ache in searing pain and the sleeve of my trench coat to actually burn.

From the deflection I move into thrusts and War continues to deflect while refusing to back down. War's attention is drawn away as he bats someone away. Someone else strikes War from behind and a chain wraps around his neck and arm. "Take the shot Lightning!" Rain shouts. I pull the Sword of Might back and as it glows bright I shout, "Holy Strike!" I thrust the blade forward, but War moves his hand and catches the glowing blade. I brace for the pain that doesn't come. Instead, the glow is pulled from the sword and into

War's hand, traveling through his arm and across this body into his other hand, which glows bright.

War slams his glowing hand into the ground, releasing the energy within. White light escapes from the cracks in the floor before the energy erupts and throws us all away. I can't hold onto the Sword of Might, as War still holds it in his grip, and tumble across the floor. Did he just steal my attack? With shaky eyes I look back to find War resting torso-deep inside a crater. He leaps out of the crater, the Sword of Might still in his hand and smoke rising from his grip. He lands on top of me. I'm slammed back into the ground with his right boot pressing into my body and forcing the air out of me. I have trouble taking a good breath. I'm unsure if it's from the sheer pressure or if more ribs are broken.

I drive the Dagger of Power into his leg and scream. Burning pain erupts in my right leg. It hurts so much. Why isn't he even flinching?

"Go on," War says. "Use Cataclysm. I will retreat if you do."

I hesitate. If I unleash cataclysm, it'll destroy my foot and may not even affect him. War rips his foot away, slicing our legs even more. I scream as he kicks my hand away and slams his boot down on it.

"Call your angel!" Úna shouts.

"You need me!" the other panicked voice shouts. "Just say you need me!"

War reaches down and pulls the Dagger of Power from his leg and tosses both weapons aside. "You are a coward," War says. He raises his other boot, putting his full weight on my arm. "And I have lost interest in you." He slams his boot down. I scream and cough blood. I hear someone shout my name. "Begone," War orders as he releases more grenades. Explosions rock the area around us, making my ears ring. War stomps on me again, forcing more blood from my lips.

"Focus!" Úna shouts. "Call your angel!"

War continues to stomp. It hurts; it hurts so much.

"Just say you need me, please!" the voice shouts.

War raises his boot again and spikes jut out from the sole. He stomps again and I start to choke on the blood in my mouth. It's getting dark. I'm going to die. I wasn't ready. Now I'm going to die. The demon hunter line will end. Everyone's died for nothing. I'm getting cold. Mom. Dad. I'm sorry. Michael. Will I get to see you now?

"Say you need me!" a voice shouts.

"I need..." I repeat, but it's hard to talk. I just want to sleep. Michael. I'm so sorry.

"Say it!" the voice shouts.

Another stomp knocks me out of the encroaching darkness. "Michael!" I scream. "I need you!"

Pain rips through my heart and the room becomes warm and bright. I see War turn his head, looking behind him. He moves away from me and pulls a large sword from his body. I turn my head and see a pillar of light. It takes the shape of a person and begins to dim. A long flowing gown covers the wingless angel. His dark brown hair is long, touching the nape of his neck. I remember that haircut. The angel looks at me in shock. He calls to me. His warm coffee brown eyes take on anger that I have never seen in them before as he turns his gaze to War. His robe shifts in a breeze that centers on him.

War groans in displeasure, "Archon."

I can't help but stare at this angel in disbelief. Am I dead or did Michael really come to my rescue?

Nineteen

"Wrong angel!" Úna shouts.

"Get away from her!" Michael demands. Wind pushes off his glowing body, washing over me. Hearing his voice again calms my shaking nerves as the wind takes the pain away. The shifting world focuses and for the first time I can really see him. I start to sob. It really is him. He came for me.

"You are not Saint Michael," War says. "How did you come to be here archon?"

"I came for Rebecca," Michael says. "Now get away from her."

War looks back to me. "That is very interesting."

Michael moves cautiously to one side with War's momentary distraction. I don't realize what he's doing until I see the Sword of Might. War returns his attention to Michael and he dives for my sword. Michael grabs it as he rolls to his feet, but before he can make any kind of demand he starts to scream and lets the sword clang back onto the ground.

"Foolish archon," War says. "Neither angel nor devil may touch the Heavenly Weapons. Tainted and blessed, they are for human hands alone. To any other their bite burns like fire." He upturns his hands, showing Michael the burns from the sword. "And those wounds are slow to heal."

I look at my hands. They still hurt with the fresh burns. I don't understand what War means. I try to pull myself to my feet. I don't realize right away that I'm being helped. Hail pulls my arm over his shoulder and supports me. "We gotta take this time to go," he says.

"No," I protest. "I can't leave him!"

"Hey, ol' boy is here to save your ass. Let him."

"I can't lose him again."

"You'll never lose me, Becca," Michael says. "I'll always be with you. Besides, how often do you get to die twice for someone?"

War laughs. War actually laughs. It's eerie. "I like you, but a seraph you are not."

Michael positions his feet to create his foundation and raised his hands into a defensive stance. "You talk a lot."

War rubs his chin. "Though, perhaps you have the heart of one." He tosses a sphere to Michael. I react instinctively, pushing away from Hail as I cry out to Michael. The Heavenly Weapons tear through the room and into my hands, but it's too late. Michael catches the sphere, but it doesn't explode. Instead it grows and extends into an ash-black staff. Michael twirls it around to get a feel for it before settling it into his hands and holds it loose against his body. He brings his left leg forward and bends his knee, keeping his right back and straight, creating a firm stance.

"An interesting choice of weapon," War says. He twirls his massive sword around and it shifts into a staff. He then enters an identical stance.

"No, Michael!" I exclaim. "You can't!" I try to pull away from Hail, but he fights against me.

"Rebecca, go!" Michael says. "I can handle this. Trust me."

"Alright, screw this," Hail says as he slings me over his shoulder. Pain rips through my body as my broken ribs shift. I drop the Heavenly Weapons as I try to relieve the pressure. I hear Jorge shout an order and the crowd follows behind us. I look past them to Michael. He and War are in step circling each other. Tears run down my face. He's right. I have to retreat. "I love you," I whisper. "Come back to me."

I force myself from Hail's shoulder, landing hard on the floor. Hail helps me up. "We ain't got time for this," he says.

"I know," I say. I wince and hold my ribs as I get up. "I'm okay." I look back to Michael, watching him trade blows with War. "I'll get you out of here."

"No," Jorge says as he walks up to me with the support of Rain. He hands me the Sword of Might. "You're getting us out. This backfired on you."

I take the sword from him. "It doesn't matter. I still have to—"

Jorge slaps me. It takes me by surprise and after the beating I've taken, it stings. "Look at yourself!" he shouts. "You're bloody and beaten. You keep holding your ribs like they're broken. You can barely stand on your own. He beat you Lightning! He almost killed you!" I can only stare at Jorge as he berates me. What am I going to say? He's right. "You lost, Lightning. Now it's time to go lick your wounds before you try again."

I take a breath. "Try again," I repeat. "I can be better prepared and try again. I need my dagger." A boy with sweat and blood covering his face hands me the Dagger of Power. I stare down at him, remembering what War had said. His childhood is being stolen from him, pulled into battles he has no business fighting. His entire life will be shorter because of it. I cup his chin in my hand. "I'll get you out of here," I tell him. "Then you need to go

263

home." He looks at me, his eyes moist with tears. He nods.

I step away from Hail and approach a wall. The Sword of Might glows and I thrust the blade into the wall, releasing the energy and blowing it out. I summon the solid white shield and focus it into the hole as a ring to keep War's chains back, allowing us to escape the room. After everyone has passed Hail helps me through the barrier and I continue this through several more walls until we're safely outside.

I sit on the ground to rest. Jorge is barking orders but getting resistance. I'm not paying too much attention. I'm in too much pain. I reach into my pockets for more ointments and first aid. Hail insists on helping me. I don't argue with him and let him dress my wounds. As he's bandaging my ankle I work on my hands and listen to the growing argument. Someone starts to scuffle with Rain and Jorge.

"Hey!" I shout. "Hasn't there been enough fighting today?"

They stop and Hail helps me to my feet. The man looks me up and down. He has tattoo's I don't recognize as Thunderbirds peeking through ripped clothes and blood. "Who the hell are you?" he asks.

"She's Lightning," Hail says. "The one that single handily kicked all your asses."

"Hail, don't," I say.

"Oh really?" the man asks. "Looks like she got her ass kicked."

"Don't change the fact that she can mop the floor with you," Hail says.

"I'd like to see the bitch try!" the man threatens.

"Stop it!" I shout. "What is wrong with you people? All your friends were just slaughtered and you still want to pick a fight?"

"Hey, that thing came for you. It came right up to you."

"How do you think it found me?"

"You called it!" someone else shouts as he pushes through the crowd. "I watched you do it after you took out Conrad."

"But you're the ones that brought him here in the first place! You hate each other so much you're willing to kill each other! That's what he feeds on!"

There is a momentary silence before someone speaks up. He's young, definitely still in high school. His eye is swollen shut and there are cuts on his face. "So us fighting brings him? We fight and he comes?"

"Yes," I answer. "That's exactly what happens."

He thinks for a moment before pulling the red and black bandana from his head, revealing a gash. "Fuck that, I'm out." He walks into the crowd and grabs a younger boy. "We're out. We ain't doing this no more. I ain't dying like that. Least if I get shot there's a body for Momma to bury."

There's sentiment to his words and others begin to walk away. Mostly they are younger members from both sides. "Where the hell do you guys think you're going?" the first man shouts.

"Let them go," Jorge says.

"You don't give us orders!"

Someone throws a hard punch out of nowhere and knocks the man to the ground. They both have similar tattoos. "You don't order us around either. Maybe you didn't notice but Conrad and Sergio are both dead. There ain't no reason to fight them anymore." He looks into the crowd. "What were we even fighting for anyway, huh? 'Cause Sergy couldn't get some pussy? Pretty pathetic if you ask me. But that thing in there? That's something we got a score to settle with."

"Are you crazy?" I shout. "That is the Horseman of War!"

"I don't care who it runs with. If it's alive it can die."

"It's not that simple!"

Hail nudges me. "Let it go."

"You don't understand."

"Don't matter. You are what you are. We are what we are. Never took shit from nothing and no one. Ain't going to start now. Scores will get settled."

"You're not going to listen."

"Not agreeing is not the same as not listening," Jorge says. "But I'm not stupid. I know we can't beat it. I know what it is. But I don't think you can beat it either. Not right now and not by yourself. Right now dude in there has its attention. When he doesn't anymore, it's going to come after you again and you're in no condition to fight." He digs out his wallet and hands me a credit card. "There's two thousand dollars on this. Use it. I'll take care of it."

"I can't take this."

"Well you are. We're going to try to buy you some time. You need to find a place to lay low and heal. I know you can do that pretty fast."

I take the card and look at Jorge. There is resolve and hope in his eyes, but I don't see the hate that was there before. "Be careful," I say. "I didn't go through so much trouble to save you just so you can die like this."

"Hail, take her as far away from here as you can."

"No, I'm okay. I can push through this and move faster on my own."

"Then get moving. You need to put some distance between us."

I nod and start off. The pain makes me limp, but I'm eventually able to fall into Quickstep. There's something different about how I fell into it, but I'm in too much pain to care. The numbing effects of the ointments are starting to kick in. I just need to keep running.

-Heaven's Interlude-

Michael traded blows with War, trying to push through the Horseman's defenses, but War wouldn't budge. No matter how hard Michael pushed, War stood his ground, not once shifting his attention from Michael, even as Rebecca made her escape.

"You impress me with your skills, archon," War said. "It seems you were some manner of warrior in life." Michael feinted a jab and spun his staff into an overhead strike. War spun his staff from blocking the feint to deflecting the overhead blow. "Very impressive."

"I practiced aikido," Michael admitted as he moved away to readdress War's form. "Wouldn't call myself a warrior though. Troubled maybe, but not a warrior. I don't see what's so interesting about that, though."

"You are an archon; newly dead and unclassified. Yet your spirit says otherwise. What is more intriguing is your ability to answer the Guardian's Plea in place of her actual guardian."

"I don't know about any of that," Michael said as he rushed forward with a quick triple strike.

War spun his staff and deflected each blow before sweeping Michael's feet from beneath him and pressing the head of his staff into Michael's chest.

"And therein lies the dilemma," War says. "You are ignorant of the Rules of Engagement and the consequences of breaking them. You mean to protect her, but you cannot."

"I can try!"

War stared down at Michael for a long moment, noting the fire in his eyes. War touched his staff to

Michael's, absorbing it before absorbing his own back into his body. "You possess potential, archon. Do not let Heaven waste it. If you insist on being her guardian, guide her from sin. I cannot have her weaken."

Michael jumped to his feet and threw a punch at War, but his form disappeared and Michael's fist struck nothing. War had vanished, leaving Michael alone to take his first eyeful of the carnage around him. He started to sweat as long forgotten screams began to echo in his ears. Tears rolled down his cheeks as he tried to push out the screams. Forgotten memories rushed back. His skin burned as he recalled his tortures in Hell for the first time since his liberation and a rage started to build inside him. "Stop," he growled. "I can't. Not again." He fell to his knees, his fingers digging into the sides of his head. "Go away!" The pain and rage grew as the memories flashed back to his consciousness. "Somebody help me!" he cried.

Michael felt warm hands on his head and a soft voice with crackling flame spoke, "I will help you, archon. I owe you as much."

The terrible memories began to fade and the phantom pains subsided. Michael wiped the tears from his eyes and saw a large flame before him. "Who are you?" he asked.

"I took the sacrifice of your flesh," it said. "I am the spirit of fire."

"My sacrifice of flesh?"

"I am the one that ripped the flesh from your bones and consumed you as the offering you were presented as. My sacrifice. I was not expecting you to call me so soon."

"Santano killed me."

"The avatar offered you to me. The fire of your soul was acceptable, so I accepted the offering. I heard you cry out through our bond and I came. I can offer my power, but could you even control it?"

Michael stared at the spirit before him for a long moment. "Could it help me find Rebecca?"

"Easily."

"That's all I care about."

The flames reached out and caressed Michael's face. "You are not ready. You do not even know of the ritual."

"Then teach me! I need to help her!"

"Of course. You are ignorant of the bond formed. Your flesh was offered to me against your will. The bond can still be broken. I will even the sacrifice. While you are here, I will grant you my power. Upon your call back to Heaven, we will return to as before. Are we in agreement?"

"Yes."

"Then we are bonded until the Keeper calls you home."

The flames washed over Michael, but much to his surprise they didn't burn. His body tensed as he filled with a burning power he didn't understand, but slowly came to accept. Michael stood and took in the new feelings. He could sense the spirit within sharing its knowledge with him. With calm finally coming over him, Michael could feel Rebecca moving away at an incredible rate. He could see glimpses of her through strange eyes that were not his own. Flames ignited at his feet, consumed his form, and died as quickly as they came. Michael was gone, traveling in a manner he didn't quite understand. There were all manner of sights passing by him as he whisked from place to place. He was scared, but let the spirit guide him.

-End Interlude-

JAK LORE

Twenty

I push through the intense pain in my foot. I'm putting too much strain on the injury for the ointments to handle. I'm not sure how far I've traveled or how much further I can go, but I can't stop. I have to get as much distance between me and War as possible. Eventually I come crashing out of Quickstep and into the snow and mud, unsure if I just pushed myself beyond my limits, or if the pain had become too much.

The world is shifting again and I consign to just lie still on the ground for a few minutes. My throat and lungs burn and I can't catch my breath. The cold wind blows over my aching body, but it feels good against the ache and heat of my body. I dig my hands into the snow to ease the burning in them. The world is slowly coming into focus and I can see trees. I try to get up but my foot can't take the weight. I cradle it and find the bandage is completely soaked in blood and dripping. I pull myself across the ground and curl up against a tree. My heart is racing and pushing into my throat. Though the world is not shifting anymore, it's not in focus. I can see my breath in the air and I'm starting to shiver. I'm cold. That can't be good.

I wipe the wetness from my forehead and dread the idea of War finding me like this. "Michael, where are you?" I whisper. "I need you." I grasp at my chest as

271

pain rips through it again. A circle of flame ignites nearby. The bright yellow fire grows into a twisting pillar before burning away. I stare in disbelief at Michael. How did he do that? He looks dazed and confused as he takes in his surroundings. I try to call out to him but am having trouble making words form.

"Whoa," Michael says as he tries to regain his senses. "¡Eso fue salvaje!" He looks around and sees me huddled against a tree. "Becca!" he cries out as he rushes to my side. He's in a panic as he tries to figure out what to do. I smile as tears run down my face. I reach my hand out to him and he takes it. His worry suddenly vanishes and he looks at me. "I can help," he says, "but it may hurt a little." I nod and close my eyes. I'm tired but so happy. My body grows warm and I hear the fwoosh of a burst of fire. Every cut on my body burns and I wince under it. Michael comes closer and wraps his arms around me. I can feel a breeze around us and the pain in my body starts to subside. I can move again without agony. I hold Michael tight and start to cry. "Está bien," Michael says. "No llores. Todo va a estar bien. Estoy aquí."

I'm not sure of everything he said. He doesn't usually speak whole sentences in Spanish without a translation for me, but I don't care. "I've missed you so much," I say.

"Yo también te he extrañado. Come on. We should find shelter. We only have a few hours of daylight left."

I nod but don't move. I don't want to. I'm deathly afraid he's just going to disappear again. I just want to hold him. Suddenly I'm lifted into his arms and I can't help but giggle as he gets up. "I think that's a good idea," he says. "Why don't you just rest and let me carry you for a while?" I lay my head against him as he makes a few false starts before deciding on a direction.

For a long while I just enjoy being held and let the stress and worry finally melt away.

Michael carries me for a long time, much longer than he ever has, and doesn't show a bit of fatigue. "Why don't you put me down and rest a little?" I say. "You must be tired."

"No, estoy bien," he says with a smile as he nuzzles his face against mine, making me laugh.

I look over him and can't help but wonder. "Michael, where are your wings and halo?"

"Aún no los he ganado."

I wait for a translation, but one doesn't come. "Michael, you have to talk English. I can't understand you."

He looks at me with a bit of surprise. "Oh," he says, almost like he's looking for the words. "Sorry. I guess I didn't realize. I've been speaking my native language more often. Everyone can understand me and I can understand them, no matter what language they use."

I smile a little. "I guess there's no language barrier in Heaven." I struggle playfully in his hold. "Come on, put me down and answer my question. Wings and halo."

Michael carefully sets me back on my feet as he answers. "I haven't earned them yet. Archons haven't done anything except make it into Heaven. I don't see a lot of halos anyway."

I grimace a little as I put weight on my foot. It still hurts, but nowhere near as much as before. "War called you an archon," I say as I start to limp alongside Michael. "What is that?"

"Basically, it's anyone that's died and gotten into Heaven. There are different levels of angels, but I haven't bothered asking too much about it. I've been busy catching up with my parents."

"Your parents are in Heaven too?" My smile almost instantly turns into a frown. "Wait, doesn't that mean they're dead?"

"Yeah. Apparently when they sent me to the United States when I was six, they never had any intention of following. They were sick and weren't sure they'd make it. That's why I never heard from them. Even my tíos didn't know. I couldn't apologize enough for hating them for so long." He wipes fresh tears from his eyes. "They've watched me grow up. They haven't approved of a lot, but they're proud of who I became in the end. They thank you for that. You're the one that gave me reason to change."

I smile and hold onto his arm. I want to be close to him, but I also need a little help walking. He's told me so many times how I changed him. I never realized how much of an influence I really was. "What about my parents?" I ask. "Have you seen them?"

"They are so proud of you. A little shell-shocked, but very proud."

"I'm glad they're okay. It's been so hard without everyone. Without you. How is everybody doing? Our friends?"

"Everyone's doing good. We've all come to terms with our death. We get to see family that passed on and get to meet family we never got the chance to know. I think Nicole's taking it hard though."

"What do you mean?"

"She was really distant at first. It was almost like being in Heaven hurt her. She's gotten better. There are angels working with her, but she's not the same. She stares out sometimes, even in the middle of conversations. She'll start crying or screaming out of nowhere."

"Has she said anything to you about it?"

"No, but there's always a high-ranking angel nearby to help her when she has one of her episodes. She spends a lot of time with them. Whatever they're doing, it seems to be helping." We come across a road and Michael only takes a moment before deciding what direction to follow.

"Michael?" I ask. "How did you know I needed you?"

"I'm not sure. It started with these strange thoughts and feelings, but they weren't mine. They were erratic. Some good, some bad. Some strong, others weak. I thought I could almost hear you. When I realized the thoughts and feelings were yours, I learned real quick not to talk about it. I talked to some of the older, I guess in charge angels, but they were just uneasy about it. They told me who to talk to, but that group was just mad. They didn't want to believe it at first. They wanted to teach me how to ignore it. That it wasn't my place.

"I didn't know what to do. There wasn't anybody I could turn to for answers. Eventually I started to focus on the thoughts and feelings when they happened. I tried to hold on to them. It was hard and jumbled at first. It got a little easier. I could tell you were worried about someone named Andrea, but I don't know who that is."

"She's an old friend of mine that moved away when I was little," I say. "She's okay now, but almost died."

"I'm glad she made it. Today I was just filled with dread. All day. After a while it started to turn to panic and pain. I could feel you were hurting. I wanted to help you, but I didn't know how. Then I heard you cry out to me. I knew I needed to get to you, somehow, anyhow. I'm not sure what happened next, but I was there and I was pissed."

"I did need you. I was so stupid."

"What do you mean?"

"I needed you so badly because I was stupid enough to think I could beat War. I wasn't ready."

"What were you supposed to do? You were attacked."

"No. I called him. It was a mistake. It's my fault all those people died. I kept being told to stop, but I wouldn't listen. My ego got over inflated. I couldn't hurt him at all, no matter how hard I fought. But you're here now. We can go find the First."

Michael stares down the road in thought. I look down it too and see a few cabins in the distance. I don't like Michael's long silence. "Becca," he begins, "I don't know how I got here, or how to get back. Eventually they're going to notice I'm missing. I don't know what will happen then, but I'll do my best to help you while I'm here."

I don't even try to hold back my tears. Is he saying he can't stay? Suddenly Michael lifts me into his arms. "No tears," he says. "I'm here now. Let's get to that house and get you cleaned up. Your limping is getting worse."

I hold onto him. "Don't let them take you away again."

Michael kisses my forehead and my tears fall when he makes no promise. I bury my face in the crook of his neck so he can't see my brow furrow. I won't let them.

We walk down the road until we reach the cabins. Michael looks over them before deciding on one. He puts me down when we reach the front door. I move to knock but Michael tells me the cabin's empty. I start to ask how he knows but stop myself. He's an angel and I guess they just know certain things. I try the handle, but the door is locked.

"I guess we'll have to find another way inside," Michael says.

Before I can say anything Michael bursts into flames and slips under the door. I hear him yelling in Spanish on the other side. He opens the door and is visibly disgruntled.

"How did you do that and who were you talking to?"

"It's some kind of fire spirit," he says. "It's helping me use its power, but has a mind of its own."

"So you're like, possessed?"

"No. It does act through me though, allowing me to use its powers. Just doesn't always give me a warning."

"That's kind of creepy."

"That's what I said. Let's get you cleaned up."

"What if the owner comes back?" I ask as Michael helps me to the bathroom.

"This is a rental unit."

"Did the spirit tell you that?"

"Yeah. No one will be here." The shower has a built-in chair, which Michael helps me sit on. "There's a washer and dryer in here. I'll clean your things and get the heat turned up."

Michael helps me out of my dirty and bloody clothes and disappears through the door. I force myself up and turn the shower on. It's cold at first but warms up fairly quickly. I put the chair up and stand under the running water, letting the blood wash off. The warm water feels good, even against the burning wounds. Most of my other wounds are gone. The bullet wounds are just sore divots that will probably be gone tomorrow. My nose feels a lot better and doesn't hurt when I touch it. My chest is still sore with little cuts along my breasts and abdomen. I take the bandages off my hands and look at the burns. It isn't so tender anymore and doesn't look so fresh, but it still hurts to the touch. I take off the blood-soaked bandage of my ankle and see the mangled wound. It's not pretty to look at and looks like it's been burned, almost cauterized. It still hurts, but at least it's not bleeding anymore. At least I don't think it is. The water is red with the blood that's washing off my body.

I take the small container of shampoo and start to wash the blood and dirt from my hair. The water is finally starting to lose its red pigment. Michael comes into the room as I'm tearing open the small packaged soap. He's completely naked and I smile as he gets into the shower with me. He takes the soap from my hand and says, "I thought you could use some help." I lean back into him with a smile and let him lather my body. He goes slow, taking time and care in washing me. Being able to lean against him as he bathes me lets me take a lot of pressure off my foot. It's nice being treated so delicately, and such a turn on having his hands all over me like this. I try to return the favor, but my wounds make it difficult to go further than his waist. I bite my lip and smile as his body responds to my touch. I stroke his excitement with a soapy hand and coo, "It still works, huh?"

"Sure looks that way, doesn't it?" he says as he positions me against the wall and gets himself under the water to rinse the soap off. "I'm sorry. I know this is a horrible—"

I pull his lips to mine and kiss him passionately. He grunts in surprise, but returns the kiss, his hands tentatively touching before softly caressing my body. I wrap an arm around him and press my right leg against him, getting it off the floor and relieving the strain on it. I can feel my own excitement rising as I pull his hand down between my legs and moan as he presses his fingers inside me. It feels so good. I stroke and caress him as he plays with me. I moan into his mouth as my excitement rises higher. I wrap my leg around him and pull him closer. I hold him tight as he makes me orgasm. I hold him tight to help support myself on my now wobbly leg. I rub my hand against him as I whisper, "I want you inside me."

"Are you sure?" he asks. "You're pretty hurt."

"Just be gentle, especially with my ribs."

He runs his hand gently down my side as he kisses my neck. I gasp as he enters me and push as high as I can onto my toes. I stand there enjoying the feeling of him moving inside me, vocalizing my pleasure. His hands caress over me, straying away from my ribs, and I tell him how good it feels. We come together for the first time that night. Not wanting to let go, I can't keep my hands off him, just like our first time only a few weeks ago. The longest break we have is when he redresses my wounds. Eventually we curl up for the night. This soreness I more than welcome. I caress Michael's face as I stare into his eyes, a smile on both our faces.

"I love you," I say.

"I love you too," he answers.

I pull close to him and fall asleep.

Twenty-One

I wake up the next morning to a nice warm room. I crack my eyes just a little and pull myself closer to Michael, nuzzling my head into the crook of his neck. The soft glow of the sun floods the room and I pull the sheet over my head. A lot of my pain is gone, but my ankle still throbs.

"It's time to wake up," a voice says softly. Michael stirs a bit, but my eyes shoot open. I sit up quickly while covering myself with the sheet. A tall man in white robes stands at the foot of the bed. I immediately reach for the Sword of Might, only to remember I left the Heavenly Weapons in the bathroom. "Do not be afraid," the robed man says as he raises a hand. There's a tattoo of a lantern on his palm. I notice folded wings behind him and take a closer look. His form is mostly hidden beneath his long flowing robe with blue trim. His long brown hair has blonde highlights and hangs loose around his shoulders. His icy blue eyes are piercing and there is a bright glow around the crown of his head, almost like a halo. Is he an angel?

Michael looks at the man and says, "You look familiar. Do I know you?"

"Who are you?" I demand. "What are you doing here?"

The man folds his hands back into his long sleeves as he answers, "I am the Keeper of Souls, the Archangel Saint Gabriel."

Realization fills Michael's face and he squeezes my hand. "You're the one that met us at the gates," he says. "You're the one that walked us through."

"That was our first meeting, yes. I think we will be having more." Gabriel waves his hand and suddenly we're dressed. Michael and I get out of bed and I hold on to him.

"Am I in trouble?" Michael asks.

"Let's say this is a special case. You've spent enough time on Earth. I'm sorry, but it's time to return to Heaven."

"No!" I shout as I plant myself between them. "You can't take him away again!" I grimace through the surge of pain in my foot. "I won't let you! I'll— I'll just call him back!" Michael holds me, to help alleviate the weight on my foot.

Gabriel sighs. "That's the other part of the problem. Michael should never have been able to hear your pleas, much less answer them. You are both young, and he is your first, yet your love for one another is genuine, true, and exceptionally strong. It harms you both."

"How can loving him hurt him? He saved me!"

"It hurts you by pushing your actual guardian away. His presence conflicts with yours. In effect, Michael is hiding you."

"Then I'll just find him on my own. Michael can protect me. Maybe you didn't notice, but he stood against War. Doesn't that count for anything?"

"It's not that simple and we don't have much time. Michael is in danger. He is hurting."

"I'm not in any pain," Michael says.

"Not yet, but you will be. Rebecca, please understand. Michael has much potential, but it must be harnessed and tempered. Heaven is the only place to do that safely."

"I don't understand why he can't do that here," I say.

"Do you want to one day have to kill Michael?"

"No! Why on earth would I do that?"

"Because if he stays, you will. He's not strong enough to keep the taint of this world at bay and it will corrupt him. He will fall and never be allowed to return to Heaven."

My arms fall to my side as tears slide down my cheeks. "That's not fair," I cry.

"Say your goodbyes. He must go."

I spin around and hold Michael tight as I sob. "I don't want to hurt you."

"Don't worry," Michael says as he holds me. "You'll never be without me. They can help me, make me stronger, right? Don't worry. Everything will be okay." Then he whispers into my ear. "I'll get stronger and come back."

"Promise?" I whisper back.

"Promise."

"It's time, Michael," Gabriel says as he extends his hand and wing. "Let's go home."

Michael kisses me and moves to take Gabriel's hand. "Be strong, Becca," he says. "I love you."

"I love you too," I say.

Michael takes Gabriel's hand as his wing encircles him. "You may let him go now spirit," Gabriel says. "His time is done and he returns." Fire ignites about Michael's body and tears away into the air, vanishing without a trace. "I will follow you shortly." Michael glows and turns into a bright light that cascades away. Gabriel then returns his attention to me. "We need to have a few words before I leave."

"Please don't punish Michael," I beg.

"He has been punished enough, as have you. I knew quickly Michael had left. I was surprised, but I had been watching him. I had been made aware of your connection. I didn't intervene on his arrival because War was impressed. If he had been in significant danger, I would have come to protect him. I chose to watch and judge for myself. I was impressed as well, especially with his temporary pact with the spirit. It helped keep the taint at bay, but couldn't stop it. I let him help you, and after calculating his time safe, allowed you the night."

"Thank you for that," I say.

"You are welcome, but you can't call him again. You have your own guardian. You must call for him. Let the dead rest."

"But I don't even know who my guardian is," I protest. "I can't even understand his name."

"Because you hold too strongly onto Michael. Let him go, Rebecca. Allow yourself to mourn his passing. He is gone. He cannot help you, no matter how much you both may want him to."

I sit down on the bed and wipe my tears away.

"Your guardian was forced away when you called out to Michael. Now that Michael's gone, he needs time to sense you, but you must help him. Wait a day or so and do not yearn for Michael. Allow yourself to grieve but do not call for him. Let him rest."

"How do I find my guardian when I can't even see him?"

"Need him more than you need Michael." Gabriel begins to glow. "You should mend your clothing, unless you prefer that style of dress."

"No, I don't. How do I fix them?"

"Focus your desire to mend the broken and feel the command word. It operates through the Dagger of Power."

Gabriel turns into a bright light that cascades away as Michael did, leaving me to ponder what he's told me. I'm alone again. I've lost Michael for a third time now. I lie on the bed and cry. The little comfort I do have is knowing that when Michael gets strong enough, he'll come back on his own, so he won't be gone forever.

Twenty-Two

I cry for hours. I wasn't ready to let Michael go and I'm worried about what exactly is going to happen to him. I try not to even think his name. I don't want to hurt him or get him in any more trouble. I don't want to accidentally call him back to Earth. How would Gabriel react if I did that? After I can't cry anymore, I pull myself to sit on the side of the bed and dry my face with the bottom of my shirt. My clothes are clean, but they're torn and bloodstained. I take the Dagger of Power and rest it on my lap. I guess it's time to learn a new ability.

I take a deep breath and close my eyes, focusing on the feel of the dagger in my hands and the desire to repair my ruined clothes. A vision starts to form in my mind. I see hands move over rips and they become whole again. Breaks fall back together into a single piece. A word echoes in the back of my mind and I feel silly for not already knowing it. I run my hands over my clothes as I say the command word, "Mend." I don't go over every stain and cut, just a single pass down my body. The bloodstains vanish and rips disappear. My clothes once again look new. This is going to be handy. I can feel it's able to do more, but I'm having trouble grasping what that is.

There was some pain as I passed over my ribs and I feel them more closely. They're bruised and feel a little out of place. The stab in my side is still tender and painful to the touch. My nose is sore but doesn't seem broken. If everything else is healing, why isn't the stab? I look at my hands and see red staining into the bandages. My stitches were falling out by this time. Why are some of my wounds healing so slowly? Do I just have too many? I go to the bathroom to change my bandages and find myself limping. I'm going to have to do my best to stay off my right foot so it can heal. Looking at myself in the mirror I see slight bruising around my eyes. I guess my nose did get broken, but it seems to be healing pretty fast.

I take the bandage around my ankle off. There's a good amount of red stained on it, but it isn't soaked. The wound burns and causes me to grit my teeth as I clean it out. It looks pretty deep and still seeps blood. It needs stitches so I get the suture kit. It hurts a lot but it needs to be done. Maybe it'll heal faster now? I do the same with the stab wound on my side. My hands are easier. I just have to change the dressings. I've renewed all my pain and I'm tired, so I decide to go back to sleep. Right now I think I just need rest.

When I wake, the room is dark. I sit up and my eyes adjust to the darkness fairly quickly. I can see the room even without light. I look around and find a clock on the wall. After a moment the hands become visible in the lightless room and I see it's after six. There's no sign of the sun rising, so it's not morning. I've slept away the daylight. I stretch the sleep away only to have burning and stabbing pain assault my side. My ribs only ache, but the stab wound still hurts. I can't use my weapons directly against War. He can just redirect everything. How do I fight him without hurting myself?

Turning on the lights, I dig out Angel's books and study into the night. I still have a lot of time before my

angel can find me. I doubt War is done with me, so I
need to be better prepared. I can't use my weapons and
Quickstep won't help me. He's too fast. I have to see
what else I can do. I remember the power I used and
what War called it. I wonder if there's anything in here
on the Sonic Scream.

I wake up surrounded by Angel's open books. The
sun is just starting to peek through the windows. When
did I fall asleep? Has enough time passed for my angel
to find me? It's been about a day. A few extra hours
can't hurt so I decide to bathe again and clean up after
myself. Besides, who knows when I'll get to bathe again?
A few hours pass as I clean and the only trace I was
here is the garbage. I take it outside with me, but don't
see anywhere to put it, so leave it off to the side. The sky
is overcast and little sunlight breaks through the clouds.
I close the door and it locks automatically behind me.
No turning back now.

I take a deep breath and scan the horizon. It's quiet.
I strain my eyes and ears, but I can only hear the creak
of trees and the sifting snow. "Hello!" I call out. "I'm
here, waiting for you!" I only hear the slight howl of the
wind in return, but I can feel something around me.
"Hello? I think— I think I can feel your presence. I want
to see you. I want to know your name."

A breath is carried on the wind. "Close your eyes," it
whispers in a soft and gentle voice. I close my eyes and
try to focus through the darkness, turning my head side
to side slightly as I do. "Relax," the voice says. The voice
is feminine. I focus on it.

"Help me see you," I say.

"Clear your mind," she says. "Let all your thoughts
go away. Open your mind's eye."

I let out a breath, trying to push out all my thoughts. I try to relax and put my mind at ease. My other senses seem to focus. I can feel the air about me, smell the wood and snow. The sensations are faint and fleeting. Shapes begin to form against my darkened sight. The roads, the trees, even small surrounding animals. The lights are dim and I smile as I make out what I think are rabbits. Then suddenly there is a large and bright light. I shield my eyes as I turn away. I keep my eyes closed and try to look up at where its face should be. I can feel hands resting on my shoulders.

"Very good," the voice says.

I open my eyes and am startled at first. The person before me is very bright and crackling with electric power. Clouds sift from her form as my eyes struggle to adjust as the light of her body starts to dim. She's several inches taller than me. Her hair is long and silvered. A large layered blue half mask with interesting designs covers a good portion of the left side of her face. I can see faint scars extending from the side of her mask around her hidden eye.

"There we go," the woman says with a smile. She cups my face with her hands. "You've been quite the little trouble maker."

I pull her hands away. "Are you my guardian?" I ask.

"I've been tasked with protecting you, yes. My name is Baraqyal."

I try to repeat her name but struggle with it.

"You can call me Berry if it's a little easier."

I smile. "Thank you. I guess I'm still having trouble with your name."

Berry ruffles my hair, which makes me laugh. "You've been through so much already. I can't believe how strong you are."

"Thank you."

288

"So, what should we do first?"

"Honestly, I just want to go home."

Berry nods. "I can make that happen." She takes me by the hand. "Astral travel is something demon hunters are taught by their angels to do. I'll teach you how to do it, but it'll take some time. You don't have any of the foundation. For now, allow me to lead you." I nod and feel the wind blowing around us as thunder cracks in the sky. I look up and see the growing storm as the world becomes fuzzy.

"Don't let go," Berry says as she tightens her grip. "I need you to focus on your home. Just stay focused on that and I will take us there. Traveling this way is fast and can be disorienting, but I'll be careful to not do more than your body can handle. Are you ready?"

"Yes," I say as I focus my thoughts on home.

"We'll need to jump. Ready? Jump."

We jump and the ground falls away. Everything is a displaced blur of color. We're moving fast, but not like Quickstep. It's different. There's a lot of pressure on my body from the speed and makes it hard to breathe. I tighten my grip on Berry's hand as she leads me through the swirling colors, sounds, and smells around us. This astral travel thing is scary, but I stay focused on home.

-Heaven's Interlude-

Raphael knelt in the war-torn factory. It was the last place he had felt Rebecca, but upon his arrival he was greeted only by carnage. She was nowhere to be found and Raphael could no longer sense her. Something was blocking their connection. He tried to quell the fires but found it difficult. His strength was slow to return, which forced him to douse the flames one by one. The battle was over and it seemed the last thought Rebecca had before their link was blocked was relief. Raphael could only assume that she was safe. There was nothing he could do for the fallen so he fell into a meditative prayer to try and break through the obstruction in their link.

A day passed and Raphael could feel more of his power returning. Suddenly the obstruction was gone and he could sense Rebecca's presence again, if only faintly. He could surmise a general location and, still unable to ignite his fire, slipped into the astral plane. A short while later he came out into a wooded area with storm clouds overhead. Something seemed off about them, but he couldn't place it. Ignoring the clouds, Raphael focused on Rebecca's presence and began in that direction. Soon her presence started fading again. Panicked, Raphael broke into a run.

Lightning raced across the sky. Raphael could feel only a lingering presence, and afraid he might lose it, forced himself into Quickstep. This brought him to the steps of a cabin, but Rebecca was nowhere in sight, yet he could still feel a lingering of her. He walked up the steps and found a bag of bloody bandages. It was where the essence was originating.

"She's hurt," Raphael said. "Why is she hurt so badly?" He sensed something else and tried to focus on it. "There were two other angels here. No— three. One is very weak. The other— is Fallen?" Raphael looked around but saw nothing out of the ordinary. "There doesn't seem to have been a skirmish. I don't understand." He called out to Rebecca several times, but nothing echoed back. "Damn it Asmodeus," Raphael cursed. "What did you do to me?" He sat on the steps and sighed. The trail had grown cold again. Rebecca was on the move, and unlike past demon hunters, Raphael did not know this one well. He couldn't anticipate her movements at all. With a sigh, Raphael accepted that not only would he need help in finding her, but also in figuring out what exactly was wrong with him.

-End Interlude-

Twenty-Three

This strange astral world I find myself being pulled through is disorienting. Though we're moving forward, the pressure of our speed hits all sides of my body. It makes it a little hard to breathe and I have to ask Berry to slow down. She pulls me beside her and our speed slows. It's easier to breathe now and though the world around us is still mostly a blur, I can see it much better. It's almost like a world sits atop another world, both there and not there. It's all around us as we move through, above, and under it all at once. Berry warns me that my focus is wavering, but even closing my eyes doesn't hide the worlds around me. It's so full of lights, shadows, and ghostly figures. I lock my attention completely on Berry. It helps me ignore the spectacular world around me.

We start to slow and Berry pulls me into an embrace. I look around at an area that is barely recognizable. I think I see my house, but I'm not sure its location. Berry steps down an invisible step and shimmers, pulling me down with her. The alien world is pulled away as I find ground beneath my feet. I blink and the remnants of that strange world fade. It's night and I stand in front of my dark and unwelcoming home. Fresh snow is on the ground and our walkway is the only one not shoveled. Footprints press into the snow in every direction. I add my prints and make my way to the front door, bracing myself for the inevitable truth of an empty home. Thankfully my key still works, so the lock hasn't been changed. The house is cold and dark, but I can see after my eyes adjust to the darkness. Walking to the thermostat I see that the temperature has been lowered to sixty-five. Though the cold itself doesn't bother me, the coldness of my home does. I reach to turn the heat up and Berry stops me.

"No," she says. "This house has been vacant for weeks. Someone will investigate if life suddenly comes back into it."

"I can't even live in my own home." I say, defeated.

"If you are cold, then utilize the abilities of the Dagger of Power. It will leave no physical trace."

"It's not that. I just can't stand how lifeless my house is. I don't want to wander around in the dark. I don't want to feel the empty cold."

"The Dagger of Power can do away with these things without drawing attention. Bonfire may be a good choice."

"You're going to have to walk me through that. I don't really understand how to use my abilities. I just kind of learn as I go."

"It's easy enough. Just focus where you want it centered and say the command word. Bonfire will provide warmth and light to a standard-sized room. It won't draw attention and it can be centered on any object."

I place my hand on the Dagger of Power and focus on my keys. "Bonfire," I say. The keys get warm in my hand and start to glow. Light radiates from them and washes over the hallway, filling it with warmth. The light is soft, like that of an actual bonfire, but stretches further. The glow of the keys dim but don't go away entirely.

Covering the keys shields the light, but the warmth remains.

"Do you think it would be okay to stay here for a while?" I ask.

"For a short time I believe so, but bear in mind, this house is abandoned."

I don't answer. I don't want to admit it. Everyone is gone and everything is different. It'll never be the same as it was before. I take in the pictures of the happy family I had always taken for granted. Now that family is gone, the pictures all that remain; pictures I may never see again. I go to my parents' room. It's clean and the bed is made, but it seems off. I look over their dresser and see Mom's makeup and perfume isn't the way she likes it. I rearrange a few pieces and can already feel the tears building. Dad's wheelchair rests in the wrong corner of the room. I move it to where it belongs and fold it like it should be. My lips quiver knowing that this is the last time I'll ever move it. A lump forms in my throat, but I fight back the sobs. I wipe my growing tears away before they have a chance to fall.

I leave my parents' room behind and climb the stairs to my room. Berry just stands by and watches. Now that I can see her, it's a little creepy. I enter my room to see it cleaner than I left it. My bed is made and my desk is cleared. The lamp is moved too far over and everything on my dresser and nightstands are misplaced. So many emotions run through me. Any secrets I had hidden in my room have probably been uncovered. I can't help but wonder what may be missing. I look for my personal and dream journals, but they're nowhere to be found.

I sit on my bed and glance at my nightstand. The only thing that's still where it should be is a picture of me and Michael smiling into the camera. I pick it up and tears run down my face. "Mom took this picture," I say as my voice breaks. I can't hold it back anymore. I lie down, holding the picture close, and begin to cry. Berry comes in at my sobbing.

"What's the matter?" she asks.

"It's just…" I sob. "It all hurts so much. Everyone's gone. My friends and family. My mom and dad. Everyone. I never got to say goodbye. I never had a chance to go to their funerals. I don't even know where any of them are buried."

Berry moves around me. "I know it hurts, but I can help take the pain away." I feel her sit behind me on the bed. She lies down beside me, curling up next to me and covers me with a dull white wing. It's a little too intimately close for my comfort. "Sleep and you will feel better when you wake," she says, holding me tight and close.

"This feels weird," I say as I stir in her embrace, trying to get out of it.

"Rest," she whispers into my ear. My eyes grow heavy and I get sleepy. "I will protect you."

Berry reaches over and takes the keys from my hand, letting the darkness back into the room. Sleep soon follows.

I don't know how long I slept, but for once I feel well rested. The anguish in my heart has quelled some, but pain still remains. The picture is still pressed against my chest and without looking at it, I place it face down on the nightstand. I look at my hands and see the dressings need to be changed again. My ankle and side still hurt and don't seem to be getting any better.

I sit up and see Berry staring out the window. The sun is peeking through a crack in the curtain. She looks over her shoulder and smiles at me. "Good morning."

"Is anything wrong?" I ask as I slide my legs over the side of the bed.

"No, I'm just standing watch. Everything's fine. How are you feeling?"

"Better. I just need to change my bandages again. Some of my wounds aren't healing. I don't know why."

"The injuries from the Sword of Might? They'll heal slowly without help."

"Why? Everything else heals so fast."

"They are War's wounds, not yours. Because of that they heal as they would on a Celestial."

"What's a Celestial?"

"The simplest answer is anything that originates from Heaven or Hell. Anything that is by natural origin, divine, such as myself or War. Only magic can help speed the healing of those wounds."

"I don't know any magic. All I have are Angel's ointments and I've been running through them too fast."

"I'll teach you, but for now let's just tend to your injuries. Wait here and I'll get everything we need."

I sit and wait for Berry to return. I pull my small trash bin next to the bed and take the bandages off my hands. Parts of the burn are starting to bubble. After a few minutes Berry returns with some bandages and a bowl. There are plants flowing over the sides.

"Where did you get that?" I ask.

"Had to do a little global travel," Berry says with a smile, "but this will help." She looks over my hands. "We might be able to get this healed in a couple of days. Maybe."

Berry takes my hands and traces something over the burns. She whispers something in a sing-song voice, but I can't make out anything that sounds like words. I feel a cool breeze over my burns and it starts to scab over right before my eyes. The area around the scab goes numb and Berry crushes some leaves and berries before applying it to the scab. She tops it off with a torn leaf and wraps my hands in new bandages.

"You shouldn't have to change this now," Berry says. "It may sting and itch though. Let me see your other wounds."

I lift my shirt and point to the new crimson stain on the bandage. Berry lifts my shirt off and undoes the bandages. She lays me down and does similar to this wound, warning that this one may take a little longer to heal. It already feels better. Berry lifts my pants leg up as far as it will go and removes the bandage around the ankle. She examines the stitch work and I flinch as she touches it. "This one is pretty bad," she says. "I'll have to treat this more than once and it will take longer to heal. I think the stitching will help though. Just try to stay off it."

Berry actually takes time to clean this wound before starting her magic. Other than it hurting more and numbing my entire foot, it's mostly the same. I try to massage the feeling back as Berry cleans up. "That won't help," she says. "You'll get feeling back in about an hour or so. When you're up for it, I'll teach you a basic healing spell to deal with the pain. That wound is going to give you problems."

"I want to know what happened," I say. Berry looks at me with a confused look. "After Santano." I add.

"You may not like the answer."

"I need to know."

Berry nods. "I will gather some articles for you then. I shouldn't be gone terribly long." She hands me back my keys. It feels like the magic bestowed on them has faded. "Stay away from windows and continue to utilize the Dagger of Power. I'll be back as soon as I can."

After Berry leaves I change into my own clothes. I don't want to continue wearing gang colors. That part—that massacre—is behind me now. I head to the kitchen and pour a glass of milk only to discover its gone bad. The bread is stale too. Everything in the refrigerator has gone bad, except for the eggs. I don't know what I expected, having been gone for so long. What's worse are the intense hunger pains that come as soon as I start looking for food. Maybe this wasn't a good idea. In the freezer sausage patties is the best I can find to cook. I make breakfast hoping Berry will be back soon. I'm not looking forward to eating alone, though I don't know if angels even eat.

The food is finished before Berry returns, so I put a plate into the microwave to keep it warm. I pour myself a glass of water and sit down. This will probably be my last meal at home. Between that fact and the incredible hunger, there's no way I can enjoy it. Berry walks into the kitchen as I finish my plate.

"Here is what I could find," Berry says as she places a bundle of papers onto the table.

"Thank you, Berry," I say as I put my dishes into the sink. "I left you a plate in the microwave. I hope it's warm enough for you."

Berry looks around briefly before finding the microwave. "Thank you," she says as she pulls her plate out. She waves her hand over it, I guess checking if it's still warm. Then her hand crackles with electrical power that dances on the plate for a moment. Berry smiles. "Perfect."

"Cool," I smile. "Could I learn to do that?"

"One thing at a time. We still don't know if you have a natural elemental affinity."

"What's that?"

"What's an easy way to describe it? It's which element is strongest with you. It's the elements you are aligned with."

"How do we find out?"

"Let's get you healed first. Right now that's priority."

I agree and sit down to read the articles she brought me. Berry was kind enough to bring the obituaries too. I read them first. Nice words, even for Nicholas, the one person that doesn't deserve it. That bastard actually tried to rape me before Santano got him. It's good to see such nice things written about my family and friends though, to know they will be missed and have all been laid to rest. It lists where each was buried and I cut them out of the papers. I'll want to visit eventually. A few people were cremated, so there's no way I can really visit them. There are no obituaries for Angel, Santano, or myself.

I spend the next couple hours reading the articles and the more I read, the more my blood boils. The high school was closed to be rebuilt and the blame was placed on arson. Reports say the gym sustained the most damage, which makes sense. That's where I fought Santano. There is speculation that explosives may have been used because of the intense damage.

Santano's sacrifices have been coined the Angel Murders. It makes me mad knowing the blame is being placed on Angel when Santano is solely at fault, but it only gets worse from there. The media has painted me a villain and a part of the killings, going so far as saying I had an affair with Angel. I read theory after theory, all with the same underlying premise. I was having an affair and that put Angel and Santano, who were working together, at odds. I think what sickens me most is the acceptance that I sacrificed my friends as a tribute to them.

I scream and tear the paper to pieces. "The only thing they have right in all this trash," I shout as I crumble another paper and whip it across the room, "is that I attacked five cops to break Angel out of jail!"

"I told you, you wouldn't like what you found," Berry says as she finally gets up from the table and puts her dishes into the sink.

"I know," I say with a sigh as I pick up another article. "They know I'm alive, so they're looking for me. They're looking for Angel and Santano too, but there's nothing left of them to find."

Berry turns on the water and starts to wash the dishes. "You'll have to stay low for now," she says. "One of the advantages you have as demon hunter is you will age slowly. In thirty years' time they will be searching for a fifty-year-old woman, not a young girl in her twenties."

"Will I still look that young in thirty years?"

"It's possible. All demon hunters age slowly, but how slowly varies. Angel barely aged for nine centuries."

I crack a smile and give a light-hearted laugh. "I guess he did, didn't he? Úna did say I wouldn't age, that I would be eternally young."

Berry stops what she's doing briefly and looks at me. I look back, wondering why she's giving me such a confused look. "We shouldn't stay here very long," she says as she goes back to cleaning the dishes. "Just until your wounds have healed some."

"Yeah," I say as I start to gather the articles, "I don't think I want to read these anymore."

"Why don't you go get some rest? I'll prepare a magic lesson for when you wake."

"I'm fine. I slept well last night. Let's just start now."

"As demon hunter, you are blessed with Angelic healing, which works strongest when you rest. So, go sleep and heal. Lessons will begin when you wake."

RULES OF ENGAGEMENT

Reluctantly I agree and hobble back to bed.

Twenty-Four

Seeing as I had already slept so well, I'm surprised when a yawn escapes after climbing into bed. I grow tired and am soon asleep. I'm not sure how long I slept, but the sun is still up after I wake. My side stings and my hands itch, but I guess that just means the spell is working. Refreshed, and amazingly not groggy from oversleeping, I pull myself out of bed and limp back downstairs. As long as I move slowly the pain is a manageable ache.

I find Berry in the living room surrounded by sheets of paper, different kinds of plants and spices, and several bowls.

"What's all this?" I ask.

Berry motions me to sit with her. "Your first lesson."

I sit on a cushion that Berry has prepared on the floor for me and look at what lies between us. There are a few sheets of paper, one written in English, the other I'm not sure. There are drawings of some kind of pictograms and charts drawn too. Separated in the bowls are peppers, spices, and water.

"The first spell I'm going to teach you is a basic pain tolerance spell," Berry says. "But before I do that, we have to discuss how spells work. We'll focus on the basics for now."

"Okay. What's the first thing I need to know?"

Berry hands me the paper with writing I can't read. "Language. Do you know what language this is?"

I look over the words. They look like the same language Angel's spells are written in. "Is this Latin?" I ask.

Berry smiles. "Very good. Most spells have a verbal component to them. Though spells can be cast with almost any language, they are most potent when spoken with a Language of Power."

"I'll have to learn Latin?"

"Eventually. Now Latin isn't the oldest Language of Power, but it's currently the strongest. I've already taken the liberty of translating this spell for you. It won't be as strong in English, but it'll work."

Berry hands me another sheet and I read the incantation aloud. "Breaks of bone and flesh hinder no more. Burning scars grow cold. Pain of mind cease. Ache and hurt dwindle. Let no pain be renewed. Numb. What's all this stuff written around the words, and why is this one line separate from the rest? May anguish and pain fade."

"We'll get to all of that in a minute. The next part is the material components." Berry takes four bowls and puts them between us, each with something different inside. Long, thin red peppers, some kind of spice, white and yellow flowers, and water. She hands me a third sheet. "This spell calls for three ingredients. The first is cayenne pepper. If you must, black pepper in its natural or ground form may be substituted. Never use both. It can cause you to lose all feeling, not just ignore pain." She puts a cayenne pepper into a stone bowl and starts to crush it with a pestle. I don't remember Mom ever having those. "The cayenne always has to be crushed into a paste, so always use a whole one. You will need to add just a little bit of water, not too much. Mix in a

303

pinch of nutmeg. The last and most important piece is chamomile. The flower itself should be dipped into the paste, covering the plant as much as possible, but be careful not to touch the paste yourself." Berry dips the flower by the stem, carefully dragging it through the paste.

"What happens if I touch it?" I ask as she hands me the covered flower.

"You'll cause a backfire. This is a simple spell, so it's not dangerous, but you'll have to start over. Now if you just need to numb a specific wound, drag the flower around the area. If you need to numb your entire body, we'll need to change the spell a bit. That will require three flowers, but if the pain is exceptionally bad, you can use up to five instead. Any more will just be a waste."

"That seems easy enough. Do I have to take the bandage off?"

"No, but don't get any ideas. That has no power right now. While it can't work through clothing, it can work through simple bandages like you're using now as long as they're not too thick. It can't work through something like a cast or brace."

"Alright, how do we charge it?"

"You don't yet." Berry hands me a bowl and pestle. "Make it. If you don't make it right it can turn sour and backfire. You have to make the consistency of the paste right. I'll be able to tell, but when we're actually casting, it should turn yellow. If it's any other color its gone bad. It's the warning that it's going to backfire, so get away if that happens."

I start to make the paste and end up going through at least six cayenne peppers before I get the consistency right. Once. Berry won't let me continue until I make six correct pastes and I waste a good hour just crushing peppers. Berry lays out the six bowls and tells me to study the incantation and pictograms while she cleans up my failures for the next step.

The first line of the incantation has a symbol in front of it and a number behind it. I find them on the pictogram and it's a simple drawing of the first step, but I don't know what the symbol means. When Berry comes back in, I ask her.

"It's a rune," Berry says. "We'll discuss that later. It's not important to this version of the spell."

"This version? You mean there are other versions?"

"There are a few different versions to this spell, but you have to learn this basic one first. After you master it, we can work on the next step, preparing a spell for later use. I'll walk you through this, so pay attention. Set yourself up to read the incantation and prepare the mixture. You're going to want to keep it on a solid surface so you can use both hands." I lay the incantation and first bowl of paste in front of me. "Now mix it thoroughly at least three times while saying the first line."

I start to mix and say the first line, "Breaks of bone and flesh hinder no more."

"Keep mixing and add the nutmeg while saying the next two lines."

I pinch in the nutmeg as I say the next part. "Burning scars grow cold. Pain of mind cease." The mixture starts to turn yellow.

"Good," Berry smiles. "Keep going, say the next line and prepare the chamomile."

"Ache and hurt dwindle." The mixture turns a bright yellow.

"Carefully dip the flower and say the next line."

I do as she says. "Let no pain be—" A foul-smelling smoke billows from the bowl, choking me. I fall over to get away from the smoke. "What happened?" I cough.

"Look at your hand," Berry says as she waves her hands through the smoke to disperse it.

I find a little bit of the mixture on my fingertip. "I touched it?"

"That, my dear, is a backfire. They're mostly harmless in simple spells, but it's why we made six. Start over."

I let out a sigh and with a new bowl begin the whole thing again. The second time goes better, but the stem of the flower breaks. Berry says I held it too far from the base. The flower is the tricky part. She has me pour water into the mixture to fizzle it. The third time I get another backfire. Looks like fourth time's the charm for me.

"Say the trigger word before you pull the flower out and it'll be charged for you to use," Berry says.

I say the trigger word, but nothing seems to happen. I decide to use the flower on and around my stab wound. The mixture seeps into my skin and through the bandage as the flower falls apart. The pain almost immediately disappears.

"That's amazing!" I say.

"Isn't it?" Berry says as she slaps the wound.

I flinch, but there's no roaring pain. "It didn't hurt."

"No, but you might feel it later. Generally this spell will last for half an hour, even for a novice caster. As you get better you'll be able to increase the duration. One more thing." Berry dips her finger into the dull yellow mixture and I immediately dive for cover, but nothing happens. "The mixture is only good once. All the magic goes into the flower, so you have to know how you're going to apply the spell and act accordingly. We're

going to do it again, but this time we'll use three flowers. This casting will be a little different."

"In what way?"

"I'll let you know. Start."

I take a new bowl and start mixing. "Breaks of bone and flesh hinder no more." I take a pinch of nutmeg and throw it into the mixture. "Burning scars grow cold. Pain of mind cease." The paste starts to turn yellow and I reach for the chamomile.

"Add the footnote," Berry says.

I quickly find the footnote. "May anguish and pain fade." The mixture turns bright yellow. That's a little early.

"Coat the front of the flowers as a bundle."

I do as Berry says, covering the front of the bundle. "Ache and hurt dwindle."

"Now take them out and roll them into a loose ball. Don't worry about the paste. Finish the spell."

I start to roll it, my fingertips getting coated with the bright yellow paste. "Let no pain be renewed."

"Coat the outside and trigger it."

I coat the outside with the paste on my fingers. "Numb." The little ball hardens in my hand.

"Put it in your mouth and swallow."

I put the hard ball in my mouth and it instantly becomes soft. I can taste the nutmeg and it has a little bite to it. It returns to a paste, making it easy to swallow. My face goes numb for a moment and all the aches in my body fade.

"I didn't realize how much pain I was in," I say astonished. "How long will this last?"

"At least half an hour. I still have to assess your abilities to determine your magical strength. There're two very important distinctions about this spell. When applied to an area, it only affects existing pain. If you get a new wound or open an old one, it won't have an effect, that's why slapping you didn't hurt. Digging my finger in would have. The full body version will affect all new injuries. Now remember, this spell doesn't heal you. Broken bones are still broken. Cuts will still bleed. It just conceals the pain."

"I understand."

"We'll save this last one for later. In the meantime, memorize the incantation and the motions."

"What will change when I learn this in Latin?"

"You'll only ever need one flower. While you can still apply it, it's kind of redundant unless there's a severe injury to a limb." Berry ruffles my hair. "I know you have a lot of questions, but one thing at a time. Just study this spell for now."

I spend some time going over the motions and memorizing the incantation. The pictograph shows things we didn't go over, but I guess that's for a later lesson. An hour passes and I still don't feel any pain. Berry is impressed that the spell is still active, but after a second hour it starts to wane. The pain is coming back as a dull throb, but Berry warns me that the pain will feel worse after the spell wears off completely. She has me use the last bowl and cast the spell again. I have to refer to the spell itself, but I cast it without any problems. Berry wants me to use the spell every two hours and says we'll move on to the next step after I can cast it from memory.

"Can we talk about my powers?" I ask.

"What do you want to know?" Berry replies.

"Everything. What can I do? I've tried looking through Angel's books and found a list, but Gabriel taught me something that wasn't in them, and so did you. When I was fighting War, a new power came out. I think he called it a Sonic Scream?"

Berry nods her head. "Well, let's start with the Sonic Scream. The concussive force can push an enemy, and the high sound wave can rupture eardrums and vibrate material."

"Can you do it?"

"Yes. It's a fairly simple technique to learn, and when paired with an air affinity can be very devastating and versatile."

"How do I do it?"

"Now is not a good time to practice. We'll have to save that for a later date. As far as other powers go, meditating and aligning yourself with your weapons will reveal more of their secrets. As you already know, new abilities can manifest in desperation in the heat of battle. I think what is more important right now is mastering what you already know."

"My Quickstep isn't the same since I beat Santano. War was so much faster too. I couldn't see him at all."

"Quickstep is a very basic technique that pretty much everyone knows, but also one of the hardest to master. War is one of the few that has."

"Have you?"

"No. While I have much control and experience with it, I'm not capable of mastering it. I'm up there in mastery, but I'm as far as I can go. The two main components of Quickstep are speed and time dilation. From what I've seen of your use, you rely more on time dilation, but you have the potential to use its speed. You fall into it with speed and move with time dilation, slowing time around you to move from place to place. When your leg is better, I want to start training your Quickstep."

"Is there anything you can teach me now?"

"Not without potentially hurting you more. Speaking of which, why don't I give your foot another treatment and then you go get some more rest?"

"Can you teach me that spell?"

"It's too advanced for you right now. Just focus on what you're already learning."

So the day goes. Practice my spell and sleep. I decide to practice my Bonfire ability too, seeing just how much I can control it. It isn't too hard. Eventually I sleep for the night and wake up to a good amount of pain. I limp very painfully back downstairs. I gather what I need for the spell and begin casting. I'm distracted by the pain and the first batch backfires. I take greater care with the second and complete it without issue. The pain is gone.

"Very good," Berry say, surprising me. She was watching. "You didn't even need to check the spell. Keep up the good work."

"Thanks," I say. "When I'm healed, what are we going to do? I can't stay here, right? So where am I going to go?"

"Perhaps it's time to start charting our next course of action."

"Úna said I need to find the First. He's where First Blood was first shed. I'm not sure where to start looking."

"The oldest civilization would be a good place to start."

"Then I'm going to need to do some research, but the local library won't be enough, even if I could go there."

"A presidential library, perhaps?"

"Bigger. The Library of Congress. From there we're going to have to leave the United States. I'm going to need money. What Jorge gave me won't be enough. I need access to all my parent's assets. I know there's insurance money and IRAs and bonds. That should be plenty. I know there's a will too so..."

"You are also wanted and the only survivor," Berry says. "Those assets may legally be beyond your reach. I can get them for you, but human law will have to be broken."

"I don't care. Break it. I'm never going to get a fair trial, right? What's a few more charges?"

"Then I'll get you what you need."

"I want to let Heather know I'm alright. Can you get a letter to her?"

"Yes, but I won't be able to get one back to you."

"That's fine. I just want to let her know I'm alright."

"Then let's start making preparations."

Twenty-Five

Berry leaves with the letter simply addressed "Heather" and I begin to pack. We'll work out the details when she gets back. Since I'm never coming home again I pack only the essentials and anything of great sentimental value. Instead of filling every suitcase I can find, I decide to limit myself to only what will fit into my parents' suitcase. It's the biggest one we have and will hold the most.

Knowing Mend is a great benefit as I can repair any damage to my clothes. I don't have to worry about ruining any of my favorite tops, which I pack into the suitcase. I don't bother taking any of my more elegant tops, skirts, or dresses—just pants and shorts. Things that'll be good to fight in. I won't have time for fun anymore, so what's the point of trying to look pretty? I leave all my makeup and only take a couple of my favorite perfumes. I throw hair bands and scrunches into the suitcase. I should probably start keeping my hair braided or in a ponytail. Maybe I'll cut it so it can't be grabbed. A couple photo albums just to remember my family and friends. Finally, the picture of me and Michael from my nightstand. A few more essentials, underwear, sweaters, and blankets, and I zip the suitcase closed. Now I just have to wait for Berry.

RULES OF ENGAGEMENT

It's nightfall by the time we work out the details. First, Berry is going to disable the security. That will allow me to break the door open without sounding the alarm or being caught on surveillance. Once inside I'll use Mend to repair the doors while Berry hacks the system and moves money between dummy accounts and into one I can access. Eventually that account will be found, but by then I'll have emptied and closed it and moved the money to a completely different bank under a new name. Everything we're going to do is illegal and it concerns me, but Berry assures me no one will be hurt once it's all done. I'll have access to what my parents left me and a new identity. While I'm not one hundred percent sure about all this, I trust Berry. Besides, at this point does that really matter? Heaven's law supersedes human law anyway, right?

We're going to take my dad's van, which Berry will disguise until we can change everything over to the new me. Carrying the suitcase, whose massive weight feels like nothing to me, I lead Berry to the garage through the door in the kitchen. Luckily the garage is affixed to the house and gets some heat from the furnace. It tends to be cooler than the rest of the house, but still much warmer than the outside in the middle of winter. The blue van sits untouched. My parents had it especially designed for Dad when he became wheelchair bound. It was made so he could drive it without his feet.

"Yes, this will do very nicely," Berry says. "This will be a great mobile base of operations. Do you have a color in mind?"

"Not really," I answer.

Berry raises her hands as they crackle with power. "Then let's go with stark white for now."

Lightning discharges from her hands and bathes the car in a display of electricity, painting over the light blue into a white. Once changed, Berry points a finger at both plates and a bolt of lightning erupts from her fingertips, washing over the plates. The numbers and letters shift and change. "There," Berry says. "That will do. If you're ready, let's be on our way." I load the car and look back towards the house. Once I leave, that's it. I'll never be able to come back. I wish I could take more. I wish I could stay. I wipe my tears away and climb into the driver's seat. Berry sends a bolt of lightning at the garage door and climbs inside. The door opens to reveal the frozen night.

"Keep your lights off and pull out," Berry says. "We don't need to call attention to ourselves."

I agree and pull out of the garage. I watch my house disappear in the rearview mirror as tears wet my face. It's dark and empty, but maybe one day some other family will fill it again with life.

We pull up to the bank a few miles away. It's been closed for a few hours now and everyone's gone. Berry asks if I'm ready. I take a deep breath. "Yes," I say. Berry exits the car without a word and heads to the back of the building. I follow behind. She finds metal on the building and touches it with a charged hand. The electricity discharges through the metal and into the building. I hear audible pops and see smoke rising from a number of nearby cameras. Berry motions me towards the back door and says, "Your turn."

I examine the metal door. I slam my hand into the side of it, hoping to be near the lock since it's not visible from this side. The door shakes but doesn't open. After a couple stronger hits, I slam my body hard against it, finally forcing it open.

"You were restraining too much power," Berry says as she enters. "Don't restrain your strength when you mean to use it."

"I didn't want the door to fly completely off its hinges," I defend.

"Then we'll have to work on controlling your strength."

I use Mend on the door like Berry taught me as she heads towards the computers. It's harder to mend the door than it was my clothes, but I manage. Berry is already typing away by the time I catch up with her.

"Their cyber security is fairly straightforward," Berry says. "It'll be easy for me to get through."

"How are you so good at this?" I ask with equal parts concern and intrigue.

"This is all powered by electricity. All I have to do is tap into Lightning's extensive knowledge."

"Lightning's knowledge? What do you mean?"

"Don't worry about that right now. That discussion is still a ways off."

I sigh. At least I'm not the one being called Lightning for a change. That's nice.

"Have you decided on a name yet?" Berry asks.

"I've always liked the name Ava," I answer. "Why don't we use my middle name too?"

Berry nods. "Well, which way do you want it? Ava Allison, Alice Ava, or some other combination?"

"Ava Allison is fine."

"Alright. I'll need a few minutes to set this up." Berry starts typing at speeds I've never seen. Electric sparks are actually discharging off her hands. "The accounts are seized, just like I thought. If you're going to have a change of heart, now is the time."

"No one will get hurt, right?"

"No one will be injured."

"Then let's break some laws."

"This will take me some time. Why don't you just relax? Maybe stay on lookout in case we get unexpected company?"

Concern falls over me. I hadn't thought about that. What if security does come? I go into one of the offices and stare at the sole car in the parking lot, mine. Does the fact that it's white make it look more suspicious? There's not much I can do unless something actually happens, so I try not to worry and pray nothing does.

More than an hour of anxiety passes. I'm staring out the office window, watching the snow fall. Berry taps a thick bank envelope on my shoulder. I spin around in the chair, taking the envelope with a confused look.

"Five thousand dollars," Berry says. "Mostly large bills."

"This will come in handy," I say. "Is everything done?"

"Mostly. The debit card is going to a false address, so I'll get it myself before it's mailed out. I'll give you one more healing treatment and then you should get going."

"Wait, you're not coming with me?"

"I'll catch up. It should only take me about a day." Berry twists her hand and sparks fly from it, leaving behind some kind of clay talisman. "The spell won't last all day, unfortunately. If you find a place to cast your spell, do it. Otherwise just break this in half. It'll release the magic inside and help heal you and keep your pain at bay, at least for a few hours. Just head south for now. It's out of the way, but let's not drive through the states where the police are looking for you. Tomorrow night stop at a hotel somewhere and wait for me. I'll find you then."

316

"Alright. I guess I'll see you tomorrow." I give Berry a hug. She seems a little caught off guard but returns it. "Thank you, Berry."

"Get going. Don't linger." She pats me on the head and sends me on my way.

-Hell's Interlude-

Carrying Demonic Rebecca in one arm, the wolf bestial bound along on three legs. She wasn't completely sure if the bestial was indeed Nicholas Rannulf, but he seemed to acknowledge the name. Though he had evolved beyond his savage base form, his mind seemed to have trouble catching up. He seemed confused, not focused, and still very instinctual. Half the time he seemed to not know what to do with her. The other half he wanted to fight. So far Demonic Rebecca had managed to keep him more or less tame to protect her, manipulating his animal instincts with his still developing mind. She managed to keep his urges in check with small gestures, but as he grew more powerful she didn't know how much longer she could control him.

Nicholas ran through the rocky terrain, keeping Demonic Rebecca pressed close against him. There were rocky outcrops all around, hiding battered bestials and frightened souls. In the distance was a rocky hill. Bestials who had failed to scale it were impaled upon the rocks below. Nicholas placed Demonic Rebecca onto his back and she wrapped her arms around his neck as he started to climb the treacherous hill. He stumbled now and again and lashed out at the trapped bestials that so much as made eye contact. Eventually Nicholas made it to the top. He put Demonic Rebecca down, and though exhausted, prowled the edges of the hill to take

317

in his self-proclaimed territory. Demonic Rebecca sat on her knees and took a breath. Her power had been growing slowly but steadily. She could feel the sin of death begin to fill her, imbuing her with strength. She closed her eyes and concentrated. She was tired of being naked.

Nicholas felt his fur bristle in a breeze. His head shot to the source and bared his teeth. Demonic Rebecca's body had a slight shimmer around it and her hair floated weightlessly in the air. Nicholas cocked his head curiously to the side. The glow brightened around her chest and hips. Nicholas instinctively stalked around her as he watched. The breeze began to fade and the shimmer dimmed. The glow took shape and darkened into a red hue. The glow turned into a crimson sports bra and red and black boy shorts. Nicholas approached Demonic Rebecca and she smiled as he rested his claws on her hips and squeezed tentatively, unsure of what exactly he wanted to do.

"Do you like?" Demonic Rebecca asked as she ran a hand through the fur on his head. Nicholas rested his head in the crook of her neck and licked at her throat and chest. "Like," he growled. Demonic Rebecca scanned the broken terrain. She could see a good distance away. Her sight was strengthening. She let Nicholas nuzzle and caress her as she took in their surroundings. She could make out various forms of bestials in the distance. The groups were small, some seeming to fight and others stalking as one. There were a few larger forms roaming alone. None seemed to notice their presence. A soft grin crossed Demonic Rebecca's face as she directed Nicholas' head and pointed. "Nicholas," she cooed. "Do you see? Challenger's coming to take what is yours."

Nicholas growled, "Mine is mine," as he stalked around Demonic Rebecca. He looked at her and she averted her eyes, something she learned to do to avoid challenging him. "You are mine."

"That's right, Nicholas," Demonic Rebecca said. "All yours."

Nicholas grabbed Demonic Rebecca by the hair and pulled her head back. She let out a gasp of surprised pleasure. "Stay," he growled.

Demonic Rebecca smiled at him. "Of course."

Nicholas rounded the hill and chose his first target, bounding down the hillside as best he could and headed off to his first battle. Demonic Rebecca's lips curled into a grin as she laid down to relax. "That should keep him busy for a while." A shadow fell over her under the clop of hooves. She pulled away in panic from the source and into a crouch.

The burned red fur of goat legs stepped before her, their dark hooves making very audible clops as they struck the ground. Demonic Rebecca looked up at a hard crimson body and massive twisted horns framing an emotionless face. Leathery bat wings folded against his back and red, bloodshot eyes peered down at her. Why had Satan come all this way?

"It seems you have a pet," Satan said as he stared down at the demonic, his emotionless tone and uncaring eyes betraying no thoughts.

Demonic Rebecca looked out towards Nicholas. "Yes, for now."

"It seems you've been very busy."

Demonic Rebecca leaned back, swaying a leg from side to side. "A girl needs her hobbies."

"Such lack of manners," Satan said. "It seems you lack the same etiquette as your virtue."

Demonic Rebecca pulled herself to her knees and bowed her head, resting her closed fists atop her legs. "Not knowing the etiquette and not using it are two different things, My Lord."

"Semantics."

Demonic Rebecca uplifted her head slightly. "What brings you all this way?"

"You."

Demonic Rebecca's pulse began to race as she looked at Satan with worried concern.

"I'm not sure if I should be displeased," he continued, "or impressed."

"I would say impressed. I have separated Rebecca from her guardian, and she is none the wiser. She continues to sin, giving me strength. She's playing right into my hands."

"What is your goal exactly?"

"What is the goal of any demonic?"

"There is more to it than that. This is too well planned. You leave yourself vulnerable, sending another in your stead. Very undemonic."

"The end game is the same."

Satan smiled, raising Demonic Rebecca's guard. "You share similar qualities to Demonic Angel. I guess, perhaps, he was not as unique as I thought."

Demonic Rebecca returned a nervous smile.

"Wouldn't a proper guard be more suitable over this bestial you have adopted?"

Demonic Rebecca is jarred by the sudden shift in tone. "I cannot call Baraqyal back from Earth. She must stay."

Satan walked to the edge of the hill and spread his leathery wings. "Baradiel was your assigned guardian, was he not? Perhaps there is something you can offer? I'm sure he would make better company."

Satan fell forward and glided away, his powerful wings flapping once to maintain lift. Demonic Rebecca stared after him. Satan had come for something else, but she couldn't fathom what. Why bring up Baradiel? She knew he would make better company, but that wasn't the point. Besides, what could she offer him?

-End Interlude-

Twenty-Six

I take I-55 out of the city. I'll need a map to chart my way. Since I have half a tank of gas and trying to get out of Chicago as fast as possible, I decide to drive until I need a fill up. I just need to get away right now. As my tank runs low, I start looking for a gas station and eventually pull off the highway into a late-night station. It's silent except for the crickets. I fill up and go inside to buy a map. The long-haired clerk gets out of his chair with the chiming of the bell attached to the door. He puts his book down as he steps forward to greet me. "How you doing?" I smile back and we exchange some small talk. Seeing all the snacks on display gets my stomach audibly growling.

"You sound hungry," the clerk laughs.

"Yeah," I say. "I guess it's been awhile since I last ate. I'll get some snacks to go with the map."

I look through the maps, but my stomach distracts me. I buy a couple energy bars just to placate it while I get what I need. I know I won't need much, just enough to deal with the growing hunger. I grab several bottles of water too. They'll come in handy later.

I make my purchases and head back to the car. I put the nozzle away and climb into the driver's seat. As I get back on the highway I realize I need a place to stay for the night and plan. I have no idea how to get to the

Library of Congress. I just want to drive a little bit farther; then I'll start looking for a hotel for the night.

I drive deep into the night before I start to feel some pain again. That's when I start looking for a place to stay. Berry said sleep will help me heal, so maybe a nap is in order. I find a hotel without much trouble and rent a room. It's one of those chain hotels and they make me pay for two nights since I don't want to be out by ten in the morning. I'm a little annoyed, but I pay the price. I pull my suitcase inside, my pain getting worse and making it a little hard to walk. I toss my suitcase onto the bed and start gathering the ingredients for the spell. After a few minutes the spell is complete and the pain is gone. I decide to take a shower and have a look at my wounds. I know it hasn't been long, but I'm curious.

I take the bandages off before stepping into the shower. There is some blood seeping from my ankle, especially when I put weight on it. The stitching is holding it together well and it's started to form a scab. My side is faring better. The redness is gone and the wound has scabbed over. My hands are even further along and the scab is starting to fall off and leave a scar. That will probably be gone sometime tomorrow. I enjoy my shower and redress my wounds. I throw on my nightgown and place the Heavenly Weapons by the bed. That's a habit I need to develop. They always need to be nearby. There's still some hours of night left, so I crawl into bed and sleep.

I wake up to sunlight poking through the room's thick curtain. Pain quickly follows. The spell wore off in my sleep hours ago and is hitting me full force. After casting the spell, I wonder what the next step is. I'm ready for it, I know that much. I pull out the spell pages and try to decipher the symbols and drawings on the pictograph. I realize the drawings are actually hand gestures. I practice them, trying to get them right, but I'm really not sure what to do with them. It looks like the spell changes even more if I try to use them. The symbols I can't figure out at all.

After spending a few frustrating hours on it, I think I have the gestures down and realize the spell is starting to wear off. It's either starting to last longer, or my healing is starting to pick up. Either way, I'm happy. I'll have to cast less often. After I subdue the pain I open the map on the bed. I take a pen and start to map my way to Washington. After finding where I am on the map, it looks like I just passed St. Louis. I can probably cut through Kentucky and Virginia and avoid Indiana altogether. It's way out of my way, but like Berry said, I don't want to be where they're looking for me, so Indiana and Michigan are out. I mark my course and fold up the map. I'll get a move on and rest once I reach Virginia.

-Interlude-

Heather sat at the kitchen table with a thick study guide opened in front of her. Her mother marched angrily into the room as her brother, Haden, called after her. Heather looked up in time to see her mother slam a letter onto the open book in front of her. "Care to explain this, young lady?" she shouted.

Heather looked at the letter and said, "I withdrew."

"You can't drop out of school!"

"Mom, what do you think I've been doing? I'm studying for my GED. I take the test next month."

"Oh, the Good Enough Diploma. Didn't I raise you better than that?"

"Mom, half my friends are dead. I'm not even in the same school with anyone I know!" Heather fought back tears as the awful memories rushed back.

"I'm sorry about your friends, but not being with them is not a reason to drop out!"

"Mom, I'm in a whole other district with nobody I know. Who am I supposed to graduate with?"

"That's not the point of graduating!"

"Yes it is! There's no difference between a GED and a diploma! They both say the same thing; I have the minimum amount of education that I'm required to have. It's the exact same thing!"

"One says you didn't care enough to finish!"

"Okay, everybody calm down," Haden said as he put himself between Heather and their mother. "I see where you're both coming from. Let's just take a breath."

"Don't you dare take your sister's side," his mom threatened.

"I'm not taking anybody's side, but you both need to listen. Heather didn't come to you because of what you're doing right now. She should have said something to someone, me or Dad, but this is why she didn't. We know how you feel about school, but listen to what Heather is saying."

"She'll make new friends."

"Eventually, yeah, but she'll never replace them. What would you do if Dad died? Would you be out dating next week? What if Heather or me died? Would you immediately try to have another baby?"

Their mother slumped into a chair with a sigh. "No. I would be devastated. I just don't want her throwing her life away. Some colleges don't accept GEDs."

"I'll make do, Mom," Heather said. "I'm working really hard, and I'm dealing with a lot of stuff. I don't need to be getting yelled at on top of it."

325

"I just really hope you've thought this through. I wish you would have talked to me about it."

"Would you have listened?"

"If you actually came to talk to me. This was not the right way for me to find out."

"I'm sorry. Between everything that's happened, the robbery, the murders, and the counseling, I'm dealing with a lot."

"Yeah," Haden said as he started rifling through the mail in his hand. "Who steals a fridge?" He stops and casts an inquisitive look over a piece of mail. "That's strange," he says as he hands the envelope to Heather. "It's addressed to you and has no return address or stamp."

The color faded from Heather's face as soon as she saw the handwriting. She knew exactly who it was from. She tried to remain calm as she tore the letter free and read it. "I need to be alone right now," Heather said as she abruptly got up and slammed the letter into her study guide.

"I'll talk to her," Haden said to his mom as he chased after his sister.

Heather ran to her room and tried to close the door behind her, but Haden was too close behind and blocked the door.

"I said leave me alone!" Heather exclaimed.

"Heather, what happened?" Haden asked. "What's in the letter?"

"You wouldn't understand."

"I would if you just told me. You can always tell me anything, remember?"

"Almost anything."

"No, anything. The fact that you don't want to tell me everything is beside the point."

"You'd just think I'm crazy."

"You're my sister. I already think you're crazy."

"This isn't a joke."

"Heather, just talk to me."

"Go away."

"I'm worried about you. Don't you think you're overdoing it a bit?"

"What does that mean?"

"You see a priest more than your counselor. I've heard you saying the Rosary a few times this past week alone. I didn't even know you knew it."

"The priest taught me. It helps."

"Heather, I'm not stupid. What else happened that night."

Heather sighed in defeat. "Fine, you really want to know?" She let Haden in and locked the door behind him. "I'll tell you, but you can't tell anyone."

"I won't."

"I mean it. Not your friends back at college. Not Mom and Dad. No reporters. No one."

"I promise; it won't leave this room."

"I haven't been honest with what happened that night with anyone except the priest, and I'm still keeping secrets from him. But I need to tell somebody the truth, just like he said. It's eating me. I'm choosing you, so you're the only one who's going to know. Keep it that way."

Haden swallowed a nervous lump in his throat. There were few secrets Heather guarded like that, so Haden knew it was serious.

"I refuse to call them the Angel Murders," Heather began. "It was all Santano. They were sacrifices."

"What do you mean sacrifices?"

"Santano sold his soul."

Haden tried to raise an eyebrow, something he couldn't actually do, but still did when he was confused. "Like went off the deep end?"

"No, he made a deal with the devil. Turns out you can really do that."

Unsure of how to take this information, Haden took a deep breath and rubbed the back of his head.

"He was trying to become Death," Heather continued as her hands started to shake. "And he was changing. Every time he killed, more of his face would strip away."

"He was carving his face?" Haden asked in disgust.

"No, it was—" A shiver ran through Heather's body and she tried to keep herself from shaking. "I don't even want to think about it. It wasn't natural. I still see his face when I close my eyes; a skull with eyes and a tongue. In the dark I can hear him laughing." Heather started to cry. "Sometimes I see him in the shadows." Haden stared at his sister as she reached for the Kleenex and wiped her tears away. She took a breath. "That's why I sleep with the lights on now," she finished.

Haden sat on the bed as he tried to wrap his mind around what he was told. He wanted to say that Heather was just traumatized, that it was all just in her head, but he had trouble convincing himself of that. Suddenly he realized why. "Wait, were you there? Why didn't you tell anybody?"

"How do you tell someone you were kidnapped by a demon?"

"I think people would get the reference."

"No, I mean an actual demon. We weren't robbed. Everything that we're missing it ate. Including the fridge. They rounded us up like cattle to the slaughter. I watched Santano murder them one-by-one. Angel and Rebecca came to rescue us, but they were only able to save me."

"They weren't working together?"

"No. It was all Santano. Angel had been trying to stop him."

"What happened to the three of them? Where are they now?"

"Angel died protecting us from the demons that were chasing us. Santano became this huge shadow and fear washed off him. Rebecca became like an angel. I was scared out of my mind, but Rebecca made me feel safe. Their fight tore the gym apart. If Rebecca lost, Santano would have become Death. The fate of the world rested on that fight. Rebecca beat Santano and sent him to Hell. I saw the world almost end that night. How many times has that happened? How many times has the world almost ended? That's why I'm so distant. That's why graduating with a school full of strangers isn't my top priority. Rebecca lost everything and is out there trying to save the world and everyone's saying she's some kind of monster. That she belongs behind bars. And what can I do? Just go on and live my life? Just pretend that I didn't see what I saw? Pretend that none of it happened? How can I do that to her?"

Haden sat slack-jawed. "That's what really happened?" he asked.

"Why do you think I haven't told anyone? Why do you think I can't defend her against all these accusations? Who would believe me? That's why you can't repeat this."

"I believe you," Haden said

"That's why I told you. You're probably the only one who will."

"That letter I gave you. That's from Rebecca, isn't it?"

"Yeah."

"What's it say?"

Heather flipped through her study guide and handed the letter to Haden. "Read it yourself."

Haden read over the letter, awed by what was written within. "Sounds like she's been through a lot."

"She has. She's trying to save the world."

-End Interlude-

I'm uncomfortable as I make my way into Kentucky. It's time for another casting, but I want to get a room first. Most of my pain is in my foot now and driving with cruise control helps alleviate the pain. My foot gets to just sit and rest. The sun will be going down soon, so I should pull in for the night. It's been a day now, so Berry should be on her way too.

I find a nice little hotel just off the highway. Other than a gas station and small restaurant, there's not much around it except open road and snow-covered trees and fields. I pay for a room for the night and struggle with the suitcase. Pain shoots through my leg as I try to drag it inside. The pain allows me to actually feel its weight. In retrospect, maybe I should have cast the spell in the car. Too late now.

Inside I collapse on the floor to get the pressure off my foot and start pulling the ingredients from the suitcase. I have enough chamomiles for a few more castings, more if I use the application version. Since it's really just my foot, that's what I decide to use. I can deal with my side, and my hands don't really hurt anymore. Unfortunately, the first batch backfires. I had gotten really good with the version I've been using, but I didn't practice the other one. I try again with the spell pages and finally get some relief. I guess all I have to do now is relax and wait for Berry. There should be a store nearby. Maybe I'll go replenish the ingredients.

RULES OF ENGAGEMENT

Twenty-Seven

This area is pretty much open country and the closest grocery store is in the next town over, about an hour away from the hotel. I buy more cayenne peppers and another container of nutmeg. Apparently, I have to go to an herbalist shop to get the actual chamomile flowers. I did pick up some seeds, though I'm not sure how I'm going to grow them. I'll talk to Berry about it. I put everything away and set up for another casting before jumping into the shower. I'll need another treatment in about an hour.

After my shower I put on my nightgown and dig through my suitcase for a photo album. I sit on the bed and start turning through the pages. It's one of mine that I started after Michael and I had dated for a while. The pictures are from the Fourth of July. I think we were in Reese Park. Michael and I had only been together for a few months at this point, I think, but we were becoming close and I really enjoyed spending time with him. I think this was the first time he went out with my family. He's standing over the grill with that long unkempt hair of his cooking skirt steak. I remember; it's just before he cut it. Lemon and salt was so simple and so much better than I thought it would be. I run my fingers over the pictures. A small smile crosses my lips. It doesn't hurt as much now, knowing he's not here. "I miss you, Michael," I whisper. "I hope you're doing okay. I can't wait to see you again."

It feels like a hand squeezes my heart, making my chest hurt. The pain lingers even as a warm light appears in the center of the room, taking the shape of a person. It's the wrong shape to be Berry. My heart jumps thinking that it may actually be Michael, but hope makes the pain linger a bit longer. The light begins to fade along with the pain and I hear Michael's voice call out to me. I put the book down and stand up, taking a step towards the light. It fades and Michael stands in a stark white robe with light gray trim.

"Are you okay?" He asks as he looks around the room.

I'm standing silent in shock, unable to move at first. Then I run and hold him. "I'm fine, you're here," I say as he holds me.

"I heard you call me."

"I didn't call you. I just said I can't wait to see you."

"Well, I heard you. I thought you might be in trouble again. The next thing I knew, here I am."

"I'm not in trouble, but I'm happy to see you again."

"Where are we?"

"We're in Kentucky."

"What are we doing in Kentucky?"

"Right now, I'm just waiting for my guardian. We're on our way to Washington."

"You look a lot better than when I last saw you."

"I feel a lot better. How are your wounds?" I upturn his hand and look at the burn across it. It's not as far along as mine, but it looks like the boils have drained.

"They're trying to teach me how to tap into my natural healing ability. Involves a lot of sleep, apparently."

"That's what I've been told. My healing is pretty far along, but my leg still has a bit to go. I was taught a spell to deal with the pain."

"A spell? You mean magic?"

"Yeah. I'll show you. It's about time for me to do it again anyway."

I sit at the little table in the room and get everything together. Michael watches in silent curiosity as I cast the spell and apply the chamomile to my foot. "Is that it?" he asks. "What did it do?"

"It took all the pain in my foot away." I say. I get up and stomp my foot. "See, no pain at all. There won't be for a few hours."

"That's cool, especially since I know how messed up that leg is."

"So, what have they been teaching you?"

"Not much really. They're evaluating me right now. Mainly a bunch of tests. They tried doing something so I wouldn't hear you, but obviously that didn't work."

I laugh. "Gabriel better not blame me for this one. I've been careful. They screwed up."

"Naw, I'll probably be the one to get yelled at."

"I'll tell him, I didn't call you. I was just thinking about you. They can't really expect me to stop that."

We both laugh and I hug him again. As I stand there enjoying his embrace, a thought crosses my mind. "Hey, do you think my parents could come visit me?"

"I don't know," Michael says. "I don't really know how that works."

"I just thought, since you come..."

"Yeah, but I'm not supposed to be able to and I don't know how I'm doing it."

"So you're not sure how to get back either?"

"Not a clue."

"So you're here until Gabriel comes to get you, and since he's not here yet, he may not know you're gone."

"Maybe, or he expects your guardian to send me back."

I smile. "About that." I walk my fingers up his chest. "You know she probably can't find me as long as you're here."

Michael smiles back. "You think so?"

"I'm not so hurt now," I say as I start walking him back. "And I'm not in any pain."

"Oh really?" He stops once he hits the bed.

"You know what else?"

"What?"

I push him onto the bed. "I'm not wearing anything under this." I climb on top of him as his hands caress my sides. "Are you?"

"Why don't you find out?"

I kiss him as his hands start to explore my back. I pull at his long gown until I can get my hand under it and up his leg. My hand caresses across what I want, but there's a soft fabric protecting it. "Seriously?" I laugh as I pull them off. "Why?"

"Never really thought about it," Michael says as he takes them from me and tosses them aside. "This is a bit unlike you, Becca."

"After what I've been through, I think a little change is warranted."

Michael pulls me down to his lips as he pulls my nightgown up to expose my naked skin. I sigh happily against his mouth as his hands travel the length of my back, down to my legs, and back up again. He pulls my gown over my head and drops it beside the bed. He starts to roll over, to put me on my back, but I push him back down. "Uh-uh," I grin. "It's my turn to take care of you."

I lay in Michael's embrace, finally out of breath. I trace my finger along his chest as I caress my leg against his.

"Wow," Michael says. "That may have been the best sex I've ever had."

"Better than Sarah?"

"Oh yeah. I don't think I've ever gone that long before; not without a break."

I smile and am pleased with myself. I was better than Sarah. That starts to sink in and my smile fades. I was better than the school slut? I push myself up and look at Michael. He sees the change of expression on my face, the shame that's grown.

"What's wrong?" he asks.

"I don't want to be like Sarah," I almost whisper.

"You're not."

"I don't want to become her. I don't want this to be all we are now."

Michael sits up and pulls the covers up around me. "We're not. This isn't why I come. This isn't why you call."

"Then why is it the only thing I wanted to do? Like you said, it isn't like me. Come on Michael, I didn't even put underwear on. I never do that."

"Do you need me to leave?"

I latch onto him, afraid he'll suddenly disappear. "No! No, I don't want you to go. I'm not mad at you, I'm just confused. What we're doing isn't wrong, is it?"

"Why would it be?" He takes my hand and holds it tight. "I love you, Becca. Being dead doesn't change that."

"But doesn't being dead make it wrong?"

"I'm not a zombie."

"You're an angel. I want you to stay that way."

RULES OF ENGAGEMENT

He takes a deep breath and we sit in silence. I have no idea what to think and wish Berry was here to help me.

I jump when an audible hum pierces my ears, breaking the silence. My heart drops and fills with relief at the Sword of Might's signal of warning. It had done this same thing when the avatar came back. This I can handle and I won't have to dwell on this morality issue.

"What's wrong?" Michael asks as I reach for the sword.

"I think it's an avatar," I answer as I grasp the sheathed Sword of Might. "Show me." The image it shows is of War. My stomach twists and makes me a little sick. He's riding atop a tank, his chains anchoring him in place. I see him coming down a familiar road. He isn't too far away. He's coming back for me. I shake the vision away and exclaim, "War has a tank!"

"What?" Michael shouts. "Are you sure?"

"Get dressed! We have to lead him away!"

We jump out of bed and put our clothes back on. I don't think I've ever gotten dressed so fast before. I grab my suitcase and rush to the car. I throw it in as I fumble with the keys. A shell hits the ground with explosive force. Pain shoots through my arm and blood stains my coat. Pieces of metal pierce my arm. I look around and see dozens of metal shards scattered over the ground, in cars, and even the building. Lights come on in various rooms as people peek through their windows and step outside. "We can't run," I say.

"Yes we can," Michael says. "Becca, get in the car."

I pull the metal out of my arm. "I have to stop the tank. Help evacuate."

The tank fires again. I rush towards the shell and focus as hard as I can. I throw my hands up and conjure the biggest shield I can. The shell slams into the

337

shield and explodes. I'm thrown onto my back as the shield shatters. Panic is starting to set into people as Michael tries to get them to leave.

I have to get closer to the tank. The shells are detonating too close. I fall into Quickstep and rush up the road. I don't want to get too close, especially in Quickstep. I stop a couple hundred yards away. "I'm right here!" I shout. I know War can see me, but he doesn't seem to acknowledge me. The cannon is aimed high and the barrel pulls back, firing another shell. I unleash Whirlwind as the tank jerks against its firing. The winds catch the shell and veer it off course, exploding on the empty road.

"You missed!" I shout.

"I'm not aiming at you," War says.

My heart drops. He's not trying to hit me; he's trying to hit the hotel! The cannon aligns and prepares to fire. I fall into Quickstep as the shell is released. Berry said there are two elements to Quickstep; time dilation and speed. The roar of the tank is a stagnant drone. The trees are locked in mid-sway. The shell, though traveling much slower, flies through the air and has covered almost half the distance by the time I race after it, but I can't catch it. It's too far ahead and still traveling too fast. My foot is starting to hurt, slowing me down and letting the shell out pace me. I don't know how, but I need to push myself. I need the speed!

Pain burns into my ankle as my feet slam into the ground. The world around me starts to blur at my periphery as I focus on the artillery shell. I see a family of three rushing into their car. My eyes widen as I realize they'll be hit. They'll die. I scream as I push myself forward, every inch of me burning with exertion as I finally overtake the shell. I leap up as I twist towards it and project my shield around it. The explosion shatters the shield and throws me out of Quickstep. My body breaks the pavement as I bound off it several times. My sight is unfocused and blurred, and my ears are ringing. I can't tell what's going on around me, but I force myself to stand and try to shake the effects away. It hurts to move and I can feel the shrapnel embedded in my body. The shield may have taken the brunt, but it couldn't stop it. Blood drips from every wound and pools on the ground beneath me. I have to stop the bleeding.

I dig into my pocket as my vision starts to focus. The roar of the tank is replacing the ringing in my ears and I hear another round fire. I can just barely see it. The Sword of Might ignites and with a swing I unleash Meteor Strike. The flaming arc looses several meteors towards the tank. One hits the shell and detonates it in the air. The shockwave washes over me and I finally find the relic. I smash it with the pommel of my sword and release its magic. A bright energy swirls around me and caresses me in a pleasant breeze. My pain steadily fades and shrapnel pieces clunk on the ground. The magic is actually pushing them out.

The tank slowly advances and is visible on the road now. As long as War has that tank, I'm barely on the defensive. I have to take it out. I've picked up its firing sequence and realize it's reloaded and about to fire again.

"Enough!" I shout as I punch the ground. A shock wave vibrates from my fist and through the pavement, causing the entire road before me to buckle and the cannon to overshoot. I focus on the speed aspect of Quickstep as I rush forward. The world around me doesn't slow, but rather blurs and in what seems like an instant I'm at the cannon of the tank. Stunned, but knowing I don't have much time, I use all my strength and bend the cannon up so it can't fire again. With fear and determination, I stare up at War.

"It's me you want!" I shout. "Leave these people alone!"

"It is your power I want," War says, "and for that they must suffer."

Barbed black chains rip out of the tank and ensnare me. They bind tight around my body, cutting through my coat and into my skin, pulling and holding me against the tank. War leaps forward into the air, covering the distance to the hotel in that one leap. I don't understand. Why does he think I won't fight him unless he threatens people? I try to pull away from the tank, but the chains hold strong. The metal of the tank buckles as I push against it, but the chains won't give. Gunfire and screams bleed into the night. I strain harder against the chains, but they just dig into my body. Then I hear Michael scream. He's hurt. No, War won't take him away from me. I won't let him! I flex every muscle in my body. The chains shatter as I scream. I turn and sprint into Quickstep before the chains even have a chance to hit the ground. The world around me is a blur and my eyes sting against the wind as I rush back to the hotel. Pointed chains blur into my tunneling sight and race at me. The world around me becomes solid for a moment as I stop to sidestep. The chains miss me and slam deep into the ground. Before the world blurs out again I take in what's happening.

Michael is on the ground and holding his side. A family cowers before War, the father trying to shield his family as War aims an automatic rifle at them, shining as black as his armor. There is a momentary blur before I slam my fist into the gun, destroying it. This version of Quickstep is hard to use; I can barely see, but War seems to have trouble countering me now.

RULES OF ENGAGEMENT

War backhands me and I'm barely able to brace myself. I land on my back and flip onto my feet. The breath I take comes with a building of power I recognize and unleash. The Sonic Scream pushes War back and knocks the family down, but does give them a chance to run. I step forward, trying to focus the scream just on War, but I can't maintain it anymore. I have to take a breath, which allows War to plant his feet. Before I can try again, War unleashes his own Sonic Scream. It's much stronger than mine, whipping me through the air like a sheet of paper.

I flip over and dig my fingers into the asphalt to anchor myself. Soon after the scream stops my body plops onto the ground. I look up to see a car flying at me. I roll away as it slams into the ground and flips over once. I roll to my feet and draw the Heavenly Weapons. Plates open in War's chest, revealing about half a dozen cones inside. I don't realize they're missiles until they fire.

They come at me too fast to react with my shield and I can only brace myself as my skin tenses. The missiles hit me and the surrounding area, knocking me again from my feet. My body burns, but I'm in one piece. I don't know how I survived direct missile hits without putting up a shield. "Leave her alone!" Michael shouts. I look up but can only see shadows through the smoke. War doesn't seem to be moving. I get up and direct the gales of Whirlwind skyward, dispersing the smoke, loose dirt, and rocks above me. Michael is trying to put War in a chokehold, but War isn't trying to fight back. What is the limit of this monster?

War pulls Michael off his back as a serrated blade forms from his gauntlet. He holds the back of Michael's neck and drives the blade into his side. "No!" I scream as I rush forward. War throws Michael aside and directs

341

his fist at me as a barrel emerges from the back of his hand. A torrent of flame bursts from the barrel, forcing me to jump high into the air to avoid the flames. War raises both arms towards me and releases flames from both arms. I pull my weight and contort my body into the space between the flames, the heat warming my body, making me sweat and my wounds burn. I bring my sword down, scraping along War's chest but leaving no wound. I can feel the burning of the blade running down my body in the exact same manner, but I can feel the wetness of blood.

I stumble on my feet as a trail of blood stains my shirt. War slams his hands into the sides of my head, jarring my entire being, causing my legs to shake and making me drop the Heavenly Weapons. He grabs me by the neck and lifts me off the ground. I pry at his hand, trying to free myself, but he isn't choking me.

"With each push," War says, "more abilities surface." He slams me into the ground and raises his fist as sharp spikes grow from his gauntlet. "Let us find the limit of your Steel Skin."

War strikes and all I can do is turn my head and brace for the blow, but it never comes. I look up and see Berry. She's caught War's fist.

"Not on my watch," Berry says as she takes War by the arm and hurls him through the air. He lands face up on a car, sounding its alarm, and lies motionless. Berry takes my hand and helps me to my feet. "Are you alright?"

"I am now."

"If you call my name, I will come. Remember that."

"I will."

Berry's attention goes to War and mine follows. War's body blurs and suddenly he's standing. Berry pushes me back as she steps ahead of me. "You need to go," she says. She sounds nervous. Is War so dangerous that even an angel fears him?

"Angel of Storms," War says. "What are you doing here?"

"Rebecca, go. I'll keep him occupied." Her body begins to crackle with power and she calmly approaches War, her fists clenched and her body flowing with electricity. I look to see people standing in awe, watching in fear and amazement. "We all have to leave!" I shout. "It's not safe here!" I find Michael and run over to him. The serrated blade is still in his side and I smell strawberries. His clothes are wet, but I see no blood. I look back to Berry and she stands toe-to-toe with War.

"You dare stand against me?" War asks.

"I do." Berry answers.

War moves so fast I barely see the actual motion as he punches Berry so hard she doesn't just fall back, she's thrown across the lot and into the hotel. Lightning erupts from the building, blowing the front open and reveals Berry standing tall and wielding a pair of war hammers. Her silver vest has hardened into a cuirass that covers her chest and dips down towards her belly, but ultimately leaving it exposed. Intricate blue designs are etched into the silver metal very similar to the designs on her mask. She has one aqua blue pauldron, a guard on her left shoulder. The shoulder armor itself is shaped as a swirling wave of water with a clear orb in the center. The orb has a dark cloud within, occasionally flashing with tiny bolts of lightning. Her right arm is protected by a simple silver bracer with the same designs as her chest and mask. Her left, however, is more heavily guarded. The armor of her upper arm is partially concealed by the shoulder guard, while a sturdy bracer covers her lower arm. A darker blue in color than the shoulder guard, silver designs race across the arm guards like lightning, flashing and glowing in rhythm of the orb. Her waist armor also leaned more towards her left side, leaving her right almost bare. One large piece covered the upper part of her leg, exposing only the inner parts of her thigh. Both her lower legs were protected by greaves, but the color reversed from the rest of her armor, silver instead of blue, with waves etched into the lower part and lightning striking from the upper. Her dull white wings have turned silver and are spread, making her look terrifying as lightning dances around her. She slams her war hammers into the ground, unleashing a loud crash of thunder and a powerful bolt of lightning that hits War dead center and sends him flying.

With one flap of her wings Berry dashes over the ground as War flips onto his feet and rushes towards her. Berry swings a war hammer and connects with War's punch in a bright and loud clash, followed by another and another. Berry easily holds her own against that monster. The wind starts to howl and thunder flashes in the sky. A storm is moving in. Is this Berry's storm? I watch her trade blow after blow with War. She's so much more powerful than me. What chance do I have against him? I look down at Michael. He's in pain. He should be bleeding, but I don't see any blood. I pull the blade from his stomach and see something clear, like water, flow out. I touch it. It's not as thick as blood, but not as thin as water either. I put it to my nose. It smells sweet, like strawberries. This is where the smell is coming from? This is the blood of an angel?

"I have to get you out of here," I say as I lift Michael off the ground. He isn't just light to me, he almost seems weightless. I carry him to the car and put him on the floor in the back. I watch as others scramble for their

RULES OF ENGAGEMENT

cars or flee on foot. I caress Michael's face. "I'm getting you out of here," I say. "Just hold on."

I get in the driver's seat and get on the road as fast as I can, pressing the pedal to the floor. War should leave once I get far enough away, I hope. Then I can focus on helping Michael.

-Hell's Interlude-

Each swing of Baraqyal's hammers was met with the gauntleted punch of War. Pain raced through her hands with each blow, but she pushed through it, numbing and healing each strike with her magic as they happened. War kicked out, his boot slamming into Baraqyal's stomach and pushing her back. She slammed her hammers into the ground to stop her momentum. A dozen chains hovered behind War. Baraqyal took a step back as energy sparked from her good eye. War directed his chains with his hand and they lashed out at once. Baraqyal slammed the heads of her hammers together, creating a shockwave that ripped through the chains. The shattered links fell around her as lightning flashed in the sky. The broken pieces of chains returned to War and molded into spheres around him as more pulled from his body. Some grew spikes while others split into spinning blades.

"If you stand as an obstacle against me," War said, "you will be removed."

"Give it your best shot," Baraqyal taunted before lightning struck her, charging her hammers with electric power. "You're in my way too."

The spheres and blades whisked at Baraqyal. She struck the ground, discharging the electrical current in her weapon and destroyed several of War's deadly arsenals. Dirt and debris mixed with smoke as several blades cut through, but Baraqyal emerged airborne above the smoke cloud. She directed a bolt of lightning from the sky as the spinning blades chased her. The bolt ripped through the blades and split the spheres. Baraqyal felt something tug at her leg and she was pulled from the sky. She slammed into the ground and rolled away as a massive blade buried itself into the shattered earth.

Baraqyal twisted up to one knee and swung her hammers at the massive black steel sword, knocking it wildly into the air. War spun the sword around with the momentum and brought it down at an angle. Baraqyal blocked the blade and pulled her hammers down, locking it against the ground. War kicked out, landing his foot against her face and throwing her across the ground. Baraqyal rolled onto her feet and held her hammers at the ready.

War stood staring Baraqyal down, his sword's point resting on the ground. "You stand in my way," he said.

"Kind of the point."

"You try to hide her from me. You can't. I will find her again."

Unsure of War's meaning Baraqyal searched for Rebecca. She almost didn't notice the demon hunter's presence a few miles down the road. She would not need to continue the fight much longer. "Okay," Baraqyal said. "So she's gone. You can't get to her, so there's no reason to keep fighting."

"Wrong. You mean to stifle her powers. I cannot allow that. I must remove you." War widened his stance as he raised his sword horizontal above his shoulder.

Baraqyal gritted her teeth and strengthened her stance, raising her hammers to defend. "Damn, he's getting serious."

War's form blurred and vanished, reappearing in front of Baraqyal with a thrust of his sword. She spun her hammers in a downward cross, just catching the blade and burying it in the ground between her feet. A thick spike burst from War's fist as he drove it into Baraqyal's gut and lifted her up and over him before slamming her hard into the ground, burying her beneath the pavement and erupting a cloud of stone and smoke. He spun his sword into a downward thrust and buried the blade to the hilt.

Lightning danced across the sky, pulling War's attention. Hovering high above him Baraqyal cradled her wound as energy danced in her eye. "You missed," she said as she directed a lightning bolt at the walking monolith. The bolt struck War with explosive force, bathing the Horseman in fire, but he stood unharmed as flames danced upon his body. Baraqyal's body crackled with power as she prepared another attack. War disappeared in a blur and Baraqyal's eye widened in panic. She didn't see where he went. With her eye dancing with energy, she suddenly felt him above her. She spun around to strike but War grabbed her face and hurled her towards the ground. Baraqyal tried to use her wings to regain control, but War's chains shot from his back as he fell in pursuit. The spiked-tipped heads pierced through her exposed body and punctured her armor. She slammed into the ground, producing a cloud of rubble as the cement and asphalt shattered. War hit the ground feet first on top of her. Baraqyal appeared behind him with her hammers pulled back to one side. "Almost!" she shouted with a swing of her hammers into War's back, releasing an electrical bolt as they struck. War was thrown forward and landed facedown.

Baraqyal could no longer feel Rebecca anywhere, but wanted to make sure she had managed to somehow escape. Using this brief pause, she flew high into the sky and looked about the road. She couldn't see the van anywhere. Barbed chains suddenly wrapped around her body, trying to pull her down as War leaped up towards her.

"We are not done," he stated.

Lightning cracked the sky. "Yes, we are." A bolt of lightning struck Baraqyal and traveled down the chain. War's forward ascent was halted in a fiery explosion and he plummeted back towards the ground, his chains broken. Hooked chains tore from his body and raced at Baraqyal. She took a deep breath and released Sonic Scream, forcing the chains to veer off course as they were pushed back. The force of the shockwave hit War hard enough to push him towards terminal velocity in his short descent. He hit the ground with enough force to create a football field sized crater, whipping stone, dirt, and pipes into the air. The explosion poured smoke and a roaring fire into the air, despite the towers of water from the shattered water lines.

Baraqyal threw her hammers at War, each turning into a bolt of lightning, lighting up the night sky in a fiery blaze. Baraqyal took off, looking for Rebecca one last time, but she was nowhere to be found. "For the best I suppose," Baraqyal said. "I'll find you, you little brat. Hopefully before War." Her form split into shades as she slipped into the astral plane, a place War could not follow.

-End Interlude-

I drive as fast as the car will go. I need to put as much distance between us as I can, but I'm not sure how long Michael can hold out. He's barely responding to me. I watch lightning split the sky behind us. How

RULES OF ENGAGEMENT

fierce that battle must be. I was an idiot to think I could take down War alone, if at all. Michael's breathing is getting shallow. I pull over, hoping Berry can handle War. Michael needs me.

I climb into the back. Michael is covered in sweat, but he's cold to the touch. I rip his robe open to find two infected gashes, one larger than the other. I reach into my coat pockets and pull out the first aid kit. I tear open the sutures. "This is going to hurt, Michael," I warn. I start to sew the biggest wound closed. The needle pierces normally, but the thread passes out of his body. I try again but the needle passes through him this time. What's going on? I try to hold him, but my hands pass through him after a moment. He's shivering, distant, and mumbling something in Spanish.

"Michael," I plead. "Please, talk to me." The car jerks into motion and pulls back onto the highway. I look to the driver's seat and see Úna at the wheel. "What's wrong with him?" I cry.

"He's dying," Úna answers.

"But he's an angel! He can't die!"

"War poisoned him so he would linger, but he will die."

"No, that can't be true." I try to hold him, but he doesn't stay solid. All I can do is cry. I don't know what to do.

"You are a very stupid girl. You know nothing of the divine or the laws. Yet you insist on fighting battles you are not prepared for and calling upon angels that are not your own. You are making deadly mistakes."

"What happens when an angel dies?" I ask between sobs.

"They return from whence they came to heal. They cannot return for a year and a day. The same is true for demons."

349

"So, he'll be okay?" I ask as some hope returns.

"I don't know. Michael is an archon. He should not be able to come to Earth, not like this. Your love is too strong, allowing him to break the rules. Everything comes with a cost. Should he die here, I don't know what will happen to him. He needs to be returned to Heaven."

"Then send him back!" I plead. "Please, send him back!"

"I can't."

"Why not?"

"I am not a being of Heaven. I am a True Form. I am something different from the divine. A Celestial to be sure, but not a divine." She looks at me through the rearview mirror. "So, what are you going to do?"

I lean over Michael, trying to cradle his head in my hands. He doesn't pass through. He's shivering and through my tears I try to kiss his lips, but there is no flesh to kiss. "I'm so sorry Michael," I say. "It's all my fault."

His eyes open ever so slightly and fixate on me. He smiles. "You're so bright Rebecca."

I smile through my tears. Tentatively, I place my hand over his heart, focusing so maybe I won't pass through him. "Please, don't hurt anymore Michael," I whisper to him. "It's okay now. I'm safe." The flow of his clear blood slows. Is he running out? "You can go now."

Michael closes his eyes and smiles. He isn't shaking so much anymore and I'm starting to get hot. He holds my hand that's placed over his heart and takes a deep breath. "You smell good," he says.

I smile and try to kiss him again. This time I can. "Go home, my love."

Michael begins to glow and light shines through the window in the dark of the night. It covers him. "Home,"

Michael whispers. He sparkles as he starts to fade. The sparkles travel the light beam out of the car and into the sky, only to vanish as soon as Michael is faded. I see my hands and look at myself. A fading light is surrounding me and I'm starting to cool. I really was glowing.

"So very interesting," Úna says.

I climb into the passenger seat and buckle in. I check the mirrors and see the storm raging behind us. I wipe the wetness from my face to find it covered in dirt and blood. I don't care. I only hope Michael is okay. "Where are we going?" I ask.

"Where do you want to go?" Úna replies.

"We were going to Washington D.C. I'm going to go to the Library of Congress and look for the First."

Úna nods and turns off the road. I don't react and just close my eyes as she calmly drives towards a tree.

Epilogue

The air was still and the starless night sky moonless. The land was barren and eerily quiet. The sound of footsteps was loud in the silence. The man stood before a large mountain devoid of any green or life, as the rest of that barren world. He vanished into the night void in his dark three-piece suit and black top hat. His eyes, hidden behind dark shades, took in the mountain. He was an older man. His wrinkling face pulled into a small grin. "This will do," he said. Slowly, he raised his arms, his hands limp, as if in preparation. His hands threw open and the mountain was blown to bits.

His hands moved, almost as if directing an orchestra. The mountain pieces moved over him, shaping themselves into bricks and steel panels and beams. The ground the man stood on exploded into a perfect square. He hovered on a metal disc, unmoved from where he was. With a flick of his hands, the metal structures began to slam themselves into the ground, creating the foundation of a building. The sheet metal and bricks slammed down, making the exterior around him. A floor beneath him pulled out of the ground and he rested on it. The material had been used, but still he stood in the darkness.

He pulled his hands close and pulled matter from the air itself. Sending the matter into the room, he created light. He looked around and smiled. He raised his hand towards a wall and machinery began to form, molecules pulled from the very air and rearranged however he liked. Soon, the room was a fully equipped laboratory with computers, alien devices, and stocked tables of tubes, needles, and burners. He walked to an empty table and with a raise of his hand materialized a dozen alien-looking containers, each with attachments to a large computer that grew from the ground behind the table.

The man pulled a smooth, baseball-sized stone-like orb from his pocket and placed it on the table. "You were always so powerful," the man said. "Let's see what secrets your Ultra-tron possesses." He placed his hands around the orb, the Ultra-tron, and it hovered between them as he raised them over the table. With slight focus and effort, the Ultra-tron began to emit light from within. It didn't glow, but was breaking. He pulled his hands apart and the Ultra-tron shattered into thirteen unique pieces. Twelve he let sink into the containers and the computer began analyzing them. He took the last piece between his fingers. He stared at it with a smile and removed his dark shades, revealing glowing crimson eyes. "I'm sure the secret lies within the Beast-tron."